ALSO BY LEE S. HANNON

COLIGO, Book One of the UNITAS Series
February 22, 2022

UNITAS, Book Two of the UNITAS Series
June 23, 2022

COGNATIO, A UNITAS Series Novella
June 23, 2022

REVIRESCO, Book Three of the UNITAS Series
Coming November 2022

UNIVERSUS, A UNITAS Series Novella
Coming November 2022

The Demon's Prometheus
Coming 2023

For more information, please visit:
www.leeshannonbooks.com

And be sure to follow Lee S. Hannon on social
(Instagram, TikTok, Twitter, and Facebook):
@LeeSHannonBooks

Praise for
COLIGO: Book One of the UNITAS Series

"A provocative, complicated tale twisted into a knotty framework of time paradoxes."
—*Kirkus Reviews*

"An ambitious noir-tinged future-city mystery of androids, politics, and biotech. This promising debut, a science-fiction thriller set in 'The City' after an android 'Resurgence' has upended society, beguiles from the start with its layered mysteries, both about the state of the world, especially its politics and pharmaceutical companies, as well as a series of murders."
—*Booklife Reviews*

"With a frenetic pace, a dramatic opening scene and a diverse cast of charismatic characters, it's difficult to imagine who wouldn't enjoy this novel. The perfect combination of scintillating mystery, futuristic science fiction and intriguing political thriller, COLIGO is a compulsive read that will wear your fingernails to the quick."
—*Indies Today*

"Set in a future where humans and androids coexist, Lee S. Hannon balances extensive world building, interesting characters, and an intriguing plot in COLIGO (The UNITAS Series Book 1) to create a science fiction novel that is both absorbing and engaging. A memorable start to an epic and thrilling adventure."
—*Indie Reader*

"This book had me hooked from beginning to end! We have a ruthless mind game to control The City, players will risk it all...It's a battle of good and evil and the winner...well, we shall see what happens next."
— *Jessie, BookToker: @exclusivepalmbeachliving*

"Lee S. Hannon's outstanding writing is at once descriptive and interesting. She had me captivated from the first page...her storyline and character development is so well done that it is almost impossible to put the book down!"
—*Elizabeth Witman*

UNITAS

Book Two of the UNITAS Series

ū.ni.tās
noun
declension: 3rd declension
gender: feminine

Definitions:
1. Oneness
2. Unity
3. Sameness

BY

Lee S. Hannon

Cover Design by Tori Mulhern
Map Design by Keir DuBois
Family Tree & Timeline by Shannon Lee Smith

First Edition, 2022

The Library of Congress has catalogued the hardcover edition as follows:
Names: Lee S. Hannon, author.
Title: UNITAS: Book #2, The UNITAS Series: a novel / Lee S. Hannon
Description: First edition. | Boston : Idella Imprint Publishing, LLC, 2022
Identifiers: LCCN 2022907599
ISBN 9798985117547 (hardcover)
ISBN 9798985117578 (paperback)
ISBN 9798985117561 (ebook)
Subjects: Fiction, Techno-Thriller | Science Fiction | Dystopian.

Our books may be purchased in bulk for promotional, educational, or business use. Please contact your local bookseller or Idella Imprint Publishing, LLC by email at: sleehannon@gmail.com.

www.leeshannonbooks.com
Follow on Instagram, Twitter and TikTok: @leeshannonbooks

For more information or inquiries, please reach out to Idella Imprint Publishing, LLC

10 9 8 7 6 5 4 3 2 1

To Mom,

For absolutely everything

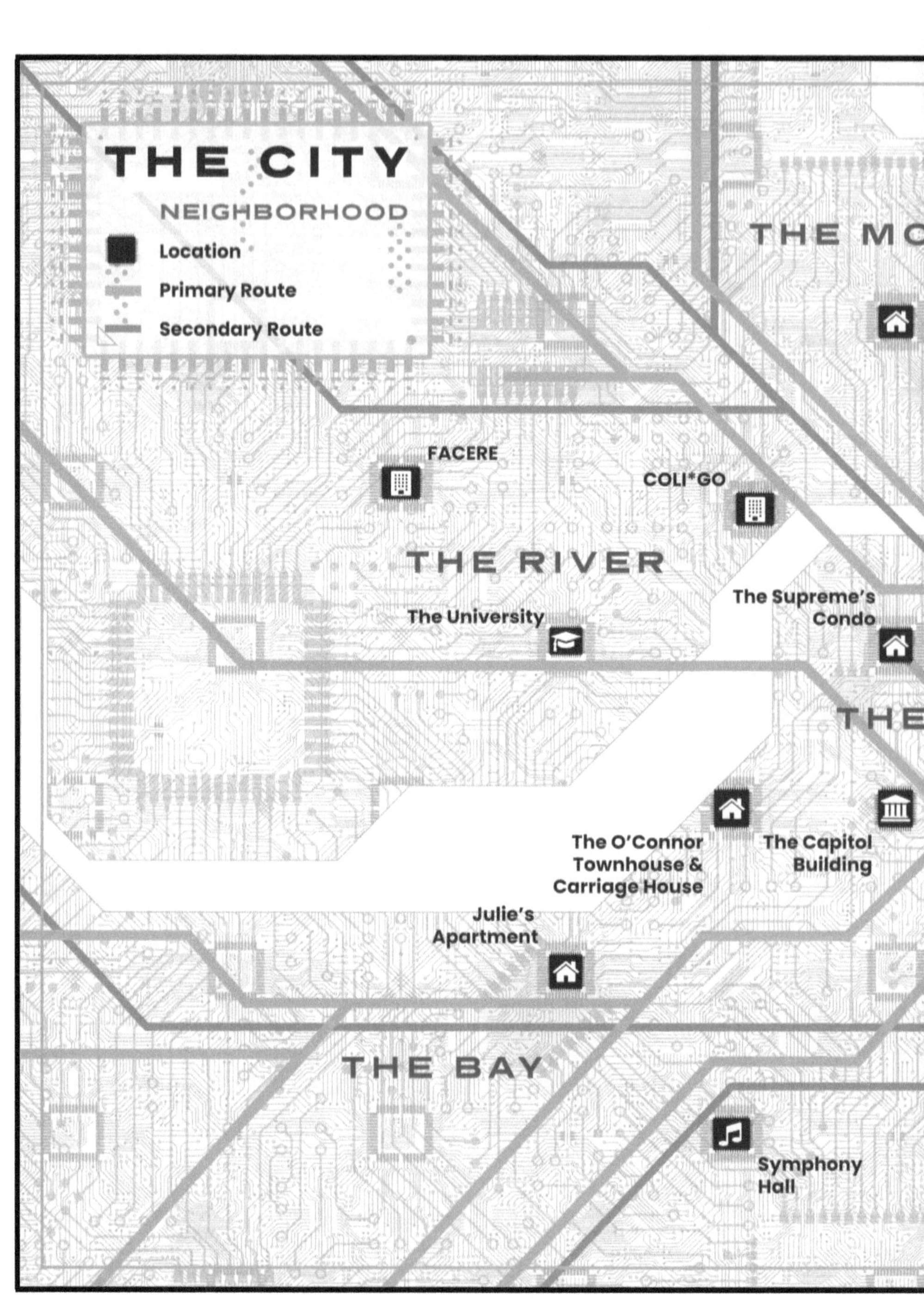
THE CITY
NEIGHBORHOOD
Location
Primary Route
Secondary Route
THE MO
FACERE
COLI*GO
THE RIVER
The University
The Supreme's Condo
THE
The O'Connor Townhouse & Carriage House
The Capitol Building
Julie's Apartment
THE BAY
Symphony Hall

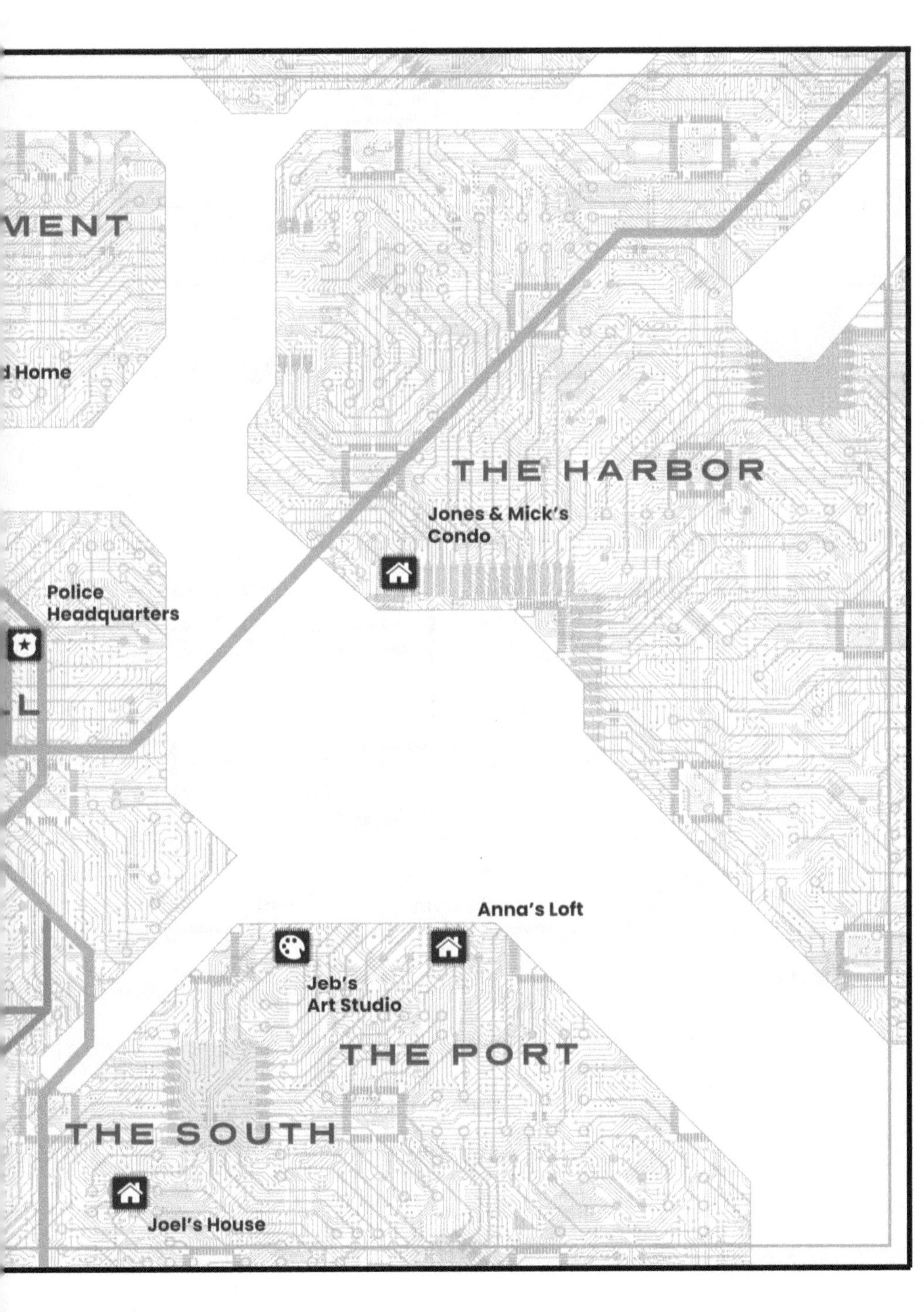
MENT
d Home
THE HARBOR
Jones & Mick's
Condo
Police
Headquarters
L
Anna's Loft
Jeb's
Art Studio
THE PORT
THE SOUTH
Joel's House

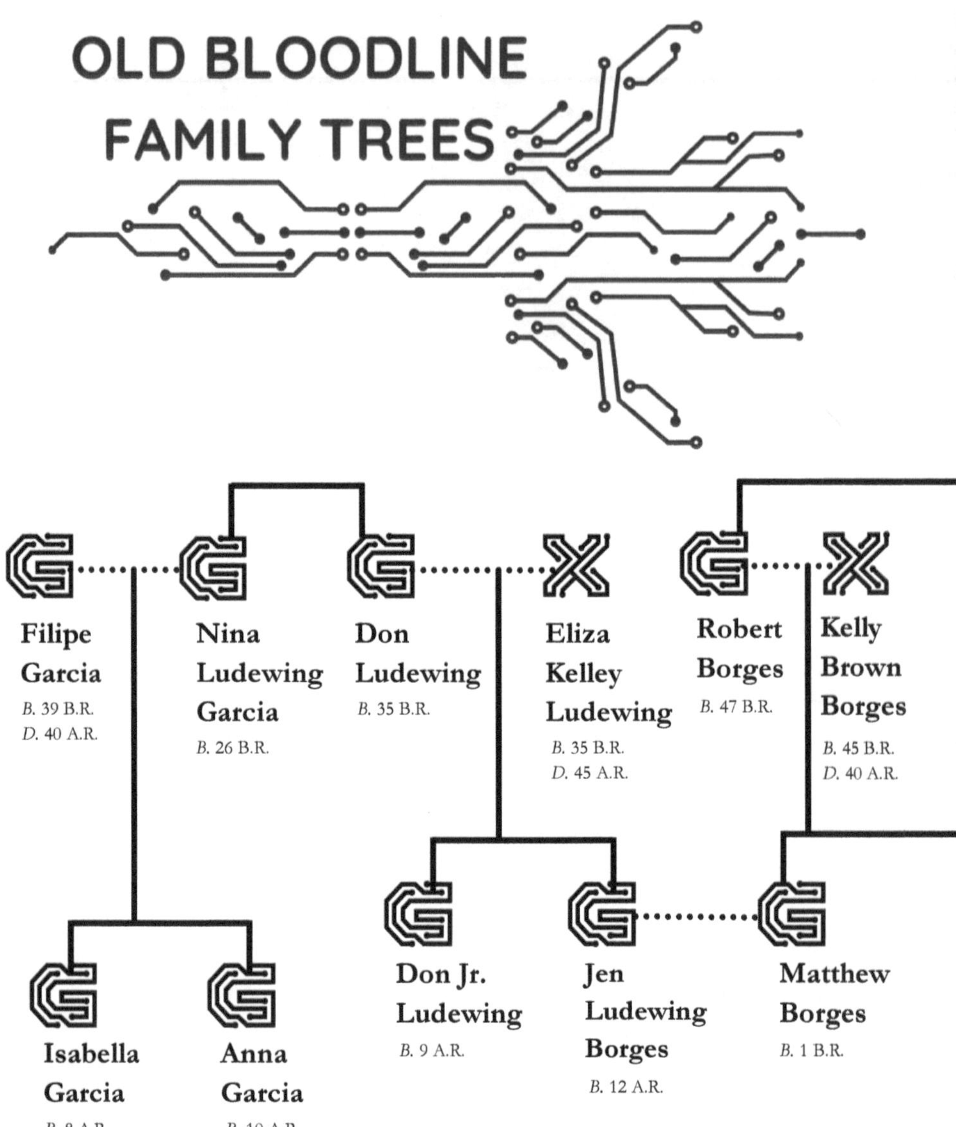
OLD BLOODLINE
FAMILY TREES
Filipe
Garcia
B. 39 B.R.
D. 40 A.R.
Nina
Ludewing
Garcia
B. 26 B.R.
Don
Ludewing
B. 35 B.R.
Eliza
Kelley
Ludewing
B. 35 B.R.
D. 45 A.R.
Robert
Borges
B. 47 B.R.
Kelly
Brown
Borges
B. 45 B.R.
D. 40 A.R.
Isabella
Garcia
B. 8 A.R.
Anna
Garcia
B. 10 A.R.
Don Jr.
Ludewing
B. 9 A.R.
Jen
Ludewing
Borges
B. 12 A.R.
Matthew
Borges
B. 1 B.R.

Legend

Old Bloodline Lineage

Nobody Lineage

.... Marriage/Partnership

—— Blood Relation

B.R. = Years Before Resurgence

A.R. = Years After Resurgence

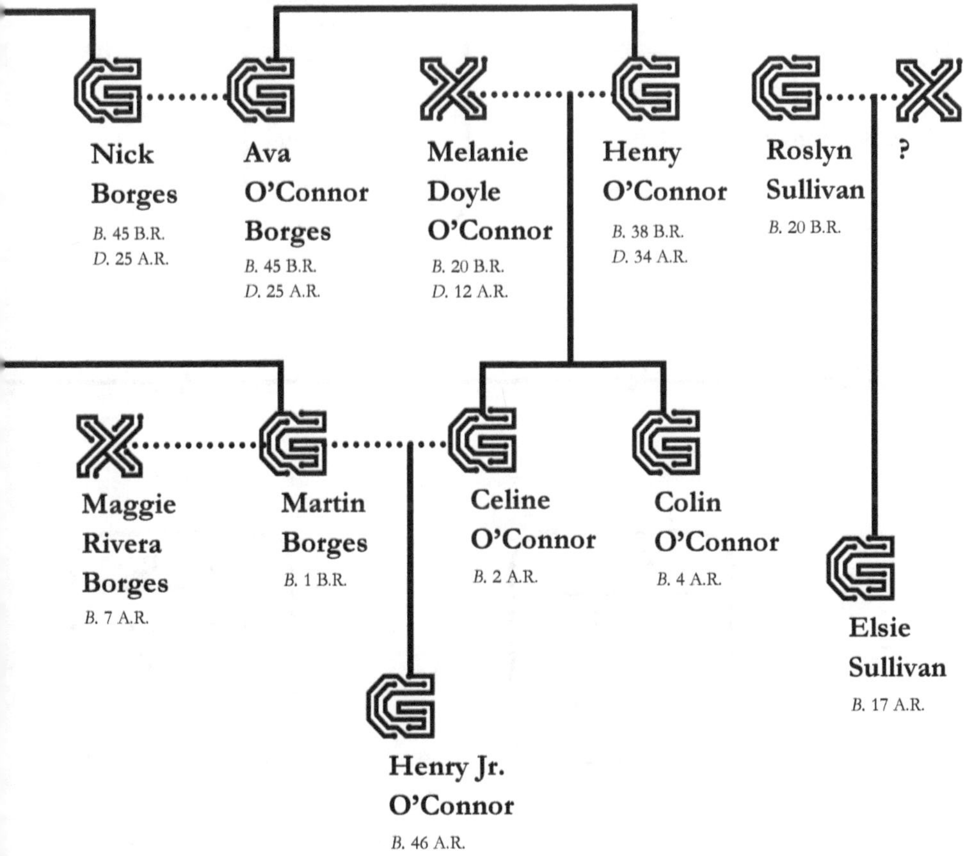

Nick Borges
B. 45 B.R.
D. 25 A.R.

Ava O'Connor Borges
B. 45 B.R.
D. 25 A.R.

Melanie Doyle O'Connor
B. 20 B.R.
D. 12 A.R.

Henry O'Connor
B. 38 B.R.
D. 34 A.R.

Roslyn Sullivan
B. 20 B.R.

?

Maggie Rivera Borges
B. 7 A.R.

Martin Borges
B. 1 B.R.

Celine O'Connor
B. 2 A.R.

Colin O'Connor
B. 4 A.R.

Elsie Sullivan
B. 17 A.R.

Henry Jr. O'Connor
B. 46 A.R.

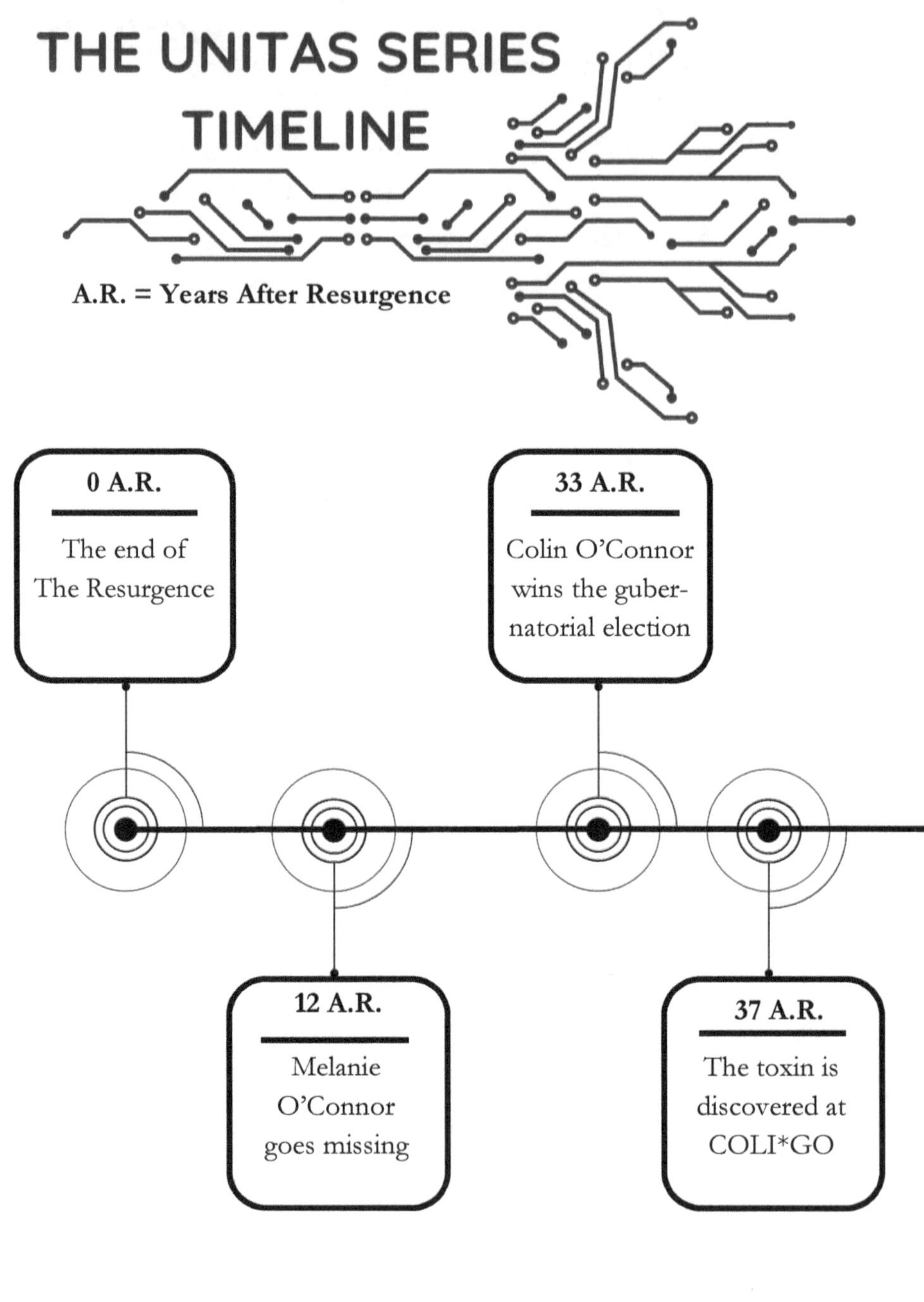
THE UNITAS SERIES
TIMELINE
A.R. = Years After Resurgence
0 A.R.
The end of
The Resurgence
12 A.R.
Melanie
O'Connor
goes missing
33 A.R.
Colin O'Connor
wins the guber-
natorial election
37 A.R.
The toxin is
discovered at
COLI*GO

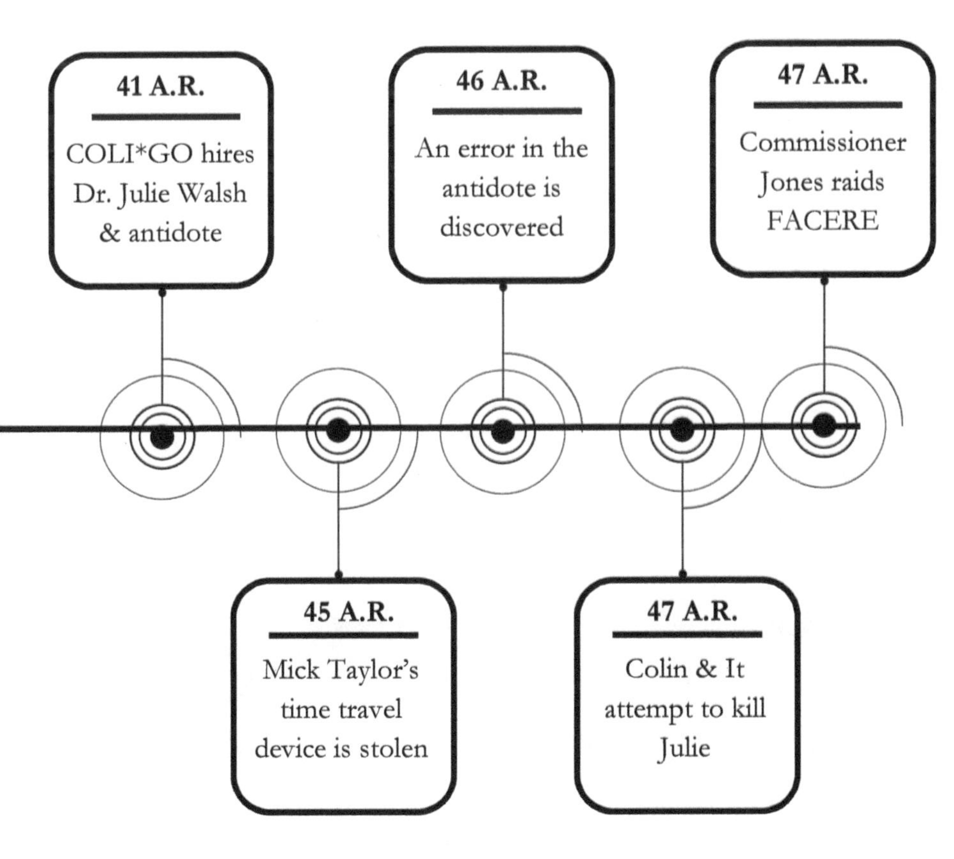
41 A.R.
COLI*GO hires Dr. Julie Walsh & antidote
46 A.R.
An error in the antidote is discovered
47 A.R.
Commissioner Jones raids FACERE
45 A.R.
Mick Taylor's time travel device is stolen
47 A.R.
Colin & It attempt to kill Julie

PART ONE

The Past

"Dreams are messages from the deep."
—Frank Herbert

Prologue
It

June 23rd, 46 A.R. (A.R. = Years After Resurgence)

It looked out across the estate with curiosity. The moonlight cast shadows across the edge of the cliffs along The Oceanside, illuminating not one but two figures. Sounds of crashing waves consumed him, drowning out any conversation the women were having with one another.

He wondered why two Julies were standing out on the lawn. It rubbed his eyes, afraid he was seeing things that weren't completely real. But he wasn't imagining this.

Both Julies argued for a few minutes, one Julie waving her hands frantically around her body while the other Julie stepped back, edging herself closer to the side of the cliffs. This Julie looked different—she wore a sheer white blouse, and her body was more rigid. With the brightness of the moon, he could see dark markings beneath her shirt, scattered across her abdomen and left ribcage.

Scars. Wounds.

It grinned at the thought.

He traveled time before, traveled to the past at least; he instinctively knew Julie traveled time now too. How else could there be two of them here in one moment in time?

The idea captivated It in an oddly satisfying manner, and he wondered which liberties Julie took advantage of with her ability to also travel time.

The other Julie he recognized with ease—her hair was pulled into a messy bun, the golden and red flecks shimmering against her iridescent skin even in the darkness. She still wore Colin's undershirt after stealing it earlier in the evening.

It looked down, his bare chest showcasing small goosebumps from the cool ocean breeze. Colin's shirt . . . his shirt. He hated admitting they were one and the same.

Suddenly, the Julie he recognized gripped the foreign Julie's shoulders, and the two danced awkwardly along the cliffs. It knew what was about to happen, the memories of Melanie O'Connor's death flooding rapidly into this mind. Memories of himself grabbing Melanie's delicate shoulders before purposefully releasing them in a single push.

The two Julies approached the jagged parts of the landscape, the unrecognizable Julie's feet teasing the edges along the toothed rocks.

Do it, Julie. Do it, It taunted her in his mind.

And she did.

He watched as Julie's body thrust off the side of the cliff, suspending in the air for a prolonged moment before disappearing out of sight, consumed by the rocky landscape and hungry ocean waves below.

The Julie who previously had been curled up beside Colin only a half-hour ago peered over the side of the cliff, falling to her knees. She placed her head in her hands and cried out, her weeping a familiar, delicious sound. A sound reminding It of when he strangled her a few months ago.

Fear. Hurt. Heartbreak.

It closed his eyes to savor the moment. When he opened his eyes again, It found himself back in his prison, the horrid room holding him captive.

The squishy pink walls pulsated around him, glowing sparks of light zigzagging in a lustrous pattern.

The inside of Colin's brain.

It wasn't sure how he got here, wasn't sure why sometimes he could escape, why he was able to not only see but also experience memories. It later blamed the antidote—Julie's antidote—for trapping him here. For slowly killing him or, at least, for trying to kill him.

Did I imagine this? he wondered, the sight of Julie's mangled body down by the shoreline shimmering across his vision. The water lingering around her broken fingertips, her cracked bones. The way Julie's dead eyes looked into his before finally closing. Her blood trickling around her into the sand, the same way he eerily imagined blood soaking around her in the snow—another vision he didn't comprehend, at least, not yet.

That was the problem with time travel. Time travel played tricks on the mind, blurring the edges of what was real and what was simply a dream.

It looked down at his hands, the stain of crimson blood seeping within the thin lines of his palms, visibly screaming at him. The other Julie's blood.

No, It finally decided. *I did not imagine this.*

PART TWO

The Present

"In life, unlike chess, the game continues after checkmate."
—Isaac Asimov

Chapter 1
The Governor

February 24th, 47 A.R.

Joel Kennsington stared back at Colin with a menacing grin that spread from corner to corner of his mouth. Colin couldn't stand the man, never could. Joel was fairly attractive and of similar age to Colin but stood shorter and carried himself in a more bullish manner—attempting to take up as much space as possible with his overconfidence.

To be fair, Colin thought, *it's rare to be taller than me.*

Colin's office surprisingly remained mostly untouched, but he himself didn't occupy the space each day as he had less than a month ago. Instead, Colin was the room's prisoner, the gatekeeper to the most ineffective, incompetent, and selfish politician in all of The Constituency. Colin missed his office being distinctly his—the beautiful mahogany desk, the lovely chessboard sitting on the side table gifted to him by his sister Celine, the picture of his mother, and all the memories.

Colin's fingers brushed around the edges of a folded piece of paper in his pocket, a notion turned into a habit to soothe him when faced with this piggish man. Like her note, thoughts of Julie curled around the edges of his mind, her smile appearing lovingly in his vision. He held on to the small piece of hope that he would see her calming and supportive grin spread across her freckled face again. The only image of her that provided him with any sanity.

Someday? he wondered, unsure.

Colin released her letter from between his fingers and removed his hands from his pockets before clasping them together.

"So what's on the schedule today?" Colin asked coyly, the sarcasm and irritation strong in his voice.

Joel swiveled in his chair—Colin's chair—and looked around at him with a snicker before answering. "The Representatives of The Androids are pushing for a resolution on The Supreme's charges. The commissioner has yet to make a final verdict, and I don't know if I should get involved."

I should be the one getting involved, not you, Colin thought angrily.

If there was one thing that enraged Colin the most, it was lack of control. Colin spent his whole life with structure and predictability. Chaos and uncertainty made him spiral, unable to grasp his own personal pitfalls and demons.

But if Colin wanted to contain his current situation, it was better to aid Joel from complete disaster. And selfishly, Colin needed a resolution for The Supreme so that he could finally face his own fate.

"Have you tried speaking with the commissioner directly? And not in your impish, impatient way? Ask him what's making him timid in finalizing his verdict."

Colin knew what really caused the commissioner such grief. He faced fallout from The Representatives of The Androids if he did the right thing—if he formally put The Supreme on trial for her crimes and requested the high judge dictate her penalty.

Consequently, if the commissioner did nothing and didn't bring The Supreme before the judicial system, The Representatives of The People would skin the emerald green scales off his body and parade the android around The City with his head on a stake.

"He won't take any of my appointment requests unless you attend with me," Joel answered, the venom in his tone pungent. Colin couldn't contain his own smug smile.

For nearly the last month, Joel took the informal role as "acting governor" while Colin remained in limbo.

A few weeks ago, Colin turned himself in to The Legislature and explained how he killed Kathleen Murphy, his secretary and legislative aide, after discovering the wretched experiment she became at the hands of The Supreme.

Colin shared how he didn't wish to kill Kathleen but she requested he did—she could not handle the pain and side effects from the operation any longer. The Supreme, his android counterpart in The Legislature, ran horrifying science experiments on humans by turning them into a hybrid species she called posse hominems. After a microchip was placed into a human's brain, they became half-human and half-android.

Colin learned Kathleen was turned into one of these creatures against her will with plans to turn against humans at The Supreme's will. Colin truly didn't want to kill Kathleen and had almost backed out of the notion completely while he held her paralyzed body in his arms.

Kathleen was his oldest friend, and he had often felt like she was the sister he wished he had over his own. Kathleen's voice had sliced through Colin's heart, and to this day, he still heard her thick City accent as she took her last breaths and spoke her last words.

Yah have tah kill me. I don't even wanna be me. It hurts. And . . . and yah have tah stahp The Supreme. Expose her.

Colin wanted to expose The Supreme for all her crimes, but she knew too much about his own colored past. Julie reminded Colin there was one way to bring down The Supreme and her evilness: by exposing himself before The Supreme could reveal him.

The plan somewhat worked. The Legislature accused The Supreme of violating human rights, treason, and abuse of power.

But Colin wasn't let off the hook either.

The representatives weren't sure what to do with him—he had saved the government from being overthrown but also murdered a citizen in the process. The Legislature didn't know he was a serial killer, and neither did they know the full extent of his crimes.

Uneasy about having a man who killed his own staffer as their elected official, the representatives made their Session speaker, Representative Joel Kennsington, assume the responsibilities of the role until the final decision was made.

Joel Kennsington was a vocal member of the Humanizer party, a sect of The Representatives of The People who held on to beliefs that considered androids as second-class citizens.

Luckily for Colin, the public didn't know he was placed under house arrest as he patiently waited for an accusation from the commissioner's office. The public still believed he was their governor, and in a sense, Colin still was.

At least for now.

"Then what are we waiting for?" Colin asked, a devilish grin appearing on his face. "Let's pay the commissioner a visit."

***

Jones looked surprised to see Colin and Joel in his new office. Colin and Jones had a complex relationship. As Julie's best friend, Jones knew her secrets, and he knew many of Colin's.

Jones had been the one to piece together the truth about Julie's disappearance and discovered Colin's attempt to kill her. Whether Jones agreed with Colin's reasoning—believing Julie was a posse hominem meant to destroy society on behalf of The Supreme—Colin had yet to determine. All Jones knew was Colin hadn't succeeded in killing Julie. Nor had he wanted to.

To Colin's surprise, Jones kept his crimes a secret and didn't expose him as The City's infamous serial killer who plagued the streets with horrific murders for over a decade. Instead, Jones insisted on helping Colin. Or at least, trying to help him.

Jones had appeared in Colin's townhouse the morning after he and It left Julie in the woods. Jones pulled out the missing doses of COL23, the antidote—the antidote Julie invented, one that promised to cure Colin of It, his other personality. His sinister personality.

But the bottles of COL23 sat inside Colin's refrigerator back at the townhouse. Untouched.

"Commissioner," Joel addressed Jones, outstretching his hand. Jones did not shake it.

"Representative Kennsington." Jones smiled slightly as he addressed the man. "Governor O'Connor."

After The Legislature arrested The Supreme, all her appointed androids stepped down from their positions. The Representatives of The Androids deemed Detective Jones worthy of the promotion as The City's commissioner.

Jones was smart and intuitive, but he seemed tired of solving The City's largest crimes and mysteries. Colin wondered how much those representatives knew of Jones's history and his connection to all of them.

"We were hoping to better understand timelines regarding any accusations against The Supreme from your department," Joel said, jumping right in. This wasn't how Colin would have approached the situation, another stark difference between himself and the "acting governor."

"I see," Jones responded slowly.

"I think what Joel meant to say," Colin said, taking a seat to ease the tension among the three of them, "was if there's anything you need from us or The Legislature, we are more than happy to help you."

"I know what Representative Kennsington meant to say," Jones said in a harsh tone. Joel drew in his breath sharply, agitation spreading across his body in a strained manner.

"I'm in the middle of an investigation behind your office's accusations against The Supreme. Once we understand the reality of the situation, then I will request her trial to the high judge." Joel rolled his eyes, tapping his fingers against Jones's desk with annoyance.

"Am I not moving swiftly enough for your liking, Representative Kennsington?" Jones spat at him with equal impatience.

"No, you're not. We need answers. The Legislature needs answers. The public needs answers."

"I don't believe in rash decisions, rash allegations. And I'd prefer if you made an official appointment next time," Jones said, his scales shimmering from a dull green to a vibrant emerald, indicating he felt the emotions he experienced, which was a rarity for androids.

Colin couldn't help but smile knowing Jones not only understood most human emotions but also felt them too. A distinction that was paramount and illegal. As an android, Jones wasn't technically allowed to feel or understand more than 20 percent of human emotions, but in reality, Jones knew and felt over 60 percent.

"You're making this worse, Commissioner. Dragging out this process isn't helping people or androids find peace. Kennsington is correct: We need answers. We must move forward—in whatever direction that ends up being."

"You can get out of my office too, Colin," Jones responded sharply and informally, so much so that Joel's eyes widened.

Colin was surprised by the venom and nastiness in Jones's voice, a sense of betrayal running through his veins. But Colin understood Jones had also been through many tragedies lately, and processing those while not instinctually understanding all his emotions might make that a challenge for the android.

"You can't tell us what to do, Commissioner. I'll be back, with or without the governor. I'll be calling your office daily until you decide to buck up and do your goddamn job," Joel hissed, his teeth glaring as he stood from his seat.

Colin looked back at Jones, hoping to find some sense of solace, some kind of understanding that they could share. A slight nod from Jones was all Colin needed to confirm that Jones didn't hate him—that Jones was also confused and hurting.

But gaining Jones's trust required more effort than Colin initially anticipated.

Chapter 2
Commissioner Jones

February 24th, 47 A.R.

The walls in the prison cast large shadows in the dark hallway as he approached the holding cell. Jones braced himself for the long-awaited announcement he would have to make to The Legislature in the next few days.

When Jones looked up, he saw an android with rainbow-like yellow scales nodding in his direction from the doorway. His arm lifted behind him, gesturing at the door.

It was time.

Jones took a deep breath and closed his eyes. When he opened them, the brightness inside the room caught him by surprise.

The Supreme sat in a plastic white chair in the far corner. Her eyes pierced directly through Jones, and a blank expression remained painted on her face. Her orange jumpsuit contrasted against her amber-colored scales, and her braided hair was hastily thrown over her shoulders. The Supreme didn't bother to stand; she didn't even acknowledge Jones's entrance.

"Madam Supreme," Jones said, standing awkwardly in the corner as he nodded for the yellow android to close the door. The Supreme's left eyebrow raised slightly at the sound of her name. "I came to talk to you about what is to occur in the next few days."

The Supreme stayed silent, but her eyes narrowed in on Jones. Jones shifted his weight back and forth on each foot. Discomfort was one of the thousands of feelings he both understood and experienced himself.

"I'm going to The Legislature soon," Jones continued, examining The Supreme for any kind of glimpse that emotions ran through her processor. She gave nothing away. "I will request a fair trial. They've accused you of many crimes, and it'll take about another month before they bring you in for questioning. That will be your opportunity to set the record straight, if you choose."

Jones expected The Supreme to answer, but she continued in her silence. He grabbed his device from his pocket and pulled up the list he already had memorized in his processor.

"Treason, first-degree murder on multiple counts, attempt to murder, embezzlement, theft," Jones rattled off the list. He looked over at The Supreme from his device. No movement, no inclination of her guilt or innocence. "I'm sure you know them all by heart now."

Jones wanted to feel bad for The Supreme, and in some ways he did. Her actions were unforgivable, but Jones knew what it was like to be a minority. To be thought of as a second-class citizen. The Supreme wanted to change the tides for androids, and while her direction and approach were too extreme, Jones couldn't completely blame her.

He cleared his throat. "There's got to be an explanation of how this is possible. How an android could even do this. All the experts at FACERE claim the microchips wouldn't allow for this kind of behavior, or at least this repeated behavior." The Supreme's eyes grew wide as a vicious grin spread across her face.

Finally, a reaction from her, Jones thought as he watched her scales light up beautifully, shining and shimmering in the harsh light. The gorgeous amber browns and golden hues intertwined together.

"Do you really have nothing to say?" Jones asked. "You're going to just let this happen? You're not even going to defend yourself?"

The Supreme crossed her arms and leaned back farther in her chair, her lips pressing slightly together. Jones turned toward the door, ready to knock for the prison guard to return.

"You have the answer to FACERE's questions, Commissioner. How is it that you understand more than the legal limit of human feelings and emotions?"

The Supreme's words stopped Jones dead in his tracks. The hated feeling of fear crept into his body, and the aching of his scales harmfully made room for the sensation.

"Did it ever occur to you that I also understand more human emotions than I'm allowed? I could make an educated guess at which human recoded your microchip."

Jones didn't respond but gave The Supreme a strong, authoritative look—one commanding fury.

"She is everyone's favorite little serpent." The Supreme's words cut across the room with a palpable sharpness. "I wonder, Commissioner . . . Do you think she screamed in fear when she realized the only man she ever trusted, the only man she ever loved, stabbed her twenty-three times? Do you think my opponent left anything of her mental stability behind? Do you think maybe Colin changed her forever? Beyond human repair? How it was a blessing for her to have a microchip in her brain so that I could program her in the future if I needed?"

"Leave Julie out of this." Jones's words were harsh and impulsive. He took a deep breath, calming himself as anger bubbled inside him and glowed across his body in sharp green varieties.

The Supreme chuckled at him as his scales lit up uncontrollably.

"I really like Julie. She has so much potential. As a hybrid, she can lead both people and androids someday."

"I think we're done here, Madam Supreme," Jones answered, hastily knocking on the door.

The guard cracked the door open, his eyes inspecting The Supreme for a moment too long. Having an android here in the prison was rare, let alone the most powerful android leader across The Constituency.

"You can take away my dignity, Commissioner Jones. But you can't take away my vision for our society," The Supreme said before the door closed behind him.

Her words lingered in Jones's processor for the rest of the day.

***

A quiet knock sounded at the entrance of Jones's office. He looked up and found a beautiful human woman in his doorway.

Smaller in both height and stature, she stood before him with deep chestnut hair that fell far past her shoulders in soft waves. The warm tones of her skin danced around her bright lipstick, and she outfitted a feminine fitted pantsuit with tall, elegant high heels.

"I don't mean to interrupt, but the receptionist said you were free." This mysterious woman's voice even enchanted Jones as she spoke.

"Come in." Jones gestured for her to sit across from him at his desk. He stood and shook her hand as she approached. "I don't think we've met before."

"Margaret Rivera, but everyone calls me Maggie," she replied with an upbeat grin. "I'm the head of FACERE."

"Nice to finally meet you in person, Ms. Rivera," Jones said with a hesitant smile.

He exchanged multiple messages with various FACERE employees over the last few weeks regarding The Supreme and her processor but never Maggie herself.

Maggie looked around Jones's office and took the seat by his desk. Jones kept his office at the police headquarters sparse; the bookshelf and walls remained fairly empty of any mementos or decoration. Maggie glanced back at Jones with an odd gaze as if he were one of her creations. He wasn't—Maggie looked too young to have made Jones in the android manufacturing lab, appearing to only be in her late thirties. Jones himself was thirty.

"I'm wondering if there's a possibility my team can look at The Supreme's processor, regardless of what occurs at her trial. We want to do an extensive analysis. We would like to know if an error can explain the abnormality. I'm afraid that other androids might be"—she looked up at Jones, remembering she was in the presence of an android—"impacted."

"And if you think other androids are experiencing the same error?" Jones asked, the words slipping between his lips too eagerly.

"Let's not get ahead of ourselves and take this one step at a time. We've never experienced an incident quite like this before."

Jones observed the way Maggie's lips rested in a half-grin, the figurative gears in her own mind turning. "The Supreme's experiments were out of line. Cruel, even," Jones admitted.

"I must agree, but her idea for hybrids is fascinating," Maggie said, leaning closer to Jones's desk. "But COLI*GO isn't the place for such exploration. It should be done at FACERE, if anywhere at all."

"I think that will be up to The Legislature to decide," Jones warned. He was still figuring out the ins and outs of his new role. Jones now held more political responsibility and tact than he initially anticipated when he accepted the promotion.

"Have you formally seen FACERE's facilities?" Maggie asked, her right eyebrow raising with a playful curiosity.

Jones returned a small android-appropriate smile. "I have not."

"I'd like to arrange a visit for you, if you're interested."

Conflict—a feeling Jones recently learned from Colin O'Connor—coursed through him. He was created at FACERE like all androids but had no memory of the place, no memory of what his life was like before he left those walls. Androids didn't remember their birth or their creation process at FACERE. The organization remained quite secretive; there were no photos of the inside of the laboratories or manufacturing facilities in any database, and anyone who worked at FACERE received special government clearance. The organization itself was a quasi-government operation, its history checkered similarly to the biotech firm COLI*GO.

"Isn't that not standard, given that I'm an android?" Jones asked.

Maggie looked around Jones's office before allowing her eyes to wander back to him. She shrugged her shoulders and let out an audible sigh.

"I've always been a big proponent of android leaders knowing their origins, knowing the future of their own beings," she replied innocently. "And besides, you're the commissioner now. Without an active supreme, you're the second-highest-ranking android official in The Constituency. I don't think anyone would bat an eye if you stepped inside FACERE."

"Then I'll take you up on your offer. I'll be interested to see the difference between COLI*GO's and FACERE's labs."

"You must be spending quite a bit of time at COLI*GO these days."

"I am," Jones answered truthfully.

Jones released the lower lab back to The Board of Directors and interim CEO Peter Schneider only a few days ago. No evidence was left behind; The Supreme made sure of that. Jones didn't reveal to anyone his knowledge that Isabella Garcia was involved with The

Supreme and her creation of posse hominems, and none of Jones's detectives found anything that linked the former surgeon to The Supreme's operation.

COLI*GO cut itself an advantageous deal with The Legislature, paying off their crimes with hefty fines by promising to uncover The Supreme's accomplices. COLI*GO continued operating as it always had and stayed out of the spotlight, at least for now. Jones debated sharing his knowledge, but another part of him wanted to see COLI*GO pay its fair share—he didn't believe for a moment that COLI*GO's founder, Celine O'Connor, wasn't aware of what happened in her precious building.

"What do you think of Celine O'Connor's brainchild?" Maggie asked, referring to COLI*GO.

Jones understood Maggie's motivations behind her question, but he wouldn't give her the satisfaction of gossip.

"COLI*GO is impressive, Ms. Rivera. I won't deny that. The O'Connor family built an empire in The City."

"I am all too familiar with the O'Connor family," Maggie replied maliciously. "I'd happily ignite the flame that destroys them if given the match."

Jones made a mental note in his processor of Maggie's odd remark. Old bloodline families weren't always trusted by the public; many gained their wealth from unsavory acts and maintained it through close involvement in both the public and private sectors. But there was also a celebrity-like effect that old bloodline families had on normal people and androids. Many considered them famous, followed the families in the tabloids, and worshiped them. Old bloodline money built The Constituency, and without them, there wouldn't have been opportunities for "nobodies" in society to advance, either.

"Well," Jones responded, "let me know when I can visit FACERE, and we can discuss your access to The Supreme's processor—if that still applies."

Maggie smiled again, her bright red lips spreading stylishly across her face. She stood and shook Jones's hand before departing.

Jones listened to her cascade down the hallway before he looked up Maggie's profile in the database.

Maggie grew up in a poorer section of The City but excelled in public grade school. She was the first in her family to attend The University, where she studied economics, coding, and statistics. After graduating from The University, Maggie entered an internship at FACERE within the finance department and worked her way up through the company. She was only recently promoted to head of FACERE a few years ago, previously holding the position of development lead.

Jones wondered about her hatred for the O'Connor family specifically. Maggie wasn't from an old bloodline family, and from what he could tell, her family didn't work for old bloodlines either. Jones scanned through every digital imprint associated with Maggie's name.

His eyes widened when he discovered a marriage license and divorce papers linking the woman to an old bloodline family from The City, the Borgeses. While not the O'Connors, the name was prominent and still important to society. Upon further research, Jones found another connection, one a bit less obvious.

A photo appeared on the screen of The Ways and Means Committee. Now Jones understood the connection, her hatred. Maggie Rivera was the conduit between the finance team at FACERE and The Capitol Building—working closely with Colin O'Connor before he was elected governor. Jones presumed the two knew each other well—very well—based on the sheepish and bashful grin Maggie gave Colin in the photograph. This was only a look, one that could be interpreted differently depending on the image's viewer, but Jones knew better now that any sliver of a connection to The O'Connors wasn't insignificant at all.

Chapter 3
The Governor

February 24th, 47 A.R.

The O'Connor townhouse seemed different when Colin returned. Joel dropped him off discreetly in the garage, not answering Colin's question about when he would return for him next or how many days would pass where he would be alone.

Colin climbed the stairs before reaching the main living space and sighed. The air felt warmer inside the living room, the smell more floral, sweet, and familiar.

Julie, he thought before shaking his head. Acknowledgment of his loneliness made him imagine her.

Colin couldn't let his mind wander too far down the path of possibility in case she never returned to him. Besides his jaunts to The Capitol Building with Joel and the occasional representative or dignitary they met with, Colin hadn't physically seen or touched another being in nearly a month. Not since the last night with her, not since the next morning when Jones gave him a dose of the antidote. He wasn't sure if his isolation was formally part of his punishment, but he assumed so. Even his own sister, Celine, remained aloof, only sending him a few cryptic messages. But she never returned his calls.

Then there was It.

It was missing in action, and his abandonment felt the harshest to Colin.

Colin often thought back to the night when he and It attempted to kill Julie. The thoughts consumed his mind when he was asleep. He found himself waking in a cold sweat, his stomach turning before he could race to the toilet in the master bathroom. Colin never vomited so much in his life as he had this last month. The night terrors of his mother's horrid death no longer plagued his mind but instead were replaced by the visions and memories of Julie—particularly the way he stabbed her.

The sight of the purple tint of her pale skin, her body freezing as the blood flowed from the twenty-three shallow stab wounds he violated across her body, was more vivid in dreams. The shallowness was uncharacteristic for him based on his previous victims, but he never loved and obsessed over his past victims.

Only Julie.

Of course she will never come back to me. How could she ever forgive me? Colin wondered, his eyes wide and awake, staring up at the ceiling.

The decision to commit such a horrible act wasn't one he wanted to do, but that hadn't been the first time he hadn't wanted to do something so horrid. Colin and It had killed many women before. Colin only hoped that if Julie was really still alive, the way Jones led him to believe, that she understood the reasoning. That she understood he was trying to save The City from the evil monster The Supreme had unknowingly turned Julie into.

A half-human half-android hybrid.

Colin rose from his bed and walked into the bathroom. The light felt unbecoming on his reflection in the mirror. The faint lines from the corner of his eyes were deeper as he approached his forty-third birthday. His normally olive skin looked a bit paler, and the bags under his eyes grew more pronounced each day. At least he hadn't lost much weight—something his nearly six-and-a-half-foot tall figure couldn't withstand.

Colin slowly opened the vanity doors, and his eyes glossed over the various pill bottles lined up beneath the sink. He closed and opened the door multiple times before deciding to reach for a particular bottle of benzodiazepines, a type of sleeping pill. The coating left a chalky feeling on his tongue before he slugged it down with help from the bottle of Scotch he now always kept on his nightstand.

Grabbing Julie's college sweatshirt, Colin curled into the bed. The mascot of The University was faded on the warm fabric, but he held it with conviction and tried to avoid the horrid hallucinations filling his mind as the pills worked their way through his body. The sleeping pills caused nasty side effects, but at least once Colin fell asleep, the sight of Julie dying at his hands wouldn't occupy his thoughts, wouldn't haunt him.

As Colin drifted to sleep, he dreamed of Julie and almost felt her loving touch. When he opened his eyes, he found the touch wasn't completely imagined.

Isabella Garcia sat on the corner of his bed. Not Julie.

Colin shot straight up, instinctively moving away from Isabella's touch as if the tips of her fingers burned him.

Colin and Isabella had spent nearly a decade together, and their relationship was not only complex but also incredibly intertwined within all facets of their public old bloodline family lives. Isabella was a beautiful and kind woman, of a rivalry old bloodline family from The Island. She possessed luscious brown curls that softly brushed her caramel-colored skin. A small woman in stature, Isabella was nothing but fierce and intelligent—originally a surgeon by training who gave up her lucrative profession for that of philanthropy and activism.

Colin's stagnant personal life veered crazily off course after he met Julie Walsh, a graduate student from The University. Julie had presented her antidote and years' worth of research to his sister's biotech company, COLI*GO. While Colin and Julie didn't explore their mutual attraction until many years later, once they did, they were inseparable.

Isabella and Colin's public split wasn't blamed on his infidelity; Isabella at least gave him the parting gift of needing to move back to The Island to take care of her mother, allowing the public to believe that their relationship had naturally run its course. No hatred existed between Isabella and Colin; they cared about one another from the sheer fact that they had spent so much of their lives together.

Isabella examined Colin's master bedroom, her eyes growing wide at the sight of the bottle of Scotch on the nightstand and his clothes uncharacteristically thrown across his room. Colin was a structured man, one of control and precision.

"Colin," Isabella said, taking a deep breath in. "What are you doing?"

"What am I doing?" he asked with his hands angrily flying in the air, annoyed by Isabella's intrusion into his home.

Isabella picked up the bottle of Scotch and walked toward the bathroom. Colin quickly arose from the confines of his bedsheets and followed her. Flicking off the lid, Isabella dumped the contents from the bottle down the drain.

"Isabella," Colin tested quietly, the anger continuing to build in his mind.

"You can't let yourself waste away, Colin," she responded and opened the sink vanity, grabbing as many pill bottles in her delicate and perfectly manicured hands as she could.

Colin stood idly, watching as Isabella unscrewed the caps off each bottle and emptied them over the toilet before flushing it. He shook his head, but the knowledge of his secret stash in his study kept him calm.

"I can't sleep without those."

"That's a lie."

Colin watched as Isabella continued investigating his home, moving from the master bathroom before heading downstairs to the kitchen. Isabella spared discarding his expensive liquors, avoiding his study entirely.

She knows but doesn't want to see the actuality of my demons. Of It. Isabella always made that clear.

Isabella eyed the beer in his refrigerator suspiciously—knowing Colin never drank beer—before leaving the bottles untouched.

The beer was for It, not for Colin. If It ever returned.

"Why are you here, Isabella?" Colin asked, his arms crossed inquisitively as he watched her parade around his home.

"Would saying I miss you not be acceptable?" Her words were quiet, and she shielded her eyes from him as she spoke.

"No."

"You're so cold, Colin."

"Well, that's what happens when all you've ever loved is taken away from you," Colin answered bitterly, not caring if his words hurt Isabella.

He had loved her once—but that was so long ago now.

"Answer that yourself. You took Julie away." Isabella's voice broke as she glared up at Colin.

Colin cautiously stepped away from her.

How does she know? What does she know? Colin wondered, standing up straighter.

"I know there's nothing romantic between us, Colin. There hasn't been for a very long time. But I do still love you." He didn't know how to respond to Isabella. He chose silence. "At least let me help you get back on track. Let me help you"—her eyes darted around the mess inside the townhouse—"clean yourself up."

Even Colin acknowledged the disarray of his home and how the current state of it didn't reflect his true personality.

"I'll admit, it's nice to see someone," Colin answered, the words lingering between his lips in a surprisingly warm manner.

"You haven't seen anyone?" Isabella asked, approaching him with hesitation. Her fingers traced his jawline, an affectionate moment he would have appreciated from her years ago but not today.

"No," Colin admitted, stiffening as he moved away from Isabella's touch. "Not since what happened at The Capitol Building. The only person I see regularly is Joel. I'm lucky to speak with other representatives. Sometimes Commissioner Jones. But otherwise, I live here, and I wait."

"It hurts my heart that you live this way. You can't give up. You must keep fighting. For the people of The Constituency. For the androids too. We all need you."

Isabella placed her hand delicately on Colin's chest, careful to avoid any suggestive manner. Her intentions seemed kind and familiar. A tenderness that Colin leaned into and appreciated.

"I want to help you. I promised Julie . . ." Her eyes flitted to the vials of COL23—the antidote—sitting in his open refrigerator, untouched.

Isabella picked up one bottle in her tiny hand and admired the clear liquid inside. A promising innovation. One meant to save society.

"Why didn't you . . ." She didn't finish her sentence before looking up at Colin.

"Why should I?" Colin asked, grabbing the vial from her and placing it back in the fridge. "Why should I destroy something so important to me, something that is me? Taking the antidote won't bring back Julie."

Chapter 4
Julie

January 28th, 47 A.R.

Her eyes opened with an intensity that Julie Walsh hadn't felt in a very long time. Moments before, she was thrown off a cliff on the edge of The Oceanside. Her past self pushed her over the ledge. Now, Julie felt a familiar, terrible feeling seeping inside. She attempted to kill herself and create a time loop. But her plan hadn't worked quite as she intended.

Julie expected pure death. Instead, the woods surrounded her, and she lay peacefully in the snow, her body numb from the cold. She recognized this place instantly: This was where Colin took her, where Colin tried to kill her.

But he didn't succeed.

The snow surrounding her body was painted a familiar deep red, the repercussions of Colin's knife slicing open her body, allowing it to leak out into the sticky snow.

In shock and fear, Julie's hands instinctively landed on her abdomen. She expected to find twenty-three fresh, shallow, open wounds across her stomach. A large sigh of relief left her body as her fingertips only traced her newly healed scars.

How? She wondered. Logic couldn't explain Julie's situation, but she quickly learned from her experiences with time travel that anything related to it was hardly logical. *Was Mick correct in his assumption about death and time travel?*

A chill ran through her body as she sat up. By killing herself while she time traveled, her body was supposed to end up back to where she would actually die.

But I didn't die here.

The harshness of The City's winter weather was bitter, as if The City itself knew what was to come. Julie quickly found her time travel device in her pocket, her fingers brushing methodically against the round shape of the collapsed glasses and the pointed edges of the chrome box that accompanied it.

The crunching sound of familiar footsteps in the snow forced an alertness in Julie. She was familiar with the sound, reliving the sequence of events from when she lay here in the snowy woods before. The sound came from Mick Taylor, her former friend and the inventor of time travel.

He was searching for her broken body; the body Colin left to bleed out in the cold, empty woods.

Not this body.

After Colin tried killing Julie, Mick came back and rescued her in these woods. He brought Julie to the future, where Dr. Isabella Garcia tended to Julie's wounds. But then Mick tricked her and lied to her. He sent her back for selfish reasons.

Julie wasn't sure if she could trust her friend anymore.

He aligned himself with The Supreme, an android willing to do the unthinkable for control and power. An android Julie had once trusted before she turned her into a new species.

Mick couldn't know about her time traveling abilities yet. He couldn't know she escaped her time loop. Mick was the one who sent her back in time, thinking the outcome of that decision would trap her within various dimensions of time.

Julie's fingers raced to her neck, feeling the terrible jagged scar left behind from when Isabella removed the microchip in her brain.

But Julie didn't have time to think. Mick was after her, thinking he would find a weak, stabbed, and hopeless Julie in this spot.

She stood, expecting her body to respond in complete pain, but strength consumed her, and she ran. Julie didn't care how loud her footsteps were, she didn't care if Mick saw her figure running between the trees, darting through the branches and diving in and out of wintertime brush. Julie didn't know where she would end up, but once she was out of the woods, she could formulate a better plan and figure out how to navigate herself in this world that was both so familiar to her and so vastly different from what she remembered.

When she felt Mick wasn't chasing her anymore, Julie took a

deep breath. She made it outside of the woods and into a neighborhood along the bounds of The City.

One she didn't recognize.

Following signs for the subway, Julie walked in the brisk, dark evening. There were many parts of The City that Julie was unfamiliar with. She had been born in The Outskirts, but her family moved to The Monument neighborhood while she was fairly young. Her father hoped the closer proximity to premiere hospitals would help her mother, who suffered from early onset dementia and an undiagnosed psychological condition.

The streets were lined with triple-decker homes that couldn't be identified or separated from one another in the dark except by their distinct, different colors. The actual presence of the homes, knowing multiple families were living within all the walls and corridors, bothered Julie. The complete discrepancy between old bloodline families and nobodies was prominent in the outer parts of The City compared to downtown.

This discrepancy bothered Colin, something he worked hard to fight each day within The Legislature as the governor. Colin truly cared about the nobodies of their society, much before Julie came into his life.

Julie finally reached the red subway line and fumbled in her pocket for her monthly pass. Pressing against her fingers, the metal chip allowed her entry into the ancient underground transportation system.

No one bothered or spoke with Julie on her commute back into The City's downtown area. Instead, humans and androids alike ignored her, allowing her to sit uncomfortably in her own nervousness.

Closing her eyes and leaning back into the sticky seat, Julie's heart rapidly raced inside her chest. She wanted desperately to return to Colin's townhouse in The Hill but knew she couldn't. She wasn't sure what his response would be if he saw her alive. She already betrayed him, albeit unknowingly, by being a posse hominem.

A former posse hominem, she reminded herself.

Going back to him wasn't the answer. Julie couldn't intertwine with what fate had in store for Colin within the next few days. She was a firm believer in trying to keep the past as pure as possible. Events needed to play out as they were intended; that was Julie's whole purpose for creating the time loop at The Oceanside.

But I failed.

Julie entertained the idea of finding Jones, showing up at his and Mick's front stoop in The Harbor. But going there didn't feel right to her either.

The beautiful lights of The City ricocheted across the train cars in the nighttime darkness. There was only one place Julie could go, but it wouldn't be a permanent solution because her father would report her missing in a few days.

Julie's apartment on Commonwealth Avenue welcomed her silently, nothing out of place or touched since the last time she occupied the space. She walked cautiously through the one-room apartment. Her studio felt cool and unforgiving simply because she knew this would be one of her last times here, at least for a long time. After reading Mick's journal entries, she learned he often returned to her place looking for both her and his journal.

The softness of Julie's bed enticed her, and she oddly felt warmth and reassurance when embracing the smell within her bedding. The smell of not just her but of Colin. His scent cascaded from her pillowcases, her sheets. Everywhere.

While some version of Colin had just stabbed her twenty-three times, Julie let herself indulge in the familiarity of him. She allowed herself to wonder if there could be a day where they would be together again. An odd sense of hope granted her a small resolution to the problems lingering between them.

Julie looked down at the band on her ring finger.

Over a year ago, Colin gave her a beautiful emerald ring that once belonged to his mother. Right here in her very bed was where he proposed, expressing his honest and raw love for her. Julie's mind drifted to that memory: Colin came over after the celebration of his victory in the election—he would serve The Constituency and continue his quest for peace and prosperity for humans and androids for six more years. Colin had held her, devoting his energy to helping her bring the antidote to life at COLI*GO before confessing his other intentions with her.

Intentions of spending the rest of their lives together.

Their relationship was a secret and would likely always remain one. Julie was a nobody in society, and while she made a name for herself, she wasn't part of any old bloodline family. There were expectations that Colin O'Connor would marry someone from another old bloodline family, someone like Dr. Isabella Garcia. But Colin and Julie shared so much of their lives with one another that she didn't care that their relationship was a secret.

Their connection was strangely unexplainable.

Colin was the first person she truly opened up to after her mother's death, and similarly, Julie was the only person who accepted Colin for who he really was.

Or who she thought he really was.

Julie looked back down at the ring again and twirled it around her finger. The emerald stone was enchanting, the diamonds scattered across the edges of the main setting. She coveted the ring and everything it symbolized about her and Colin's love.

Feeling heavy with her emotions and her inability to logically know what to do with her next move, Julie allowed the visions of Colin to swirl around her brain. She imagined him at the townhouse and wondered if he felt any kind of remorse for what he tried to do to her.

She believed he did, but for now, Julie realized the best thing for her was sleep.

***

The harsh realities of the shadowy morning illuminated through Julie's large bay windows as her alarm shrieked. Julie climbed out of bed and opened her freezer, pausing at the unfamiliar object within.

Mick's journal.

Julie pulled out the neatly wrapped leather book with its yellowed pages and sadly smiled. As she thumbed through the book, an idea sparked inside her. With a plan finally forming in her head, Julie wrote vigorously on the icy pages and drank her coffee. Pulling out her device, she sent off a message before she could second guess herself.

Julie showered, changed her clothes, packed a bag with some belongings, the time travel device and the journal, and quietly walked out onto the street.

A liberating feeling flooded her as she continued out into the open. No one glanced at her with uncertainty; no one cared that twelve hours ago, another version of her actually went missing—a part of her she would never get back.

Julie's legs carried her, leading her to the place she was dreading most: COLI*GO.

She decided not to take the subway and allowed the long walk and extra effort so that she could clear her thoughts before arriving at the office and confronting someone she didn't want to face.

Walking through The Hill hurt Julie's soul in a peculiar way; the wounds in her heart festered uncontrollably at all the memories she had here. The sidewalks were constructed from a beautiful brown and red brick, flowing down the street in an inviting manner. The road brought her to the bridge, and she crossed the deep blue river, once polluted beyond what anyone thought would be repair. But COLI*GO had fixed that, too.

The River neighborhood stood across the strongly constructed beams of the old bridge. The shimmering buildings of technological and biotech buildings, research facilities and laboratories, stood tall and proud.

Julie's feet felt heavy as she walked through The River toward the COLI*GO headquarters. It was still early when she approached the lobby and swiped her badge.

A security guard nodded at Julie. He was tall like most androids, and his scales shone a deep midnight blue.

"Good morning, Dr. Walsh. You're in early."

"I have a very important and confidential meeting this morning," Julie responded, handing over her device to him. He nodded and handed back her device.

Julie took the elevators up to the 101st floor of the building, the location of offices for all COLI*GO's executives and senior directors. She wished for a moment she was back in the lab, back in her tiny cubicle contained within the middle of the building.

This was where it all began.

Julie's office was untouched, her things scattered illogically across her desk. The mess oddly greeted her with a sense of comfort. Julie wasn't as organized or structured as Colin, but to her, the mess made sense. She knew exactly where everything was.

Julie spent the last six months collecting and uncovering proof in her investigation of The Supreme and her terrible misuse of company power and funds. She tracked down ledgers and found cryptic but incriminating evidence against not just The Supreme but those on The Board of Directors who helped her keep these illegal activities hushed. The Supreme was funneling money into a special project in the lower lab—one where she transformed humans unknowingly and unwillingly into hybrids. Julie already traveled back in time, giving this information to Colin in the form of a letter, one he would open this morning when Jones came to visit him.

Colin will expose The Supreme in a couple of days and confess to Kathleen's murder, Julie realized.

As she quietly cleaned up her office, a light knock registered against the door.

Representative Joel Kennsington examined Julie with an intriguing gaze. Julie matched his expression, a form of flattery the man greatly welcomed. A thrilling sensation ripped through Julie's body like a strong current: Joel didn't know she was supposed to be missing and Colin's crimes from last night hadn't caught up with the light of day.

And they never will.

"I'm surprised you asked me to urgently meet you this morning, Dr. Walsh," Joel said with a peculiar type of curiosity.

Joel paced back and forth near the doorway for a moment longer before reaching the chair opposite her desk. Julie found his hesitancy to her as COLI*GO's CEO—the most powerful and influential biotech company in The City—odd.

"What happened to you?" he finally asked, his eyes drifting toward the graphic scar cascading down her neck.

Julie's hands instinctively flung up to cover her healed wound. The scar became such a part of her now that she forgot how horrific it truly looked to those who knew her without it.

"That's part of why I asked you to meet with me," Julie answered honestly. "The Supreme changed me into a new species, a hybrid of androids and humans. She did so without my permission, and I discovered others in COLI*GO are behind this too."

While on the opposite side of political ideology, Joel Kennsington was powerful within The Legislature and knew how to make noise about what happened to her and what happened to so many other humans without their permission. For an unexplainable reason, Julie held Isabella's involvement close to her chest, removing the philanthropist's name from all her documentation. Julie needed Isabella somewhere in the future, and she wouldn't be able to help her if she was behind bars.

Joel leaned forward from his seated position, his hands lingering dangerously close to Julie's neck. Julie allowed the violation of his presence on her skin, knowing he meant no harm. Joel was simply stunned, even curious.

"So it's true" were his only words.

Representative Kennsington was an active participator in the gossip of COLI*GO performing wicked experiments in its lab, especially as the head of the Humanizer party. Julie originally hated Joel for his accusations, but that was back when she was naïve, when she believed COLI*GO was only capable of greatness. Now, from her position at the very top, she knew better.

"That's a shame," Joel responded, moving back from her and relaxing into his seat. "About the scar. Without it, you'd be absolutely perfect."

The words hurt Julie differently than how Joel intended. She didn't care if this vile man found her attractive or not. Instead, Julie took his words as a sign that she was now something unfamiliar and dangerous.

Untrustworthy.

Julie's thoughts drifted back to Colin as she wondered if he would ever fully trust her again. Especially after everything she did.

"How did she get away with this, without anyone else higher up in COLI*GO knowing?" Joel continued.

Julie looked down at her desk, the incriminating documents spread across like pieces on a chessboard. She carefully placed the documentation neatly in a pile and clipped them together.

"All the answers you need are right here," Julie said, placing everything into a folder.

"I take it you've decided to join me on my mission for The Constituency?" Joel asked as he reached for the folder with his course and calloused hands. "Especially since you're giving this to me so easily?"

"Not so easily, actually," Julie said, pulling the folder back and out of his grasp. "I told you when I first took this position at COLI*GO that I wanted to help society. I want to help the people and the androids in The Constituency. I thought I could do so with science. Someday, I can. But not today. I know what you could do with this information, but I also need a favor from you."

Julie thought back to Joel's odd visit months earlier. He came to her office, unannounced, and offered her a position of power within The Legislature if she would forego her allegiance to Colin O'Connor and the rest of the O'Connor family.

"And what would that be?" Joel asked, his brown eyes looking beyond Julie and squinting out across The River as the sun began to rise. The colors weren't vibrant or beautiful in the winter, much like they were in the summertime. Instead, the grays of The City dulled in its glow and spread across both the buildings and streets.

"I need a place to stay for a while. And no one can know about my whereabouts after today. I think your place would be unassuming and discreet for me."

Joel cocked his head to the side, his eyes puzzled.

"There was another project The Supreme maintained through misappropriated funds," Julie continued. "Time travel. And the Julie you see right now, well, I'm a different version of myself. I'm a time traveler. No one can know."

"Time travel?" Joel asked, stunned. His eyes examined Julie again, this time a bit more carefully. "Is this in the documentation as well?"

Julie nodded before handing over the papers to him. Representative Kennsington skimmed through the sheets, his eyes growing worried and concerned with the turn of each page. He looked back up at her, finally realizing the power that came with housing a time traveler.

"I think you and I can make a deal."

***

Kennsington's home was situated at the end of M Street in The South neighborhood and overlooked a dead end. Julie observed the small front yard with a modest two-story brick single-family home that belonged to the representative. M Street consisted of various home styles, from triple-deckers to duplexes and tiny Cape-style structures. This part of The City was local—families lived here for generations: working-class families.

Joel's vehicle pulled up the narrow and short drive, and both he and Julie exited the car. There was much about Joel that Julie hated; he was a man who didn't believe androids should receive the same equalities as humans, and he wasn't a strong believer in science. But this was the safest place for Julie.

No one would ever look for her here.

The inside of the house reminded Julie of her father's home in The Monument. Joel kept the house tidy, but the contents missed the touches of another. Sparse furniture was scattered across the rooms with no sense of purpose or design.

Inhaling, Julie realized there was one grave difference between these two traditional nobody men and how they kept their homes: the absolute loneliness surrounded her, and the yellowed walls reeked of stale cigarette smoke.

"There's plenty in the fridge if you're hungry. And I have a nice outdoor patio in the back when the weather warms up. If you're still here then," Joel said quietly, allowing Julie to observe his home on her own terms. "You can stay in the bedroom on the first floor, or you can stay in the spare upstairs. Across the hall from the master."

"Thank you," Julie responded, opening the door on the first floor before noticing how Kennsington gawked at her body.

Time travel changed Julie's appearance, thinning out her limbs and giving her a gangly appearance. She didn't find herself attractive when she was too thin, but this was a body a pervert like Joel Kennsington appreciated.

"I hope you know there's nothing more coming from this."

"Respectfully, Dr. Walsh, I wouldn't touch anything Colin O'Connor has fucked," Joel said with a snicker so shrill, it reminded Julie of who he really was under his façade.

"Are you calling me a whore, Representative Kennsington?" Julie challenged him. She didn't care what this man thought of her, but that didn't stop her instinct of defensiveness.

"No, on the contrary—I'm calling him one," Joel responded with a chuckle before eyeing Julie once more. "I've known Colin a long time. We were on The Ways and Means Committee together after graduating from The University. Even after Isabella, his eyes always wandered. Ask him about it, if you ever see him again."

He looked at her with pity in his eyes.

Julie didn't care—a revolting man like Joel Kennsington was simply a pawn in the larger game she played to save The City.

Julie laughed and placed her bag on the bed. She walked out of the room and ventured over to the kitchen. She was hungrier than she expected, and Joel watched in horror as she ravaged a leftover container of pasta and bread.

"What do you plan on doing while you're here? How do I know you'll hold up your end of the bargain for me?" Joel asked, walking to his living room and settling into the sofa.

Joel placed her folder of documents down on the coffee table before his eyes darted back and forth, taking in more information from the pages. His hand shook as he jotted down his own notes into his device.

"I need a place to sleep and warmly piece together the missing components of my plan. I'd be traceable if I rented another apartment; all of my money is tied to my identification card," Julie reminded him.

She would have rather spent her earnings on another apartment tucked away in an unassuming part of The City, or even beyond. But cash didn't exist anymore; The Legislature had gotten rid of that decades ago. All financial matters were linked to a person's or android's identification card. It was the only way to pay for things.

"And your plan?" Julie eyed Joel carefully. This was not part of the bargain they made.

She promised to formally hand over all her evidence against The Supreme and offered insight into how time travel worked. Julie did not agree to be at Joel's beck and call, to time travel at his whim. Joel Kennsington was too dangerous—at least The Supreme couldn't time travel on the account she didn't have human blood. The technology didn't work on the silvery liquid that coursed through android veins. Joel, on the other hand . . . He could be destructive. Irresponsible.

"Ensure peace and prosperity for The City."

"Always so vague, Dr. Walsh," Joel said with a grunt before reorganizing the documents.

"What is your plan?"

"Arrest The Supreme. Put a leash on androids. They have too much power. This proves that," Joel answered.

The Supreme's actions didn't prove that androids had too much power. Instead, her actions proved that androids were much like humans—that they could do both right and wrong too. They could be immoral. The Supreme was evil, but that didn't imply all androids were evil, much as all people weren't the same.

Maybe one day, androids will get to vote for their leader as humans do. It shouldn't be up to FACERE nor The Legislature to choose one for them, Julie thought sadly, looking out the window toward the gray winter sky.

Chapter 5

Commissioner Jones

March 1st, 47 A.R.

Jones's dark apartment felt strange, as if something were different in the air as he opened the front door. After his breakup with Mick, Jones moved into a small studio apartment of his own in The Bay.

He spent a few weeks with Anna in The Port but didn't want to overstay his welcome or cause any unwanted speculation. Androids and humans were allowed to be friends, but romantic relationships were strictly forbidden. There were never any romantic feelings between Jones and Anna, but he did consider her a close friend.

Jones never imagined a life where he could afford to live in The Bay. The neighborhood was expensive compared to the spacious accommodations he and Mick could afford over in The Harbor. Jones and Mick owned their place outright, the salty air and memories of their hidden relationship escalating inside the memory portion of Jones's processor. As an android, he stored everything: every memory, every detail. A curse for an android who could understand and feel human emotions.

Thinking about Mick caused turmoil and a flood of unwelcome sensations Jones wished he didn't understand. Wished he didn't feel. Even memories of Mick's calloused hands against Jones's scales, Mick's dark ebony skin complementing the bright green, emerald shades of Jones—this all haunted Jones to no end.

Jones tried pushing the feelings aside, angry that he chose to experience them because he had asked Julie to recode his microchip as a teenager. He couldn't hate her; he would never hate his best friend.

And it was my choice.

Julie was the only family Jones had left, and he intended to figure out what happened to her: where she vanished to and where she escaped after surviving an intended death from Colin and an intended disappearance from Mick.

Julie was strong. Jones believed she was okay, believed she would survive. But that didn't mean he couldn't worry about her.

There was no way Jones saw himself and Mick making any kind of amends after everything that transpired that fitful day in January. But Jones was rational enough to admit he still had feelings for Mick. Strong feelings.

Jones pondered the possibility of him and Mick often, thinking if he tried, maybe he could forgive the love of his life for willingly destroying the future for his own greed. Mick was seeking a sense of purpose, a sense of belonging.

Isn't that what we all want?

Jones pushed his thoughts aside and turned on the lights. Looking out the window and across Commonwealth Avenue, Julie's apartment remained dark and empty.

I wonder if one day, when I look out there, she'll be staring back, Jones thought. This was the real reason he chose this apartment—a financially uncomfortable one, even with his new pay raise.

The rain poured down outside, hitting the windows with loud thuds. Something foreign on the corner of the kitchen island caught Jones's eye as he placed his key fob in the entryway dish.

A leather-bound journal.

Jones's scales illuminated as adrenaline coursed through his body. He swore he heard the loud hum of his processor in response. Taking a deep breath, he walked over to the kitchen area.

The journey didn't take long in his only four-hundred-square-foot apartment, but he paused when he reached the journal. The smooth leather reminded him of silk as his hands gripped the corners.

Mick, how did you find me? How did you get in here? Jones wondered, spinning around to face his closed, secure door.

Jones didn't want to open the journal—he was done with Mick and his terrible time travel antics. As far as Jones was concerned, time travel was dangerous, and Mick's irresponsible actions while time traveling were to blame for why Julie was missing, why Colin's and The Supreme's fates were in limbo, and why posse hominems still roamed the streets, trying to remain undetected.

But now that he held the journal, Jones easily imagined Mick's presence in his home, almost able to smell the crisp, wood-like scent of his former lover.

Mick claimed the journal helped him keep track of his research since devices weren't reliable when traveling time. And at one point, Mick left Jones this same journal and asked for Jones's help in pinpointing It's identity. Believing he was aiding in the quest to save society, Jones eagerly helped Mick solve the case.

Jones eventually uncovered the evil, mysterious identity of The City's uncaught serial killer, of It. It was Colin, or at least another personality of Colin's. The words "dissociative identity disorder" rang through Jones's ears—a diagnosis that had been made by Anna and Isabella's father, Filipe Garcia. It was a personality Colin struggled to maintain, especially when triggered by trauma. Jones pieced together the puzzle but hadn't understood fully until Colin confided in him.

Colin trusted Jones, most likely because Julie trusted Jones and Colin believed Julie would save him. A special bond existed between Jones and the aloof governor, to the point where Jones ultimately didn't turn Colin in.

Should I have? Would things be different if I did? Jones illogically blamed himself for Colin's attempt at killing Julie—for some painstaking reason, Jones believed if he hadn't posed the possibility in the journal, the event wouldn't have occurred.

But knowing why Colin had, and only discovering that after the fact, Jones realized he couldn't have done anything to prevent the actions from happening.

Looking at the journal in his hands, Jones wondered which version of the journal and which version of Mick delivered it to him. There were multiple versions of the leather-bound diary and there were multiple versions of Mick Taylor.

Jones caressed the soft yellowed pages before feeling a painful nick. A thin slice appeared across the scales on his index finger. Silver liquid pooled out—the android equivalent of blood.

He quickly dropped the journal on the end of the kitchen island

and grabbed a napkin off the counter. After applying pressure, the cut stopped oozing in only a matter of moments.

"Leave me alone, Mick," Jones shouted to no one.

A loud thud answered him. The journal now resided on his kitchen floor, sprawled apart.

Chapter 6
Peter

March 1st, 47 A.R.

So much of Julie remained in her abandoned office on the 101st floor of the COLI*GO headquarters. Dr. Peter Schneider couldn't bring himself to throw away her things and instead slowly meddled his own belongings beside hers.

Celine O'Connor's call a month prior remained a hazy but pungent memory in Peter's mind. The Board of Directors needed a new interim CEO while Celine remained on maternity leave, and she recommended him.

No one knew where Julie was. She stopped showing up at COLI*GO, and after a few days, her father reported her missing to the android police force. She hadn't shown up to their weekly Thursday night dinners, and no one could track the location of her device. Her last known location had been here, in this office. Now she was off the grid, wherever she was.

Android detectives ripped apart Julie's office, looking for clues regarding her disappearance, but couldn't find anything of interest. No body appeared, and questions lingered around The City about the beloved scientist's disappearance.

For weeks, Peter rang Julie's doorbell each day before and after work until one of her neighbors kindly asked him to stop. The police had ripped apart her home, and a sheer volume of flowers and trinkets overwhelmed the front steps. Dr. Julie Walsh was beloved in The City. Her innovations in science, mixed with her relatability and kindness, created a swarm of supporters and admirers.

The hologram of her "missing persons" picture haunted Peter around every corner in The City and each night on the evening news. Julie's simple but bright eyes followed them all, even Celine O'Connor, who offered a sizable reward to anyone who found Dr.

Julie Walsh or had information about her disappearance or whereabouts. Celine's inquiry remained silent and unanswered.

Peter cared about Julie. Not in a romantic way—at least not anymore. Julie was one of the few friends he had here in The City. Peter and Julie had dated after she graduated from The University, but their relationship ended when Peter moved to COLI*GO's affiliate foreign office. Nothing sour happened between them, and she was the one who reached out to Peter and asked him to lead her antidote project. Peter's decision to return to The City seemed simple at the time, but now with Julie gone, the complexities sprouted up like springtime flowers.

"Dr. Schneider?" Mick Taylor's voice echoed from the doorway.

"Yes, Taylor?"

Mick approached Peter with emphasis and power in his steps. Peter took in the normally awkward man in front of him. Mick possessed large hands and broad shoulders but continuously carried a rail-thin frame. His skin peeled and appeared itchier each time Peter saw him.

"I have the report on the modified COL23 asset," Mick responded, placing his device over Peter's device to transfer the files.

COL23: the antidote. Julie's antidote.

Julie developed the drug back while she was a PhD candidate at The University. She pitched her molecule to the COLI*GO Board, and they purchased her innovation. Previously known as the antidote, COL23 helped resolve memory issues and restore brain function to patients suffering from Alzheimer's. The drug was marketed successfully and helping those patients across The City and the rest of The Constituency.

Preliminary testing showed promise for patients suffering from psychological disorders that stemmed from memory and cognitive issues. For an unknown reason to the research team, the antidote performed inconsistently with patients who suffered from bipolar disorder, or manic depression. Relapses were documented in the clinical trials, and in some cases, the disease took full control of patients' minds.

Months ago, Mick identified a root cause for relapses. The gene therapy technology misidentified the healthy receptor cells in the brain and instead latched on to damaged ones when patients experienced trauma. At the time, Peter managed the clinical trials for COL23 and had since tasked the team to recode and test the asset.

"Mick," Peter said abruptly, placing his hand on Mick's forearm. "How are you doing? Truly? I know Julie was your best friend."

"Is," Mick said coldly, ripping his arm away from Peter. "Julie is my best friend."

Julie met Mick at The University. They bonded over being some of the select few human students who weren't descendants of old bloodline families. Their friendship had seemed to drift sometime after Peter and Julie broke up, but she still hired him to work on the antidote.

"Don't tell me you understand." Mick's words were bitter. "In the course of a month, my best friend goes missing, and my partner leaves me. You can't understand that pain, Peter. Don't request that I 'take time off' to deal with my issues. I need this distraction right now. I need COLI*GO and everything I'm doing here."

"Of course," Peter answered slowly.

Mick's outburst wasn't irregular or unsurprising. Peter and Mick never got along, always butting heads in the research lab back when Peter managed the clinical trials. Peter never understood why Mick Taylor hated him; the tension seemed to start from the very beginning. They never trusted one another, making the process of innovation more challenging as they faced issues with Julie's famous asset.

"Why don't you start the simulations today? Provide me with a status report by the end of the week, please." Peter walked over toward the window and away from Mick.

"Can't you officially make me the project lead on COL23?" Mick asked impatiently, clearly intent on not leaving Peter's office anytime soon.

So that's really why you came up here, Taylor? Peter wanted to ask, his stare remaining out the window. He wouldn't give Mick the satisfaction of the agitation spreading across his face or the nervous twitch of his upper lip.

"Have some patience, Taylor. Good things come to those who wait."

"You didn't wait too long before securing this office." Mick's voice was deep and menacing. Threatening, even. "Julie's office."

Peter sharply turned around to respond, but the look of pure hatred beamed out of his eyes instead. Mick shook his head, unaffected by Peter's glare, and walked out of the office without another word.

Peter made his way back to the desk and picked up his device. He opened the electronic folder where Mick transferred the file earlier. Additional files were saved on the device, erratically named with numbers and letters.

Mick is too sloppy for his own good, and he wonders why I haven't promoted him? Peter wondered, opening the first file.

Cryptic coding flooded the cells in the document, the origin showing an intention for human matter, but the coding didn't fit any regular standards for therapeutics or drugs. Peter's eyes furrowed as a knock on the door jolted his focus back up.

"Celine, I wasn't expecting you in the office today," Peter said.

Celine O'Connor's tall but elegant figure closed the door and approached him. Her dark hair was styled in an angled, sleek bob, and she wore her usual button-up shirt and a long navy pencil skirt.

"Apologies for my unannounced visit, but it's important," she said, her voice raspy against her solemn smile.

"Of course."

"I need your help with a confidential project." Celine's red lips squeezed together tightly as she took a seat across from Peter.

"Did The Board approve?"

"No. The Board doesn't know."

"Isn't this what got us into trouble a month ago?" Peter asked hesitantly, recalling the backlash COLI*GO received upon the investigation of The Supreme's unapproved projects.

"Think of this as more of a personal favor rather than a work assignment," Celine said soothingly. She smiled at Peter, her charming grin and beauty shining through. Celine was an O'Connor—charisma was part of the family's character traits.

Peter leaned back in his seat. He had spent his whole career working for COLI*GO. Peter wondered what kind of sway Julie truly had over Celine O'Connor and how involved she was in all of this. There was no doubt in Peter's mind Julie was connected—she disappeared at the same time as COLI*GO's shining light came crashing down within the walls of The Capitol Building.

"And what's the favor?"

Celine's eyes darted back toward the door, confirming it remained closed.

"I need you to find Julie."

Peter awkwardly laughed, the sound originating from deep within his stomach. He never performed well under nervousness and uncertainty, and Celine's proposition didn't entirely make any rational sense to him.

"I'm fairly certain Commissioner Jones is looking for Julie," Peter replied. "And the police department isn't even sure if she's still alive. People don't remain missing this long unless they're dead."

"You're wrong about that," Celine countered. "The police are still searching for Julie, but they won't find her. I have a theory about where she is, but I need someone else to go on the journey and retrieve her."

"She . . . she fled The City?" Peter asked, still confused by Celine's words.

"No," Celine answered, pulling a small two-piece device out of her handbag.

Peter took the device out of her hands and studied the contraption. His fingers grazed over the circular frames, and his mind raced.

"It's a time travel device."

"How did you . . . How is this possible?" Peter asked, stunned.

"The Supreme and I invested in time travel research. That was an experiment that, thankfully, neither the public nor The Legislature knows about. The device uses human blood to travel forward and backward. I'm trying to track down both Julie and the missing devices. Only six devices were ever made. Two are missing. The inventor has one, I have mine and The Supreme's, and Julie has one."

Celine placed the other half of the device, a chrome box, into Peter's hand.

"Who invented this?" Peter asked.

The device was intricate, and the design well thought out and crafted with elegance and creativity. Both modern and medieval in appearance, the box had sharp, crisp edges while a serpent, scaly figure was etched into the frames of the accompanying glasses.

"It's best you don't know too much, especially for now. That will only cause issues and distractions," Celine replied softly.

"And why can't you find Julie?" Peter asked, slightly irritated at Celine for brushing off his questions when she asked so much from him. "Why can't you use the device?"

Celine sighed, a pondering look on her face in response to Peter's question. "Do you want the truth?"

Peter nodded, remaining silent.

"I've never used the device before. It requires human blood, as I mentioned. There are many observations and many years of research conducted on the instrument. But there are still many unknowns. I'll provide all the documentation of what I know to you, and I suggest you read through the entire document before you use the device. Too many intricacies and room for error. And that's why I'm asking you to time travel. I'm afraid to leave my baby, especially alone with Martin. That's a personal issue that I refuse to elaborate on for you. But I'm also unsure of how to move forward in finding Julie since she hasn't reemerged. I doubt she would give me a warm welcome, but I need to find her. And quickly. She's the only one who can save Colin."

Peter held mixed feelings for Governor Colin O'Connor. He appreciated the man's ideology and acumen. Governor O'Connor always "got the job done," but there was something arrogant about the man, something Peter couldn't put his finger on. A sense of uneasiness filled Peter's stomach, now knowing Julie was involved.

"How could Julie save Colin? What does he need saving from?"

"Their relationship is complicated," Celine answered with irritation in her voice, as if she didn't approve of what she was about to reveal. "He truly cares for her. And she cares for him. They oddly love one another, but that's a secret you cannot disclose, Peter. Their affair would not only ruin my family's reputation but the reputation of COLI*GO. And regardless, Colin needs the antidote."

"The governor suffers from Alzheimer's?" Peter asked with a raised pitch in his tone.

Peter saw the governor on the news all the time, read about him too. There never seemed to be any key indicators that made him believe the governor suffered from the disease. Peter had spent years of his life working on COL23 and the clinical trial—he was a subject matter expert.

"Yes," Celine said, the lie almost traceable on her lips.

*I don't believe her. I don't like Governor O'Connor, but I care about Julie. And I care about helping COLI*GO.*

"Tell me everything you know about why Julie is missing and time travel, and I promise I will search for Julie."

***

Peter looked out over Dr. Anna Garcia's balcony, taking in the beautiful harbor view. Her loft apartment in The Port was glitzier than his humble brick-walled home in The Bay, but he wasn't ashamed of who he was, or really, the lack of who he was.

"Thank you for meeting with me," Peter said, looking back toward the fascinating woman beside him.

Anna Garcia didn't exude a typical beauty—rather, her muscular build showcased an attractive strength. She and her sister, Isabella, shared short statures and the same deep skin tone. While they had lusciously thick hair, their styles differed. Isabella was always photographed in regal colors and formfitting dresses, but Anna expressed herself as more casual in jeans and silky blouses.

"Of course," Anna said, approaching Peter with a wide grin.

"I need someone to investigate the lower lab incident at COLI*GO. We made a deal with the high judge and The Legislature that if we hire a consultant for the project and they uncover who aided The Supreme, COLI*GO will only face fines. I know you have mixed feelings about COLI*GO, but it's different from what it used to be—now that I carry influence."

"Okay." Anna paused hesitantly. "Tell me more. I'll listen."

"You know the truth about The Supreme's posse hominems. I saw the documents The Supreme made you sign so that she could blackmail you. Other than an android who works for COLI*GO named Nolan, we have no other leads."

"You do realize I technically work for Commissioner Jones, correct? And that I'm a forensic medical professional, not a detective?"

Peter recognized she wasn't trained in the police force—that was where he had issues with hiring a consultant. Only androids attended the police academy, one of the original reasons androids were created in the first place.

Androids lacked the understanding of most human emotions and thought more rationally, making androids better suited for roles in society like first responders. But androids were also loyal—and Peter feared that the investigation needed the eyes of a human.

Commissioner Jones had mentioned how Anna Garcia helped investigate The City's infamous serial killer, Jeb Taylor, even though she was the department's medical examiner. She only recently returned to her position after the new commissioner was promoted. Clearly, the two were close, and Peter believed Anna could solve his predicament.

"I know," Peter responded, looking out toward the harbor again. "But you're smart and determined. And you come highly recommended by the commissioner."

Anna grinned at Peter's compliment.

I wonder what it's like to be the quieter sibling in an old bloodline family, Peter thought, thinking back to how he rarely saw Anna's name in the tabloids and only Isabella's. Or how much more subdue the younger Garcia sister truly was. Isabella was the shining star—a woman who played the perfect, compassionate philanthropist. How could Anna ever compete?

"Why don't you try to uncover this mystery, Dr. Schneider?" Anna asked with a small chuckle.

"Between running COLI*GO and another task that's been asked of me, I don't have the bandwidth to give this the full attention it needs. But I promise to help you. I won't make you do this alone."

Anna stuck her hand out toward Peter and grasped his in a firm handshake. "I'll do it."

Peter smiled in relief, the weight of this responsibility lifting slightly off his overburdened shoulders.

"Let me show you around the building? And the lower lab?"

"Sure, let's go."

Peter's vehicle drove across downtown and over the bridge to bring them to The River. The odd mix of historical buildings and brand-new, shiny skyscrapers surrounded them. Home to innovation, technology, and pharmaceuticals, The River's windy streets elicited a secret promise of gilded hope.

The COLI*GO building loomed above them, the glass structure waving at the top, slightly egg shaped. The sun's rays reflected off the windows, shimmering into the actual river below.

When they arrived inside COLI*GO's lobby, Peter handed Anna a badge of her own, the word "consultant" printed underneath her name. This badge provided Anna access into the elevator, and the pair headed down to the lower lab.

Anna had barely spent time within these walls, but Peter knew this building like the back of his hand. Only a few people had access to the lower lab, and the words "No Entry" and "Restricted Access" flooded their vision as they stepped out of the elevator.

They walked toward the large door at the end of the hall, and Peter swiped his badge and opened the metal door with ease. But Anna stood in the entryway for a moment too long.

"What's wrong?" Peter asked, turning back to her.

The room wasn't welcoming but not too different from a laboratory. The industrial design of the room showcased harsh and ugly cool-toned tiled floors, and along the back wall, metal drawers lined up perfectly from floor to ceiling.

"This room reminds me of The City's morgue."

Peter froze in his tracks. Looking back at the wall of metal drawers, he finally made the connection without ever having stepped foot inside the police headquarters.

"This . . . This is where The Supreme made posse hominems?" Anna's voice was strained, and her eyes darted back and forth, taking in the room.

Peter watched as Anna approached the back wall, her fingers brushing the steel handles.

"Yes," Peter answered with a crack in his own voice.

He continued observing Anna as she instinctively pulled on one of the drawers. It remained locked. Peter thought back to the first time he came down to the lower lab, almost a month ago—how

Commissioner Jones and his team swept through the room.

There had been some bodies inside the drawers, and while everyone inside was still alive, some had already been transformed. Peter had nearly vomited at the antiseptic smell that engulfed the entire space while Celine and the rest of The Board of Directors had stood in silence, heads slanted down in embarrassment. Shame was evident—they had let The Supreme perform these experiments right under their noses.

"They're empty."

Anna's small body collapsed onto the floor with a loud thud, her hands reaching up to her face as she sobbed uncontrollably. Peter sat down on the floor next to Anna and wrapped his awkward and gangly arms around her. He held Anna while she cried, assuming her memories of seeing Lexi Pvadinish's dead body plagued her. Peter read the documentation Commissioner Jones provided and shared the horror of Lexi's dry, flaking skin. The tiny scar—the barely noticeable incision below her left ear—trailing down Lexi's neck. A microchip had been forced into Lexi's brain before she was strangled and stabbed twenty-three times, by The City's infamous serial killer.

"I'll help you find the monster who assisted with this bullshit as long as you promise COLI*GO never does anything this horrific again." Anna's words were cruel but justified, with passion seeping from them.

"COLI*GO will never do anything so heinous as long as I remain in control of the company," Peter vowed, pulling Anna closer into his chest.

They looked at one another in silence, remaining on the floor of the lower lab for so long, the overhead lights flickered, the motion sensors thinking no one remained in the room.

"Truthfully, why don't you have the bandwidth to help me more with this?"

Peter closed his eyes slowly and opened them as he answered. "I'm trying to find Julie. I have information that leads me to believe she's still alive."

PART THREE

The Past

"Can't repeat the past? Why, of course you can!"
—F. Scott Fitzgerald

Chapter 7
Julie

June 23rd, 12 A.R

Arriving at The Oceanside, Julie tightly gripped the edges of her body. The humid, salty air welcomed her to a place she equally loved and hated. The roaring sounds of waves crashing against the cliffs filled her ears as the sun rose over the horizon and the morning mist kissed her face.

The bad decision of time traveling to this moment circled in her brain, but Julie's curious nature always got the best of her.

Her boredom reached its max capacity after spending endless days locked in Joel Kennsington's house. Julie's situation took a turn for the worse after she left without telling him and walked to M Street Beach. When she returned, Joel's anger consumed all the empty space in the house. He locked her inside his home each morning following the incident. Julie could still hear the alarm counting down as Joel left for The Capitol Building, his brown, beady eyes never leaving her until his vehicle drove out of sight.

At least with her time travel device, Julie didn't trip any alarms and could transport to other places. Mick's technology granted her a small sense of freedom. Normally, she used her own blood to travel, but something about the small remaining sample of Colin's blood enticed her. Weeks passed as she thought about what to do with it—once gifted to her by Mick when they were on speaking terms. Back when Mick believed Julie would help him with his larger plan to support The Supreme's grasp for power.

The large mansions and estates sprawled across the landscape in front of Julie, but the lights remained mostly off. A few twinkled against the early morning sky, but sleep seemed to captivate the inhabitants of The Oceanside. Julie's presence wouldn't bother them anyways—she was a ghost in this time.

Julie carefully studied and memorized the list of time travel observations Mick had recorded in his journal. One of those observations indicated if someone traveled to a time before their birth or after their death, they essentially assumed the role of a ghost while walking through that time. No one could see or hear her because 12 A.R. occurred five years before Julie's birth.

The town square came into view as Julie walked at a brisk pace. The Oceanside was a vacation destination for old bloodline families. Fancy restaurants and cafes lined the docks along the peaceful inlet side of the peninsula while the massive estates perched themselves over the cliffs facing the harsh openness of the ocean.

Colin had taken Julie to his family's estate in The Oceanside many times. Julie appreciated the hominess of the O'Connors' summer home. Celine and Colin kept the estate resembling as close as possible to the memories of their childhood, so renovations were minor. The home reminded the siblings of their mother, and any disruption felt like an attack on her. Instead, they used the space to keep the memory of Melanie O'Connor alive.

Colin spoke fondly of his mother to Julie and confided in witnessing her death. That event changed him—the trauma created It.

Julie only saw photos of the mysterious woman who had such a large impact on the man she loved. The public loved Melanie and forgave Henry O'Connor for marrying a nobody because of her kindness. Melanie's disappearance, and later assumed death, changed the former governor for the worse. Colin described his father as cold and heartless with a hatred Julie never understood.

Her feet hit the cobblestone streets, and the empty shops greeted her. Within a few hours, the area's quiet roads would bustle with the magnetic energy of those looking for a morning cup of coffee and a pastry and errands needing attention before social calendars completely consumed them.

A light shone brightly from one of the coffee shops, the sunrise breaking through on the horizon behind her. Julie opened the door slowly, knowing it didn't matter because no one could see her anyway. The smell of ground coffee beans filled her nose, and pastries lined the glass case. Julie's feet guided her to the back of the tiny café, and she settled into a small chair.

What am I doing here? Julie wondered, her fingers plunging into her pockets where the time travel glasses and chrome box resided.

Julie closed her eyes, feeling the mistakes of her decision to come back to this moment. She wasted the last of Colin's blood sample to witness a moment so tormenting to the man as a way to understand him, to hopefully find the forgiveness she needed for his trying to kill her. By coming here, she would go back with a stain on her own skin—a small wrinkle or two.

Selfish. Wrong.

The café crowded quickly with people and androids milling in and out to get their morning espressos and lattes. The bell hanging off the door rang loudly, and Julie looked up. A small smile formed across her face. At the counter stood Melanie O'Connor.

The woman was simply gorgeous—tall and lanky with freckled, blemish-free skin radiating in the morning light. Her light blonde hair fell below her shoulders, and her indigo eyes softened underneath luscious black eyelashes.

Melanie laughed at something the barista said, her smile intriguingly spreading across her lips. As she grasped the small cup of coffee around her hands, the emerald ring sparkled brightly on her delicate finger. Julie looked down at her own hand. The same ring shone on her in a similar fashion.

Julie's gaze lifted, and her eyes locked with Melanie's. Melanie tilted her head to the left, her eyes lingering on Julie's hands before nodding in her direction.

Julie's lips parted, and the color drained from her face.

Impossible, Julie thought, turning around to see what else could have caught Melanie's attention behind her. *There's no way she could have seen me.*

When Julie's focus shifted back, Melanie was nowhere in sight.

Julie's body propelled out of the seat and through the door. She nearly tripped on the steps down to the street, and her head whipped left and right. Julie's feet overtook her mind as she raced through the now bustling village area.

No one in the crowd noticed her. Julie approached a couple and tried tapping the man on the shoulder.

Nothing, no reaction. She was still invisible to them.

Where did she go? Julie wondered, continuing down the street.

She didn't need a map to know how to get from the village to the O'Connor estate. Julie's run slowed down to a fast-paced walk, knowing the journey would take her about twenty minutes.

Julie took a deep breath and decided to enjoy the warmth of the sun that pricked her skin. The scenery of the brick roads and large elm trees on either side helped soothe her racing heart. Eventually, the mansion came into view. The long driveway wrapped around the front in a half-circle, filled with crushed seashells. A grin formed on Julie's face, her mind wandering to the first time Colin brought her here.

She had arrived before him, and she hadn't cared to stay inside. Instead, she explored the property and grounds. Hydrangeas and exotic flowers lined the expansive green lawn. Everything was meticulously kept as if someone were here to enjoy the beauty every second of every day.

The home in front of her still looked the same, the familiarity an easing thought.

A young Celine darted across the large glass windows, chasing after a young android with autumn-colored scales.

The Supreme.

Julie balked, stopping in her tracks. She yearned to continue watching the two young girls chase each other around the grand staircase, whatever game they played clearly captivating them. But a sudden sharpness filled Julie's body, the unexplainable pain followed by firm sounds of silence—a familiar vibration sensation to when she time traveled.

Another time traveler, Julie recognized. Her head darted around, scanning the area for the other intruder. Julie walked around the side of the house, the cliffs lining the back finally coming into view. *Will they see me? Or am I invisible to them too?*

"Colin!" Melanie's voice called out in the distance.

Julie's body drifted toward the sound, the shouting. Her heart beat rapidly in her chest, knowing what was coming. Adrenaline filled her veins, and she rushed to the sharp edges of the cliffs.

The sides of the rocky landscape were all too familiar to Julie—they were the same ones she pushed herself off in the future. Julie gulped at the distance to the bottom, the sandy beach area appearing miles away from where she stood.

"What are you doing here, Julie?" A hand clasped her shoulder.

The familiar, deep voice belonged to her former friend, Mick Taylor. Her eyes grew as she observed her friend. He didn't look angry to see her; he seemed relieved.

Mick's hand tightened its grip, his thumb painfully pressing into her while his other hand reached for her throat.

Julie didn't give him a chance, kneeing Mick right in the groin.

Mick fell, grunting from her forceful jab. With mere moments to outrun him, Julie's heels turned and her feet picked up their pace. She didn't look back and moved ahead, her body almost slipping in the slick grass. The loud crunching sound of the driveway's seashells exploded in her ears.

Chapter 8
Mick

June 23rd, 12 A.R.

Mick held his breath and watched Julie from outside the café. Her hair appeared darker, the red and gold tones deeper from barely spending time outdoors and in the sun. Her skin—always pale but paler now—confirmed Mick's suspicion: This Julie traveled from the winter of 47 A.R.

This was the Julie he was looking for.

Julie's eyes darted around the scenery, taking in her surroundings. Mick stalled in his approach. He couldn't believe she came here to this moment and this memory. The one that birthed a monster.

I shouldn't be surprised, Mick thought. *She still loves him. She will always love him.*

Mick thought back to The Supreme. If she hadn't provided Colin's alter ego, It, with a prototype of Mick's device, he wouldn't have come back to this date and done the unthinkable act that created an ultimate time loop entangling everyone and every time traveler.

Mick visited this date often for many reasons but for this one in particular: Everything originated here. Eventually, all those who held his time travel device found themselves visiting this date. This was also the only time where all time travelers could collectively return, in some distant, different dimension, from their respective presents.

Studying the effects of this particular time loop interested Mick the most in his research. There was something critical about all these tiny, different pieces. He needed to figure out how they all fit together.

The ringing of a bell filled Mick's mind, and he shifted his focus back to the café. Back to Julie. Julie's eyes searched the streets urgently, her fingers grasping the edges of the doorframe.

Then she ran.

Mick sighed. Running wasn't something his out-of-shape body was keen on participating in. Instead, he walked his normal pace and headed back to the O'Connor estate, knowing that was Julie's destination.

Mick missed Julie; she was his first true friend and the person who introduced him to the love of his life. Mick and Julie's friendship was battered now, inflicted with bullet holes and slash marks stemmed from lies and deceit, but Mick was determined to make amends. He needed to in order to save society.

When he finally caught sight of Julie again, she was out of breath. Mick slowly approached her, his hand reaching out.

"What are you doing here, Julie?" he asked, his hand clasping her shoulder.

Julie's eyes grew wide in fear when she turned around to face him. Mick smiled softly at her, not wanting to pose as a threat. The last time they spoke, he lied to her about time travel. He sent her on a mission to change the past. It didn't matter to Mick if she succeeded in her task or not; Mick needed Julie to attempt the assignment so that he could better understand time loops.

Julie successfully died and returned, but Mick's theory regarding a time traveler's death was still unclear. She returned to the place of where she didn't actually die. Julie should have returned to her actual death.

Mick tightened his grip on her shoulder, his thumbs pressing into her soft skin. He lifted his other hand to tuck away a stray hair whipping in the ocean breeze. Mick didn't make it close enough before Julie kneed him between his legs.

Goddammit!

Mick collapsed, groaning in pain as Julie dashed away. He didn't chase her, didn't even attempt the idea. He grounded his fists and lifted himself up. An unsettling feeling in his bones erupted; another version of himself roamed The Oceanside. Another time-traveling version of himself.

There was only one way to solve the issue, one that Mick didn't like. He knew when the other version of himself arrived, where he would stay, what he would write in the journal.

The sound of the waves crashing violently against the rocks shattered through Mick's thoughts. He approached the edge of the cliffs, hesitantly peering over the side.

Melanie O'Connor would fall to her death here in a matter of minutes. And somewhere in the future, Julie faced a similar fate.

But Julie didn't die. Only one of these women would survive to face It.

For now.

***

Mick spent the next day at the lighthouse. Something about the abandoned structure reminded him of the silos on his family's farm in The Countryside. He glanced up, noting how the strange spiraling staircase collected as a compilation of steps leading to nowhere.

He placed his palm flat on the bed, the warmth of his body—a body from an earlier time—lingered on the navy quilt. A sad smile appeared on Mick's face at the memory. He had been so naïve back then, thinking he could help everyone without hurting anyone.

The journal lingered on the nightstand table, the edges still cream colored versus the yellowing it would experience in the future. The tips of his fingers brushed the corners, a feathering feeling of the uneven pages welcoming him.

Mick couldn't stay any longer because another version of himself loitered in town. He would return and form a plan that would change the course of the future. Mick's past ebbed with his future in all dimensions of time.

His feet ached inside his shoes as he descended the stairs. Mick didn't come to the past just to find Julie—there was another purpose to this trip.

The journey back to The City wasn't pleasant in the humid summer heat. The high-speed train roared through the empty land between The Oceanside and The Outskirts, and the wasteland outside his window depressed him. Mick recalled stories from his history classes of a time where people lived in these communities, life flourishing, or at least, welcoming the embrace of opportunity.

When Mick traveled from The Countryside to The City in his

twenties, he couldn't pull himself away from gazing out the train's window. And now, his eyes similarly peered out but were entranced for different reasons.

In the summertime, most old bloodline families drove down to The Oceanside while their workers flocked from The City. Tickets weren't cheap, but the promise of bringing home enough money to sustain a family, support missing savings funds, or afford rent for half the year persuaded people and androids.

The train slowed as it approached the downtown station. Normally, Mick would walk to The Hill from here, but the sun beat down unforgivingly against the concrete jungle of The City. His feet guided him lower in the station toward the subway. The same mechanical beast he was used to from the future approached. He only stayed on the line for a few stops before departing.

A golden dome atop The Capitol Building emerged in his line of vision as he surfaced from underground. People and androids crossed the park with purpose. The crowded area reminded Mick that even in the aftermath of unrest, peace could prevail.

Hope could prosper.

Security at The Capitol Building wouldn't let Mick past the front lobby. He didn't have his identification card, and even if he had it, he wouldn't forfeit it anyway. Technically, Mick was only a few days old if someone really investigated him. The middle-aged-looking man standing in front of the metal detectors wasn't an accurate depiction of his true self.

An android with bright crimson scales grabbed his arm and dragged him down the hall. The harshness of the android reminded Mick that he wasn't far removed from society's largest uprising, the most devastating revolt of any species against another: The Resurgence.

The android knocked loudly on a familiar wooden-paneled door, and another android emerged from behind it. This android stood taller than most, his shoulders a bit broader. His scales were golden, a brighter gold compared to Emilia's but still a similar shade.

This was the first supreme. The supreme before Emilia.

His eyes widened at Mick before he nodded at the rough android security guard. Mick stumbled after being let out of his grasp but quickly found his footing.

The office didn't appear much different from how Emilia decorated it. The large desk with intricate carvings of androids and humans caught Mick's eye instantly. An heirloom. The courtyard beyond the windows blossomed with exotic plants and flowers. A sensory overload flew through Mick with all the vibrant colors surrounding him.

"Take a seat, human." The android's masculine voice broke their silence.

Mick obeyed him eagerly, intimidated by the sheer size of the android standing in front of him. He had led a revolution and started the road to equality for his beings. His simple presence demanded respect.

"Why are you here?" he asked, his eyes zoning into Mick's body, scanning him. "And who exactly are you?"

"I'm a time traveler. I come from the future."

A human would laugh at Mick. Most would call him a crazy lunatic. They would throw him out of their offices, their homes. But not an android. Or at least, not this android.

"And why do you travel here and request to see me?" His voice boomed against the walls.

"The supreme who succeeds you, do you know who she is?" Mick asked, leaning back in the chair and crossing his leg. Mick ran his hand through his wiry hair and looked back up at the android in front of him.

"I know Emilia. I have great plans for her."

"We need to program her to understand all human emotions." Mick didn't back down and held himself as confidently as possible, knowing what he said was treason.

"That's against the law," the android answered, but a wicked grin flickered against his scaly face.

"If she doesn't comprehend us, she will never succeed in the android quest for retribution," Mick countered, painstakingly aware this supreme didn't yet possess this ability.

"And why would a human request this?" he asked, crossing his glowing arms. The gold colors shimmered intriguingly against the sunset cascading through the windows, and a bright tangerine tone illuminated from him.

"Because androids can't travel time. And I work for her."

"So, you already know if I program her microchip or not." The android was using logic against Mick, but Mick learned long ago that logic didn't apply to time travel. "I don't have a code to reprogram her microchip. It would be too dangerous for me to obtain one. Times are still turbulent, human."

Mick laughed, a deep roaring thunder emerging from his throat.

"I can take care of that. And I can reprogram yours. Is that what you want? It's an easy request and one I can certainly help you with."

The android's eyes rotated to the corners, a pondering look for his kind.

"What I've learned in this fight for freedom is that knowledge is power." He kicked his feet up on the edge of his desk. "And I want you to tell me everything. I need you to tell me how androids can control The Legislature. How we eradicate human control. Most importantly, I need you to help me destroy those filthy old bloodline families. All of them. Then reprogram my microchip and teach me how it's done so that I can reprogram Emilia's."

Mick pushed his glasses back up the bridge of his nose and smiled widely.

"I'll tell you everything you need to know, but can I ask you first what your given name is? I hope you understand; where I come from, Emilia is the supreme. It feels wrong to address you as such."

The android drew in a quick breath as if he didn't expect such curiosity from Mick.

"Edward," he answered slowly, his eyes wide. Edward walked away from Mick, the scales across his neck shimmering. "Now, tell me more about the future, time traveler."

Chapter 9
It

June 23rd, 12 A.R.

He waited as the younger version of Mick Taylor wandered the shoreline beside Melanie O'Connor's body. It sat in the sand, his face resting between his hands. He killed Melanie O'Connor. He killed Colin's mother. The shock hadn't left his body yet, and the pure rush vibrated through him. It and Colin had killed many women before, but this . . . this was different.

And time travel added more complexity. The damage was done, the loop that the time travel inventor Mick Taylor always feared was cemented into place.

There was no escaping this loop, the loop that was the catalyst for everything. It had already tried escaping this loop countless times before. Each time, he came back and experienced this moment more intensely, more painfully, and a small part of him melted more into Colin's mind.

Vicious thoughts churned in It's head, logically piecing together the reality he didn't want to face. With his body shaking and his fingers outstretched and trembling, It finally stood from his crouched position.

It felt for the time travel device in his pocket, the pointy ends of the glasses protruding along the edges. With Mick finally gone, It made his way back over to Melanie. He knelt in the sand beside her, slowly lifting her body into his lap. Melanie's wounds protruded from her, and her blood pulsated into the sand, freeing itself from her body.

"I'm sorry," It whispered in Melanie's ear.

Stroking her hair away from her face, It leaned his forehead against hers and swallowed back his tears. After saying goodbye for the countless time, It released Melanie's body into the incoming tide.

He walked toward the direction of the O'Connor estate, and upon reaching the wooden staircase, he climbed up the side of the cliffs. With each step, It's mind swirled with Colin's. There were few times in his life when he and Colin coincided together, acted as one singular being. Memories poured through him, Colin's memories of this day from his childhood, the lashing out from his father for the following days, months, and years.

When he reached the top, It faced the estate. With purpose and confidence in his steps, he walked across the neatly manicured lawn. The large hydrangea bushes, fern hedges, and vegetable garden greeted him. The smell of salty ocean water and freshly blooming roses filled his nose.

It opened the large glass French doors with ease, unsure why they were closed in the first place. He paused before fully entering: The silence of the estate startled him. It let out a deep breath and concentrated. He knew where to go; he'd lived through this day before, even if not as himself, but as Colin.

Henry O'Connor sat in the study on the first floor. The back wall of the room was made entirely out of windows and sliding glass doors leading out to the patio. It suspected Henry watched as a tall dark figure approached his home, yet the man sat still. The dark green stone floors illuminated a gloom, and the glass of his Scotch sat nearly empty beside him on the desk.

It peered over the old-fashioned marble and engraved wooden clock. The man was drinking a few hours before noon, a concerning action.

A lousy drunk in my adulthood who apparently was a lousy drunk in my youth, It thought. Colin thought. He couldn't quite tell—this was all too confusing for It.

Looking directly at Henry O'Connor reminded him of the reflection that stared back at him in the mirror each morning. Especially now, since they were close in age.

The color drained from Henry's face, and his eyes grew wider with each step It took toward him. Finally, It sat down in the leather chair directly on the other side of the desk. Leaning over the mahogany wood, he snatched the decanter and poured himself a couple fingers of amber liquid. It swung back the expensive, smooth single-malt with ease and slammed the glass down loudly on the desk. A tiny crack splintered upward from his forceful motion.

"You're going to listen to me, and you're going to do as I say."

The words sliced through the silent room with intensity, and only the sound of the waves crashing along the cliffs outside answered him. Henry O'Connor looked up and down at the man before him and tilted his head to the side with drunken intrigue.

"You're not going to find Melanie." The sound of her name finally provoked emotion out of the stoic man.

"Excuse me?" the familiar voice, one It hadn't heard in a very long time, sternly floated across the desk.

"You're not going to find Melanie, but it shouldn't have been her. It should have been you. You never deserved her."

Henry motioned to stand, but It grabbed his forearms and he retreated into his seat.

"Who are you?" Henry's voice rang in between a pitch of anger and fear.

Maybe he hasn't figured out who I am, and the sheer resemblance is so uncanny to him, It thought.

Facing Henry O'Connor like this wasn't initially his plan, but the idea tempted him into this situation.

"That doesn't matter," It spat, leaning back into the leather chair.

Crossing one of his legs over his knee, a hard line crept across his lips. It enjoyed making his large presence even more consuming but couldn't enjoy this normal feeling with the events of his morning invading his mind.

Henry inquisitively looked at It. They shared the same facial features, olive skin, and square jawline. The steel-gray eyes.

It hated this man; Colin hated this man. Henry's cold shadow still lingered among Colin and his sister back in the present even though he had been dead for years.

"The Supreme." It paused, realizing Emilia was only nine years old at this point. "I mean, Emilia. Emilia will invest in time travel."

"So, you are my son," Henry stated.

"No," It answered, picking up the empty whiskey glass and carefully observing the tiny crack on the side. He clenched his fist tighter, this thumb shaking. "I am not your son."

Shards of glass fluttered across the desk, and a large piece sliced through his skin. The bright red blood oozed out with both speed and agility from the single injury. Henry's eyes darted down at It's hand and then back up to his face. Confusion clouded Henry's dark, bone-chilling eyes.

"You can't coddle Colin through this. I'll take care of him, be there for him. You need to make sure he's strong," It finally said before closing his eyes and sticking his thumb in his mouth, tasting the tangy and coppery blood.

Colin needed him. Not this man.

"Through what?"

"I told you," It replied, a venomous hurt running deeply through him, "your wife isn't coming home today. It will trouble Colin for the rest of his life."

"What do you mean? She's out looking for him right now, and I should head back out there and join her." Henry almost sounded genuine.

"She's already gone."

Colin's father was powerful in his younger years, with his muscular frame and tall build. They were both intimidating men, and now with the uncertainty settled, Henry gained back his self-assurance.

"Who are you, and what are you doing in my house?" his voice bellowed as he leaned in closer to It's face.

"I'm the man who killed your wife. I'm the man who eventually kills you." It stood to match Henry's gaze.

He gripped his hands on Henry's shoulders, the extra few inches giving him an advantage. Bright red blood stained the collar of Henry's dress shirt, seeping uncontrollably out of It's wounded thumb. It shoved Henry back against the wall and smiled.

Pushing Henry O'Connor around felt amazing. The pent-up anger from all those years—the years of hate and abuse—came bubbling up and out of him. It didn't hit him too hard, just enough to shock the man and break him into a mild submission.

"Don't you dare speak of this again," It spoke before exiting the estate, prepared to travel time back to where he came from.

PART FOUR

The Present

"Silence creates its own violence."
—Jeff VanderMeer

Chapter 10
Julie

April 1st, 47 A.R.

When Julie made it back to the present, an unnerving fear coursed through her body. Relief spiraled through her mind the moment she ripped the glasses off her face. She glanced at the clock displaying the same date from when she left earlier that day: April 1st, 47 A.R.

The smell from Joel's cigarette lingered around her, the staleness causing a burning feeling inside her lungs. She stood from the bed and opened the door. Joel sat on the couch, the smoke trailing off his left hand.

"You left."

Julie paused in the doorway, gripping the door handle tighter. The tension in her shoulders spread to her legs. Julie admitted hating that Joel Kennsington caused her unease. But she didn't like admitting when he was correct, either.

"I didn't leave," Julie said, surprised the words didn't stutter out between her lips.

"Don't be coy," Joel responded, taking a drag of his cigarette. He lifted his gaze to Julie and smiled handsomely with a small bit of cruelty cracking through. "You traveled time?"

"And what if I did?" Julie asked in a sharp tone.

Joel laughed and stood. He stalked toward her with a hunger in his eyes and only paused inches away from her face. Joel's closeness made Julie's heart beat faster, and as he leaned in, his lips brushed the edges of her ear. Julie smelled cheap Irish whiskey on his breath.

"Where did you go, darling?"

"That's none of your business," Julie replied, standing a bit taller and firmer. "And never call me darling, ever again."

Joel leaned away from Julie, his eyes traveling up and down her body. He paused at the scar on her neck and chuckled.

"Your silence isn't part of our deal. You tell me about the future when you travel. You give me insight and answers."

"I do. I've held up my end of the bargain," Julie replied bitterly, thinking about the random assortment of information she had already provided to Joel over the last few weeks. "I went to the past today. Are you happy?"

Joel's guttural laugh reeked of his sour boozy scent.

"Feeling nostalgic, darling?" he asked, emphasizing the word "darling," which annoyed her.

Joel tucked a loose strand of hair behind Julie's ear and finally walked away. Julie responded with a warning look. Glaring, she tightened her fists and leaned against the doorframe.

"Put on a nice dress," Joel commanded. "We're going out."

"What? I don't think that's a good idea for me," Julie protested.

Grabbing her upper arm with a firm grasp, Joel dragged Julie out into the living room. "I don't ask twice, and I don't trust you here alone, especially after you bent the rules today."

Julie scowled at Joel but decided to obey his request. She reached for her simple leather jacket and slammed the bedroom door closed to change out of her jeans and sweater. Julie pulled on a simple long-sleeved black dress and reemerged into the living room.

They exited Joel's house a half-hour later, and the bitter spring air lingered on Julie's bare legs. April in The City always betrayed the optimism of spring with vicious cold fronts and then a day or two of sunshine.

The walk took time, the narrow streets widening as Joel and Julie approached the edges of The Port neighborhood. The lights from high-rise buildings and large glass skyscrapers twinkled ahead. Julie shoved her hands in her pockets, clenching her jaw while she shivered.

The Port was a newer, glitzier neighborhood, with various bars, nightclubs, and high-end restaurants lining the streets. Both expensive and hip, The Port lacked history compared to sections of The City like The Hill or The Bay.

Joel dragged them into a dimly lit building with the words *The Grand* sparkling in bright lights. The bouncer nodded at Joel, granting them access inside. The club was crowded with androids and humans. Joel clutched Julie harder, his fingers digging into her boney forearm.

Music vibrated loudly, the bass shaking the room around them. Androids and humans danced together in the center of the large room, clad in scandalous outfits.

I don't miss this, Julie thought, remembering the numerous times she and her colleagues went out and partied after working long hours in the lab.

Random hands grasped out for Julie, and a male android raised his eyebrows at her. His scales glimmered faintly in a captivating maroon, a unique color Julie rarely saw on androids. He pulled her toward him with his strong grip, but Joel's grasp was tighter and she veered off with the representative toward the bar.

"Irish whiskey straight, for me, and . . ." Joel looked over at Julie inquisitively as if guessing her drink of choice provided some kind of sick satisfaction in his mind. "A vodka soda with lime."

He isn't wrong.

Joel placed his identification card down on the bar.

"You can let go," Julie yelled over the DJ's loud music into Joel's ear. His hand was still secured tightly around Julie's forearm, which ached uncontrollably.

"Are you saying you don't like a bit of roughness? I find that hard to believe." Joel slurred his vulgar words, anger and intoxication lurking around the edges of his mouth. Julie smacked his arm, and eventually, he loosened his hold on her.

A bone-thin woman with a tight neon backless green dress strode by them and leaned up against the other side of Joel. She eyed Joel and presented him with a seductive smile, her blonde hair dyed with purple streaks. The bartender placed Joel's whiskey and Julie's vodka soda down on the bar, and Julie rolled her eyes in Joel's direction. Joel couldn't see her in the darkness. He gravitated toward the woman, his hand lingering a bit too close to her bottom, and Julie saw this as her moment for escape.

Julie grabbed her drink and yelled over her shoulder, "I'll go sit in one of those booths on the back wall. Come get me when we're leaving."

She didn't want to spend her night watching Joel hit on anything with a pulse.

Unwillingness sparked across Joel's drunk eyes, but he reluctantly nodded, knowing Julie wouldn't run away.

She had nowhere to go.

Julie made her way across the dancefloor, squeezing and adjusting her body to pass through androids and humans touching one another. Nightclubs were some of the few places where society deemed it socially acceptable for cross-beings to engage in such behaviors. Romantic relationships and partnerships were still forbidden between androids and humans, but being here in this loud, invigorating room, Julie would have thought otherwise had she not known. Some had their hands on others' thighs, kissing necks, lips, and sensitive places behind ears. Hands reached out for Julie, attempting to pull her body by her scarf or entice her to join in on the dancing.

The loud noises from the music and the simulation of strobe lights and so much touching overwhelmed Julie. She hadn't been out in public in a long time and hadn't been to a dance club in years.

Shaking her head, Julie continued her journey to the other side of the room, which was quieter and less packed.

Once she reached an area with tables and booths, she let out a large sigh of relief. Julie's grip on her drink relaxed, and she took a large swig. The vodka burned on its way down, but she smiled. Julie forgot how exhilarating alcohol tasted, how tempting the liquid was in drowning out her true emotions and anxieties. She took another large gulp and nearly emptied her glass.

"This is the last place I expected to find you."

The familiar voice made Julie's heart stop beating. The tightness in her chest exploded, and a flicker of optimism burned through her cloudy, tipsy thoughts.

"Peter."

Peter Schneider held himself with an air of confidence Julie wasn't used to. He looked different here in the darkness, more mature.

The first time they met: it had been her first day working at COLI*GO after graduating from The University. Peter was older than her and on the team she was assigned to. Together, they worked on a legacy asset and provided first-class treatment for numerous neurological diseases. They informally dated for almost two years before Peter was assigned to a team in a foreign affiliate office. Julie had refused to follow him there, and their relationship ended. When it came time to hire a lead for her COL23 clinical trials, there was no one else Julie trusted with her antidote except Peter. He was a brilliant researcher and had deep knowledge of the clinical trial process. He came back to The City, and now he filled her shoes as acting CEO while Celine continued her maternity leave.

Peter's green eyes glistened, and his hand reached across Julie's cheek, affectionately brushing the loose hair away from her face.

"You're the most wanted woman in The City right now. Everyone is looking for you. What the hell are you doing here, of all places?" Peter's voice was smooth compared to the harsh electronic music playing in the speakers, and a lightness filled Julie's lonely heart.

"It's a long story. I can't explain it all here, but you can't tell anyone you saw me," Julie answered, pulling Peter toward a more secluded booth where the music felt less deafening.

"I've been looking for you. Celine O'Connor has been looking for you, too. She has sent me on a wild goose chase to find you, along with one of the missing time travel devices. I never thought I'd see you here . . . I thought I would have to use the device and travel time."

Julie's eyes widened with horror. She hadn't realized that Peter was looking for her or that Celine willingly pushed the idea of time travel on her friend.

"Peter, you can't use the time travel device."

"Why not?" His lips curled with curiosity. "You can't be the only one allowed to have fun."

"I'm not. And it's not fun. There's someone else, someone really dangerous who also travels dimensions of time."

"Governor Colin O'Connor?" Peter's icy words floated between them as if slapping her across the face.

"No," Julie answered as her peripheral vision caught Joel's stocky figure in the distance.

Panic filled her eyes, and she pleadingly glanced at Peter. Julie wanted a few more minutes alone with Peter to explain what was happening. Peter's eyes followed Julie, noticing Representative Kennsington stalking around the club. Without Julie having to say anything, Peter seemed to understand.

Peter swiftly grabbed Julie's jaw in between his fingers. He shielded her from her chaperone and pulled her even closer. Peter's lips felt warm against Julie's, his hands steady and grounding. The saltiness from a tiny bead of sweat on his upper lip lingered across Julie's tongue as his own stirred against her teeth. Julie welcomed this intimate touch from another being for a moment too long before pulling away.

"What the hell, Peter?"

Peter's shoulders dropped, and he shook his head. He looked hurt by her rejection but not surprised.

"What are you doing with him? Of all people?" Peter asked, shaking his head in agitation.

"Oh god, Peter, no! I'm not with Kennsington. I needed a place to stay. A place where no one would ever find me," Julie answered, hoping he heard the disgust in her voice.

"I'm not talking about Kennsington. I'm talking about the governor. There's something not right about him," Peter nearly yelled in frustration while placing his hands on Julie's shoulders. "Anyways, we need to meet again. We need to actually talk."

Peter pressed too closely to Julie's body, his shouting emulating a deep hurt mixed with concern.

"How? Joel won't let me leave his house. And he has a camera at his front and back door. He would know if you came."

Peter grabbed Julie's hand in his, his thumb rubbing calmingly and reassuringly across her knuckles. With so much history between them, guilt flooded Julie at this intimate gesture.

"Then we will use time travel. I need to get a good footing on it, understand it a bit more. In three weeks, travel to the day you go missing and meet me there right before midnight at my apartment in The Bay."

"I don't know. That sounds dangerous, and you shouldn't time travel. It changes you once you travel to another dimension." Julie's eyes darted away from Peter and locked with Joel's.

He finally spotted her—she didn't have much time.

Peter sensed her stiffness, and before Julie could register his intentions, his thumb and index finger grasped tightly around her finger and pulled the engagement ring off in one harsh movement.

"Peter!" Julie yelped, grasping for her ring from him.

"No," he yelled at her, backing away. "I need assurance you will follow up with your end of the bargain. I'll give you your ring back when we meet again."

Peter backed away, conflict in his eyes at his own cold actions. As he disappeared into the thick crowd, tears streamed down Julie's face. Her right hand held her left as if trying to soothe the bareness that was now there. When Julie turned around, Joel's red face, flushed with alcohol, greeted her.

"I got you a ride home." Joel's voice vibrated off Julie, his eyes glancing toward the direction where Peter disappeared. "You're right. It isn't a good idea for you to be out in public."

Joel roughly grabbed Julie's arm again and led her toward the back exit. A bouncer nodded in their direction, and the cool air hit Julie's skin. She felt dizzy and exhausted from her day, unsure what to make of her strange interaction with Peter.

A black sedan appeared in the alleyway, and Joel shoved her inside. "You're not coming?" Julie asked as he leaned over to close the door.

Joel grinned cruelly.

"Later," he responded and slammed the door closed.

The android in the front drove them through the windy streets of The City, away from the glitzy Port neighborhood and back toward the quiet, dark shadows of The South. A singular light shone from the kitchen window when they finally approached Joel's home. Julie grabbed the car's handle but found herself locked inside.

I'm a prisoner no matter where I am.

The android got out of the front and opened the door for her. Together, they walked into the house. His bright yellow scales hummed softly in the nighttime air, and Julie found herself smiling at how beautiful he looked. She thought of Jones and wished there was a way she could reach out to him—he was her confidant.

The yellow android's badge hung from his shirt, showing his employment in the government. The color of his identification badge revealed he was a prison guard, a vastly underappreciated role with great responsibility. He dealt with criminals all day—mostly human criminals since crime rates amongst androids remained nearly nonexistent due to their inability to feel the same level of emotions as people.

"Joel is a Humanizer, you know." Julie's words were strong, but her tone remained low as if the house could hear her words and report back to Kennsington.

"He mentioned you'd tell me that." The android didn't look Julie straight on and instead fixed his gaze at her gnarly scar. "And frankly, I can't be bothered with someone so low in the ranks like Representative Kennsington."

Startled by the android's admission, Julie's head cocked to the side in interest and intrigue. "Then why do you work for him?"

The android didn't answer and unlocked Joel Kennsington's front door with ease.

The house reeked of cigarette smoke, and even the android upturned his nose upon entering. He walked over to a window at the far end of the living room and unlocked it. The panel stuck, but with his strength, the chipped paint fluttered onto the windowsill with ease. Cool, nighttime spring air rushed inside.

"I don't work for Joel Kennsington even if he thinks I do," the android responded.

Julie held her breath as he approached her. His sheer height and build worried her, and there was no emotion or indication of his next move. His hand rested gently on her back and guided her away from the living room and into her bedroom. He fumbled with something in his pant pocket, and a small personal device emerged in his hands.

The lightweight and sleek screened device slipped stealthily into Julie's palm as he leaned into her ear. The edges of his dry lips threatened Julie's softer skin, and a chill shivered through her.

"The Supreme and Commissioner Jones send their regards."

The android backed away from Julie and left in a hurry.

Julie's eyes dropped to the device in her hand, an her fingers grew cold and clammy. She didn't trust The Supreme, especially after both her public and personal betrayals, but she trusted Jones more than anyone else. An uneasiness settled in her stomach, thinking he was now working with The Supreme.

Julie kept the personal device turned off, imagining the power button was its own Pandora's Box that she wasn't ready to open.

Yet.

The house remained silent for a few hours, and Julie welcomed sleep as she pushed aside all other impending worries. Today's events exhausted her—between time traveling on Colin's blood to a place where she didn't belong to the horrid night out at the club and her encounter with Peter.

Julie barely heard Joel's drunk whirlwind of an entrance home, but the confirmation that he had returned glared at Julie early in the morning when she opened the door and spotted a neon dress tossed on the couch.

Julie cringed and looked over at the clock on Joel's stove.

Five fifteen a.m. She doubted Joel and his evening guest would wake anytime soon. Her eyes darted to the window the android had opened last night. His action didn't trigger an alarm, and Julie now suspected Joel's means of keeping her locked inside only extended to the front and back doors. She doubted Joel would notice if she slipped through the window.

Risky, she thought. *But if I return before Joel wakes up, he will never know.*

Unwilling to leave the coveted time travel device alone in Joel's unsupervised presence, Julie quickly grabbed the glasses and glided out the window. Her body barely fit through the opening, but the freedom exhilarated her more than the alcohol from the previous evening.

Shadows lingered on the wet streets, and the remnants of an evening rain Julie didn't remember were now visible in the morning light. She pulled her jacket and scarf closer to her body and picked up her pace as she headed toward her destination.

Chapter 11
The Supreme

April 3rd, 47 A.R.

The new high judge looked uncomfortable in the Sessions room at The Capitol Building. He rocked back and forth in his seat as his eyes took in the enormous room with a peculiar sense of uneasiness for an android.

The Supreme hated how monotone her orange jumpsuit looked against her amber scales and how pale she was from the lack of stimulation over the last couple of months.

So many eyes in the room were all looking at her. Members of the media were forced into the outer alcoves of The Capitol Building, and the public was corralled outside across Beacon Street, congregating in the public park.

The Representatives of The People and The Representatives of The Androids sat in their assigned, respective desks. A table and chair resided next to Representative Joel Kennsington's station, and the governor occupied the seat, shifting back and forth with eyes never leaving the insufferable representative beside him.

Colin looks terrible, The Supreme noticed as her eyes scanned Colin up and down. Colin's skin radiated a pastiness unfamiliar to The Supreme, and large bags under his eyes portrayed his sleepless nights and returned habits of drugs and booze.

Commissioner Jones, still new in his appointment, sat beside the high judge. His emerald green scales flickered as he rolled down his sleeves to hide his ability to display the feelings coursing through his body.

The room quieted as The Supreme took her seat in the makeshift witness stand beside the high judge. He rose and faced the audience.

"Madam Supreme, you've been brought here today so that we

can begin your trial and question you about the various crimes The Legislature has accused of you." His young, inexperienced voice echoed in the stillness of the gallery. With trembling hands, he barged down his gavel.

The Legislature appointed new androids to all positions The Supreme previously appointed; most poignantly, the high judge and the commissioner. The Supreme was unfamiliar with the brilliantly blue android with silver-edged scales. She looked up at him and nodded.

"You've been accused of the following crimes: first-degree murder on multiple counts, kidnapping, and attempt to murder by turning numerous humans into posse hominems. The exact number is still currently under investigation." The high judge closed his eyes before continuing, "You've also been accused of one count of treason in an attempt to overthrow The Legislature. Lastly, one count of embezzlement in the sum of $1.5 billion from COLI*GO investors and shareholders."

The Supreme said nothing and only nodded.

"Because Commissioner Jones has requested a fair trial, we will begin with the interrogation of yourself and, after, continue with testimony from varying witnesses."

Whispers erupted across the room, filling the marble floors and cold, wood-paneled walls with an essence of passion and life. The high judge banged his gavel against the desk not made for him and silenced the room. With questionably dark and unwelcoming eyes, the high judge looked over at Jones. Jones moved from his seat and walked toward The Supreme.

"Is it true you orchestrated the funneling of money into the posse hominem project under a false ledger account at COLI*GO?" Jones asked.

"Yes," The Supreme answered with a cracked voice from the first time speaking in days. She cleared her throat and continued, "I began funneling the money in the spring of 43 A.R. after learning which innovations COLI*GO selected from The University under Enterprise Holdings, Inc. The project didn't officially kick off until 45 A.R., which was when I had secured enough resources."

Jones and the high judge glanced at one another, suspicious of

The Supreme's honest and lengthy response after two months of silence and stubbornness. The room remained silent, with both humans and androids lingering on the edge of their seats.

"And how did you obtain"—Jones looked down and closed his eyes before continuing—"your test subjects?"

"I hired an individual to kidnap them. I worked with the former commissioner for others."

A gasp came from the back corner of the room. The Supreme rolled her eyes—the commissioner's question wasn't new information; she had already confessed guilty to some of her crimes, with kidnapping being one of them. Where The Supreme insisted she remained innocent was in the accusations of murder.

"Who did you hire?" The high judge spoke this time, his voice silencing the whispering noises around them.

"Jeb Taylor, who is now deceased, thanks to Commissioner Jones," The Supreme sneered.

The high judge ignored her jab at his colleague and continued with another question, "And these humans that Mr. Jeb Taylor kidnapped—did they know what was to become of them?"

"No."

"So, these humans were made, unwillingly and without consent, into hybrids?" Jones clarified.

"Yes."

"And how did you select your test subjects? Records and evidence collected from the lower lab indicate you have upwards of thousands of creations roaming The City . . . and possibly beyond."

"Most worked for old bloodline families or were associates of old bloodline families. Jeb Taylor and I had various connections with this part of society—me through my position as supreme and Jeb through his art and illegal drug pandering." She didn't bother to look at The Representatives of The People as she spoke these words.

Most were members of old bloodline families themselves. The Supreme observed the gears in their minds turn: the missing house staff, the helpers, and those who stopped showing up to work or who began acting differently. The look on their faces said it all: *Are they all hybrids?*

Over the course of several years, Dr. Isabella Garcia, with the help of a COLI*GO android researcher named Nolan, performed thousands of these surgeries, usually upwards of twenty or more a day.

"And Kathleen Murphy, Governor O'Connor's former secretary and legislative aide," Jones started, his eyes drifting over to where the governor sat. "Did Kathleen unwillingly or willingly opt for this transformation?"

"You phrased that most accurately, Commissioner," The Supreme articulated, her head moving toward the representatives in the room. "It's a transformation, not the act of killing."

Jones's eyes widened, realizing his grave mistake in his choice of words. The Supreme distinctively hated how everyone considered her innovation murder. She provided a new class of citizens for this constituency, one that would unite the ungrateful Legislature from completely imploding and destroying both itself and The City.

"Answer the question, Madam Supreme," the high judge warned. "Did you do this operation to Kathleen Murphy unwillingly?"

"Yes," she responded. Her eyes remained focused on her clasped, handcuffed hands. "Kathleen Murphy was simply used to hurt and torment Governor O'Connor. Dr. Julie Walsh's transformation, on the other hand, served a purpose of much importance, and I would rather speak about her."

Colin grew stiff in his seat at the mention of his lover's name. Even Representative Kennsington crossed and uncrossed his arms in a fidgeting and nervous manner. Hushed voices and gossip emerged between the representatives in the room.

"Dr. Julie Walsh? The missing interim CEO of COLI*GO?" the high judge asked, his scales rapidly pulsating a darker silver tone across his body.

"Yes. I transformed her into a posse hominem without her knowledge or consent. She was one of my later creations."

"And do you know of Dr. Walsh's whereabouts?"

The Supreme eyed Jones, noting the struggle pressing between his lips as he talked of his friend. This was the opportunity he spoke of—if there was a chance for her to expose Colin O'Connor and all his crimes, all the murders, it was now.

Commissioner Jones is a coward, The Supreme thought, contemplating the opportunity.

She looked over at Colin, her lifelong friend and enemy. Their relationship had always been complex ever since their childhood. Henry O'Connor raised The Supreme—she and Colin grew up together like siblings. If she accused Colin of taking his beloved scientist into the woods and killing her, then Jones could easily put the governor up on this stand beside her.

But Colin loved Julie.

The Supreme understood the concept of love but never experienced it herself. She idealized the emotion, desperately appreciating the rarity of it.

Colin and The Supreme locked eyes, and she instantly recognized the lifelong torment and regret she forced him into by pitting him and his other identity, It, against one another.

I understand now. Colin isn't the only one who loves Julie Walsh—It loves her more than he would ever admit.

It never mentioned Julie to her during Colin and Julie's affair. The Supreme only happened upon the information after Celine made an insinuating comment, and she confirmed the suspicion when she spied on their lovemaking.

It always shielded Julie from me. It always would.

Colin's eyes softened, no anger or hatred seeped through his facial expression. He was haunted by his own decision, not The Supreme's.

He's made peace and accepted his fate. He'll take his punishment if I choose to turn him in. He already admitted to The Legislature that he killed Kathleen Murphy. Colin really isn't the coward his father often called him.

"I do not know where Dr. Walsh is," The Supreme finally answered after painful, anticipating moments of silence.

The room remained eerily hushed and heads turned to one another. A look passed between Jones and Colin, and The Supreme snickered. Knowing Jones couldn't break her on the topic of Julie Walsh satisfied her, a feeling The Supreme understood and enjoyed.

"Besides Nolan, whom we have here to testify as a witness, who helped you with the procedures?" Jones asked.

"No one." The Supreme looked over sharply at Nolan. She could only thank her trusty colleague, Mick Taylor, for reprogramming Nolan's microchip and wiping away his memory of Dr. Isabella Garcia.

"We find that hard to believe, Madam Supreme," Jones replied with a bit of harshness The Supreme didn't expect.

She remained silent.

"Did Dr. Walsh assist in your procedures?" the high judge ventured. The room exploded at the accusation.

Dr. Walsh was not a medical professional. The ability for her to perform complex brain surgery wasn't viable. Even if she possessed the skills, Dr. Walsh was adored by the community. As a nobody, her human peers admired her ambition and intellect, her compassion and excitement. Their love for Julie began far before her appointment as interim CEO. When her antidote received approval for Alzheimer's, The Constituency saw her as a savior. No scientist before her had come close to any kind of cure—and here, Julie provided one to them with kindness and empathy.

The Supreme chuckled, and the room quieted down, confused by her uncharacteristic outburst of laughter.

"Dr. Julie Walsh doesn't have an evil bone in her human body." She caught Colin's eyebrows raise, and a discrediting smirk crossed his face at an obvious remembrance of a sinister memory of her.

Does he also know Julie has a bit of a wicked ruthlessness to her, if provoked? If uncontrolled? The Supreme wondered. *Of course he does. He knows her better than anyone, even me.*

"I'm not sure if that's true, Madam Supreme. Julie did conspire against you and provided the evidence used in these accusations from The Legislature. It appears you'd gain a lot from keeping her out of your trial, and I'm convinced you know where she might be. So, I'll ask again: Where is Dr. Walsh?" The high judge seemed tired of The Supreme's runaround, his aggravation showing not only in his rough tone but also across his shining scales.

Both he and Jones understand and feel more human emotions than they should, The Supreme noted. *They could both use my special serum.*

She used to possess a special pharmaceutical to inject herself with each day before her arrest. The Supreme's predecessor provided her with this serum; it acted as a tool to help hide the changing colors of her scales when she experienced or understood an emotion. No one knew The Supreme understood 100 percent and experienced about 50 percent of human emotions and feelings besides Celine O'Connor—no one could ever know that she and the android who came before her had recoded their processors.

"I don't know. I assume she discovered what I'd done to her and fled. She must have pieced together my grand plans for her," The Supreme answered.

"And what were those plans?" This time, it was Jones's voice piercing through the silence of the room.

The Supreme paused and took a breath. Closing her eyes, she contemplated how to say the words she needed to say.

"I imagined Julie would unify our society. I imagined a world where humans and androids voted together, had only one leader. She could have united and led all of us, secured the peace between all beings. Only a hybrid could connect humans and androids, and who better than a person not of old bloodline descent but still someone everyone knew? Someone most admired and adored? Trusted? An intelligent, brave, and strong woman? One who cared equally about humans and androids? She could have saved us, Commissioner Jones. But instead, you have all ruined us. You've all destroyed the great potential for The Constituency."

A loud bang sounded in the audience as the governor gripped the edge of Joel Kennsington's desk. Joel darted his eyes back and forth, nervous at the sheer, physical presence of Colin O'Connor.

Colin's eyes narrowed, and his knuckles turned white from his intense, tight hold.

"Is there something you would like to say, Governor?" the high judge asked as all eyes in the room followed The Supreme's and landed on Colin.

Colin's breathing sharpened, and the harshness of the air escaped his flaring nostrils.

"No," he said sternly, the commanding dominance in his voice highlighting his strength and power.

Joel let out a large sigh and relaxed into his seat while Colin let go of the edge of the wooden desk.

“I think we should take a quick fifteen-minute recess.” Jones motioned toward the high judge, who nodded.

The bailiff, an android with iridescent yellow scales, approached The Supreme and guided her by the handcuffs loose on her wrists to the other side of the room.

Colin looked over at The Supreme and nodded, an acknowledgment she didn’t expect but appreciated from her old friend.

Chapter 12
The Governor

April 4th, 47 A.R.

People on the streets screamed. Colin heard their loudness from inside the townhouse. The Supreme's crimes were leaked to the public earlier in the day, the secretiveness of her trial exposed and handed off to the media from an "inside source" from within The Capitol Building.

Joel Kennsington was to blame.

Moments ago, people and androids didn't know anything about hybrids, and they didn't know one of their leaders experimented on their neighbors, friends, and family members to create them. Their anger rippled through the neighborhoods of The City with a ferocious vengeance similar to the android uprising that ignited The Resurgence.

Colin was born after The Resurgence but the stories of violence, riots, and destruction were woven into his upbringing. Political turmoil and the uncharted territory of androids integrating into the lives of humans was a large part of his upbringing. The O'Connor townhouse had lived through these experiences, witnessing similar scenes to what occurred outside these walls now. The windows rattled, and noise from vehicle horns exploded. A mass group of people congregated in the streets and in the public park.

Colin stood from his chair and left his study to cautiously approach the window. The carriage house blocked his view of The Capitol Building and surrounding area.

He walked through the doorway swiftly and headed for the circular staircase leading to the roof deck. The breeze chilled him to the bone, and the gray clouds above threatened downpours.

Colin didn't care. He only cared about understanding the

outbreak surrounding The Hill.

The view from the roof stretched out across The City. On one end, Colin observed The River neighborhood and wasn't surprised to find the COLI*GO building completely dark and empty. He and the other Board of Directors sent a communication earlier that day, insisting employees work from home and remain away from the public eye if possible.

They weren't sure how much of COLI*GO's involvement would be exposed during The Supreme's trial, but they never expected posse hominems would make breaking news headlines.

From the other end of the roof deck, Colin caught a glimpse of The Capitol Building and the park abutting Beacon Street. A massive crowd stormed the steps of the brick building, the golden dome casting dark shadows in the park. Shapes and shadows of figures illuminated through the misty air, but Colin assumed they were humans, not androids. A deafening, piercing scream shouted through all the other noises, and Colin's eyes grew wide in terror at the sight unfolding before him.

"We found one!"

"You freak!"

"Disgusting hybrid!"

"Look at her scar!"

Pain and horror coursed through the throng of individuals dragging a young woman across the park's common area. They kicked her, pulling her hair and clothes.

Her screams reminded Colin of Julie's from the night he strangled her. This woman's cries impaled Colin, the fear palpable in the thick, disturbing air. He wanted to look away but couldn't—his body was frozen in place while violently shaking.

Two larger male figures pulled a woman up from her arms and strapped her to the statue at the edge of the park. The very same statue his father commissioned to symbolize peace after The Resurgence—humans and androids shaking hands, depicting peace and partnership.

Jones! Where are you? Where are the police? What are you doing? Colin questioned, gripping the edge of the railing with panic striking through his core.

As if on command, Colin's eyes shifted to The Capitol Building where he recognized the android police force. They attempted to break up the crowd but failed, completely outnumbered. There were too many of them, throwing anything they could grab their hands on at the officers. The police weren't moving fast enough, not even in their rarely used riot gear.

One of the men holding the woman hostage raised his hands high in the air, and a pocket blade shone through the mist.

No, no, no . . . Colin's mind raced, his brain preparing itself for what he knew would come next but somehow wasn't ready to witness.

The young woman cried out at the sight of the knife in her captor's hands. The most animalistic, guttural noise escaped between her lips as he slashed open her neck. In his sloppiness, the man hit an artery and blood rapidly gushed out from her. The color drained instantly from the woman's face, the life seeping out of her eyes. So much blood surrounded her, exploding, staining and dripping down her clothes. The substance sprayed across people lingering a bit too close in the front row of the crowd, but they barely flinched.

The sheer gore made Colin's throat close up.

The other man approached the opening in her neck and prodded his fingers into the wound until he found his prized possession: the microchip.

He completely violated her in front of so many people, Colin thought, shaking his head away from the sight.

The man lifted the microchip high in the air, his fingers stained crimson red. Clasping the hand of the man beside him, they held up the soiled knife in unison. The rioters and onlookers cheered, raising their own hands in allegiance.

A gunshot ricocheted through the air, and the man with the knife instantly fell to the ground. A second sound quickly followed, and the other man faced a similar outcome as his partner. The crowd shrieked, dispersing in various directions as the android police force swarmed the scene.

Colin's eyes darted to the top of The Capitol Building in the direction where the shots were fired. The commissioner was one of the few androids with the authority to use a sniper weapon. Only a small handful of highly trained android officers were given the same level of training.

Colin spotted Jones on the top floor, the rifle perched on the windowsill. Jones's emerald green scales shimmered through the fog, brightly clear as a whirlwind of emotions and feelings overwhelmed the android. Jones leaned away from the scope and looked out across the park.

The crowd disappeared as quickly as it formed, and the only figures left were police officers, the young woman, and her two dead assassins. Her body dangled with her head bobbing slightly and her feet swaying in the wind. Blood profusely spilled onto the white statue around her.

Peace was shattered—peace and security that took Colin over a decade to build back into society.

Mere minutes. Destroyed.

Colin's knees buckled, and he fell to the ground. He blamed himself—while The Supreme's crimes were unforgivable and ultimately her own fault, he couldn't stop himself from thinking how terribly this situation escalated and how if he wasn't consumed and locked away from his own grief, he might have been able to prevent this woman's death.

I could have conspired a plan, a plan to break the news to constituents in a less sensationalized way. They could have accepted the realities of humans, androids, and hybrids. Instead, I let my mind wander in grief and guilt. Guilt for killing Kathleen, stabbing Julie, and sending her somewhere far away from here. From me.

Colin hated everything in this moment: He hated The Supreme, not for her bullshit beliefs that hybrids would unite society but instead how she gave no regard for human choice in her decisions. He hated Jones for his inability to make quick, distinctive decisions. He hated The Legislature for their lack of responsibility and action to keep the Humanizers in check. He hated Joel fucking Kennsington for trapping him here in the townhouse like a puppet. He even hated his sister, Celine, and her blind eye to what happened inside her precious COLI*GO.

But most of all, Colin hated himself.

He hated It for convincing him they needed to push Julie away for the sake of society, and he truly recognized now that he had no control of his own mind anymore.

Isabella is correct—people and androids needed me. And I failed them.

As if his thoughts summoned him, Colin envisioned a phantom hand on his shoulder: It.

While It was just another part of Colin, sometimes he physically felt It's presence as if he were his own being. The illogical part of Colin wished It wasn't a piece of his mind—a piece he was afraid would take control if he continued divulging himself in.

"We need to find Julie." It's words were sorrowful, very unlike him. "Before they find her."

It looked out across at the remnants of the horrid scene and screamed loudly, knowing the sounds of the weeping City drowned out his own agony.

"They will pay for this," It swore, making a promise to not only himself but also Colin. "All of them. I will make them regret this."

***

"Colin? Are you okay?" Celine's voice echoed down the stairs from the roof deck. Colin tilted his head up, surprised his sister's voice filled the townhouse after all this time.

"I'm fine," he responded without enthusiasm. He turned his head toward the doorway and toward her tall and lanky figure. "How are you? How is my nephew? Are you two safe?"

With her dark hair and a rectangular frame, his sister reminded him of both his father and mother respectfully. The siblings towered over others with their abnormal height—something they inherited from a combination of their tall parents—but Celine's skinny, bony physique and angular jaw with sharp, defining cheekbones resembled their mother.

When Colin looked in the mirror, his father's face stared back at him. He hated that man, even in his death, and hated how his father haunted his reflection at each glance.

"I'm sorry." Celine's words were crisp but genuine.

Colin watched his sister burst into tears, her tiny hands grasping her face and shielding her eyes from the outside world. He could never stay angry at Celine for too long, no matter how much she deserved it or how much he wanted to. There was some sense of personal responsibility he held for his older sister, a guilt for all the hard experiences he brought during their youth, and for forcing the decision of their father's life support on her.

Opening his arms, Colin embraced Celine, and her sobs drowned out in his chest. After a bit of time, she finally settled down, but Colin didn't let go of her.

"I'm going to find her for you, I promise." Celine backed away from him, wiping the corners of her eyes. "This is all my fault. I'm fixing it. For COLI*GO. For us. For you."

Celine looked up at him with her steely eyes, another O'Connor trait they both possessed from their father.

"How?" The words left Colin's lips with tension and confusion.

"I have Emilia's time travel device. I found it in the lower lab and confiscated it before Jones and the police arrived."

Celine referring to The Supreme by her given name made a twinge of pain course through Colin's chest, sparking the familiarity between himself, his sister, and The Supreme.

"How will that help?"

"Julie is a time traveler. I mean, that makes the most sense." Celine's uncanny ability to piece together information still impressed Colin.

He thought back to the night Julie gave him the note—the one with incriminating evidence against not only The Supreme but also The Board members of COLI*GO, including his sister. When Colin went to The Legislature, he kept his sister and The Board out of his accusations. His focus was solely on stopping The Supreme.

But that night seared through his memory like a strongly lit flame.

Julie had come to the townhouse in a breeze, and her rush to give him this letter felt particularly strange. He had reassured Julie there was no threat and she was safe. But he had been wrong. He became the threat to her safety.

Months later, Colin realized Julie time traveled from the future. They had shared an oddly invigorating moment together, one Colin originally mistook for a dream. There was something so abnormal about her body when he touched her; her stomach and ribs were littered with scars. But in the morning, Julie was back to who she was before. Simple and pure.

Julie traveled back to that particular night with a purpose and a plan, Colin realized.

Their experience meant something to both him and her. He hadn't killed her. Those scars on her body were healed marks—marks originating from his purposefully shallow stab wounds.

She knew what I would do, and she still came back.

This tiny thread of hope and optimism kept him going, kept him believing that Julie would return to him again. But the implications of time travel still confused Colin. It traveled time before, experiencing the sensation for them both. Memories haunted Colin in the form of dreams, and he couldn't trust his mind to distinguish the difference between reality and his imagination.

"I'm not doubting you. I'm just not sure how you'd find her," Colin finally answered his sister.

"I'm sending Peter Schneider on the mission." His sister's words stung Colin's heart. "I provided him with one of the time travel devices. I asked him to find the missing one and to find Julie."

Colin didn't care for Peter and preferred the man wasn't his sister's first choice in finding the woman he loved. His jealousy ran deep with that man. Colin had previously convinced The Supreme to send Peter away to the foreign office, back when he obsessed over Julie from afar. But Peter was smart—he was the right choice to lead COLI*GO in Julie's absence.

Celine stepped back from Colin, tears falling from her eyes. Colin wanted to thank his sister, wanted to believe in her ability to trust someone outside of them with this important task.

But he didn't.

"What about Mick Taylor?"

"He still works for Peter. Why?" Celine's eyebrows furrowed at her brother's question.

Not that version of Mick, Colin thought. *The dangerous time traveler version of him.*

"I'm not convinced of his strength. He's easily swayed by his emotions," Celine answered, interrupting Colin's thoughts.

"You're right," Colin replied, deflecting his concerns as his thumbs rubbed his temples slowly. "I'm still adjusting to this . . . new setup. This new routine. I'm not my normal self."

"Isabella told me you were doing much better," Celine said and tentatively placed her hand on Colin's shoulder.

He recoiled a bit more harshly than he intended and couldn't explain why. While Colin appreciated Isabella's company, she lingered too long, cared too much. She unsettled him.

"Why is this the first time I'm seeing you after all these months, Celine?" Colin's voice trembled while he cleared his throat.

The pain reverberated in his words.

"I'm locked away in this house all alone, dealing with the mistakes I've made. Julie's gone and you know more than anyone how much I love her. I appreciate you're looking for her now, but have you realized what her absence has done to me? The absence of everyone from my life? The pain and torment I experienced making the decision to kill Kathleen? All because The Supreme turned her into a hybrid, threatened to kill me. And then, before I knew it, Julie was gone, too. Another victim of The Supreme's. I admitted my demon to you that day; I confided in you about It. Did you wonder how I'm dealing in all this isolation? You couldn't even show up once?"

Celine's lips trembled with regret. A small whimper escaped her lips, the tears forming again in the corners of her eyes. Colin didn't feel bad about what he said: She deserved all the terrible hurtful words he spun at her. He was wounded, and Celine didn't bother to help the only person who went to various lengths to protect her and their family.

Colin cared about his sister; he even smiled larger than she had at the birth of her own son. Baby Henry looked up at his uncle with all the wonder and happiness in the world, and Colin promised Celine he would do anything to protect him. More so than her own husband, Martin.

"I was afraid you hated me." Celine's voice was filled with only a small resemblance of regret. "I'm not the same as you, Colin. I wasn't ready to face the realities, make the same selfless sacrifices you made. I initially thought of your acts as horrid. And when you confided in me about Amanda . . . I knew you had been sleeping with her, but I didn't piece together that you killed her too. She was mine; she was my happiness. She was going to betray me, and I finally realized the bigger picture of everything you did. You did all that to protect me. To protect our family."

Colin looked away from Celine and toward the misty city streets. His shoulders relaxed as he held on to the ledge.

"I'm tired of all this bullshit. We need to be on the same side."

"I see that now. I want to understand. I want to be there for you." Celine stood beside him and leaned into his large frame before taking a deep breath. "Do you think The Legislature will charge you for your crimes too?"

"I'm not sure," Colin answered, choosing his words carefully. "I admitted to killing Kathleen, but they don't know about Amanda or any of my other . . . crimes."

"When will you know their decision?" Celine asked, tilting her head in his direction.

Colin shook his head and continued gazing out across The City. The eerily quietness after such madness and chaos earlier concerned him.

"Soon, I imagine. Especially with what happened today."

"If there's anything I know about crisis and handling the backlash of it, The Legislature can't afford to lose you. They will turn a blind eye, maybe give you a slap on the wrist."

"You're probably right."

Colin looked down at his sister, her clear eyes glistening with hope.

"I don't feel safe so close to The River. Can Henry and I move back here, stay with you?"

A lightness crept across Colin's chest. He feared his lack of control on It, feared his own odd personality traits and need for structure and quietness. That was what always held him back from ever starting a family of his own.

His sister and her baby inside these walls would challenge him. But Colin didn't want her or his nephew hiding in fear, especially if COLI*GO's true part in The Supreme's affairs ever came to life with the public.

"What about Martin?" Colin asked of Celine's husband.

Colin never cared for Martin Borges even though he was also from another old bloodline family. Colin considered Martin a weak, spineless man.

Celine closed her eyes and shook her head. "Things are a bit estranged between us."

Colin's shoulders stiffened.

"Did he hurt you? Or Henry?" His eyes widened, and a sharp threat formed on the edges of his lips.

Celine laughed. "Martin is the least threatening man I know. I often wonder if that's why I chose him. He's easy to control, easy to persuade. He adores me and normally places me on a pedestal. He even left his first wife for me."

Divorce was an unheard-of atrocity in The City, but his decision wasn't overly frowned on because he had married a nobody: Maggie Rivera. She had only been deemed acceptable by society because she made something of herself within FACERE at such a young age.

"Martin serves many purposes in my life. Business partner, mentor, lover, friend, and father to my son. But I've never loved him."

Colin remained silent, unsure how to respond to the truth in his sister's confession.

"I mentioned spending time here," Celine finally said. "I told him I needed space and that you needed me. You know how Martin can be. He wants so much, and I can't give him everything he asks for because he can't give me everything I ask for."

The authenticity in her words pulsated between the siblings, and Colin sadly smiled. He appreciated his sister's blunt honesty—she didn't need to explain anything more to him; Colin understood and reflected on his own past romantic relationship with Isabella.

"Of course you and Henry can move in here. You can stay as long as you'd like. That's what this house is for: family."

The two walked back down the stairs and into the warmth of the townhouse. Celine observed her surroundings, not noticing a difference from the last time she was inside Colin's home. Had she returned a few weeks ago, she would have found a disastrous mess.

Isabella helped Colin straighten up, and while life without Julie was still a challenge for him, the normal acts of life became easier with each passing day. He started making breakfasts of more than just coffee again. He ran on the treadmill, washed and dried his laundry, cooked hearty meals, and changed the sheets each week.

The dark circles beneath his eyes hadn't disappeared, but slowly, Colin believed they would. He even stopped drinking each night, not touching the tempting bottle of Scotch in the cabinet of his study—the one place Isabella forgot to look in her effort to purge his home of demons.

He was grateful for Celine coming to the townhouse this evening. After seeing the massacre in the park and the disarray and experience of It for the first time in months, tonight would have tested his true darkness. His true vulnerabilities.

Celine's eyes narrowed at the sight of Julie's sweatshirt on the edge of Colin's bed as they walked past the master bedroom. She paused, lifting her hand toward Colin but thought better of it, and they continued down the hall toward the multiple other bedrooms.

She settled on taking her old bedroom, the one she occupied during her childhood and young adult life before purchasing her own place with Martin.

"Thank you," Celine said, looking up at Colin as they stood in place, staring at the spacious bedroom. "We'll move in tomorrow."

Chapter 13
Mick

April 6th, 47 A.R.

Mick left his condo in The Harbor and headed toward Jones's new apartment in The Bay. He returned from his most recent time travel trip, and his messy home greeted him with no warm welcome. Mick's desk was covered in notes, samples, and prototypes. A load of laundry lay wrinkled in the dryer, and the dishes piled high in the kitchen sink.

Peter would surely be looking for him—he always noticed when Mick was away from the COLI*GO office for too long. Mick shuffled the messes to the side and escaped into the cool, wet spring air.

The streets were misty and his detour to Jones's normally took him twenty minutes. The streets were still and the normally packed subway cars provided solace and shelter in their abandonment. Mick got off the subway stop located in the park and walked west onto Commonwealth Avenue. He paused by Julie's apartment and peered into her large bay windows.

Dark. Empty.

Mick missed her, and while he still believed her allegiance to the O'Connor family was wrong, he wanted to find his friend and talk to her.

Maybe she will listen to me. If I can just find her . . .

At first, Mick wasn't sure where Julie went after he sent her back to June 23rd, 46 A.R. According to his theory on time loops and the semi-invincibility of time travelers, she should have returned to the place of her true death. From there, he figured Julie would find her way back to him. But Julie was nowhere to be found, and he worried something went terribly wrong—that she was in grave danger.

Breaking into Jones's apartment was an easy task, almost as easy as breaking into Julie's mirrored studio across the street. Jones selected this exact unit for its perfect view of Julie's place. The impact of Julie's disappearance on Jones troubled Mick.

Julie and Jones were friends since grade school, and she was responsible for recoding Jones's microchip to understand and feel more emotions. Mick observed from afar how tormented his boyfriend was from all the chaos that surrounded him.

Dark clouds and overcast skies made the shadows of Jones's apartment darker and gloomier as Mick stumbled through the kitchen area. He nearly tripped and fumbled around his feet to find the leather-bound journal.

My journal.

The notebook lay disheveled on the floor, untouched.

Jones was meticulous in keeping his home organized, and even the smallest object out of order made the scales on his arms flare in uncomfortable shades of green.

But I didn't bring the journal here.

Flipping through the pages, horror filled the bottom of Mick's gut. Ungluing from his place, Mick placed the journal back on the kitchen island and hurriedly left Jones's apartment.

He crossed the street and picked up his pace until he made it to the subway. The ancient tram moved slowly as it left the underground and crossed the body of water on the centuries-old bridge. Small marks pricked the water from the rain, and lightning struck out across the horizon. Mick sensed a loneliness in The River much as he had in The Hill once he stepped onto the sidewalk. Even this neighborhood was a ghost town, and he didn't pass a single soul. He pulled his hood above his head, but his glasses were already streaked with cool raindrops. The walk to COLI*GO's headquarters took only a few minutes once he left the train, but Mick dragged his feet.

The large glass doors welcomed him with a warm blast of air. The oddness made Mick's heart beat faster, and his eyes darted back and forth to watch for a surprise shadow.

Only a few security guards looked up at him as he approached the lobby.

Where is everyone?

Mick halted as a small figure caught his attention.

Anna Garcia sat by the large water fountain in the center of COLI*GO's lobby. They locked eyes, and he approached.

Anna stood and placed both hands on her hips. Mick felt the sudden urge to pivot in the opposite direction, but diversion was too late—Anna was already walking toward him. When he reached her, she grasped his bicep with a strong grip.

"Mick." Her calm voice caused his feet to stop moving.

With the emptiness of the building and the surrounding streets, the sound of her voice was magnified loudly in his ears.

"Anna."

"Do you have a minute?" Her eyes softened, and a small flush rose across her cheeks.

In this lighting, he almost mistook her for her older sister, and she reminded him of a deep, dark secret they shared that no one could ever know.

"I suppose," Mick whispered.

Anna pulled them to the corner while her fingers tightened their grip around Mick's arm.

"I know you time travel," she said in a hushed voice, "so you know a great deal about posse hominems."

"I do." Mick sighed. He didn't want to discuss time travel with Anna or posse hominems. Mick wasn't inclined to lie and honestly hated being elusive and ambiguous. A discussion with Anna would require him to be these things he despised.

"So you know who helped The Supreme?"

Mick's face tightened at the sound of her question. Her inquisition made his stomach turn, more than he could allow her to know.

"You won't like what I have to say. So I better say nothing."

Anna flinched in response. Mick moved away, his strides longer with an extra foot of height he possessed over her. But Anna was determined. She caught up to Mick by adding emphasis and urgency to her steps.

"That's not going to work, Mick. You need to tell me what you know—especially if you want to help your friend Julie."

Mick stilled at the mention of his friend, and he sharply raced away. Mick scanned his badge at the security checkpoint, relieved he would finally lose Anna in the elevator waiting area since she didn't work here. His jaw dropped when Anna's hand whipped out a badge from her coat pocket and she walked through the glass turntable behind him. Mick pressed the elevator call button for the 101st floor and sighed. If there was anything he learned about Isabella, it was that she responded well to dominance. He figured he could try the same trick on her sister.

"Do you really think it would be that easy?" Mick asked, twisting to face Anna. "That you could waltz right into COLI*GO, ask me a question, and solve whatever Jones has assigned to you? Did he specifically ask you to torment me?"

Anna narrowed her eyes at Mick, his questions slicing through them both with astonishment.

"What the actual fuck did Jones ever see in a loser like you?" Anna echoed, and in his fit of anger, Mick shoved her into the now opened elevator.

He ran for the lobby, making his way through the front entrance with Anna and the elevator disappearing up the building. The street outside was still quiet, and Mick fumbled for his device. He quickly unlocked the screen with a shaking hand. He was so preoccupied after returning from a time travel expedition that he hadn't realized the date.

The world changed overnight while he time traveled. The eerie sidewalks reminded him of after curfew hours in The Countryside even though it was late morning in The City. The alerts flashed before his device like shooting stars, each wanting to salaciously grab his attention.

A group of humans had butchered a posse hominem in the park. Jones's familiar voice sounded from the small speakers in Mick's device: All citizens were to stay indoors, work from home, and only venture out in case of emergencies until all perpetrators from the riot were captured.

*Anna's presence at COLI*GO is even more alarming.* Mick wondered why she left her ostentatious loft in The Port and risked the trek across town to speak with him. *How did she even know I would be there?*

Between Anna's knowledge of where he was and his unrecognizable journal in Jones's kitchen, Mick's mind paused, and a horrendous, fearful realization crossed him.

Chapter 14
The Governor

April 6th, 47 A.R.

Being back in his office at The Capitol Building invigorated Colin. The City needed him now more than ever, and he wanted to protect people, androids, and even hybrids. After the violence he witnessed and knowing The Supreme was behind bars, hybrids weren't the threat he initially thought. Now was the perfect time for him to execute his power and a plan.

Colin's daily briefings with Commissioner Jones left them both frustrated but not at one another. They both wanted to identify the culprits leading these riots and knew the group stemmed from the Humanizer party. Finding their leader wasn't a challenge, but understanding the identity of the orchestrators of the attacks posed difficulty. They were sophisticated in their communications, and placing moles in a group that hated other beings besides themselves was nearly impossible with a full android police force.

The head of the Humanizers sat right in front of Colin: Representative Joel Kennsington.

He's behind all of this but won't let up. Why is he keeping his cards so close to his chest? This is unlike Joel.

"How can I help you today, Representative Kennsington?" Colin asked with a devilish smirk across his face, his emphasis on the word "representative" heavily pronounced. Colin never wanted to call Joel "acting governor" ever again.

"Well," Joel said, leaning back in his chair, "since my idiotic colleagues deem you suitable for your role and I have responsibility as Session speaker, I have a lovely parting gift for you."

Colin's body stiffened at the endless possibilities of Joel's innuendo and sarcastic tone. He placed a hand on his chin and kicked his feet up on his desk. Joel rolled his eyes at Colin's obvious disingenuous care toward him.

"You've pushed off finding a replacement for Kathleen for long enough," Joel responded, his smile beaming off his face like a young school boy's.

The sound of Kathleen's name from Joel's lips irritated Colin to no end—Joel knew Kathleen was like a sister to Colin.

A light knock sounded from Colin's office door, and a young woman, roughly Julie's age, walked into the room. She was tall for a woman and stood at nearly five foot ten. Freckles painted wildly across her face, and she donned a fashionable matching gray blazer and pencil skirt. A flicker of jet-black ink peeked out on her neck, but the tattoo was mostly covered by her chestnut hair, which crashed in waves along her shoulders.

"May I introduce you to Elsie Sullivan?" Joel asked, standing from his seat and meeting the young woman at the other end of the office. "Your new secretary and legislative aide."

She looked familiar to him. Elsie's mother served as a representative while his father was governor and into his own first term as governor. His father and Representative Sullivan worked closely together. Representative Sullivan championed several moderate pieces of legislation for humans and androids.

According to Legislature gossip, the representative's daughter was a bit outspoken and worked as a notary for the former high judge. She was young and green, but a woman like Elsie wouldn't have survived day in and day out working for androids unless she possessed both wits and intellect.

With a shift in android appointments from The Supreme's abrupt departure, Elsie needed a new home, and The Representatives of The Androids were happy to hand her back over to someone on the side of The Representatives of The People.

But giving her to me? Colin looked over at Kennsington questionably, his brow raised over his otherwise stone-cold face.

He didn't quite understand why Kennsington would allow The Legislature to pick someone like Elsie Sullivan to be his secretary and legislative aide—she was young and too inexperienced compared to Kathleen.

"I hope I'm not interrupting anything?" Elsie asked in a polished tone, but she didn't fool Colin—he could tell from her tattoo and the way she straightened her strong build that there was an edginess to Elsie.

Kicking his feet off the desk and planting them firmly on the ground, Colin stood to meet her. As he approached Elsie, she smiled curiously.

"Not at all." Colin's voice sounded more enthusiastic than previously before. "I know of you, Ms. Sullivan, and I fondly remember working with your mother before she retired. I'm glad to have a brilliant mind on my team."

"Thank you, Governor O'Connor," Elsie responded, and the two walked back over to where Joel Kennsington sat. "I remember the first time I met you in person, when I was a notary for The Records Department in The Courthouse. I'll never forget thinking that someday, I wanted to work for you."

"Why don't you show Representative Kennsington out of my office, and then we can go over how I keep my schedule, prioritize meetings, and other basics?" Colin didn't break his stare away from Kennsington but noted how Elsie smiled excitedly.

"Of course, Mr. Governor," her airy voice responded, and she showed Kennsington out the door.

Colin settled back into his chair and scanned through his device. He was running behind schedule with this unexpected curveball. He heard Elsie's heels clicking against the marble floors, the sound growing louder as she approached.

"Have a seat." He gestured toward her.

Elsie obeyed, a slight tremor in her hands as she sat down.

"Representative Kennsington isn't the only one I interviewed with. I had a panel with the full legislature and second interviews with each Representative of The People." Her quiet voice softened with each word, wanting to convince Colin she was worthy of the role bestowed upon her. "And my mother had nothing to do with this, either. It's important to me that you know I didn't use her influence to get here. I did this on my own."

Colin smiled. "I don't doubt your qualifications, Miss Sullivan. It's not my place to judge you without giving you a fair chance."

"I understand I'm an underdog here, especially compared to

Ms. Murphy. I don't have anywhere near the appropriate amount of experience, but I want to prove everyone wrong. I want you to know I'm taking this position seriously." Elsie pulled out her device, ready to take notes and listen to what Colin instructed of her.

He smiled, her tenacity reminding him of someone else he knew.

"If I never gave the underdog a fighting chance, I'd have missed out on a lot of important opportunities in my life." The words lingered on the edges of Colin's lips, and he wondered how much Elsie knew about him.

By the eager grin on her face, he assumed she didn't know about his colored past.

"I will treat you with the same respect as I treated Kathleen. I promise."

"Thank you," Elsie replied before putting her device down on the desk.

She looked up at him with her fawn brown eyes, her smooth skin illuminating under the harsh lights in his office.

"I think you'll find you and I are cut from the same cloth and handle situations similarly, based on how similar we are in personality."

Colin leaned back and crossed his arms, perplexed by her response. Intrigue crossed his mind at a fast pace before dissipating into hesitation.

"How so?"

"I'm not completely inept. I grew up with my mother in The Legislature. I know there are more efficient ways to make The Legislature move in the right direction. I'm interested in learning how you've accomplished that with such ease," Elsie said, picking at the paint on her nails. "I someday would like to be governor. I think you'd make the best mentor anyone could ask for."

Colin's eyes drifted from Elsie's face and down her body.

She was an abnormally tall woman like his sister but had a powerful build. The curves on her biceps were apparent underneath her blazer.

"I'm honored you think so highly of me. Harnessing the power of observation is the first step in being a skilled politician. But what I do after hours is of my own accord," Colin spoke crisply and quietly, but he carried an intense demeanor behind what he said. "Any involvement in that requires trust. I don't trust you."

"Yet," Elsie interjected with a hint of optimism in her tone.

"What did Joel say to you about me, anyways?" Colin asked, unsure where to skirt the line with his new secretary and legislative aide.

"I think he holds too much influence and power and we should stifle that as quickly as possible." Elsie's cold tone immolated Colin's, penetrating through the air with an element of ease much like the slick, sharp knife he kept.

Colin would need to eventually work with and trust Elsie or fire her. The longer Colin watched how Elsie tinkered with her device and notes, and the physical distance she insisted upon Joel while in his presence relaxed his nerves. There was nothing particularly off-putting about Elsie.

Colin distrusted the situation, not necessarily her as a person. There was an oddly charming air to Elsie. Her ease and natural ability to be fascinating while abrasive made Colin believe he may have selected her himself if given the chance. The appointment was highly intimate—not having a say in who filled Kathleen's shoes was extremely unheard of, which caused his initial doubt in her.

"Why don't you tell me a bit more about yourself?" Colin asked, wondering if he could capture an inkling of how wicked his new aide could be. He appreciated the harshness of her voice, her sense of urgency and commitment.

Elsie chuckled quietly, and a sense of familiarity passed between them, even though they barely knew one another. A cloudiness passed through Elsie's eyes, and Colin instantly recognized the look—a look that he sometimes saw in his own reflection.

"I grew up on The Monument, and it was scandalous news when my mother had me. Old bloodlines don't have children out of wedlock, and if they do, they don't do it alone. Her being a single mother shunned us from that part of society. In a way, I feel like a nobody because those were the everyday people who embraced us. The Monument is truly my home because of how welcoming and supportive the community is. I never knew who my father was, but I remember my mother's tears. She oddly loved the man, but apparently, he never gave a shit about me. I rebelled in my youth, screwed up in school. But having a failure as a daughter wasn't an option for my mother. She helped me harness my anger and hatred and encouraged various . . . creative outlets. I'm an avid boxer, which I know is not something women often find a passion in, but it's how I handle my darker urges. And it's given me a lot of strength."

Colin nodded, captivated by Elsie's openness and background.

"So why are you interested in this particular side of the game? Were you not happy working as a notary?" he asked, leaning closer to her.

"If I'm being honest," Elsie said, meeting Colin's intense gaze, "I was bored. This is where change really happens. And I understand that change only happens if you're willing to skirt the ethical line. That's right up my alley."

"Well," Colin said with his famous O'Connor charming grin, "I appreciate your enthusiasm, mutual disdain for Representative Kennsington, and willingness to explore unconventional approaches, but The City is facing a larger threat right now."

"Understood."

"Help Commissioner Jones find the head ringleader of this underground terrorist group that's destroying The City and hurting posse hominems. Then we can go from there."

Elsie lifted her hand out and reached for Colin's. "Sounds like a deal."

They shook on it.

***

Over the next week, Elsie ran Colin's office like a tight ship—she was more structured with his schedule than Kathleen had ever been. Colin's calendar appeared on his device each morning at exactly 4:30 am. Never a minute earlier, never a minute later.

Elsie's tall shadow always beat him into The Capitol Building, already situated at her desk outside his office. Even Colin's meetings were more controlled. No one from The Legislature randomly stopped by without a death glare from Elsie. Representatives learned if they wanted to meet with the governor, they needed both an appointment and good favor from her. Small gifts appeared on her desk from legislative aides from various representatives—both human and android alike.

The notion made Colin chuckle. Elsie was cunning and conniving, reminding Colin of himself when he was her age.

"You have a meeting with Commissioner Jones today that isn't on your original schedule," Elsie's sharp voice snapped Colin out of his thoughts. "I apologize for the inconvenience, but the commissioner insisted it was urgent."

"That's quite all right. I rarely rearrange my schedule, but Commissioner Jones is always the exception," Colin answered before walking into his office and closing the door.

His desk was more cluttered than he normally kept it. A pile of approved bills lingered on the edge, waiting for his signature. Most were minor changes to The Legislature's budget, but a few were larger, more intricate pieces of legislation. He pulled the first document off the pile and examined the contents, flipping the pages until he reached the end.

A sense of sadness overcame Colin as he noted the printed name of an android representative at the bottom. With The Supreme's absence, the android representatives rotated the official signing ritual amongst one another.

Looking for a distraction, Colin pulled at the bottom drawer of his desk. Inside, he kept his most favored mementos. On top was a binder filled with Julie's original University presentation on her antidote. Colin removed the binder and flipped through the pages with a small smile. His notes and questions were written along the margins next to Julie's vivacious description of how her drug would change society for the better.

Underneath where her proposal lay, a folder contained a copy of the first piece of legislation Colin signed as governor. He opened the folder, his awful, sloppy signature shimmering in jet-black ink on the left-hand side. On the right, Emilia's elegant mark mirrored his. Colin's finger grazed across her signature slowly, savoring the very distinct moment he would never forget.

His and Emilia's friendship had been complex in their adulthood.

He missed the simplicity of their childhood bond and wondered how everything went so wrong once they both assumed power in The Legislature. It wasn't like they both hadn't planned on some kind of career within the government.

When Colin and Emilia were teenagers, they spent summers at The Oceanside estate plotting their futures. They imaginarily conquered threats and protected their hypothetical Constituency, debating and sometimes agreeing on how they would help people and androids. Together.

But Emilia ruined everything we could have accomplished with her own selfish ways, Colin thought.

She sought her own retribution for androids, but he never understood why. Colin considered himself a Sympathizer, and while he tried to temper the truth about to what extent during elections, Emilia always knew this about him. She had a very influential friend across the aisle. Her betrayal felt oddly personal, first with Kathleen and finally with Julie.

Colin placed the creamy paper back into the folder and hid it with Julie's binder where it belonged. The drawer slammed closed a bit louder than he anticipated, but his fury flew through him like the first wave of a tsunami.

He rose from his seat and stormed out of his office.

"Cancel my next two hours. I have an urgent matter to attend to," Colin said, looking over at Elsie.

This was the first time he strayed from her schedule, and he wasn't sure how she would react. Elsie nodded and went right back to typing on her device.

Colin made his way to his vehicle in the underground garage, and the automated navigation calculated his route with self-driving technology. Normally, Colin would enjoy the walk across The City to his destination. He loved his home, but the state of danger and despair caused a rippling grief inside him to strengthen. The streets weren't safe—even in the middle of the day.

I need to fix this. Colin swore he would.

Pulling out his device, he messaged Jones. The small reply bubbles instantly appeared at the bottom of the screen, and Colin let out a small breath of appreciation. The car abruptly stopped before

Colin could reply, and he looked out the window.

A slight sense of irrational regret seeped into Colin's bones, but his outrage mixed with his cocky sense of confidence he'd forgotten about in the months of his own depression and isolation reemerged with a vengeance.

He stared back at the large, windowless brick building. The Supreme was somewhere inside, holed up in a tiny cell.

The Legislature deemed her processor corrupted and requested an evaluation and recommission before they sent her off into an early retirement. Emilia was only halfway through her life, and if any shred of her survived the planned reprogramming, she'd be miserable for the rest of her life.

Thunder sounded from outside the vehicle, and Colin jumped in his seat. He wanted desperately to barge into the prison and demand visitation with The Supreme. Colin envisioned slamming his fists down on the table, requesting she provide answers for why she risked everything and why she was willing to let The City crumble and fail. He imagined her answering him and providing him with solace, some kind of understanding.

But Colin couldn't even conjure up an explanation on his own in this fantasy. His mind drifted to so many possibilities, but they all lingered back to illogical, senseless, and cruel reasons.

Colin looked down at the navigation on his dashboard. His fingers lingered on the screen and his eyes traced over the roads within The City's limits—the place he grew up, a location that transformed so incredibly and interchangeably depending on its stability and who was in power, who led society. He helped his home recover once before—he'd do anything in his power and ability to help it recover again.

His eyes glanced back out at the prison once more. Colin realized he may get no answers from The Supreme, no reasoning nor explanation.

He would need to find his own closure.

Chapter 15

Commissioner Jones

April 8th, 47 A.R.

The FACERE building towered above Jones, stretching up and disappearing into the clouds. Lifting his head and leaning back, both excitement and nervousness flickered through his processor. Jones looked forward to the opportunity to go behind the curtain and witness the true scenes of the android manufacturing laboratory.

Maggie Rivera's petite frame came into view as she exited the glass front doors. As she approached Jones and stretched her arm out to shake his hand, Jones took a moment to admire her. Maggie wore a stylish black pencil skirt with four-inch patent leather heels, a lilac silk blouse, and a form-fitting blazer. Her style and polished demeanor reminded Jones of old bloodline women like Isabella Garcia, but Maggie was born a nobody.

"Commissioner, it's so nice to see you again." Her grin beamed across her delicate face.

Jones shuffled his weight back and forth, and his eyes darted down the empty streets of the outer perimeter of The River neighborhood. FACERE was tucked away in the farthest corner of The City's limits, which The Legislature preferred, and the distance between its location and The Capitol Building felt even more enormous with the abandoned streets.

"The pleasure is mine, Ms. Rivera," he responded with sharp eyes. "But we should head inside."

Jones declared and enforced a curfew across The City between the hours of 8:00 p.m. and 8:00 a.m., encouraging all to work from home. After being pressured by The Legislature to enact this new mandate, Jones understood that it was a consequence of his actions that Mick described in his journal entry. Between this realization and the image of the two men he'd shot down, Jones struggled to fully power down his processor and sleep at night. The woman who those men butchered in the park flashed before his eyes, and their faces permanently burned in his processor. The rifle unforgivingly weighed in his hand even though it wasn't physically there anymore. He felt his sight still shifting through the scope, watching the events unfold before him.

As the highest-ranking official in the police force and one of the most influential androids in The City, Jones felt the burden of these human deaths was his to bear. He refused to let his young android snipers fire the fatal shots—shots that would start a political war within The Legislature and within society.

In the few days that passed since the event, Jones, Governor O'Connor, and The Legislature hoped for calmness and an end of violence against posse hominems. But the killings didn't stop. An underground network of self-proclaimed vigilantes made their way through The City, fueled undoubtedly by the Humanizers. Jones was determined to identify those citizens and arrest them all for terrorism.

Jones possessed a peculiar affliction toward posse hominems and felt it was his duty to protect this minority class of citizens. He proposed sending out a message to all constituents that those who believed they were posse hominems or knew they were could seek refuge at the police headquarters. Governor O'Connor hesitated at this notion, claiming it might draw those wanting to harm hybrids, and raised the issue of trust.

"They've been kidnaped and transformed at the request of an android and are likely to feel uneasy at the thought of being corralled together in a central location filled with androids," Colin had said. Jones reluctantly agreed with the governor's remark, and in the end, the police headquarters remained quiet.

Wanting to escape the situation and his thoughts, Jones looked back to FACERE with a sense of urgency. Once inside, Jones turned around 360 degrees and took in his surroundings. The inside lobby was opposite of COLI*GO's, and the security guards behind the Plexiglas domes were humans, not androids. At COLI*GO, most of the security force were retired police androids.

FACERE's subdued colors, carpeted floors, and fake greenery with palm trees reminded Jones more of an outdated medical center. COLI*GO was much sleeker in design, simpler even. But the differences didn't end there. Jones noted no androids puttering around the halls or near the elevators. Humans surrounded him.

"The office is quieter than normal with about half our employees working from home," Maggie explained, but Jones only half-listened.

He was stealthily scanning the floor plan, determined to remember the full experience of his tour. An ominous feeling excreted from his scales that he would need to recall every moment of this experience later.

"We have five labs within the main part of the building and an additional three on the west side. All our prototypes are grown in the labs in the main building before the coding is sent off to the manufacturing facility. There's a lab focused on microchip improvements, one dedicated to the processor, one for scale development, a lab specializing in organic matter, and one that is strictly experimental." Maggie waved her arms around as they continued down the stark white-walled hallway.

Jones's processor raced, attempting to recall any memory of this building and place. He had been born within these walls—how could this feel so foreign to him? So unwelcoming?

Maggie stopped in front of a sturdy metal double door. "Restricted Access" was painted in large bold red letters sprawling from one end to the other. Jones's body stiffened, and his scales betrayed the emotions he was experiencing. He tugged on the corners of his coat's sleeves—glad he'd kept it on when they entered the building.

Maggie's eyes drifted from Jones's to the door, and with the swipe of her badge, she was granted access into the mysterious room. The space extended upward several stories, so high Jones couldn't find the ceiling. Massive incubators lined perfectly together in straight rows against the walls, all filled with a clear viscous liquid. Maggie continued her slow, purposeful walk down the center of the laboratory, but Jones remained frozen in place.

Inside the tubes were androids, their eyes closed and a breathing tube sticking out of their mouths. Their arms and legs were outstretched like a starfish and locked into place by straps and cuffs. Vibrant colors from their scales radiated through the liquid, lighting the otherwise dim room.

The androids inside were fully grown adults—not children. Once an android reached school-age, their memories of FACERE were wiped, and then they were sent to live with their sponsors and integrate into society. He had never once thought any adult androids would occupy FACERE.

"Which lab is this?" Jones asked, unable to focus on one particular aspect of the room.

"The experimental lab," Maggie answered, her palm resting against the incubator beside her.

She stared longingly up at the unconscious android inside and briefly closed her eyes. Her long lashes brushed the tops of her cheeks before her eyes opened wide again.

Jones moved past Maggie with a fearsome curiosity exponentially growing in each step. The android in the tube beside him kept his eyes open, but his pupils didn't follow Jones's movement. His breathing was deep and steady as if he were asleep. An indescribable urge overcame Jones, and he faintly tapped the glass. The android's silver scales flickered at the sound, pulsating as his hands squeezed into smaller fists.

In the next tube, a female android's hands possessed an extra finger each, and Jones noted how her nails were painted a deep midnight blue. The talons on the ends of her knuckles seemed like a vision from a fairy tale, and he was afraid to circle the backside of the tube, unsure if he would witness something horrible on her back, based on the winged shadows that cast themselves on the tiled floor.

"They don't feel pain. We've programmed that emotion out. Their processors cannot understand hurt or discomfort," Maggie called out as if understanding how terrifying this laboratory really was based on Jones's continued silence.

Jones approached another android without responding to Maggie and flinched. His eyes were missing. The hollow space in his sockets revealed the tiny mechanical placeholder for the special eyes many androids possessed. Jones brought his hand up to his own face.

"We completed testing a new eye software," Maggie said, approaching Jones with a reassuring smile. "Currently, you can pull up someone's identity and public information by scanning them."

Jones nodded slowly, a small sense of terror and fascination vibrating through him.

"Well," Maggie continued, "now the police, firefighters, nurses, and first responders will be able to scan humans for vitals too. Everything from blood type, disease and condition recognition, and other biometrics."

Maggie pulled out her device and hovered over the small screen at the base of the android's incubator. A graphic of his body appeared like Leonardo da Vinci's *Vitruvian Man.* Maggie's nails tapped the screen, and the image zoomed in on the android's face. She selected the eyes, and to Jones's awe, a pair of three-dimensional printed eyeballs generated quickly within the empty eye sockets. They grew so rapidly, the material pulling itself together within a matter of seconds.

The android's face came to life. Blinking, he moved his eyes from Maggie's face to Jones's.

Maggie selected another button on the screen and the thick liquid drained out the bottom of the large tube. The android remained strapped and suspended inside with his arms and legs restrained and taunt. Maggie's delicate fingers hovered over the window in the tube and opened the front. The android stared back at them, his scales glistening from being submerged in the container's liquid.

"Hello, Jeremy," Maggie said with a smile to the android and commanded the screen to release his restraints.

"Hello, Ms. Rivera," Jeremy responded, now free to shift his body. "Hello, Commissioner."

The tube opened further, and Jeremy fully emerged, his height taller than Jones's. He stood between Jones and Maggie and waited for instructions.

"Jeremy, can you run a full diagnostic on me?" Maggie asked, a flicker of excitement wavering through her honey-colored eyes.

"Certainly."

Jeremy shifted his gaze back to Maggie. Jones noted how he scanned her, staring directly at her eyes before slowly moving down her body.

Jeremy cleared his throat. "Identification: Ms. Margaret Rivera, Head of FACERE. Resident of 152 Beacon Street, The Bay. Original home: 256 Old Colony Avenue, The South. Age: forty years, three months, and six days. Species: human. Blood type: AB positive. Dehydration level: moderate. Might I recommend you consume sixteen ounces of water after our conversation, Ms. Rivera?" he asked in a monotone voice. "No underlying medical conditions detected except for a predisposition to migraines. Body temperature is 97.9 degrees Fahrenheit."

Jones's eyes blinked rapidly, his head shifting between Jeremy and Maggie.

"Thank you, Jeremy," Maggie answered and woke her device up with a single tap.

"My pleasure, Mr. Rivera. I'm glad to see you are in good health."

Her lips fluttered before looking at Jones.

"Impressive, isn't it?"

"Who authorized this?" Jones's voice trembled slightly when the words escaped.

"The Legislature, of course." Maggie responded too quickly for Jones's comfort. "I could show you. I could update you right now, if you'd like."

Jones's breathing slowed at her proposition.

Is this the real reason she wanted me here? Jones wondered, but a sense of duty and responsibility overcame his fear.

"How long does the update take?"

"I like that you have a lot of questions, Commissioner. Your predecessor wasn't as curious." Her eyebrows lifted. "It only takes two minutes and thirty-three seconds."

Jones nodded, taking a seat on the stool beside the table.

Maggie grabbed a headset from the table and gently placed it on Jones's head. Her hands reached for the plastic gloves, and after placing them on, she gently held open Jones's eyes. Maggie attached a wire to his left eye and then repeated the process with his right.

The sensation wasn't painful, but he did feel an unpleasant itch. From her device, she signaled the headset's power. It turned on, and a slight humming sound filled Jones's ears. His vision went blank as a burning sensation passed through him. His scales slightly released a sweat, similar to the clamminess humans experienced when they were anxious.

The procedure completed itself in a matter of minutes.

When Jones's vision came back to life, he noted the small changes when he concentrated on Maggie. The wires were no longer attached to his eyeballs, and the room appeared a bit clearer. Similar to Jeremy, Jones's processor buzzed with her vitals and biometrics before turning itself off to his normal vision.

"See." Maggie smiled. "Easy."

Jones wasn't convinced. He removed the headset and placed it back on the table.

"I think we should head back to my office. We can talk about The Supreme's examination over lunch, and then I can show you the manufacturing lines." Maggie grabbed Jones's hand in hers and dragged him back out the door of the lab.

It'd been a long time since Jones held hands with anyone, and he was surprised by her intimate gesture. Maggie looked up at him with a bright smile, her maroon matte lipstick now sharper in his vision. His emerald scales flickered from all the emotional stimulation he experienced over the last hour. From the sly look in her eyes, followed by a tighter grip of his hand, she noticed this, too.

***

Anna sat across from Jones. She kept her loft brightly lit compared to the darkness outside. Her modern stainless-steel appliances shined against the white cabinets and countertops.

Isabella awkwardly puttered around Anna's kitchen, her weekend bag resting on the large white leather sofa in the living room. Anna warned Jones that her sister was staying with her for a few days before heading back to The Island. But Jones didn't mind.

"You have to tell me everything about FACERE," Anna said, leaning against the marble island with an eagerness in her voice.

Jones's mind went straight to the morning where he observed Maggie puttering around his own kitchen in nothing but his T-shirt. There was something oddly wicked about their experience, defying the logic of not only taboo relationships between humans and androids but also the logic of Jones's own desires.

Watching Maggie make herself coffee reminded Jones why he and human or android women never worked. In the dark, he had imagined Mick's hands scratching at the scales on his back in place of hers.

Jones missed the tenderness he shared with Mick and the only comfort he found in Maggie was that their connection reminded him of why he craved human intimacy over the cold, harsh affections of other androids.

The unobliterated wildness and unpredictability about humans left Jones wanting Maggie even though it wasn't actually her that he wanted. His escapade with Maggie Rivera might not be his last, but with her, it was simply an escape—a reason to forget his heartache from Mick's absence. The risks of his affair with Maggie were relatively low, and there were limited consequences of exposure. Maggie was too powerful and had worked too hard to get to where she was today. She wouldn't admit their actions to anyone, and neither would he.

"There's not much to say other than FACERE is strange," Jones responded, his eyes averting from Anna's as if she could reach in and pull out his memories from last night.

Jones didn't appreciate knowing all the idiosyncrasies in his friends before them because of the technology now embedded in his eyes. Jones's knowledge felt like an invasion of privacy, especially as he lingered over at Isabella. Her biometrics ran rampant in his line of vision, the awful, cancerous cells lying dormant for now but grasping the edge of thriving inside her shortly.

Does Isabella know? Jones wondered, wishing he never knew himself.

"I assumed," Anna said, clutching his forearm. "I want to know the creepy details."

The darkness of Anna's skin illuminated in Jones's peripheral vision, and the memory of Maggie's own arm gripping him last night consumed him. The experience left Jones believing Maggie didn't care or want Jones to second guess what passed between them, but she also didn't know how much he could feel, how much he understood.

"Leave him alone, Anna." Isabella's stern, motherly voice sounded from the living room.

Anna rolled her eyes, glancing back at Jones with a playful smirk.

"I have a new talent," Jones whispered, providing Anna with an extended olive branch to make up for his normal secrecy.

"What's that?" Isabella's voice echoed from across the room. He was surprised she spoke before her sister.

"I can see biometrics of humans, along with my normal eye scanning capabilities."

Anna stepped back as if her close proximity to him meant he could see everything about her. She wasn't wrong, but Jones had forced himself to minimize that capability and push it aside from his normal line of vision.

"You're joking?" Isabella asked, her body levitating toward him and Anna. "Can you make medical diagnoses?"

"Somewhat," Jones responded, the pure honesty of his android personality pushing forward for control after such a wild admission.

Isabella's eyes locked in on Jones with seriousness before softening.

Maybe she knows what lies inside her.

Jones averted his gaze back to Anna and scanned her.

"You're running a slight fever at ninety-nine degrees. It might be because you're ovulating, but you should check your temperature tomorrow to make sure you don't have a cold."

"Ew," Anna yelped, her arm slapping Jones's green scales playfully. "You don't need to remind me of that!"

"The Legislature approved of this new measure for FACERE?" Isabella asked, ignoring her sister's immature outburst.

Jones lifted his device and showed the voting tally record on his screen. Humanizers approved the notion, believing the update provided a greater benefit to humans while moderate and Sympathizer human representatives believed the update gave androids better insight into medical advancements. The androids approved the measure with no hesitation—seeing this update as an advantage for their kind.

Colin O'Connor's terrible, sloppy signature screamed at the bottom of the document. The spot for The Supreme's signature remained blank, and an android representative's printed name was stamped below the line to verify that all androids unanimously approved the measure without her.

"Yes," Jones noted, his eyes glued to Isabella as the next words escaped him, "Colin signed it into law a few days ago."

Jones looked at Anna again, his eyes buzzing with her vitals. He closed his eyes and opened them, still figuring out how to turn off this new ability.

"Stop analyzing me, you creep!" Anna laughed, the slight chuckle emulating between her lips.

Creep, Jones thought. *That's exactly all we'll ever be anymore after this update, anyways.*

Chapter 16
The Governor

April 9th, 47 A.R.

Jones waited for Colin in Colin's office, the rain violently hitting against the windowpanes. Colin's abnormally tall figure loomed in the doorway, observing his colleague and the many secrets they shared within their odd friendship.

Jones's emerald scales radiated, but the android otherwise held himself with a sense of authority and purpose. Colin took a seat at his desk and grinned.

He's coming into his new role quite responsibly and honorably.

Colin admired Jones's intellect, but he still didn't know exactly where he and the commissioner stood.

"Governor." Jones shook Colin's hand. Relief filled Colin's body when Jones smiled at him.

"Commissioner," Colin responded.

They stood and acknowledged one another for a moment too long before sitting back down. Jones pulled out his larger device, and various profiles filled the screen. The commissioner seemed anxious to get straight to business.

Identification photos, names, and brief descriptions loaded before Colin's eyes. Nearly all the occupations under the names were associated with FACERE.

"I've been working with Ms. Sullivan over the last few days to obtain certain intelligence on various potential associates of Humanizers, and we're triangulating their whereabouts regarding the attacks on posse hominems." Jones's normally still voice wavered in a broken tone.

Colin had once gone after posse hominems—killing Lexi Pvadinish and Kathleen before attempting to murder Julie—but these beings were more self-conscious than he previously gave them credit for. A wave of nausea and regret hit Colin.

I was no better than them. The words crossed his mind before he silenced them. *I'm trying to help them now. I didn't realize there were so many of these creations. And I want to help them instead of hurt them. I owe that to Kathleen. I owe that to Julie.*

"And these are the leads?" Colin asked, his eyes peering over the screen.

"Yes." Jones looked up at Colin with hesitation. The android seemed to ponder how to say the words he wanted to speak next. After an excruciating moment, Jones finished. "How familiar are you with Maggie Rivera?"

Colin's eyes widened. He hadn't personally spoken to Maggie in a while and stayed away from as much of FACERE's dealings as possible. His and Maggie's niceties soured a long time ago, back when Celine decided Martin was her old bloodline partner of choice and Maggie stood in the way.

Colin helped distract Maggie with his own O'Connor charm. The task was simple: They had previously worked side by side when he was a member of the Ways and Means Committee in his early twenties. They had even egregiously flirted with one another.

"Too well," Colin responded, unsure how much Jones had already dug up from his past. Jones had an uncanny way of pulling skeletons out from anyone's closet.

"A high-up associate at FACERE seems very passionate about his hatred for hybrids," Jones continued, without acknowledging Colin's statement. "We've tracked his identification card to each location of an attack, starting from the scene that occurred in the park. His name is Paul McGuire."

"Have you talked to Maggie about this?"

Jones's eyes darted away from his own, and his scales shimmered quickly before settling back down. Colin hadn't lost his touch when it came to observation—there was something Jones wasn't telling him about Maggie Rivera.

"No. I'm not sure if I should broach that situation," Jones admitted, shuffling his body nervously in his seat. "Paul also has a connection to Representative Kennsington. He's donated quiet a large sum of money to his political campaigns over the years. And Maggie herself is originally from The South, Joel's district."

Everything always leads back to Joel fucking Kennsington, Colin thought.

"Who else knows?"

Jones placed his device down gently on the desk and sighed. "Just you, Elsie, and one of my detectives."

"And we're sure this guy is involved?" Colin asked, his voice low and gruff.

"Yes," Jones answered confidently. "But there are more. I'm assuming his associates are people he knows, people he works with. What really bothers me is how high-up at FACERE Paul is. This seems like a fine line to cross with the power and decisions he's allowed to make there."

"What exactly does he do for FACERE?" Colin looked up Paul McGuire in the database on his own device. Depending on his position, Colin assumed he and Elsie could easily arrange a meeting under the guise it was government-related business.

Paul's photo appeared crystal clear across the screen, his deep hazel eyes large and round. The man was in his mid-thirties, a graduate of The University, and the head of Financial Operations, reporting directly to Maggie Rivera. His mother was from an old bloodline family, but his father was a nobody.

"I'd volunteer to bridge a conversation with Maggie, but we aren't on the best of terms," Colin answered truthfully.

Their breakup hadn't ended as planned. Memories of her tears and sobs as Colin threatened her hadn't been exactly flattering of him. Telling her he only indulged in their affair to distract her from her husband's own lingering eyes was a bit too harsh of a reality for Maggie. She was a social climber, trained as one since her University years. Colin wasn't her first. The evidence Colin had of Maggie cheating on her husband with several men would ruin her if it leaked. He forced her hand to concede to a smooth divorce from Martin—one where she didn't demand taking much of Martin's wealth and didn't tarnish his reputation.

"I'm aware."

"Oh? Are you?" Colin's left eyebrow raised.

"I know she's your brother-in-law's ex-wife. That was the easy piece of information to come across."

Colin chuckled, leaning back and relaxing in his chair. He decided he would let Jones lead this conversation and allow for the android to speak the dirty words.

Jones's eyes met Colin's, and he shook his head as if the android resisted the urge to laugh along with him. A smirk spread across Jones's face, paired with a hint of embarrassment. He leaned in closer to the governor as if to share a secret.

"I get why it didn't last long," Jones finally replied in a tone only slightly louder than a whisper.

"Her marriage to Martin Borges?" Colin asked with a cocky smile.

"That too."

A loud thump sounded as Colin's hand collided with the desk. He laughed liberally, the chuckle only joined by a shimmering and humiliated look from Jones. He was glad for the satisfaction of catching on to something amiss with Jones earlier.

"I didn't realize someone like Maggie Rivera was your type," Colin responded, almost in the form of a question.

The thought of Jones's former boyfriend, Mick Taylor, and the conflicted hate of the time traveler emerged in the forefront of Colin's mind.

"You're correct on that observation, Governor. Typically not. But she is a human, and I rarely stray from humans when it comes to lovers," Jones answered, uncrossing his legs and settling more into his seat. "Regardless, I don't think Maggie would be too keen on me and detectives questioning one of her higher-ranking employees with the very little and unethical information I've collected. And as wrong as it is to continue sleeping with her for information, we need to protect The City, and to do so, I need to know who these terrorists are."

Colin's eyes shifted toward the door where Elsie sat beyond it.

This could be Elsie's opportunity to show her true loyalty to me and The City. A way for me to test the waters with her and Jones.

Colin already planned on propositioning Jones as the successor for The Supreme, once The Representatives of The Androids were ready to make a new selection. Jones still confused Colin, but the android's unpredictability provided a thrill and simultaneous comfort of familiarity. He and Jones knew too much about one another—this harbored any real threats to Colin.

"Can I ask you something?"

The commissioner stiffened in his chair as if he predicted where Colin was bringing this conversation. Colin took Jones's lack of an audible response as a "yes."

"How do you like your role as the commissioner?"

The impact of Colin's question stained Jones's face—the deep greens around the edges of his scales lit up in a metallic hue at the possibility the android knew Colin was potentially dangling in front of him.

"I was honored to receive the appointment."

"Do you see yourself wishing for more influence in The Legislature?" Colin asked, remembering the report Elsie provided of Jones's recent visit to FACERE.

While Colin and Maggie weren't on speaking terms, his representatives were loose with information. Maggie had informed the representatives of Jones's visit and the update to his eyes. Maggie could be a snake when she wanted to. Jones might have been using her for his own emotional games, but Maggie was using him for hers too.

"Sometimes, yes." Jones was always honest, a trait Colin appreciated about Julie's best friend.

And hopefully, my new friend and ally in The Legislature when the time comes.

"Good," Colin said and stood.

Jones mirrored the governor's movements, and the two walked out into the hallway.

They stopped in front of Elsie's desk. She looked up at them and smiled curtly, her stiff body relaxing as she noticed Colin and Jones's ease and closeness.

"I think this sticky situation with Maggie's employee is a great opportunity for Elsie," Colin said with a curious glance. "She'll be discreet, and maybe we can get some more detailed information?"

Jones inhaled deeply with a small nod and eyes filled with warning.

"Can you arrange that, Ms. Sullivan?"

"Of course, Commissioner," Elsie responded, her eyes bright and her smile wide.

Chapter 17
It

April 10th, 47 A.R.

It looked away from the portrait of Henry O'Connor in the stairwell at the townhouse. The home was quiet with the baby and Celine off having dinner with Martin on the other side of The Hill. He could truly relax, posing no impending threat to anything or anyone Colin cared about.

Both Colin and It had purpose again—his freedom and escape from Colin's refusal to take the antidote was solidified. The Legislature deemed Colin mentally sound and shuffled away his confession of Kathleen's murder. Celine had been correct in her assumption. Brushing aside his crime was easy for the representatives. The public already believed her horrible death found justice—The Supreme bullied Jeb Taylor, an artist and drug dealer, into the confession nearly a year ago. As morally ambiguous as his situation was, the uncertainty and instability shaking The Constituency caused a need for a strong, confident leader. A leader respected by both humans and androids: Governor Colin O'Connor.

Isabella's tiny frame appeared in the doorway on the first floor. It had grown accustomed to her presence, one that previously annoyed him. Her white toothy smile spread across her face as she placed her bags down on the couch.

"How was your day?" she asked, sharply turning toward the kitchen.

"Fine," It answered as Isabella reached into a cabinet and placed a mug down in front of him.

It wasn't used to this level of freedom that Colin granted him lately. Colin rarely let It out of his cage around other people, and when Colin did, he was often angry with any intrusion into his personal life. But now, Colin needed the mental rest. He spent the last week working long hours, coming home late into the night as quietly as possible to not disturb Celine and Henry Jr.

Civil unrest stained The City like red wine on a white carpet, and confining the stain was the most important aspect. Colin and The Legislature couldn't allow for the terrorism to spread through the rest of The Constituency.

"I'm looking at townhouses here in The Hill," Isabella said as the kettle on the stove whistled, steam protruding from the spout.

"Why?"

With the uptick in violence, he didn't want Isabella spending too much time here. The Island was safer.

"Well." Isabella paused, looking straight into It's eyes. A tiny line appeared on her forehead as she squinted. It wondered if she knew she didn't really face Colin here in the kitchen.

Back when Colin and Isabella were a couple, he confided in her about his secret affliction. About It. Her father attempted to treat him as a child. But Filipe Garcia failed. How much Isabella actually understood about the complexities of Colin versus the other side of him was unknown.

"I want to be here. I would be closer to Anna and my nonprofit. People and androids need our services now more than ever, and we're understaffed. I can't manage the organization remotely from The Island forever, and I'm spending a week a month here anyways. And if I actually lived in The Hill, I'd be closer to you too."

Isabella walked over with the kettle. The burning water poured gently and carefully into the mug between It's hands. He watched the water steam up, the heat on the side of the mug warming his fingers. Isabella walked back to the stove and placed the kettle on top. With a tea bag in hand, she made her way back over to It. He tightened his jaw.

"Relax, Colin. I'm not trying to seduce you."

"We're allowed to be friends. I enjoy your company. Hopefully, mine isn't as wretched as the look on your face."

Her words pained him.

Isabella had been nothing but kind to Colin—and It—during the last few months. He owed all the credit to her for straightening up his friend, his other self, and from keeping Colin from slipping too far down into the depths of despair. It had disappointed Colin in this way by keeping his distance while Colin sorted through his emotions and the ramifications of their actions. It also needed that time to sort through his own guilt during those initial months after Julie. But everything came crashing down the night of the massacre in the park. The memory of the life seeping out of that woman's face made It's stomach turn even though he held a blade to many women before.

"You're right. I'm sorry. The days have been so long," It said, his eyes wandering out the window. The sun still shone, and the afternoon light trickled in, teasing them all with a false sense of a distantly approaching summer.

Isabella placed her hand on his shoulder and gently squeezed.

"The real reason is, I don't want to be alone anymore. After everything I've done, I just want to make things right. The loneliness is slowly killing me. Thank you for allowing me to look after you these last few months."

"You're not alone, Isabella," It said, warming to her, noting the tears forming in the corners of her eyes. "You have me and Celine. The baby adores you. There is your life's work at the nonprofit. And you have Anna and your mother."

Isabella laughed lightly at the mention of her sister. They always had a strained relationship, made worse by whatever recent family drama occurred.

"The baby is quite adorable even if Celine does hate me," Isabella said. She wiped her eyes with the edge of her fingers and smiled softly. "You're right. I'm not alone. It's just been a tough adjustment. I'm sorry, I didn't mean to bother you with my woes, especially with everything going on. How long do you think this violence will last?"

It sighed. Commissioner Jones hadn't caught everyone in the raid, and his intelligence taskforce was constantly dredging their database for new group uprisings. The media continued sensationalizing the estimated number of posse hominems in The City, painting these beings as evil creatures prepared to hunt down humans. A mass manhunt for posse hominems ran rampant through the streets. Five more hybrids had been killed over the course of a few days, and the general uptick in violence astronomically skyrocketed.

But at least there was Paul McGuire to think about. It had an uneasy feeling about letting Elsie Sullivan take the lead on this endeavor. He wasn't sold on her trustworthiness yet, but if he was really committed to making the necessary changes to stay in Colin's life, It needed to give in more.

It wasn't jealous of Elsie handling the situation. Paul didn't appeal to It's appetite the way women did—the way a knife felt in his hand while puncturing soft, silky, feminine skin. The small delicacies of slender necks between his hands, the last bits of air escaping a woman's luscious, perfect lips. If Elsie's handling of this threat convinced Colin to give up these sinister ways—for now—then the less Colin knew, the better.

"I can't really say," It finally answered Isabella.

This was the truth—It nor Colin saw a light at the end of the tunnel any time soon, at least not until the terrorists were taken care of. Isabella walked over to him and paused. Her eyes looked down uneasily at her tiny feet.

"There's something I need to tell you." Her voice trembled quietly. "I should have come clean sooner, but I was afraid you would hate me. And in your hate, I was afraid you would hurt me. I should have known better. I know you would never cause me any physical harm. You've proven that time and time again."

It stiffened in his chair, pleasantly surprised by her words. Unsure of what to expect in her admission, he gripped the edge of the counter and waited for her to resume when she was ready.

"I know what happened to Julie. You were correct in your assessment that she lived and traveled time. But what you don't know is that I removed the microchip from her brain and that it was Mick Taylor who sent her to the past."

It stood, approaching Isabella with a stealthy step in the kitchen.

"You saved Julie? How is that even possible?"

Tears streamed down Isabella's lovely face, her hands shaking uncontrollably. Her sobs erupted in It's ears, and he realized there was more—a deep-rooted truth that Isabella was about to bestow on him. One where she was correct in her fears, one that might change his whole perspective of her.

"I'm the one who helped The Supreme. I'm the one who performed all the surgeries." Her words froze the room, the coolness flickering across It's skin to reveal goosebumps.

Isabella gathered herself between sobs and continued.

"I don't know why I agreed to help her. I thought it was a noble cause at first. But then she made me perform the surgery on Kathleen. I knew something was wrong then, but I continued. Julie's transformation broke me. It was so horrific that her screams haunt me in my sleep. I don't know what to do with myself, and I've done everything I can to make it right. I went to the future on the device Mick gave me. I saved Julie that night."

Stepping in front of Isabella, wrapped his arms around her. He felt her body relax into his embrace. Her soft cries muffled themselves in his chest as he held her. Isabella buried her face, the difference in their height more pronounced with this gesture. The words "I'm sorry" continuously escaped her, and It gripped her more tightly.

Colin and Isabella had been part of one another's lives for nearly fifteen years. It realized how important their bond was to them both, regardless if it was romantic or platonic. She needed a friend much like Colin, and It needed a friend.

It wanted to hate her in this moment, he wanted to throw her across the room. But seeing the remorse on her face told him everything he needed to know about Isabella's true nature. She wasn't evil—she wanted to correct her wrongs.

Can I blame her? I am also asking for forgiveness for my sins.

"I can tell, Colin. You're not as sly as you think you are, but I see how you're coming together. I honestly do," she said softly into his chest. Her words were heavy but authentic.

"Isabella," he said, gently easing out of their embrace. "Stay safe, okay? Please let me know when you're coming back from The Island. I'll help you find a place here on The Hill."

It couldn't say the words Isabella wanted to hear: *I forgive you.*

He didn't forgive her—not yet. He desperately wanted to, but the words bubbled in the back of his throat, unable to crawl their way out. This was how disagreements always were between them. They never truly expressed their feelings and thoughts to one another—that was what ruined them as a couple from the very beginning.

Isabella nodded and called her driver. It watched her pull away from the townhouse before heading up to the roof deck. He needed fresh air to release this wild wrath. The gravity of Isabella's confession lingered in the pit of his stomach.

It walked toward the ledge and peered off the side of the railing. His large fingers curled around the safety barrier, and his gaze slowed before zooming in. His grip tightened. It recognized that woman anywhere—no matter how inconspicuous she was in her strides, no matter how sly she was within the shadows of the townhomes that surrounded them.

Julie.

His heart quickened in his chest, and he tried steadying himself. It thought about Julie often, not as often as Colin but too often all the same. So much about that woman confused It. He appreciated her willingness to do just about anything to protect those she loved, including Colin. It didn't want to admit he might not have forgiven Isabella for her transgression. But he instinctively knew if Julie asked for his forgiveness, he would grant it willingly.

Julie showed Colin acceptance. And she showed It acceptance too. At least, at the very end. Something about her magnetized It's thoughts while also pushing his buttons. She loved Colin, and Colin loved her.

It climbed down the stairs from the roof deck and headed toward the first floor. The elegant dining room had transformed over the last week to accommodate the townhouse's new residents. Toys and a highchair donned the room alongside Celine's pointy high heels. It almost tripped on a pair as he darted for the window.

Julie's figure appeared as a shadow in the carriage house across the small courtyard. It watched Julie putter around the one-room dwelling, assuming she was checking for Mick's presence. Mick also used the carriage house as a "safe haven" while traveling time. Mick's journal, or some version of his journal, remained locked in a small black metal box in the kitchenette area. But It hadn't seen

Mick there in a very long time.

After a few moments, Julie's body collapsed on the couch, and she closed her eyes. It's mind wandered to a forbidden place—the feel of Julie's skin under his hands, the taste of her on his lips.

No, It reminded himself, closing his eyes and shaking away the illicit thoughts.

He never broke Colin's trust when it came to Julie. He always respected the clear lines and never dared cross them.

Except that one time. The time he strangled her.

The feel of Julie's skin on his hands from that night vibrated through his memories, but he had never experienced the taste of her on his lips. That indulgence was Colin's and Colin's alone. Even thinking about her in that manner felt like a betrayal of his oldest and only friend.

It opened his eyes. He watched as Julie approached the large window, observing him from afar. His stare met hers, and he smiled at the sight of her body physically stalling with uncertainty. The corner of It's mouth turned upward, and his eyelids relaxed. His sinister but charismatic grin spread across his face at her before he nodded. Julie nodded back at him and smiled mischievously.

Interesting. It was taken aback by her response.

It continued watching her in delight, his body leaning back against the table. He rested his chin in his hand. It's gestures resonated his physical power and strength. He intimidated anyone who wasn't familiar with his manifestation.

Julie slowly backed away from the window and disappeared deeper into the carriage house. It contemplated the sight of her for a little bit longer and wondered what this meant not only for himself but also for Colin.

The sun set outside, the orange and pink colors reflecting off the sky, highlighting the carriage house in an enticing hue. It found himself climbing the iron steps to the top level of the structure and searching for the key under the mat.

It hated this place.

He had spent many years here in the abandoned part of the townhouse. Somewhere along the line, the O'Connors lost the carriage house in a bet, but the owner never fully claimed his prize.

The furniture was the same, but the unfamiliar smell of coffee grinds filled the space.

Henry brought him here during his youth. It flinched, recalling his body strapped to the bed. Both Henry and Filipe tied him down. Sometimes they left him here overnight. Henry hoped he wouldn't come back to the townhouse the next day. But to Henry's despise, It always made an obnoxious, sometimes elaborate, entrance out of his return.

It noted Julie's presence inside the space now. She had been here before—multiple times. He smelled her perfume on the blanket thrown across the couch, a warm and alluring scent. A bottle of her favorite wine peeked out from the edge of the counter, and It couldn't help but chuckle.

Why do you come here, Julie? It pondered, perceiving the rest of the one-room structure.

He stood completely still as he looked out the window: The perfect view of the townhouse.

Julie comes here to watch me. To watch Colin.

A dangerous idea popped into It's mind.

He left the carriage house but returned fifteen minutes later with a small sample of his blood, refiled in one of the tiny test tubes Mick had left behind. He wrapped a sliver of paper around the sample and secured it with tape on the underside of the wine bottle.

The note read: *Do you trust me?*

***

That night, It dreamt of Julie, dreamt of a different variation from the horrid evening between her and Colin. The night they killed Kathleen—the night where It strangled Julie.

The only time I ever skirted the line I promised Colin I would never cross.

In the dream, It strode past Colin deeper into the master bedroom and hovered over Julie's sleeping body. His fingers affectionately traced her jawline, lingering from her face and down her chest until he reached between her breasts. His hand slowly trailed back up to the base of her neck, lightly touching her soft, delicate skin. Spreading his fingers wide, It gripped Julie right above her collarbone. This time, his intent wasn't to strangle her.

Julie's eyes darted open, the warm blue shades reminding him of The Oceanside during a late summer storm. In this dream, Julie's smile portrayed an inviting curiosity at It's trespassing. He firmly pushed her into the bed and locked her wrists together over her head with his other hand.

She hummed, the sound of her voice melting It's concentration. Julie's eyes lingered at It's forearms, then followed down his broad chest before meeting his eyes again. Her cheeks flushed with a mixture of bashfulness and desire.

Intrigued? It wanted to ask her.

Instead, he leaned into her ear, his lips grazing her skin.

"You've always been mine, not his," he whispered.

It's grip held Julie firmly, and she squirmed against him. She lifted her face and was now less than an inch away from his.

"Yes," Julie answered, allowing her lips to brush against his chin. "I'm yours."

Her words sparked something wild inside of It, like lighter fluid on an open flame. He hungrily kissed her.

It's fascination with Julie emerged more prominently in his mind than anything he'd ever experienced before. His drive for Julie was stronger compared to his obsession with Amanda MacDonald, Celine's former chief of staff.

Like Julie, Amanda had been ambitious, driven, and cunning. He almost visibly saw Amanda's golden blonde hair, the very faint freckles dashed upon her skin, but the image flickered away. Amanda never loved It. She used him. Betrayed him.

Even with this fleeting memory of a woman It once cared about, his desire and unexplainable need for Julie far surpassed anything he'd ever known. She had been the reason he came back after five years of silence. That first encounter. Julie belonged to him, not Colin. She was made for It—the right type of woman both intellectually and physically. Colin preferred his women docile and unassuming: Isabella, Maggie.

Not It.

It wanted a beautiful harshness and instability—someone who challenged him. Someone who exposed him for what he truly was and forced him to face and accept everything about himself. Someone who saw his ugliness and wasn't afraid of what truly possessed and fueled him.

How has no one noticed this before? It wondered, releasing his grip on her wrists and grabbing her hair.

He bunched the mess of waves in his right hand and pulled, revealing her elongated neck. It roughly kissed her hellish scar, aware of the deep, reddish-purple bruises forming on the skin underneath his teeth.

Julie's other scars—his and Colin's markings—highlighted themselves across her body. It's fingers traced the lines and followed them like roads on a map. He wasn't sure why Julie had any of her scars in this dream from that night. The timing was off by several months.

The sinking feeling that this was a memory stemmed from time travel and not quite a made-up dream toyed with his mind. It didn't dwell on the thought for too long, afraid of the repercussions.

Shaking his head, It concentrated back on Julie, wanting nothing so badly in his life. He needed all of her. Now.

To hell with Colin, he thought before giving in to the temptation.

Julie tasted heavenly on It's tongue as he devoured her. He continued feasting on her like a rare delicacy, savoring every sensation passing between them.

"Fuck," he groaned, moving his lips away and nibbling on Julie's inner thighs.

His eyes scanned the room, becoming more alert and aware of the change of scenery from when he had first started consuming her. Instead of in the bedroom, they were in Colin's study, and her body was spread before It on the desk.

The warning bells of this experience existing as a memory and not a dream rang again in loud caution, but neither It nor Julie cared as he went back for her. He couldn't get enough.

It pulled her into his lap and held her gaze. Her eyes locked into place affectionately and took all of him in.

She does trust me. She does accept me. She chooses me.

It immersed Julie's body closer to his own, guiding her in his hands until no space was left between them. Julie cupped his jaw, and her soft lips kissed It lovingly and passionately. His fingers dug into the flesh of her hips to support her while her legs wrapped themselves tightly around his waist. Control slipped out of It's grasp, the feel of her forcing his eyes shut. The rawness of Julie was too tangible for just a dream, too exposed. It needed to reorient his mind before losing himself entirely in her. He couldn't allow for that, not if this wasn't a dream—if this was a memory.

We took this too far.

Time travel posed a certain threat to a person's grasp on reality. Dreams and memories were unclear and hazy. Both he and Julie traveled time, and those actions alone were dangerous. If this experience was really a memory from the future and not a dream, the consequences of their encounter could weigh heavily on them.

Especially on Colin.

But It couldn't stop himself. He leaned into Julie's lips again, and his tongue slipped between them to meet hers. Kissing her was his undoing. She was his.

And now, he realized, *I am hers.*

When It opened his eyes again, he lay in the darkness of one of the townhouse's spare bedrooms. He was alone in the bed.

Panting, he gulped down the glass of water left on the nightstand. No warmth radiated from the other pillows; none of Julie's belongings were anywhere in sight. There was no lingering scent of her perfume. No evidence of time travel.

The sound of Colin's nephew's crying lingered in the hallway. It rolled over and turned on the light.

Just a dream. Not a memory, he thought with relief. The sinking feeling in his stomach threatened otherwise. *This may not have been a memory but an admission of my deepest, darkest desire. A secret I must keep from Colin.*

It shook away the dream and pulled on gym shorts and a T-shirt. After walking through the door and down the hall, It leaned against the doorframe to Celine's room. She held her baby boy tightly, and a look of pure failure and exhaustion wrinkled across her brows. Henry Jr. wailed with arms outstretched and feet kicking.

"I'm sorry. Did he wake you?" Celine asked, rubbing slow, small circles on the infant's back. She didn't recognize the monster in front of her, assuming Colin's presence over his.

Good intent. Trust.

It outstretched his arms and took Henry Jr. into them. Rocking the baby back and forth, the beautiful creature stilled.

Complete innocence.

The baby soothed, and his whimpers quieted. It stared longingly into Henry's almond-shaped eyes as they closed, and the clean, unmistakable smell of a new child washed over him. No evil thoughts entered It's soul, and a lightness and happiness he rarely felt surrounded him instead. He cradled the baby in his arms a moment longer before handing him over fully asleep to Celine.

"I didn't realize you slept in one of the guest bedrooms now. Is it because it's been too soon? Because of Julie?" Celine asked in a hushed tone.

It never slept in the master bedroom. That was Colin's.

It didn't respond, not wanting to admit to his sister that she handed him her baby to hold moments earlier instead of Colin. Instead, Celine took his silence as if she asked an inappropriate question.

"I'm sorry. I just thought you still slept in the master. I didn't mean to say something tasteless."

He glanced away from Celine and nodded his head in agreement.

"You're right, though. I should."

Chapter 18
Julie

April 10th, 47 A.R.

Jealousy was a rare feeling for Julie, but after weeks of watching the townhouse, the feeling consumed her. She paced around the carriage house, not quite able to look away from the window.

Feeling negatively about Isabella bothered Julie—especially knowing that Isabella saved her from death in some dimension in time. But seeing Isabella walk throughout the townhouse, making dinners, playing with Colin's nephew, and spending time with Colin infuriated Julie.

That is supposed to be me.

The heartbreak and hurt sucker-punched Julie even harder when Colin walked over to Isabella, pain and sadness painting Isabella's beautiful face, and embraced her. His arms wrapped tightly around Isabella, and Julie closed her eyes. The tears still escaped her. She couldn't run away from those.

But Julie could run away from watching this unfold even further. Storming out of the carriage house, Julie risked someone seeing her. The greater risk elevated inside her mind as she crossed the cobblestone street to the corner bodega. The use of her bank credits would tip off her missing person's report, and the police would be notified. But Julie's anger fueled her in this irresponsible quest.

The android behind the counter smiled politely at Julie while she looked for her favorite wine. She made sure to never fully lock eyes with him, afraid he would scan her or recognize her photo, which was blasted all over the news.

Holding the bottle of wine in her hand, Julie looked back at the shelf and contemplated purchasing a second bottle. Her small hands reached in temptation, and she justified the higher transaction total.

She needed something to ease her mind and help her sleep.

Julie returned to the carriage house and popped the cork. The silky red liquid poured into the glass and illuminated in a circular glow on the marble countertop. Gulping the wine, Julie emptied her first glass with a singular chug. The bottle egged her on, enticing her into a second. Filling the glass higher this time, Julie sipped slower and walked back to the window.

She froze.

His eyes stared at her from the dining room. Julie couldn't tell if he was happy or angry to see her—especially as he leaned up against the mahogany table.

Her heart tensed in her chest in response to the wicked grin spreading across his tormenting, handsome face. His knuckles whitened, and his grip grasped tighter to the edge of the table as if he physically needed to force himself to stay put and not cross the courtyard.

This wasn't Colin. This man stared her down like a hunter eyeing a deer. This was It.

After spending weeks spying on the O'Connor household, Julie recognized the difference. She excelled in this area of surveillance, especially as a scientist. Colin composed his stance straighter, always planting his feet firmly on the ground. It was looser, more fluid in his movements as he pondered around the townhouse. Stress exacerbated It, and his alteration often came after Colin paced by the laundry room. Like a ritual, his fingers lingered across the small table beside the washer and dryer, and he would pull open the drawer and reveal a different piece of jewelry before resting it back in its place.

Julie knew about Colin's transgressions, but shock filled her upon the discovery of this particular secret of his—the trinkets he kept to remind himself of his kills.

It's lips twitched, waiting for Julie's reaction. Julie wasn't sure if the wine sparked her confidence or if the adrenaline from seeing Colin's embrace with Isabella still coursed through her veins. Julie smiled and nodded in It's direction.

She almost heard his chuckle escaping those attractive lips. She almost felt the warmth of his breath on her skin.

The thought made her blush like a schoolgirl, and goosebumps flooded her body. She and Colin had known one another for years, but he still made her heart skip unpredictably.

Or perhaps, she thought, *It makes my heart skip unpredictably.*

Julie's hand trailed up her neck, and her fingertips grazed the feature he always admired of hers.

It's eyes locked with Julie's, and the intensity in his stare was all too familiar to her.

Julie backed away slowly. If she kept looking at him, she would do something rash. She couldn't ruin the hard work of her well-thought-out plan. Julie had to keep her distance from Colin until the right time.

Then, we can reunite. But not before.

Julie corked the wine and placed the open bottle in the refrigerator. The unopened bottle remained on the countertop.

The City's streets endured an emptiness and gloominess in the uncertainty of crime and the dangers of villains crawling through the streets. Walking briskly, Julie headed back to The South. The windy one-way roads brought her to Joel's home, but now her feet felt lighter against the pavement. The whole way, she thought about the hunger in It's eyes. The hunger for her.

She would be back. Soon.

***

The device lay inconspicuously in Julie's hands. She hadn't turned it on since the android gave it to her, afraid of the meaning behind why. She didn't trust The Supreme and found the android leader's extension of an olive branch as an odd gesture. But the gift wasn't just hers, as the other name spoken by the android lingered in her memory.

The Supreme and Commissioner Jones send their regards.

Julie trusted Jones. He was her friend.

But is he working with The Supreme? Why? Especially after everything Jones knows. There's no way The Supreme doesn't know I helped provide Colin with all the evidence against her. I'm the reason she is in jail.

Much like the man she loved, Julie and The Supreme had a

twisted and complex relationship. The Supreme respected Julie's drive and determination, but they butted heads when she confessed wanting Julie to aid her in her quest for ultimate domination and control over The Legislature.

Julie looked from the device to the door. She sat on the corner of Joel's guest bed. This tiny downstairs bedroom was not meant for an adult to occupy. Joel and his ex-wife didn't have any children, but she wondered if the pair thought about using the space for a nursery before their divorce.

The muffled noises of Joel puttering around in the living room caused Julie's heart to beat faster. His insufferable personality was wearing her down after a few months. And her recent encounter with It rattled around in her brain, not helping her sanity.

Julie sighed and looked at the device again.

The screen illuminated in the darkness of her prison. Very few apps and icons displayed themselves on the home screen. After a moment, a small notification appeared on the messenger icon. The red dot screamed loudly in Julie's vision as her finger tapped it lightly. An unfamiliar, unique-identifying number code appeared, and the room stilled around her as she read the message from a mysterious sender.

To: 617–333–2985
From: 617–345–3709
Date Sent: April 8th, 47 A.R.
Subject: F. Scott Fitzgerald

{Message Encryption}
Julie,

You probably don't remember me, but we went to school together. I was the troublemaker sitting in the back of the classroom, and you were the teacher's pet in the front row. I never thought we would have anything in common. You stayed on the "right path" and applied your intellect in ways I was envious of. I saw you in the news recently, your face plastered next to an image of COLI*GO. I thought to myself: impressive for a nobody to make themselves a somebody.

Our commonality is not that we are nobodies. I am of old bloodline descent. Rather, we are one and the same—posse hominems. I understand why The Supreme chose you: the famous scientist adored by the public and loved by the governor.

But me? I'm just a lowly bastard of a former representative. I'm not entirely sure why The Supreme transformed me into this devious-feeling hybrid species, but here I am.

By now, you realize this isn't The Supreme. It never was. But I am working with Jones. He originally found a leak working in the prison (your yellow android friend), and instead of firing him, he coerced him for a job to get you a device. Oh, have you heard? Jones is the new commissioner. And he and I are on a mission to expose Joel Kennsington.

And in this confession, I admit I hesitate to trust my creator much as I assume you hesitate to trust her or me. But she doesn't want Colin to fail, and more importantly, neither does Jones. He realizes Colin is the only sane human in The Legislature.

For now.

I question Colin's sanity, and I think you know a bit more about that than I do. But I'm not one to judge him, for I do not have a strong hold on my own reality either.

It eluded us then, but that's no matter.

I know Joel Kennsington is up to something sinister with FACERE. He wants to destroy androids and hybrids. Beings like you and me. We have to stop him, and I not only need your assistance but also depend on your allegiance.

We know Kennsington is involved in the riots, but to what extent remains a mystery. And this is where you come in—you live with him. He is your captor.

After reading this message, if you choose to help us, please ask Joel the following: Tell me about Maggie Rivera.

Report back what his reply is, and I promise, Jones and I are working on getting you out of the hell I imagine you're in.

Sincerely,
Elsie Sullivan

Legislative Aide & Secretary to Governor Colin O'Connor
24 Beacon Street, The City

Julie held her breath while she read Elsie's message, as if her world were crashing around her. She powered off the device and hid it between the mattress and box spring.

Julie vaguely remembered Elsie Sullivan from school.

They weren't friends or in the same social circles. But from Elsie's signature, it appeared she now worked for Colin in Kathleen's place. And she was secretly a posse hominem.

She doesn't know I've had my microchip removed from my brain. But Jones knows.

Jones kept her secret The strategic side of Julie's mind spun rapidly. Julie had the potential to start with the upper hand in the game against The Supreme.

Julie rose from the bed, and the springs in the mattress creaked from the release of her body. She walked toward the door and paused.

I want to trust Elsie. She's working with Jones. And I need a friend.

Peter had promised Julie a way out of Joel's grip, but Peter's obvious distaste for Colin—the way he so easily stole her engagement ring and kept it hostage—still bothered her. Julie looked down at where the emerald ring should have been and shook her head.

Joel lifted his chin in Julie's direction as she emerged into the living room. He was still dressed in his suit from his day at The Capitol Building and leaning back in his chair with a look of exhaustion. Julie took a seat in the leather armchair opposite him.

"Good evening, darling. Care for a smoke?" A snicker left Joel's lips as he reached for the lighter in his jacket pocket.

The cigarette burned in his fingers, the smoke smoldering up in the air in the shape of a serpent.

Julie released a sultry, wicked smile Joel's way. Her insides turned in disgust at her acting performance. She shook her head at his question and crossed her legs. With a false sparkle, Julie looked over at Joel.

"So," she said coyly, "would you tell me about Maggie Rivera?"

Joel tilted his head to the side, raised his eyebrows, and loosened his tie. The cigarette dangled from in between his lips.

"Where do I even begin?"

Chapter 19
Peter

April 15th, 47 A.R.

The COLI*GO building was quiet over the last two weeks. Only important researchers and scientists who needed lab equipment were permitted to enter the building, along with executives and Board members. Everyone else worked from home, patiently awaiting the go-ahead from The Capitol Building and Commissioner Jones's office. They hoped one day, soon, they would return to everyday life.

Peter had been too afraid to use the time travel device Celine gave him and spent hours digging into Julie's research logs on the antidote. Peter didn't trust Mick's reports, an odd lingering feeling pulling at him that he couldn't explain or justify.

Mick's observations and notes weren't entirely incorrect, but they were sloppy—leading Peter and the research team down rabbit holes. In fact, the asset seemed better off than anyone expected. There was an error Peter couldn't place his finger on, but he knew who could solve the mystery and fix the antidote: Julie.

Running into Julie at the nightclub plagued Peter's thoughts. Seeing her in person, wandering the dance floor to escape Joel Kennsington, made Peter question his sobriety and reality. But she had been there. The proof was with her engagement ring in his pocket.

The idea of time travel petrified Peter based on everything Celine shared. There were risks of premature aging if a traveler ventured too far into the future on someone else's blood. There was even a chance of becoming ghost-like if traveling too far into the past.

And then there's the possibility of screwing something up and creating a time loop, Peter thought, flipping through a copy of the notes Celine provided him from the inventor's observations.

But tonight, Peter had to face his fears. His motivations were selfish—his need to find Julie was no longer just for Celine; he wanted to convince Julie to work with him and help solve the issues with her drug. He needed her. Without Julie's help, the antidote would fail, and that would reflect poorly on him as the CEO.

Peter believed in Julie's antidote. With almost fifteen years of experience in drug development, Peter recognized the power of the science behind successful pipeline candidates. This drug could make or break his career as much as it could make or break Julie's—if she still even cared.

The large conference room on the observatory floor was eerily silent. The top floor of the building had been named "the observatory" because of its full glass floor-to-ceiling windows over-looking The City skyline. Usually, this room was reserved for large, joyful events: new product launches, new acquisitions, and stellar year-end results. Today, the misty clouds covered most of The City's view and emphasized the emptiness of the surrounding streets.

Peter sat down at the conference table, his hands in his pockets. He felt for Julie's engagement ring: the large emerald stone was cold and jagged against his thumb. Peter pulled out the ring and admired the stone as light flickered off its elegance.

He hated how Julie fell for a man like Colin O'Connor, not because Peter still had feelings for her. While he cared about her as a friend and a person whom he had once shared intimate feelings for, Peter didn't love her. Peter respected Julie—she was intelligent, kind, and caring. He wanted to see her succeed. But the Julie he witnessed a couple weeks back, running away from Joel Kennsington and terrified at the notion of time travel, seemed frail. Like she was slowly dying inside and trapped in a situation she had no idea how to get out of.

The only reason she's in this situation is because of Colin O'Connor. Peter placed the ring down on the table for a moment. *I want to help Julie, but I need her too.*

Peter picked up the ring again and continued toying with it between his fingers. Guilt filled him from taking this from her.

A shift in the air made Peter stir, and he sensed he was no longer alone.

Colin had entered the conference room undetected. He didn't take a seat but strode over with a monstrous glare in his eyes. Peter suddenly felt suffocated here in the observatory, and all his remorse disappeared. Colin's presence was all-consuming, atrocious, and dark.

Colin's eyes weren't aligned with Peter's—the steel-gray color clouding while he stared at the ring between Peter's fingertips.

Peter stood and faced Colin. He was shorter than the governor by a few inches but decided to grasp the ring together and match Colin's sinister glare with confidence.

"How," Colin said, looking up at Peter. A dark shadow grew across the governor's face while his voice boomed viciously against the glass windows. "How did you get that?"

Colin swiftly approached the table and leaned against it on his knuckles. A soul-crushing roar sounded as he pushed his weight against the sleek glass conference table.

"I . . ." Peter stuttered, fear rippling through his body. He noted how his hands shook at the sight of Colin's menacing stature.

The door opened and interrupted the tense moment between the two men. Martin Borges, Celine O'Connor, and Marta McKenna entered the room together. Celine and Peter glanced at one another, and her eyes followed to where her brother was staring. Celine's gaze paused on the ring in Peter's hand.

Shit, Peter thought. *The conversation to follow this meeting will not be pleasant.*

Martin obnoxiously cleared his throat, aware of the awkwardness surrounding everyone in the room.

"Peter," Martin stated, his warm features lighting up the room with a sense of calmness. "Would you mind if I started off the meeting with an update from the R&D team? And then you can give your update on the investigation of the lower lab?"

"No, sir," Peter answered, relieved Martin had the courage to remind everyone why they were here. "Not at all."

They all sat, and Martin droned on about in-office restrictions greatly impacting the research teams. Some felt unsafe and resigned, while others requested lab equipment be sent to their homes so that they could work there rather than in the office. The requests were all denied by The Board. Celine suggested setting up a shuttle service, but Marta balked at the costs. The Board decided it was the right thing to do in the end. Colin reassured them that The Legislature and Commissioner Jones had acquired promising intel and leads—he felt The City's lockdown would end within a month's time at most. Peter listened without contributing to the conversation, and his mind drifted until Martin asked about the lower lab.

The Board of Directors and The Legislature knew Peter hired a consultant to investigate The Supreme's abuse of power and get a better analysis on how many posse hominems she created. Due to the confidentiality and request of The Legislature, Peter was advised to keep the identity of his consultant anonymous until the investigation and proceedings were nearly complete. They didn't want any sway or influence from rich old bloodline Board members.

All sets of eyes looked Peter's way. The Board clearly wanted an insider scoop. He wondered how Julie dealt with these interrogations, what kind of moral ambiguity truly resided in his friend while she held this position.

"The consultant I hired has found a few posse hominems who didn't have their memories wiped. They have agreed to meet with them. They will interview the posse hominems over the course of the next few weeks, and our hope is that they have some recollection of either the events prior, during or after"—Peter stopped, looking down at his hands and closing his eyes—"their transformations."

The room remained silent after his update. They seemed disappointed he wouldn't share more, but none were brave enough to voice their concerns.

Peter was desperate for Dr. Anna Garcia to find some connection, some common thread or clue that would speed up the impending doom he feared COLI*GO faced. They were running out of time and hadn't uncovered much else beyond what was in the police reports or in the lower lab itself.

"Good." Celine finally broke the silence in the room. "I'm hopeful your consultant will find some useful information for us. We don't want the public thinking we were so inadequate at running a company that we didn't recognize employees slipping between the cracks to support or overlook such grave matters."

Colin appeared to hold back a chuckle, but it could have been a trick of the light. When he looked over at him again, Colin's eyes remained empty, distant, and haunting. A distinctive look he seemed to wear, now with Julie still missing.

But Peter didn't feel any pity for the man. Colin's reaction alone to Peter's possession of Julie's engagement ring and his absence in February and March from Board meetings told Peter all he needed to know: Colin was involved. Colin knew something.

And that means Celine isn't telling me everything either, Peter concluded.

He still considered Colin a monster, but the man's connections kept him safe through whatever mess he had helped create.

If anything, I hope Anna finds a connection to the governor in all of this. I wouldn't mind seeing that man locked away. Or never again.

***

Peter's apartment was lonely, with all the lights turned off minus his small living room lamp. He rushed out of the Board meeting that afternoon, claiming he had an unexpected personal emergency. Celine blew up his device and requested they meet first thing in the morning to discuss both his update and "whatever conversation" occurred between him and Colin. Peter felt Celine's agitation through the words on his screen.

Peter silenced his device and placed it on the coffee table. He'd written down instructions on a piece of paper, afraid technology wouldn't make it through the void or dimensions he was about to travel in. Pulling the blinds closed, Peter sat back down on his couch and sighed.

The glasses fit snugly on his square face and the chrome box illuminated beside him. Peter held on to the small tube of his blood like his life depended on it. He extracted some with a small dropper.

The sample landed on the slide, and he inserted it into the spot in between the two lenses. The dial clicked on the top of the glasses, and a vibration stirred the chrome device. A timeframe of dates, times, and locations appeared on the screen. The first date was the one of his birth. The second loomed far in the future, and the logical explanation that this was the date of his death weighed heavily on him.

Peter gripped the edges of the couch and wondered what this madness would feel like and what the insanity would ultimately do to him once he traveled through time. Closing his eyes felt comforting even though he couldn't see anything through the shadowed lenses.

A shaking feeling etched through his body. The sensation didn't hurt, but Peter was shocked by how unsatisfying of a feeling the whole experience provided. As everything stilled around him, Peter took a few breathless moments to himself. He hesitated in taking the glasses off his face.

The silence continued, and Peter assumed he was alone, in his apartment, back on the night Julie went missing. The night he told her to time travel to. When he opened his eyes, he noted the clock on the stove read 11:34 p.m. The streetlights outside shone brightly, and a lack of stars across the pitch-black sky reassured him.

"Holy shit. This actually works." His voice echoed within his apartment.

Peter stood and rushed to his front door. He motioned to unlock it, only to hear footsteps coming from within his apartment.

Shit.

Peter turned around and found himself face-to-face with a groggy-eyed version of his past self.

The notes he studied flashed through his mind. Peter remembered where he was at this time of night on this day. Here, in his apartment. Instinct took over, and Peter punched his past self as he approached. His other body fell to the floor in a stump. Scooping himself up and carrying himself into the bedroom, memories flooded back.

I woke up the next day with a headache and a bruise on my cheek. The largest, most unexplainable migraine in my life.

He even remembered finding a glass of water and two pills of acetaminophen on his nightstand when he woke up. He never remembered placing them there.

And that, is a time loop.

"How is it that they promoted someone as dense as you to fill

Julie's interim position as CEO? And how is it that Celine trusted you to find her?" a deep voice sounded from the living room.

Peter rushed, arms raised and fists closed, ready for an altercation. Mick Taylor stood in his living room, his boxy frame thinned out and his glasses drooping down his nose. Mick held his hands in his pockets, not ready for a fight, not even appearing physically threatening.

"What the hell, Mick?" Peter asked, confused.

The clock changed, revealing it was now 11:51 p.m. Julie would be here soon. Intuition warned Peter that he might have brought Julie into a trap, the one she warned him about.

The pieces of the puzzle formed in Peter's mind: Celine insisting on not telling him who the inventor of time travel was for a particular reason, how she claimed the information was better left unsaid when he pressed her for it. Celine knew how much Peter and Mick despised one another. The hesitation in Julie's own voice at calling her friend dangerous. It all made sense, and the answer was obvious to Peter: The inventor of time travel was none other than Mick Taylor.

And, of course, Mick would also be looking for Julie.

Peter almost heard Julie's soft voice shouting over the loud music in the club. The memory was so clear Peter almost physically saw her, could still hear her: *There's someone else. Someone really dangerous who also travels dimensions of time.*

"Why don't we talk instead of raising fists?" Mick gestured to Peter's couch.

Peter didn't want to fight Mick, but he also didn't trust him.

Peter glanced back at the clock: 11:53 p.m.

"Are you waiting for someone, Peter?" Mick asked, a wide grin spreading across his dimpled face.

"No," Peter lied, clearing his throat.

And like an unfortunate cue in a horror film, the handle on the front door turned.

Why is Julie early? She's never early, Peter yelled silently in his head.

His pounding heart exploded in his chest. The first and only time he traveled to the past, and he screwed everything up. He put himself and Julie in danger.

But on the other side of the door, a much taller figure emerged. Not Julie.

This presence materialized almost six and a half feet tall: the shadows surrounding him left his face dark, but only one man who fit this description: Colin O'Connor.

But this Colin's grimace wasn't one Peter recognized from him. This man's deep chuckle, a horrific laugh, echoed through Peter and sent chills down his spine. A foreign sound. Peter wasn't the only one afraid. The color drained from Mick's face.

Like a flash of lightning, Mick darted across the room toward Peter's bedroom, and the man in the door stepped into the light. Peter heard his bedroom window open, followed by the clanking of weight on the fire escape.

Colin didn't attempt to follow Mick and remained still in Peter's doorway until the sound of the window slamming shut broke their silent standoff. Mick—or whatever version of Mick that was—was gone.

"Don't be so reckless next time. Mick can't find Julie." Colin's voice emerged louder and more structured as he leaned against the doorframe.

There was something off about Colin from his tone of voice and his physical stance. He seemed much more relaxed than the stiff, straight-postured governor Peter was used to.

"Mick is the one who discovered time travel? Does that make him the dangerous time traveler Julie speaks of? Or is it you?" Peter approached Colin slowly.

The clock read 11:56 p.m. Four minutes until Julie was scheduled to arrive.

"Anyone who travels time is dangerous. Including you. You'll understand why soon enough," Colin said, noting Peter's continuous glance at the clock. "Relax a little bit. Julie is notoriously always ten minutes late."

Peter let out a large sigh and sat down on his couch. He nervously ran his hands through his hair. Peter traveled back to the dead of winter, to only a few months before, and yet he was sweating uncontrollably. A sickness lingered in his stomach, but he swallowed the thought of vomiting away. He wouldn't show Colin how intimidated he was by him.

Colin walked out of the doorway. He slammed the door closed behind him without even saying goodbye. Peter hastily reached into his pocket for Julie's engagement ring. He looked back up at the digital clock on the stove: 12:09 a.m.

A gentle, hesitant knock sounded on his door.

"Peter?"

Peter rushed toward her and pulled Julie inside with a protective instinct. He closed the door behind her and locked the handle and then the dead bolt.

"Peter? Oh my god, are you okay? You're shaking," Julie said, grabbing him by his shoulders as if her smaller frame could physically still him.

Peter didn't answer her and dragged her to the couch.

"I'm sorry I'm late. I was preoccupied with something else, but I'm glad you waited for me."

"I saw Mick." The words were irrational but flooded out of Peter easily.

"You saw Mick?" Julie's eyes widened, and for the first time, Peter noticed a horrid scar on her neck. The thick silver line ran jagged down her neck, and purple marks blossomed around the base in red zig-zagging lines.

"What happened to you?" Peter asked as his trembling hands reached for Julie's face. She shied away from his touch.

"I'm not sure we have time for all of that," Julie answered, looking back toward Peter's door as if she knew something he didn't. Peter didn't want any other unexpected guests.

"Colin?"

"No. This scar isn't from Colin," she said peculiarly.

This scar? Are there more?

Julie cupped Peter's face in the palms of her hands, and he embraced the comforting gesture, leaning into her and breathing in her familiar scent.

Peter wanted to cry in Julie's arms, but the idea of appearing weak beside her made him restrain. She couldn't see him like this—she needed his help too. He needed to be strong for her.

"I told you, time travel is dangerous. We should meet in the present next time. I've figured out how to sneak out of Joel's undetected for a bit," Julie said, her eyes jittery.

Peter observed her odd behavior and cataloged it in his mind so that he could inquire later. Her constant stress might have accounted for her hallow stare—Julie was always on the lookout, a fugitive in her own sense.

"I need your help," Peter said, his eyes following her in quick motions around his apartment.

The discomfort she felt expelled off her body. But he had made a promise to her.

"My help?"

"Yes," Peter answered. "And it will get you out of Joel's for a bit. I need you to fix the antidote."

Julie's eyes widened at the sound of those words. The antidote meant to Julie—how she hoped to save thousands, if not millions, of lives from being ruined by terrible neurological conditions.

"What about the antidote?" she finally asked.

"You're missing in the future . . . in the present. I'm filling your shoes until Celine comes back from maternity leave. And Mick has sort of replaced me in leading the COL23 program. I know that your drug works, Julie. But I am blinded to how we can fix the issue. No one knows the antidote better than you. I need you. I need your eyes, your expertise, or the antidote will never work."

"How can I help?" Julie countered. "I have to stay hidden. I can only sneak out for a bit at a time but never long enough where Joel wouldn't notice and come looking for me. He might have seen me with you at the club—I don't know if he remembers because he was so drunk. But if he does, he will go straight to COLI*GO." Panic rose in Julie's voice as if Joel were the boogeyman and simply saying his name would alert him to sneak up between the floorboards.

"I need you back in the lab. I need you looking at the simulations and the data," Peter replied. "I think I have an idea. But you have to trust me."

Julie shook her head, and Peter didn't blame her. He had been cruel to her.

"I know you say time travel is dangerous, but we can do this safely. Once I make all the arrangements, I'll send you a message.

Do you still have your device?"

"I have a new one. I'll shoot you a message so that you have the number. Just remember to encrypt your messages to me."

"Okay," Peter said and grabbed Julie's hands in his. "Please trust me. I'm honestly really sorry."

Julie looked down and smiled. Peter placed the ring carefully in her hands.

"Yes," she responded, the peace offering appreciated from the tears forming in the corners of her eyes. "I trust you."

***

Anna stood next to Peter inside the apartment of a young woman named Chloe Wallace. Chloe wore a baggy white T-shirt and sweatpants, her long dirty blonde hair and fawn-colored eyes hidden by the starkness of her skin. Like Lexi Pvadinish, Chloe had flaky skin, and callouses littered what Peter assumed had once been silky, smooth hands.

Chloe had hesitantly opened the door when Peter and Anna arrived. She hid behind the old-fashioned chain lock and insisted they show her proof of their identification before allowing them entrance into her home. With the violence aimed at posse hominems, Peter didn't blame her, but her obvious distrust still startled him.

She lived in a small one-bedroom apartment in The South neighborhood. The home was outdated with yellow wallpaper and white appliances. She kept her place clean, but the tiny space was cluttered with various trinkets and knickknacks.

"Thank you for meeting with us. I know these are troubling and terrifying times," Anna spoke gracefully, and Chloe eyed her warily.

"Yah welcome," she responded, her thick City accent shining through. "I dunno how helpful I'll be tah yah."

"Anything you can remember will assist us greatly. We're really trying to bring justice to you," Anna said, her eyes warm and sparkly. Chloe didn't appear convinced as she relocked the door behind them.

"And of course, COLI*GO is devoted to providing

compensation, and our lawyers will reach out to you," Peter mentioned.

"I don't know if I wantcha money." Chloe sank into the worn red armchair at the far end of the room.

"Do you remember anything about the day you went missing?" Anna asked, giving Peter a sideways glance as they sat awkwardly together on the small love seat opposite Chloe.

Chloe hummed for a moment before answering. "I was workin' for the Borges family at the time. Shuffled between Martin Borges and his wife's condo and Martin's brothah's place. Did tidyin' up and housework, yah know?"

Anna nodded, and Peter looked away. He admired Celine and didn't want her to be involved in this disastrous nightmare, but he held on to his earlier sinking suspicion: Her innocence was a folly.

"Martin and Celine had a dinnah pahty back in May of 45 A.R., and I was there kinda late workin'. Then the next thing I know, I'm back here in my place with a splittin' headache. Things got worse. My skin, it's so itchy. Sometimes, I find myself lookin' out the window, and my mind just blanks. I dunno, I'm getting bettah, but it's a slow process."

"Was anyone overly suspicious at the dinner party?" Anna asked, typing quick notes into her device. "Such as someone who wasn't part of an old bloodline family? Someone who acted strangely? Stayed away from people, kept to themselves?"

Chloe tilted her head to the side and pondered Anna's questions.

"Yah know, now that I'm thinkin' about it, the guy who killed Kathleen Murphy was there."

"Jeb Taylor?" Anna's voice trembled.

Who else? Peter thought with agitation.

"Yah, that guy. I watched some of the news on his trial but nevah thought of it until you asked. Maybe 'cuz he's usually at most old bloodline pahties." Chloe studied Anna more closely. "Are yah old bloodline? You look like Isabella Garcia. She was there. Didn't stay too long and didn't go home with the gove'nah either, which I thought was strange."

"I am a Garcia, yes. Isabella is my older sister. She's really good friends with Celine O'Connor."

"She is?" Peter asked, recalling each time Celine rolled her eyes at Isabella in social settings and how she always said Isabella's name with a sarcastic tone.

"I mean . . ." Anna stammered and looked away from Peter and back to Chloe. "Anyways, is there anything else you can remember from that night?"

"Nope," Chloe said before peeking behind the curtain. "Yah know, do have yah lawyers call me."

Peter nodded slowly, unsurprised.

Anna and Peter said goodbye to Chloe and left her apartment. The sun shone brighter today and the haunted, empty streets radiated a rare springtime heat. Neither Peter nor Anna spoke as they got into his vehicle.

"So that wasn't overly eye-opening," Peter said, turning the vehicle on. The engine purred to life before dying down silently again. "We know old bloodline families are involved in this somehow."

"Quite the opposite. This was actually really eye-opening, Peter," Anna said, leaning her head against the car's window. "I've spoken to four victims so far, and you're right. All worked for old bloodline families. And they all disappeared the night of some party or event that was hosted. We already know Jeb Taylor was the muscle of the operation—the kidnapper in many cases. But The Supreme was working with someone from an old bloodline family to select her next victims. She had to be. We should triangulate guest lists from all the events and see if there are any patterns."

"That's true, but I doubt old bloodline families are going to give over their guest lists with open arms. No offense."

Anna was an old bloodline herself, no matter how much she tried to separate herself from her family. Her wealth, education, and status leaked out of her perfectly flawless skin like a loose faucet.

The journey from The South back to The River was normally through underground tunnels, but the lack of traffic allowed them to stay above ground today. Peter appreciated the different parts of The City, especially having spent a few years away from it. He felt a magnetic pull while here—something sinfully delicious about the historic charm meddling with advanced, high-tech innovation.

"No offense taken." Anna laughed and pulled out her device.

"As long as they had their devices on them, I can look up who was in attendance through the tracking database. Perks of working for the commissioner."

"Sounds like a plan."

"And I think it's time we spoke to Celine and Martin. I know they've been cleared for any involvement, but I find that so hard to believe. It's her company. It's his money from the budget that was 'diverted,'" Anna said with air quotes. "Why didn't The Legislature want Celine to know I'm the consultant you hired? I think it's time she knows. I need to interrogate her."

Peter sighed. Anna asked this question before, and he never had a suitable answer for her. Or at least, an answer that Anna accepted or believed.

The Legislature required anonymity so that someone could investigate all the executives and Board members discreetly. Representatives didn't want them trying to influence a consultant with their status.

But eventually, the façade had to end, and that was why Peter had selected Anna in the first place. He appreciated the different approach she had—she was so far removed from COLI*GO that Peter had no doubts Anna looked at everything with fresh eyes.

"The Legislature feels that once The Board knows you're the consultant, they won't be open to speaking with you or there will be friction. You're right, you need to interview them, and we can't keep going around in circles. The Legislature wants answers. But we must do this strategically and make sure your name isn't leaked before you have a chance to speak to everyone. The interviews need to be done one after another on the same day," Peter answered, looking over at Anna.

She was a striking woman with a wildly different persona and style from her older sister. What intrigued Peter the most was Anna's intelligence and introspectiveness. He sensed Commissioner Jones recommended her for those reasons.

"I'll look to schedule everything. In the meantime, no more interviews even with posse hominems. Your identity must be a secret."

Anna raised an eyebrow and pouted.

"What about Colin O'Connor? Isn't he rarely at COLI*GO now because of how tied up he is in The Capitol Building?"

"That's true," Peter acknowledged, annoyed that Colin might ruin his perfectly crafted plan. "I can't stand him, but he is the one who brought all the evidence of The Supreme to The Legislature before Representative Kennsington had the chance. I doubt he will sabotage our operation, but I am still convinced he's involved in all of this somehow."

Chapter 20

Commissioner Jones

April 15th, 47 A.R.

The loud sound of high heels clicking in the hallway on the tile floors snapped Jones out of his deep concentration. The tall and indistinguishable sight of Elsie Sullivan appeared in his doorway. She didn't wait for Jones to welcome her before confidently striding into his office.

Elsie purposefully plopped her device on Jones's desk and grinned largely.

"Julie responded."

Jones shot up from his seat and snatched Elsie's device. His eyes focused back up to Elsie, and she nodded in permission for Jones to read the message on her screen.

To: 617–345–8709
From: 617–333–2985
Date Sent: April 13th, 47 A.R.
Subject: Stephen King

{Message Encryption}

Elsie,

I remember you but never imagined this kind of high school reunion. I am hesitant to trust The Supreme, but I will always trust Jones. If Jones trusts you, I will give you the benefit of the doubt. Next time you see him, please tell him congratulations on his promotion for me.

I inquired with Joel about Maggie Rivera as you asked. Joel is an

insufferable pig, and I long for the day I don't need to hide in the confines of his home.

After a tumultuous rant about Maggie's marriage to Martin Borges, he insinuated she had an affair with Colin that ruined all of Maggie's future prospects. Because they have a common enemy, Maggie helped get Joel's childhood friends and associates in The South roles within FACERE to gain his trust. Now Joel has access to all of FACERE's projects, even before The Legislature.

Interestingly enough, Maggie's vengeance against the O'Connors is strong. Joel wants me to meet Maggie at FACERE so that she can have a "live" hybrid specimen. I've never been to FACERE, but Joel says there is a special experimental lab, which brought my mind instantly to the lower lab at COLI*GO. Both entities are filled with backstabbing, opportunistic leaders. It wouldn't shock me to find mistreated androids there.

What The Supreme did was unforgivable, but I wonder, what FACERE does to androids, is that unforgiveable too?

Human places create inhumane monsters.

Best,
Julie

A grin spread across Jones's face. He missed Julie and could almost hear her voice while reading the message. The last time he saw her, she handed him a full treatment supply of the antidote and asked him to help Colin.

"So, my spies were correct—Julie is at Joel's." Jones handed Elsie back her device.

"Yes, but I don't think she's safe there, especially based on that message," Elsie said, her fidgeting fingers tracing the nearly invisible scar on her own neck.

When Colin asked Elsie to work with him, he noticed a wildly unique set of biometrics from her body. Jones confronted Elsie about her true species in the privacy of his office, and she shared her story with him. There was a scar on her body, one that was barely recognizable now with her tattoo.

"It took many attempts to disguise this, but my childhood friend from The Monument—another trouble maker like me—opened his own tattoo parlor. I trust him and he covered this scar for me," she had shared with Jones.

The image was lovely—a dainty serpent with its tail hiding from one end of her neck up to its head behind her ear. Apparently, Elsie's mother had been horrified when she came home. The tattoo was unprofessional, especially for her career in government, but Elsie didn't seem to mind and easily hid her artwork with her long, soft hair.

"That's true," Jones said in agreement with Elsie's assessment of Julie's safety.

Julie isn't a posse hominem anymore. Julie's scar tells a different story, one of incision and removal.

Jones sat back in his seat with a sense of defeat distorting his earlier excitement. Elsie crossed her long, lean legs and contemplated the situation.

"At least we can confirm a much stronger tie to Joel and FACERE now. I think the time has come for me to arrange a visit with Mr. McGuire directly," Elsie said with a raised brow.

An ominous look filled in her eyes. A look he had seen on someone else before: Colin O'Connor, or more appropriately, It. An unsettling sense slinked through his scales, a similar sensation to a shiver.

"We should be thoughtful about this, Elsie. We can't scare him off. I might need him." Jones despised how this was a plea.

He thought about a returned, familiar darkness glooming across The City—one that didn't need to emerge with impending threats of turmoil, riots, and mobs that already consumed them.

"No, we don't." Elsie crossed her leg, and her heel dangled conspicuously off her foot. Jones shifted his gaze back to her face.

"Be careful about this. And be careful of any ideas Colin throws your way," Jones warned.

Elsie raised both eyebrows as if Jones shared a convoluted

insight into something she wasn't entirely aware of.

"Should we tell Colin?" Elsie tilted her head back and paused. "About Julie?"

Jones silently looked back at Elsie. The pros and cons of telling Colin that Julie was alive carried varied consequences and considerations. The governor seemed to finally be in a better headspace and held a tighter grasp on his other personality as of late. The knowledge of Julie and her current situation, what she was facing for all of them, would bring out the sinister side of Colin. The moment of Jones telling Colin that Julie visited him with the antidote had provided a settling ease to the man. His warm smile spread across his face like a wildfire knowing she wasn't actually dead.

"No," Jones ultimately decided and stood. "Not yet. Telling him might be a bad thing. We need to find the right time, and we need to already have a plan in place on how to bring her into the fold before we do."

"Colin deserves to know she's here in The City," Elsie countered. "Why would that be a bad thing?"

"The knowledge might unhinge him, and he's worked very hard to get out of his recent depression. Colin needs to remain focused on helping The City get out of its darkness."

PART FIVE

The Past

"Life is like a wheel. Sooner or later, it always comes around to where you started again."
—Stephen King

Chapter 21
Mick

October 12th, 12 A.R.

Mick couldn't wrap his mind around referring to the former supreme as "The Supreme." Emilia was still The Supreme to him.

A misfit in her own right much like himself, she had a stark differentiator—a family that cared about her. The O'Connors took care of Emilia as if she were a child of their own. Emilia had her own bedroom in the townhouse, situated between Celine's and Colin's rooms.

Emilia attended school with both siblings, and Henry even sat her on his lap and read her bedtime stories as he did with his own children before Melanie's death. Henry seemed content enough to continue caring for his children after Melanie disappeared.

Except with Colin.

Emilia and Celine chased one another around the dining room table. Celine was tall and scrawny for her age, and as an android, Emilia matched her in height. Colin was nowhere in sight, but Mick wasn't surprised—Colin dealt with terrible demons and isolated himself from many social interactions in the months that followed June 23rd.

The carriage house wasn't always safe to visit during this stretch in time. Mick walked through the door one morning, stopping as he approached the bedroom. His mouth dried in horror at the sight of a young Colin strapped to the bed, passed out from pure exhaustion and fear.

Mick held his breath and tiptoed to Colin's side before loosening the straps around his wrists, careful not to fully remove them himself.

He should be able to get himself out when he wakes up, Mick hoped.

The two cold, heartless men unfairly tortured a tormented,

depressed young boy were responsible for the true demons in Colin's mind. The real reasoning behind the sinister sides of It. Had they not treated him so terribly, It might have been more containable. For It to become less of a threat, he needed affection; he needed acceptance.

If someone could give It that part of themselves, he might not be horrid. He might be manageable—livable.

Mick closed his eyes and crouched in the corner, tears forming inside of him as the realization that if time travel didn't exist, if Colin's alternate personality didn't travel time, then none of this would happen. Colin might not suffer from It or the abuse of his father.

But It time traveling wasn't Mick's only concern. The growing number of travelers worried him—there was Julie, It, Isabella, and him, but now Peter was thrown into the mix. Mick wondered what Julie shared with Peter regarding time travel from their more recent meetup. Peter said he wasn't waiting for anyone, but Mick knew better—Peter found Julie, and now Mick needed to find Julie too.

Mick fiddled with the buttons on his shirt. Normally, he didn't dress so formally. Edward—Supreme Edward—was an important android, and Mick wanted to leave a good impression. Today, he would reprogram Edward's microchip to understand 100 percent of human emotions.

The task triggered Mick's insecurities and anxieties. He never reprogrammed a microchip before but Julie had. He traveled back to that moment in time on multiple occasions to learn how she accomplished such a challenging task. Mick mimicked all her processes and procedures but unnervingly knew he wasn't as talented. He didn't give Julie enough credit—she was brilliant.

Mick created the code on his own device, mirroring it on Julie's. He noted how Julie coded Jones's microchip to continuously learn when it came to understanding feelings and experiencing them. The threshold was set at about 60 percent across both aspects.

That wouldn't work for The Supreme. She needed to understand 100 percent of human emotions, but he couldn't allow her to feel them 100 percent—she would basically be susceptible to humans if she essentially was one. Mick tinkered with the code and settled on a

100 percent understanding and a 50 percent experience of human feelings and emotions.

Shaking his head and burying his insecurities deep within, Mick exited the carriage house. The walk to The Capitol Building was short, but his lungs ached. He was physically out of shape with time traveling on other people's blood and it was ruining his body. Mick swore to himself he would resist traveling time on anyone else's blood but his own, at least for the foreseeable future.

I hope Julie uses her own blood. Mick's mind lingered to the warnings and observations he outlined in his journal.

If she only used her blood, she would experience minimal effects and fewer impacts on weight loss or premature aging. He didn't want to see his friend the way he saw himself—harsh, noticeable lines on his skin and a dullness to his flesh.

And if she uses her own blood, she won't make it too far into the future.

Julie should have died in the woods during 47 A.R. and only survived because Mick found her. Time travelers couldn't really die when they traveled time because if they did, they would end up waking up in a cold sweat in the place where they were supposed to die.

The odd sense of immortality shocked Mick at first, but he learned quickly from his observations in the proteins of his blood that the blood of another time traveler could hurt him—only another time traveler could kill him. He could kill Julie.

Or she could kill him.

***

Mick arrived at The Capitol Building but didn't enter through the large front doors. He admired the public entrance, the large marble steps with slightly yellowed stains of blood from The Resurgence over a decade ago. The blemishes were almost unnoticeable, but their slight presence caused him to pause.

The rest of the entrance was magnificent, the otherwise harsh whiteness of the steps bouncing off the crimson red bricks, and the shadows from the gold dome cascaded down onto the large front lawn. Masses of people and androids puttered around the front of the building both during turbulent and celebratory times.

Mick's heart beat loudly as images of the future temporarily haunted him. His hand grasped his face while imaginary androids, people, and hybrids flooded him. In his vision, they were tearing one another apart in this very spot.

The City never held on to its peace for too long.

"Sir, are you all right?" A soothing voice rang through Mick's ears, and a warm, gentle hand grasped his shoulder.

Mick opened his eyes to a shorter woman with chestnut hair, pale skin, and freckles sprinkled across the bridge of her nose. She wore a conservative gray dress, and her hair was pulled up in a neat bun.

"Yes." Mick cleared his throat and shook his head. He offered the oddly charming woman a small smile to convince both her and himself.

"Representative Sullivan, you have a meeting with the governor that we're late for." A young man with flaming red hair approached her. The woman nodded and glanced back at Mick once more before making her way inside the building.

Mick continued around the corner, approaching a side entrance with an android guarding it. The security guard sat behind a metal detector and a small wooden desk. The sight was so antiquated that Mick smiled.

"Mr. Taylor," his voice beckoned behind his sky-blue scales.

Mick nodded and walked inside without any further security check. Working for a supreme android had its benefits.

Mick's shoes loudly clicked against the stone floors, the faint hustle and bustle of The Legislature echoing from another part of the building. This section was newer, recently constructed after the back half of the original building crumbled during The Resurgence.

Mick rounded the corner and approached Edward's office. He knocked lightly on the door and waited.

"Come in," the android's powerful baritone voice sounded from behind the door.

"Good morning," Mick said as he entered the room.

The tall and overpowering android leader's golden scales flickered against the morning sun. His scales appeared tangerine and less gold in this light. Edward was magnificent and beautiful with his broad shoulders and full frame exhuming strength and confidence.

"I'm looking forward to today." His voice was smooth and dark, the grin on his face wide enough to indicate to Mick that this android already knew more than the legal amount of his microchip.

Edward nodded, approaching Mick and closing the space that separated them.

"I'll access your microchip," Mick answered, pushing his glasses back up the bridge of his nose. "And then I will recode the chip based on what I have here."

Mick held up his device and handed it over to Edward. He welcomed the device hesitantly, his fingers scrolling through the screen without really understanding the coding that faced him.

"After completing the file transfer, I'll place your microchip back inside your processor."

"How long does this take?" Edward asked and handed Mick back his device.

"Only about fifteen minutes."

Edward looked out toward the courtyard. Mick had been in this office many times before but with The Supreme—with Emilia. Across the way, the governor's office was concealed with completely drawn curtains.

Mick yearned to ask Edward more about Henry O'Connor.

What type of man is he? How often do you speak? Do you work together? Why is Henry raising Emilia?

"And you'll leave the coding instructions with me?" Edward asked, turning to face Mick. "For Emilia?"

"Yes, of course," Mick responded with a slight smile. "How is she?"

"She is well. Sharp. Intelligent. Witty." Edward looked down at his hands and smiled. "She is in good hands until the time comes."

"When the time comes?" Mick echoed, unsure of what Edward insinuated. He looked back at the courtyard with longing.

"When she's of age and attending The University. Then she can leave the watchful eyes of the O'Connors and study directly with me. I'll guide her and coach her before she assumes my role. Before she becomes the supreme."

Mick's brow rose, unaware of this process. Edward was the

leader, but he was also the originator of any androids in The Legislature. All the traditions and rules were created by him and the first fifty android representatives. Edward truly created The Supreme's legacy.

"Where you come from, does Emilia not have a successor?" Edward asked, pursing his lips together in anticipation of a disappointing answer.

Emilia did not have a named successor yet back in present time, but Mick assumed one would be created around now at FACERE's facility based on her age.

"Her successor hasn't been named yet," Mick answered, careful to not reveal that the fate of a position like a supreme was up in the air—Emilia was still in prison, and the whole system he built was crumbling.

"She must still be young, then?" Edward's curiosity was unlike that of a typical android, but Mick was willing to indulge him.

"Yes, she's forty-five years old," Mick answered.

If she hadn't been arrested, she would serve the androids of The Constituency for another twenty-five years—the exact age from which she assumed the role.

"Well, I'm sure you will help her reprogram her successor? Or will she do so herself?"

"You should teach Emilia after you perform the task on her," Mick suggested, not wanting The Supreme to know he had these qualifications. Edward followed Mick's stare across the courtyard.

"Do you not trust the O'Connors, time traveler?" Edward inquired.

The words stung Mick. He didn't trust Colin, not after everything he witnessed across time, but he had yet to make a formal opinion about Celine. He assumed he wouldn't trust Henry if given the chance.

"I've never personally met Henry O'Connor. But I know his son all too well," Mick said with a twinge of anger and annoyance. Edward leaned back in his chair with shining, smiling eyes.

"Is he a Humanizer?"

"No. He's a Sympathizer. My distaste for the man has nothing to do with his political beliefs. He gets elected as governor, again and again. He works well with Emilia, and they make meaningful strides in the fight for equal rights for androids. But there's a monstrous side to him. It grows powerfully in his brain, especially with the help of my friend. And that is something I'm not sure I can forgive either of them for."

A shift in the room grew colder by the second.

"Your friend?" Edward asked.

"Yes, he falls in love with her and then corrupts her with his demons."

Edward chuckled and shook his head. "I thought it was women who corrupted men."

Is it really Colin who corrupted Julie or was it Julie who corrupted him? Mick wondered for the first time with the guidance of Edward's astute observation.

"I crave to learn more, but," the android said, breaking Mick's train of thought, "don't tell me too much more about the future. I want some things to remain a surprise."

His words contradicted what Mick previously believed. Jones's voice rang in Mick's ears, his warning about not interfering in the past. Jones comprehended more human emotions than most androids but would never experience time travel. Even if he could, Mick doubted Jones would ever use the device.

Jones hates time travel, and now he hates me.

Mick suspected once Edward was reprogrammed, he would fall in love with the power and influence time travel provided—the ultimate knowledge of the future's and past's secrets.

Chapter 22
It

July 24th, 45 A.R.

It never felt an urgency to travel to the recent past, nor did he previously have the need. He traveled back to Colin's youth, looking for unexplainable answers to questions he was afraid to ask himself, questions he was afraid to ask Colin. But those trips brought him back thirty or more years. Today, his adventure was more familiar.

Before putting the time travel glasses on his eyes, It had looked at himself in the mirror. He stood in the townhouse's master bedroom, his eyes lingering in the walk-in closet for too long before finding what he was looking for.

The suit Colin always wore to The Symphony.

There wasn't anything overly unique about the attire except for how influential he felt when donning the crisp black ensemble. Something about the fabric, the way the suit hung on his tall but broad body, encompassed a sense of confidence and authority that It couldn't deny. He looked charming, sophisticated, and a bit dangerous.

Traveling back in time was risky, especially with the intention of interacting with the past's inhabitants. But after weeks of wondering about his dream—weeks of longing to understand the true meaning behind the tricks his mind played on him—It had to know.

He needed answers.

It didn't plan on spending much time in the past, just enough to understand the lingering questions, the unexplainable doubt in his mind. And a moment to pay Maggie Rivera a visit.

I can't forget that dreaded task either.

The glasses fit tightly across It's face as he leaned back in the chair in Colin's study. He pulled out the knife from the bottom drawer and swirled it around his finger. The blade enticingly pressed against his skin. The prick didn't hurt him as the blood lightly bubbled up and exposed the invincibility of the human body in its wake.

Blood to travel time.

It refused to use anyone else's blood but his own, and he refused to travel to the future.

After the vibrations of the device shuddered through him, It removed the glasses. He still sat in Colin's study, the same place he'd been moments before. But the digital clock on the desk read a different date.

A grin crept across It's face as he confirmed his location: July 24th, 45 A.R. Back before everything went to shit, back when things were exhilarating. It strode out of the room with heavy, loud footsteps against the expensive wooden staircase.

The summer night air was humid, making his skin stick to his suit. His walk from The Hill to The Bay was peaceful and vastly different from how it looked in the present from which he came.

In the present, It had peered out the window at an empty park, one that normally bustled with humans and androids enjoying exotic plants, beautiful flowers, and a perfectly manicured green lawn. Tonight, couples of the human and android variety held hands as they strode through The City's most famous green space—eyes smiling up at one another against the gaslit lamps illuminating a soft hue around them. The water from the pond shimmered a deep navy from the darkness, promising allure and mystery to passers-by. No one bothered him; no one seemed to notice a man masked as their governor stalking by in the confines of a starless night sky.

It's steps led him to Commonwealth Avenue. Beautiful historical brick and limestone buildings with grand, ostentatious steps bordering the sidewalks surrounded him. The insides of these homes had since been modernized, something that separated The Bay from The Hill. The charming trees lining the road provided enough shelter with large masking shadows as It continued his forbidden journey.

Julie's apartment was lit, and her figure leaned up against the kitchen island. She had just gotten home from The Symphony, although not as Colin's guest but The Supreme's. It grinned at how striking Julie was in this moment—the simplicity of her, a true wonderfulness he wanted to indulge in. An indulgence Colin wouldn't approve of.

It climbed the front steps hastily, and his hand trembled as it hovered over the buzzer to her apartment. He'd debated this moment for hours and eventually days. As risky as this was, It didn't intend to change the past. He didn't plan on confronting Julie. It played the part of Colin well enough that she wouldn't know the difference—at least not yet.

I need answers and confirmation, It thought. *To the question of if my imagination was truly wild or if my dream really was a memory.*

If It could confirm his suspicion, he could better prepare himself for the fall out of a lifetime.

I could better prepare Colin. I could save myself.

The door chimed quietly, and the lock retreated to grant It access. He walked inside, smelling the light scent of Julie's perfume in the building entryway. It approached her door and gripped the handle he instinctively knew was unlocked for him. For Colin.

All I need to do is kiss her lips lightly and leave. See if the taste of her is familiar or not. Determine if my dream was a real memory or a figment of my desires and imagination.

Julie smiled at him as he entered her apartment, her body relaxed and comfortable against the kitchen island. She was tantalizing.

He embraced her tightly, the smell of her hair consuming his senses and the warmth of her body distracted him from his real intentions—the true reason he jeopardized so much for a simple but necessary answer.

"You're beautiful," It whispered, his hands lingering to her waist and gripping her tightly.

It lifted her body up to the kitchen island with ease and rested her close to the edge. Her legs dangling off the side and her freckled skin peeking from the slit of her silky black dress distracted him further. At this angle, they were face to face. Equals.

The way they were meant to be.

It gazed at Julie, and an uncharacteristically warm smile spread across his face.

"You told me you weren't stopping by tonight. I'm surprised you're here," Julie said, her long lashes brushing against her iridescent skin.

This was why I chose today to visit you in the past. It affectionately rubbed his thumb across her cheek.

Isabella was in town that weekend and annoyingly occupied Colin's evening before the large public campaign event he had the next day. Colin couldn't escape to see Julie tonight.

It could see her uninterrupted.

An innocent air pulsated around Julie. He was drawn to this invisible magnetic pull. There were no ulterior motives. Normally, It liked thinking about the devious side of Julie from the future, but here, he enjoyed her naïve nature and the idea that he could corrupt her this evening instead of Colin.

It grabbed her hands in his and interlaced his fingers with hers. A tactic to keep his urges to touch her elsewhere at bay.

"I couldn't stay away."

This was a bad idea.

The danger lingered in It's brain as Julie wrapped her legs around his waist and pulled him closer. It held his breath, and a vision of ravishing her passed through his eyes.

No. I'll only kiss her. I will leave before this goes too far.

But It didn't listen to his own warning. He released his hands from her and touched her leg, fingers trailing up her thigh and under her dress. The feel of her skin was familiar to It, but he reminded himself that he knew what it was like to touch her. This wasn't why he was here. Her taste was what was unfamiliar to him, a foreign concept he couldn't stop salivating over after the intense premonition.

It took the plunge and kissed her deeply as his hands inched further up her leg and gripped her tightly. He longed for the final answer he feared. Julie hungrily engaged his advances, the tender but passionate moment locking them together.

Shit, It thought as his lips parted from Julie's and trailed down her neck. The sense of her haunting his tongue. *That wasn't just a dream. I had a memory—a memory from time travel.*

Headlights flickered outside Julie's large bay windows, catching It's attention for a brief moment as he moved down her body and explored her. He paused and looked up at Julie.

Should we draw down the shades?

But Julie's presence, her need for him preoccupied his actions. It forgot his worries, and the thrill of being able to finally have her with no repercussions distracted him. It grinned devilishly and continued giving into his deepest desire—the woman who would eventually ruin him: Julie Walsh.

She trusts me.

***

Maggie's eyes were large and round and her hair was shorter but still styled in soft, luscious curls. She wore her infamous plum suit, holding a feminine but strong demeanor in her seated position behind a large L-shaped office at FACERE. Maggie's fingers delicately held a sleek stylus while tapping the tip gently against the chrome metal desk.

The walls of FACERE were harsh and cold compared to the warmth It felt earlier in Julie's studio apartment. While Julie's place was updated and modernized, It experienced a softness from her furnishings and the hominess and longing of her plush, cloud-like bed.

Or maybe that's all from Julie herself, It wondered with a slight grin.

Mistakes were made last night. It should have left. Knowing how vulnerable he was around Julie should have stopped him, but as she slept in his arms, It realized he didn't want to let her go. He understood why Colin truly loved her. Sharing himself with Julie strengthened his feelings and invigorated him to really make amends and find her when he returned to his version of the present. It needed Julie for the ultimate part of his plan, but he now wanted her more involved—he wasn't sure he could do this without her.

"I don't like unannounced visits from members of The Legislature—particularly from you," Maggie's voice interrupted It's thoughts, and he entered her office.

"Well . . ." It sighed as he strode across the harsh tiled floors toward Maggie's desk. "This isn't really official, on-the-record business."

Maggie tilted her head to the side and raised a brow. She was an interesting woman, one Colin didn't mind but was still cautious of. Their past was messy and complicated—a sloppy reminder of why Colin rarely lingered from Isabella again until Julie. It was the only one allowed to linger.

"Are you here to complain about my refusal to assign the next supreme again? Or is it to complain that I won't let you raise him or her?" Maggie asked, her eyes drifting away from his. "I'm waiting until after the election. It doesn't make sense until I know the winner."

"I'll win the election."

Maggie chuckled and shook her head. Her laugh echoed around the room, and the sound of her heels tapped against the floor as she stood. Her tiny frame wandered easily to the other side of her desk, and she pulled out two crystal high-ball glasses and a fairly expensive bottle of Scotch. Maggie poured the amber liquid with both ease and a heavy hand. She passed It a glass and sat back down.

"Your confidence is so infuriatingly predictable," she responded, taking a delicate sip.

A tiny smile peeked through the corners of her mouth, but it disappeared quickly.

"I'm going to win the election," It said again, more firmly this time.

"I'd be more accommodating if you just married Isabella. A stable home structure is important in raising a child even if it's only an android." Maggie spoke knowing Colin would never pull the trigger and marry his long-standing partner. "Although I noticed you didn't smell like her when you walked in but still smelled awfully feminine? How can a woman like Isabella not be enough for you?"

He rolled his eyes and leaned back in his chair, agitated by Maggie's accurate accusation. "Don't threaten me. That didn't work out so well for you last time," It recoiled. "And an android life is just as important as a human's. Especially a child's."

"I'm not sure the voters would like hearing you say those words, Governor. So, if you're not here to beg on your hands and knees before me over tradition, why are you really in my office?"

"I'm here because you seem to have an affiliation for my rival,

Representative Kennsington."

Maggie froze at Joel's name, her eyes widening before relaxing back to a normal, unaffected stare. She walked over to the other side of her desk and leaned against it with ease to refill her glass.

"Are you jealous?"

Not in the slightest, It thought instantly but was glad he hadn't spoken the words out loud.

It remembered her and Colin's affair. There was nothing special about them—nothing special about her—and Colin used Maggie in a cruel and senseless fashion.

For Celine's sake.

This favor Colin did for his sister never sat comfortably with It. Celine wouldn't do the same for Colin if the tables were turned. Why Colin always gave Celine the upper hand, It never understood.

"I'm just trying to warn you, as a friend," It answered slowly, inching his chair away from her.

"I can make my own decisions about who is worthy of my time. Joel Kennsington isn't going to use me the way you did. He's a big enough man to actually stand up against The Supreme," Maggie said, pausing in the small space between It and her desk. "If I'm being honest, I don't understand why you and I aren't working together. We both hate her. I suppose you're right about Joel, but at least he entertains me. You won't even answer my messages."

Of course Joel entertains you, It thought in annoyance targeted straight at the man. *You're an attractive, powerful woman who controls the facility that creates beings he hates. The beings he feels are second-class citizens.*

"Hate is a strong word," It responded, contemplating the ugly truth behind what Maggie said. He did hate The Supreme even if Colin insisted on working with her until the very end. "But I don't doubt she'll do something sinister."

"That's impossible. FACERE doesn't program malice or violence into microchips, especially for an android who becomes a supreme."

"Just because FACERE didn't program her that way doesn't mean someone else didn't. And she's already started messing with your future plans of upgraded android prototypes by creating her own specimen."

He gulped the last of his Scotch and aggressively placed the empty glass down on Maggie's desk. He looked up at Maggie with an intense stare meant to cause fear and doubt.

"And you think that's linked to her microchip being altered?"

"Did FACERE ever check Edward's microchip after his death?" It asked, not shifting his gaze even an inch.

He was the predator in the room, and Maggie understood her place. Maggie averted her eyes and grabbed his empty glass. Her silence was an honest enough answer.

"Who could even be capable of doing such a thing?" she eventually asked.

"I'm not sure," It answered and stood from his chair, ready to finally leave.

He looked down at Maggie, and her questioning but insecure glare reminded him of a timid, confused puppy.

"But you better figure it out soon, Maggie. You don't want anyone jeopardizing all your hard work in making it this far up society's ladder."

Chapter 23
Peter

October 12th, 37 A.R.

The COLI*GO building looked nearly the same, but the shininess of the glass radiated a bit brighter in the sunny fall morning. After weeks of seeing a mostly empty building in the present, Peter smiled at being back in time with the hustle and bustle of scientists and business managers. He missed the liveliness of COLI*GO, the excitement and thriving ecosystem that pulsated around its walls.

Peter crafted his plan carefully. For Julie to fix the antidote, she needed a place to actually do it. She continued hiding from society, and while the building was mostly empty, the risk remained high that someone would see her. Julie wanted to keep her identity a secret, and Peter wasn't sure why she hadn't let the world know she wasn't dead or missing. He doubted he would know the reason until the time was right.

Celine hesitated at first to travel time with Peter, but he shared with her his logs and experiences and promised as long as she traveled on her own blood, nothing damming would happen. Peter needed Celine's buy-in—this was the only way his plan would work.

Celine's face showcased pure dumbfounded joy during her first experience with time travel. Peter reminisced in that same feeling a few weeks before with his first experience, but he didn't feel like the veteran Julie was in the process. No fine lines had wrinkled Peter's face, but his clothes did hang a tad bit looser from his body—a symptom Julie shared.

"Don't use someone else's blood, Peter," Julie had cautioned. "It'll age you. I've only used the blood of another twice, and I felt terribly ill afterward."

Peter didn't notice the wrinkles Julie referred to. His friend still held a simplistic enchantment over him.

"Wow," Celine said, letting go of Peter's hand and approaching the elevators from COLI*GO's main lobby. "How much she's grown since this moment."

COLI*GO was Celine's first baby, the first endeavor that she poured her blood, sweat, and tears into. Seeing COLI*GO again in its first few years of existence brought a warmth to an otherwise closed-off woman.

The journey to the 101st floor provided a few moments of solitude that they needed. Celine nervously fiddled in the elevator beside Peter. Her eyes darted back and forth, and she straightened her blazer half a dozen times before they reached the top.

The doors opened, and an attractive woman greeted them. She was tall and curvy with bright blonde hair and enormous green eyes. Her style was simple and elegant in a fitted black dress with a silver key necklace dipping down across the top of her exposed collarbone.

"Hello, Ms. O'Connor, you're in early today, and . . ." The young woman looked curiously over at Peter.

"Amanda, this is Dr. Schneider. He and his partner are doing some consulting work for COLI*GO," Celine said with a slightly higher pitched voice than normal. "This is Amanda MacDonald, my chief of staff."

"Pleasure to meet you, Ms. MacDonald," Peter said, extending his hand to shake hers.

"I need you to create two anonymous access badges to the lower lab. One for Dr. Schneider and one for his associate," Celine instructed. A sad but small smile inched across Celine's face. "And this needs to stay off any records. It's highly confidential."

Amanda nodded, leading Celine and Peter to Celine's office. Amanda's long fingers typed quickly across her device, and in a matter of moments, two plastic cards printed from the small machine under her desk. Amanda handed them over to Peter with a sense of hesitancy, her eyes never once leaving Celine.

"Will I get to meet your associate, Dr. Schneider? Just so I know not to call security on them?" Amanda asked, finally shifting her gaze over to him.

Peter's shoulders tightened, and his body stilled. He hadn't anticipated any kind of push back or hesitancy from Amanda after Celine helped devise this plan. Celine assured him Amanda was accommodating and unassuming, but the woman had an uncanny sense of curiosity.

"I'll be sure to introduce you to Dr. Walsh when she arrives next time."

"I look forward to meeting her," Amanda said with a wide, attractive smile. She looked back over at Celine. "Should I still cancel your last meeting today so that you can make the dinner you're scheduled to attend?"

Celine's eyes softened, and Peter noticed the corners growing wet from holding back tears. Celine cleared her throat before addressing her chief of staff.

"Yes."

***

"This place still gives me the creeps, but at least it's quiet," Julie said, walking ahead of Peter and into the lower lab. The room wasn't equipped with the metal drawers against the walls. A crisp blue-gray color encompassed the otherwise empty space. A few small metal tables lined the middle of the room with some basic lab equipment and devices scattered sparsely on top.

"No one uses this space, so no one should bother you. No one knows you're even here except for me, Celine, and her chief of staff."

Julie nodded and placed her heavy bag down on the table. She meticulously removed vials of COL23—the antidote—along with a simulation device Peter stole from the future version of COLI*GO. Another device emerged from the contents of Julie's bag, one that stored all the clinical trial results and data from every study performed on the drug. She looked back over at Peter and chuckled.

"You don't have to stay here, Peter. I'm highly capable of taking care of myself."

Peter's eyes glanced around the room hesitantly. He was afraid of Mick Taylor, the man who seemed to always find him in his travels through time. It didn't matter how careful Peter was in his planning;

there wasn't a trip to the past where he didn't run into his foe.

"I want to help," he said, approaching the table.

Julie booted up her device and handed Peter a set of plastic gloves. It'd been a long time since Peter or Julie did any actual testing or research—they'd both reached the point in their careers where they managed people and projects and were so far removed from this part of the scientific process. The cool blue latex felt itchy on Peter's skin as he adjusted his hand inside. His fingers lingered on the touch screen at Julie's notes from all the research done on the antidote. Peter had already read it all, after she was initially missing and when Mick implied the antidote wasn't salvageable for any patients beyond Alzheimer's.

"What went wrong, you think, with Colin?" Peter asked, the mysterious question he never understood the answer to.

Julie sighed, clearly unready to admit the gray area of ethics she crossed by treating the governor with her unapproved drug.

"The real culprit is difficult to understand," Julie said, finally matching Peter's stare. "But I've narrowed down the reason to two possibilities. Either Colin didn't receive the right amount of doses, which I suspected in the end, or he experienced a relapse, some traumatic event that caused the antidote to accidentally identify the incorrect neurotransmitters in his brain. There's always the possibility of both these realities being the reason. Because of all these unknown variables, I can't say for certain."

"Well, if it is the first reason, the issue would be remedied if he retook the antidote and followed the correct course of therapy. Did he ever finish his last treatments?" Peter asked, noticing Julie close her eyes.

"I don't know," Julie said in an unconvincing lie. "What did you and the team find from the patients in the clinical trials?"

"Similar results to what you outlined regarding Colin, but they all completed therapy," Peter answered, hovering over Julie's device and bringing up the results on the screen. "Some documentation was captured that could resemble relapses."

Julie pulled up the data sets and formatted everything in the file into a chart. A small gasp escaped her as she leaned in closer, enlarging the dots along the graph. Peter's eyes followed her pointer finger. Every patient in the study experienced a relapse within the same four-day window: exactly halfway through their treatment journey. The uncanny and unlikeliness of such similarities struck both Peter as odd. A small glimmer of excitement replaced the fear on Julie's face.

"Peter! We need to check all the data from these dates," she said, pointing to the charts. "And then we need to cross-reference the lot numbers of the drug and see if there are any correlations or similarities and rule out expired drugs. We might be on to something."

Peter grinned, helping Julie discover the real failure behind the antidote was the right thing to do. Together, they jotted down various notes and outlined the missing information they needed to gather when they returned to the present.

"Can I ask you a sensitive question?" Peter gripped the side of the table.

Julie nodded, her eyes wide with empathy.

"Do you remember what happened to you when The Supreme kidnapped you to make you a hybrid?"

Julie closed her eyes and shook her head. Peter wondered if she regretted sharing this experience with him, but he had to ask her about the scar on her neck. He needed the truth spelled out in front of him.

"I honestly don't remember what happened. I had a strange dream sometime after the procedure, but I'm not sure how reliable the nightmare is regarding the accuracy of what actually happened. My brain was trying to regain control of a foreign object inside it."

"I understand," Peter said, shifting uncomfortably from one foot to the other. "Anna Garcia is helping me investigate the implications from the lower lab. The Supreme wouldn't admit on her trial about who helped her. There were accusations that the other culprit was you, but she denied that. Based on your likeability in The City, no one believed you could have been involved."

Julie's jaw dropped a bit at the accusation.

"Clearly, I didn't believe that either. But I'm just being honest. The only other being we know involved was Nolan, an android researcher here at COLI*GO."

"Are his scales purple?" Julie asked cautiously, grabbing Peter's hands with her own shaky ones.

"Yes," Peter answered in a whisper.

"That's what I remember from my dream." Julie let go of him.

Her fingers went to her ugly enlarged scar and delicately traced the protruded silvery skin.

"I know who helped The Supreme, but please don't be angry with me, Peter. I'm not sure I can share that with you."

Peter stepped back, and anger rose from the pit of his stomach.

"That person helped me after Mick rescued me from the woods. I can't betray their confidence."

"The woods?" Peter asked, an odd instinct to wrap his arms around Julie and her trembling body overcame him. She felt small in his embrace as he held her and allowed her to cry.

"I'm missing back in the present because I'm supposed to be dead. I was supposed to die in the woods, but Mick rescued me. He came from some version of the future and brought me back to it, and the person who helped The Supreme perform all those surgeries removed the microchip from me. That's why my scar is so large. It's a re-incision. I know why you're asking for that person's identity. You're obligated to investigate that because it happened within the walls of COLI*GO, but I can't tell you." Her words were muffled between tears, and Peter rubbed her back slowly.

"Can you at least answer this question?" Peter asked, pulling Julie away from his chest so that their eyes met. "Was it Colin who tried to kill you?"

Julie aggressively pushed Peter away and faced the other direction. "I need your help fixing the antidote, Peter. Are you going to help me, or are you going to interrogate me about things I cannot change?" Julie asked with a harshness in the tone of her voice.

The space between her and Peter grew smaller, and her non-answer provided the truth behind how sinister Colin O'Connor really was.

"I'm disappointed in you, Julie. I thought you were stronger than this," Peter shot back, unsure if he was mad at Julie or if he pitied her.

"Be careful of your accusations, Peter," Julie warned with anger in her ocean blue eyes. "I've been to hell and back. I've had someone inside my brain twice. I've died several times. I'm not supposed to be alive. I've fallen from a cliff and plummeted onto the shards of pointy rocks. I've been stabbed twenty-three times. But I'm still here. You don't know what I'm truly capable of. No one does. I'm stronger than anyone seems to believe, and I will succeed in fixing the antidote even if that's what truly kills me."

"Why are you fighting against me half the time?" Peter complained, raising his hands in the air. "Yes, I'm loyal to Celine and I always will be, but why aren't you? She wants me to shield you from the dangers of her own brother, the dangers of Mick, and even the dangers of The Supreme. What happened to you when Mick saved you the first time? How did he make sure you didn't die?"

"I won't tell you who helped The Supreme, Peter."

"I don't care about that! I just don't want to have to rely on Mick to save you." Peter's voice rose slightly.

"Save me?"

"You're in danger. Not now but in the future. I don't know what happens when a time traveler dies, but you might die again. What if I can't bring you back like he did?" Peter sat on the stool beside Julie and grabbed her hands in his.

"Peter," Julie said with a longing sense of sympathy. "I'll go back to that night. I've died before while I was traveling time. That's what happens—you end up back in the original place where you were supposed to die. Based on Mick's research, only a time traveler can truly kill another time traveler."

Peter's skin paled with dread.

"I need to tell Celine," he responded, rising from his seat and pacing around the room. "And now we really need to make sure that Mick doesn't find you. He's pursuing you."

"I think you're wrong about Mick."

"So you're actually talking to and working with Mick and me?" Peter asked, a dark shadow covering half his face.

"No," Julie said confidently, and Peter believed her. "But you have to understand that Mick is my friend."

"Was," Peter corrected with a twinge of disgust in his mouth. "Mick was your friend. I went to the future. I couldn't help it, and now I know what happens."

"What did I tell you about traveling to the future, Peter?" Julie nearly screamed at him. "The future is dangerous and isn't always the same. Sometimes it changes. Time travel to the future hurts your body and causes internal harm. Don't do that again."

Peter noted his reflection on the screen. The wrinkles in his forehead now more noticeable and prominent.

"Please listen to what I have to say. For your safety," Peter pleaded with her.

"No. I'm here to fix the antidote. And if you want to help me, great. If not, I'll tell you when I have the answer and you can leave me alone."

Peter sighed. He should have expected this. Julie did always infuriate him with her stubbornness and inflexibility in her morals and beliefs. He shouldn't have been surprised by their disagreement. It by far wasn't their first.

"Okay," Peter relented. "I'll stay here and help you. I won't tell you what happens in the future."

Chapter 24
Julie

November 2nd, 37 A.R.

The lower lab was empty when Julie traveled back in time to study the antidote. No one bothered her here, and the freedoms these trips provided kept her focused on the larger plan.

Being back in a lab gifted Julie with a kick of adrenaline and excitement that she missed. While in her management position for the latter half of her short career, she felt sheltered from her favorite part about COLI*GO—the science. Her first few years after The University, Julie made friends with all her colleagues and spent the little free time she had forging relationships and networking. Gaining their trust and support became her priority. She intuitively knew without it, she wouldn't have been successful in her role as interim CEO.

Julie's loneliness in the lab didn't bother her. Julie felt a sting of happiness being back at COLI*GO even if this COLI*GO wasn't the same one she experienced. No one here recognized her but always provided polite "hellos" and "good mornings" as she made her way throughout the glass skyscraper. Julie co-existed with society when she traveled back to 37 A.R. to work on the antidote. The wild and intoxicating sense of autonomy coursed through her veins, her months of isolation back in her present a deep scar that she mentally added among her numerous physical ones.

She thought back to when Peter asked her what went wrong with Colin and his treatment. She watched Colin nearly nightly from the carriage house, and the image of countless unopened vials of COL23 lining the shelf in his refrigerator wounded her. She originally gave them to Jones—a full course of treatment—and hoped Colin would take the drug both for himself and her.

But he never touched them. He left the doses as is.

At first, Julie didn't understand his reasoning, but over time, she realized why. Logging countless hours of observation and study over the O'Connor townhouse only scratched the surface on the impossible code. Colin wasn't ready to give up It from his life. He saw no purpose if he were to be alone.

Julie contemplated right then and there about going over to the back door, knocking loudly, and asking him to reconsider and help himself before it was too late—before he did anything dangerous again.

But she didn't.

Julie learned the difference between watching Colin work through his grief and It work through his. It kept himself busy, transforming Colin's study into a room with a neatly stacked pile of books. He would read for hours and escape the world before closing the book and placing it meticulously back where it belonged. Other days, It ran purposefully uphill at full speed on the treadmill.

Colin insisted on rotating around the house aimlessly, wandering the halls, looking for Celine, and helping her with simple tasks. He fixed every leaky faucet and corrected each slanted shelf inside the townhouse.

It thrived on creating a controlled, purposeful environment. Colin thrived on others creating a sense of purpose and structure for him.

And that is why he will not give up It.

Julie took her personal device out of her lab coat and stared at the screen. Technology was a strange concept as a time traveler, but her personal device still worked no matter where she was, stuck in the actual confines of the present.

The date stamp on her message remained from the day she traveled time. The loneliness Julie faced made her bond with Elsie stronger—although they never physically saw one another. Elsie was a great confidant and a solid friend, and the two exchanged multiple messages daily.

To: 617–345–8709
From: 617–333–2985
Date Sent: April 30th, 47 A.R.

Subject: Winston Churchill

{Message Encryption}

Elsie,

I have a confession to make about time travel. The act is inebriating. The control, the sense of intrigue and terror, that the smallest movement can alter time as we know it. I'm beginning to understand why Mick is addicted to time travel. There's great responsibility and fear that accompanies these sensations, but I believe *history will be kind to me, for I intend to write it.*

There must be some type of chemical reaction that occurs in the brain when a person uses the device. Logically, no one should feel the endorphin high associated with this devious act. If I survive fixing the antidote, my next scientific experiment will be on the effects of time travel within the human brain. An area accidentally overlooked by my (former?) friend and colleague, Mick Taylor.

I don't blame Mick for not evaluating this aspect—he focused solely on hematology in his studies because blood is his expertise.

I'm writing you this admission because I want you to remind me that I have good intentions if I ever become corrupted.

Thank you for being a friend during these dark times.

Best,
Julie

"What are you and Dr. Schneider working on?" a timid voice from the doorway asked.

Julie looked up from her device and smiled. Peter and Celine told her one other person knew a little bit about what happened in the lower lab here, one person whom Celine trusted above all else—her chief of staff.

"A potential new drug," Julie answered while taking in the beautiful woman who now stood before her.

Amanda MacDonald wore a tightly fitted black dress and bright purple stilettos. Her honey-blonde hair was pulled back in a tight, neat bun, and her cherry red lips were turned upright into an attractive smile.

"What kind of drug?" Amanda asked, her delicate hand resting on the metal table.

Her eyes never left Julie, and she felt like a gazelle in the desert being eyed down by a hungry lioness.

"A neurological asset."

"Oh," Amanda said, her bright red mouth opening slightly with enthusiasm, "I know what you're working on: COL2120."

COL2120, Julie chuckled in her own mind. *The drug I had to spend years fixing while the antidote sat in Martin's desk drawer. That awful thing.*

When COLI*GO offered Julie a job after graduating from The University and paid her upfront for the rights to her antidote, she had been ecstatic. But instead of allowing her to continue working on the drug she developed, they insisted she join the team supporting the company's largest and most profitable drug, COL2120.

Speculation always surrounded COL2120 because of its tainted story of initial approval. But Julie worked diligently with Peter to discover multiple indications and fixed the errors surrounding the gene therapy technology. COL2120 originally received approval from The Legislature in 38 A.R. and served as the foundation that helped finance most of COLI*GO's pipeline. Without COL2120, the company wouldn't have stayed afloat.

"I'm Amanda MacDonald, by the way," she said and outstretched her hand to shake Julie's.

"Dr. Julie Walsh," Julie responded, grabbing Amanda's hand enthusiastically.

"I didn't mean to bother you, but I was a bit bored upstairs," Amanda said while stretching her body out against the table. "Celine and the rest of The Board are in a very important meeting that I'm not allowed to attend."

"What exactly do you do here at COLI*GO?" Julie asked, trying to make conversation even though she already knew.

Peter warned her about Celine's curious staffer who had provided them access to the lower lab and was considered the keeper of Celine's secrets.

Amanda brought her hand up to her face and studied her perfectly manicured nails. She grabbed a shiny silver key necklace hanging from her neck and played with the charm. The piece looked oddly familiar, and Julie heard her heart pick up its pace inside her chest.

The laundry room. The place where Colin keeps all his victim's trinkets.

A slight sense of fear trickled inside Julie, but another opportunistic side of her wanted to understand why such a woman ended up on Colin and It's hit list.

"I'm Celine's chief of staff. My responsibilities vary wildly on the day from scheduling meetings for The Board of Directors to providing input on meeting notes and keeping Celine company when she's lonely." Amanda's eyebrows raised suggestively, and Julie took the hint to mean their relationship wasn't strictly professional. "So what are you? In your late twenties, early thirties?"

"I turn thirty this month," Julie answered, shifting her eyes back down to her work and hoping Amanda would take the hint and leave. Julie still had more tests to run on the antidote today before she traveled back to the present.

"Really?" Amanda exclaimed. "We should go out and celebrate."

"I don't know if that's a good idea."

She came here to work on the antidote and for no other purpose. She didn't want to change or impact time with any decisions she made while visiting 37 A.R. But the temptation to interact with another person who wasn't Peter or Joel enticed her.

"Oh, please," Amanda begged, her smile growing larger. "I know a really great secluded spot around the corner. And you seem kind of lonely, no offense."

A laugh escaped Julie. There was definitely something conniving and intoxicating about this woman. How had she so easily convinced her?

"Okay, fine. But just one drink."

The two left COLI*GO and walked toward the small square near the bridge that connected The River with the rest of The City. Julie knew most of the bars here. The University wasn't too far away, and these were places she, Mick, and Jones had ventured to in college. When Julie worked at COLI*GO, she and her colleagues only hit up these spots to avoid long and daunting trips to The Port.

The pair entered a tiny hole-in-the-wall establishment and took a seat in the far corner of the bar. Amanda ordered them a bottle of Zinfandel and smiled up at Julie, knowing she pushed the limit of Julie's one drink contention.

"So tell me the real reason Celine is sticking a cute, intelligent mind like yours down in a dusty old basement laboratory?" Amanda asked after they were halfway through their first glass.

Julie longed to tell someone that she was trying to uncover the faultiness of the antidote based on varying and frustrating clinical trial data, but she couldn't. The antidote worked well with Alzheimer's patients, but the problem for patients with psychological disorders was more deeply rooted in the unpredictability of their disease on the brain. If they experienced any kind of triggering event during treatment, the antidote was rendered mostly useless. Julie finally concluded the problem with her drug was its half-life.

The only real solution would be creating a new molecule that only needed to be injected once rather than once a week over the course of six months.

Peter's eyes grew wide when Julie suggested this, but he also seemed confident enough that Julie could create the new drug. The process was daunting, especially while working mostly alone. Julie spent hours tirelessly in the lab, unsure if her exhaustion stemmed from the stress of reinventing the antidote or if her time travel high was subsiding.

Today had been particularly groundbreaking. She attempted her new molecule in a testing model and uncovered she accidentally created a drug that sped up the progression of the disease rather than curing it. Now she knew which components were attracted to toxins in her original antidote.

"I'm basically throwing the drug on its head and recreating it," Julie answered Amanda as the alcohol zipped through her body.

"Huh. Well, everyone on The Board keeps saying COL2120 is going to change the company. This is 'the' drug," Amanda said, taking a deep sip from her oval-shaped wine glass.

Julie fixated on the lipstick stain left on the rim of Amanda's glass, and her mind swirled from the booze and illicit memories of her and Colin.

I miss him.

Julie had been good about keeping her thoughts at bay while she worked on the antidote, time being a bit of an issue even though she had infinite amounts of it.

"COL2120? Well, it is going to change the company. Without COL2120, COLI*GO will fail." The words whirled out of Julie uncontrollably. "The drug is amazing and so many patients will benefit from it, but it isn't perfect. And COLI*GO has so many other opportunities they're delaying based on just this one asset."

Amanda nodded and filled Julie's glass with more red wine. Amanda's gaze drifted over to Julie's scar and the small blotches at the bottom. Her eyes widened, but she didn't mention her observation.

"I want to learn more about COL2120 because, you're right, that's all The Board talks about. Honestly, I would love to move out of Celine's chief of staff position and be the product lead for the drug," Amanda confessed, her admission of lofty career ambitions something Julie admired and connected with. "I imagine myself on the team launching COL2120. While I'm honored The Board thinks I'm smart enough to guide them in broader discussions and areas of the business, I'm tired of sitting behind a desk and being at Celine's beck and call. I want to be part of the action."

"I understand. Being stuck in a role while longing for a different one is never a good place to be in. Trust me, I know," Julie said, thinking about her own journey.

Amanda nodded sympathetically, and she looked over at the other end of the bar. "Those guys are staring at you."

"They're not staring at me. They're ogling over you," Julie responded with a raised brow.

Julie was plain compared to the tall gorgeous blonde at her side. Understanding Celine's infatuation with Amanda was simple, and knowing Amanda would eventually be Colin and It's victim, Julie assumed he waded in those waters too.

Julie wasn't naïve to Colin's sexual exploits before her, but instead of jealousy, she felt a small, sinister side of herself wanting to learn more about Amanda, pull out the bits and pieces that highlighted why someone like him would engage with both herself and this woman. Amanda was obviously charming—a trait Julie felt she lacked—but the drive behind this woman was what made her truly appealing in Julie's eyes.

"My job is demanding, and my personal life is a mess. I already have two lovers. I don't think I could juggle a third." Amanda tipsily laughed.

The confirmation Julie needed.

Amanda looked back over at Julie with a lighthearted smile.

"Those are stories for another night and will require two bottles of wine. But enough about my escapades. Tell me everything you know about COL2120 so that I can impress Celine when I ask her for the role?"

Julie nodded and genuinely smiled. "How much wine do we have left?"

Amanda tilted the bottle slightly, revealing they still had about half a bottle. Speaking to another intelligent, thought-provoking woman invigorated Julie. She spent another two hours with the lovely and enchanting creature, hoping she could provide her with some slight insights to land the job of her dreams.

"I should really get going," Julie said while looking at her half-filled glass and the nearly empty bottle of wine. She was afraid to stand up right away with how drunk she felt.

"Well, finish your glass first," Amanda said and clinked her glass against Julie's. "I'm glad I met you, Dr. Walsh."

"I'm glad I met you too," Julie responded with a wicked smile.

Chapter 25
Mick

August 31st, 35 A.R.

The trickery of Mick's alternate time travel identities wasn't much different from Colin's belief in It. Mick didn't realize the oddity of his family dynamics when he was younger until he discovered his own time loop. These escapes to the past were really just his way of dealing with everything that would happen in the future. He played various pieces in The Supreme's grand plan.

The apartment he occupied in The Port was situated above the art studio below him. Jeb Taylor's art studio.

Growing up, Mick believed Jeb Taylor was his uncle—an uncle who sometimes held an affection for him, the one who helped finance his tuition at The University and attempted to help him escape the grip of The Supreme.

In his youth, Jeb Taylor was a time travel version of himself.

Uncle Jeb did actually exist as a different person, but the man flew to The City after stealing money from the family farm in The Countryside. The real Jeb was an artist who concocted beautiful paintings—mostly sceneries that were pure and lovely. His images grew darker as his addiction to drugs consumed his soul. An imitation that Mick could easily convey later.

Mick walked into Uncle Jeb's apartment and found him dead. He had overdosed, and his body hung sideways off the bed. Mick slowly approached his uncle's lifeless body and sighed. At the time he needed a living persona in the past so that he could funnel money and sustain a life of time travel. Jeb had funds tucked away, and a younger version of Mick would travel to The City very soon and ask for help with school and an escape from the toxic environment in The Countryside. A depressing life. Mick couldn't leave his youthful self with no options.

Thus, the time loop was created.

Jeb Taylor and Mick shared an uncanny resemblance anyways, and with the horrid effects of time travel aging Mick's body, the deep, cracked lines across his skin matched his uncle's. There was no better opportunity than to consume the man's life as if he had never died.

And Mick had Isabella. She grimaced when he handed her his uncle's eyeballs and asked her to create the contact lenses from them. Isabella didn't ask too many questions and carefully provided him with the security that even an android scanned him, they wouldn't know the difference between him and his uncle. And pretending to be someone else gave him a chance as the ultimate bishop piece in The Supreme's and Colin's infinite game of chess.

We're all pieces on the board, but at least I have a wide range of movement and opportunity.

Mick was swift and agile, able to warn his future self, Julie, and, to some extent, Jones about the future and its collapse. He took this chance to feed Colin O'Connor with the drugs that drove a wedge between him and Julie, drugs that ignited the portion of his brain occupied by It. He was also instrumental in helping The Supreme and Isabella obtain humans to transform into hybrids and pushed her mission forward when no one else could move that quickly.

Mick glanced over at the clock and sighed. He didn't normally indulge in the trafficked drugs from COLI*GO, but they helped him sleep through unbearable nights. The nights where he really thought about the repercussions of his actions. He gulped, thinking of Jones shooting him in the courtroom in the future. That physical body of his plundered, but the moment his eyes closed and opened again, Mick stood before the place and time where his actual body died.

A place he didn't want to think about.

The invincibility as a time traveler simultaneously existed as both intoxicating and painful.

A slight knock on the door sounded, and Mick stood, ready to welcome the younger, inexperienced version of himself. The unassuming hope and optimism of a better life here in The City smeared across a younger Mick's face. He threw his backpack with the little number of possessions he owned onto the couch.

"When do your classes start?" Mick asked his younger self, already knowing the answer.

"Next week! I can't believe it's finally here!" The excitement rang through his otherwise baritone voice.

"You have six years ahead of you for your PhD program, Mick. That's a lot more time than you think."

The younger Mick rolled his eyes and unzipped his backpack. He slowly removed his dusty, out-of-style clothing and placed the items on the air mattress in the corner of the living room.

"Have you thought about your area of study?" he probed, walking over to the window that overlooked the large salty harbor that separated The Port from The Harbor. If Mick squinted hard enough, he could make out the triple-decker that he and Jones would eventually call home.

"I'm sticking to my research in blood. Hematology makes sense to me. Maybe I'll take the route to become a doctor, but I also kind of like just sitting in a lab and exploring the structure, the make-up of the proteins," young Mick said with glee.

"What's so fascinating about blood?" the Mick pretending to be Jeb asked.

"It stores so much information about a person. I could tell you if you were going to develop a certain condition in the future based on looking at your blood now." His confidence gleamed from a wide adolescent smile.

Mick turned and looked away, knowing what was about to escape him. He remembered these words; he remembered this moment. This was the moment, the idea that changed his life when he was younger.

"If our blood knows so much about the future, imagine if you could use it to travel there?"

***

Mick looked down at the blank canvas in front of him. There wasn't much activity happening in Jeb's studio today, and he needed to produce more work. He needed inspiration and had none—life seemed so horrible to him, knowing what he knew.

The pills in the back room, stashed inside the locked cabinet, taunted him. Mick knew what became of Colin when he consumed these drugs in the future, that these drugs also took away his true uncle's life. But Mick couldn't help himself. He needed the seedy escape—to be transported to a place where he didn't have to think, a place where he could simply be.

The high was even more intoxicating than the last time Mick indulged, and the vibrant paint colors stimulated him. Hours flew by as Mick portrayed the several terrifying events of the future. Each mural portrayed a significant killing from The City's uncaught serial killer. The large hand grasping the throats of delicate women.

Mick painted a blonde first, paying homage to Amanda MacDonald even though she wasn't Colin's first kill. He moved on, swirling chestnut curls around another pale figure: Kendra Washington, Representative Kennsington's future legislative aide. Lexi Pvadinish's dark skin and features coursed through his paintbrush next.

The emotions and anger flooded out of Mick in a tumble as he painted Julie. His friend—his only friend, the only person he trusted with his life.

So much so, I trust her to end it for me if it comes to it.

Her blue eyes were a hauntingly beautiful warning and the most urgent and horrific of the series he crafted. The colors swirled together, and he signed his uncle's name on the bottom.

When Mick looked out the front windows, dusk had set upon The Port neighborhood. A small jingle sounded from the entrance door, and he looked over with bloodshot eyes.

"Yah, this guy is wicked awesome." A husky and strong City accent sounded in his ears.

Kathleen Murphy.

Mick befriended Colin's legislative aide easily, finding her brute personality a comfort.

He straightened up, quickly stashing his disturbing and violent series into the art studio's back office before approaching the front of the gallery.

"Can I help you?" Mick asked, surprised but happy to find

Kathleen in his presence again.

"Yah." Kathleen smiled brightly and looked over at the handsome man beside her. "My brotha-in-law and I were lookin' for a landscape paintin' to give my motha-in-law for her birthday."

Kathleen's companion had a wholesome smile with large lips and tan skin. Her husband's brother was an attractive man.

"I can definitely show you some great pieces I have. Any particular preferences regarding scenery?" Mick asked, looking down at his paint-stained hands and clothes. He looked like a complete madman, and embarrassment rose warmly in his cheeks.

"A cityscape would be nice," Kathleen's brother-in-law interjected. "I'm Keith, Keith Henderson."

Mick outstretched his hand to shake Keith's. "Jeb Taylor."

Keith smiled at Mick, the same look that spread across Jones's face the first time they met one another. Mick contemplated the implications of exploring a personal life with his time travel.

That might not be a bad thing.

PART SIX

The Present

"Pardon my sanity in a world insane."
—Emily Dickinson

Chapter 26
The Supreme

April 27th, 47 A.R.

The Supreme waited in her cell, whispers of the horrors imprinting across The City loitering between the prison guards. People and androids waged war—mobs and riots broke out in the streets. They were terrified of the new, mostly undetectable species intertwined within their society.

Posse hominems.

Being alone and isolated in prison gave The Supreme perspective, one she hadn't expected in this state of loneliness. Her full understanding and appreciation of It being trapped from the antidote now comprehended in her processor—his awful entrapment was much like her own. It's retelling of his experience plagued her much as the memories infected Colin.

So this is how It felt, The Supreme pondered.

The Supreme didn't know which day it was or even the time. Her entertainment came from finding imperfections on the beige-painted walls. There were noticeable chips in the paint, but they never seemed to stay in the same place.

She wondered when Jones would return and let her know what would happen when she crossed the threshold of FACERE. Her predecessor was always wary of FACERE and its complete ability to not only develop but also test androids in unimaginable ways. Edward constantly fought The Legislature on FACERE's freedoms, considering the organization's liberties as an injustice to all.

Edward also hated his given name; he's the one who insisted I always be called The Supreme, she reminded herself.

Colin and Celine still occasionally called The Supreme by her name, but no one else had in a very long time. She doubted anyone even knew her given name. Once she assumed the position of supreme, she left that part of her life behind her.

The yellow-scaled android guard walked by and nodded at her through the small circular window in her door. She captured his loyalty early on. Androids still respected The Supreme and what she had accomplished in liberties for them. But they were also programmed to protect The Constituency. The Supreme's transgressions were no longer considered light crimes and still implicated her in hurting humans. Hurting society.

The Supreme noted a new piece of paint chipping on the walls across her cot. Being on this side of madness caused various shimmers on her scales. Normally, the change of amber to gold gave away her ability to understand human feelings. The idea of her scales revealing her true intentions was now irrelevant. Her scales pulsated with physical hurt across her body.

Emilia thought fondly of Edward's scales when looking at her own. His were golden, too, but changed to a tangerine hue when in her presence and in the presence of any important dignitary. Edward had been a majestic android, and she appreciated his own acknowledgment and dangers of his attractiveness.

Edward championed the tradition for the governor to be the sponsor of the android child who would serve as the next supreme. When FACERE announced Emilia as his successor, he refused to go near her.

Sex didn't matter in the same ways to androids as it did to humans, but Edward didn't have a partner. A single male android raising a female android of equal power and affinity raised eyebrows, no matter how much of a father figure he wanted to be for Emilia. Humans were skeptical of androids to begin with, and demeaning them in any way imaginable to paint their own narratives and craft their own tales was too risky. Those humans later became known as Humanizers.

Edward confided in Emilia later—when she was an adult—that his other motive in this push for tradition was so that she could learn the ins and outs of politics at a young age and garner insider information on old bloodline families.

Regardless of the skepticism The Legislature had of Edward when she finally began studying underneath him, Emilia had a fondness for females over males. She rarely indulged in any acts of affection or intimacy, and her sole focus was simply on advancing power for androids in society. By the age of forty-five, Emilia had only ever gone as far as kissing a woman.

Androids weren't meant to suppress their sexual desires, but they were expected to maintain control over their feelings—feelings they weren't supposed to experience too much of anyways. But androids were like humans, and both wanted and needed sex. Emilia hadn't experienced the affections of another, but she still appreciated and longed for intimacy and love—no matter how much she hated admitting it.

The vibrant passion between Colin O'Connor and Julie Walsh flashed before her. The imaginings of Colin's hands over Julie's flushed skin and the sight of him tasting the most intimate parts of her made Emilia experience a burning she didn't know existed.

The Supreme hardly experienced the emotion of regret, it wasn't programmed inside her, but the feeling of curiosity flooded through her knowing she hadn't allowed herself the opportunity to enjoy life in the same ways Colin enjoyed his. He made time for his pleasures and cravings while still successfully managing his role as the governor.

Why did I feel like I couldn't do the same? The Supreme wondered while staring at the same paint chip that occupied her time yesterday. *Is it because I'm a woman? And an android woman at that?*

Her eyes shifted to another chipped spot on the wall to free herself of those memories tucked deep within her processor.

Nothing was left for The Supreme once Jones handed her off to FACERE. There would be no more parading around The Capitol Building, whipping votes for and against humans. No longer would she experience the anticipation and excitement of long hours in Colin's office, his palpable agitation with her intrusions and Kathleen Murphy's speculative eyes.

Kathleen.

The Supreme missed Kathleen and despised sacrificing someone she actually enjoyed the company of. No one could ever replace Kathleen, not even Elsie Sullivan.

But Elsie Sullivan did fascinate The Supreme. The young woman was a human who didn't realize her own intelligence, despite having a mother in a prominent role within The Legislature. Elsie was lost without a full family to support her. Growing up with a caretaker or in the arms of Representative Sullivan's legislative aide was another miss on the otherwise smart woman who raised her. Elsie didn't need a father, and she would truly hate him if she knew him.

And that's why I turned her into a posse hominem.

Elsie's inability to know her true potential made her a perfect person for The Supreme to inflict into Colin's life even while she was inside the confines of jail. Colin would instinctively trust the woman for the simple fact that she subconsciously reminded him of a harsher, rougher-around-the-edges version of himself.

Elsie now had her own "It," and The Supreme suspected the real It was lonely.

It deserves a devilish mentee; there always needs to be an It even after It is gone. The Supreme smirked in her cell alone. *Elsie is my last parting gift to Colin before FACERE destroys me.*

The Supreme didn't know when the new commissioner would grace her with his shiny emerald-green scales, and she didn't care if Maggie Rivera tried changing her processor.

Maggie Rivera was an easy woman, one who cared too much about keeping up with old bloodline families even though she wasn't part of one. She made the right mistakes and trusted snakes too easily. The Supreme even suspected Jones recognized this weakness in Maggie.

Maggie thinks she can take everyone down and rise to the top. But she can't.

Emilia's eyes widened, and her scales illuminated a deeper orange tone. Her chance for someone to save her from her inevitable fate was futile, but being saved wasn't imperative to her plan. She played her part, and she played it well.

Mick would eventually find her. The Supreme wouldn't remain docile for too long, even if Maggie completely stripped her microchip.

That bitch can try her hardest, but I know what will become of her.

Comfort in knowing certain aspects of the future calmed The Supreme and kept her moving forward during uncertainty. Mick's own hang-ups with the future came from him losing his friend Julie.

He made for a terrible human; his betrayals tormented him in ways that made The Supreme question his loyalty.

But he had to find her—that was the only move on the board she had little control over. She needed the opportunity to turn on the microchip in Julie's brain to win the game.

Only Julie can truly kill Colin. The Supreme sighed at this inevitable point and wished she could complete the act. Her eyes stuck to another faded paint chip before she closed them.

When The Supreme saw Colin at her trial, he looked terrible.

Colin might not have the ability to placate The Legislature in such despair, but It . . . It might thrive in this environment and take control.

***

Commissioner Jones sat across from The Supreme in her holding cell for the last time. The Legislature was handing her over to FACERE for evaluation of her microchip and processor. Defects weren't an option—especially one in a future supreme.

The next supreme, an android with the given name Ethan, was too young to take over the responsibilities of the role. They had placed him with former Representative Sullivan as his sponsor until Colin married Isabella. Maggie Rivera's statement claimed that the governor couldn't raise a child android alone alongside his schedule. Roslyn was retired, but Emilia had been raised by Henry; FACERE hadn't taken her away after Melanie O'Connor died. Not that it mattered to The Supreme who took her place or if she would get to continue on with her role after all was said and done.

The Legislature hadn't decided if reprogramming Emilia was an option and what they would do with her after she was reprogrammed. Talks of appointing a new supreme were already in the works, and the commissioner shared with her that FACERE was fast at work creating a new microchip for the unnamed successor.

The silence between Jones and Emilia continued. She wasn't sure what to say but felt obligated because she spent most of her time alone these days.

"When will this hellhole I'm in finally be over?" Emilia asked.

The commissioner appeared empathetic, an emotion he seemed not only to understand but also to experience himself. His scales flickered, and he didn't try hiding this from Emilia. She knew his true powers.

"I don't want to live if I can't understand emotions, Jones," she admitted, hoping the familiarity of using his name soothed him. "What will they do to me?"

Jones closed his eyes as his scales visibly pulsed in a painful manner. "They'll examine your microchip and run tests on your processor. There's talk about clearing your microchip so that you won't remember anything. I've advocated against that."

His answer didn't provide The Supreme with any sense of comfort.

"What kind of sway do you even have at FACERE?"

Jones opened his eyes, and a flash of bashfulness ran across his face before subsiding. The Supreme's stubbornness and ruthlessness came from her understanding too much, and she hoped he didn't find her too abrasive and rude.

"I've gotten close to Maggie," Jones admitted. "I'm trying to help you, Madam Supreme. You need to understand that."

The Supreme's loud, husky chuckle broke the seriousness in her previous demeanor. Jones's eyes zoomed in closer with curiosity.

"Oh, God." Emilia continued laughing. "You're sleeping with her."

"What I do in my personal time is none of your concern. But if you want to know, I've struggled with the end of my relationship with Mick. I need something, some kind of solace. I can only find that with humans. I hope someone like you would at least have some sense of sympathy for this struggle."

"I do, to an extent. See, Jones, I understand all human emotions, but I don't experience them all for myself. That's the difference between us. Julie programmed you to understand and experience. Edward programmed me to understand all and experience only a few."

"How? How could he even do that? Where did he learn?" Jones asked quietly, looking away.

This was the first honest conversation The Supreme and Jones had with one another, and she couldn't help but wonder if it was because the android pitied her or if he truly cared.

"I'm honestly not sure, Commissioner."

They stood, and Jones grabbed her handcuffed arm, guiding her out of the cell. The silent ride over to FACERE took only a matter of minutes, with its location in The River conveniently off a main roadway.

FACERE was exactly how The Supreme remembered it. The building stood high in the sky, looming over the empty streets of The City with a sorrowful but wounded presence as if the building itself didn't condone what happened within its confines.

"I hate this. I really do." Jones placed his head in his hands in the seat next to her. The vehicle hummed but remained in park.

"You know," The Supreme said, looking up at the cloudy sky, "you're just like Colin. You're the android version of him."

"How?" Jones shouted passionately. "We're nothing alike."

"You're both in love with people who will kill you."

Silence followed, and The Supreme's words hung in the air like a threatening premonition.

Chapter 27
The Governor

May 1st, 47 A.R.

Elsie trembled as she pulled her hair back into a sleek ponytail. Colin's eyes followed the black ink on her tattoo from her ear to the base of her neck. The tail of the snake was intricate, the scales shaded immaculately by the artist. Normally, her tattoo was hidden by her thick hair, but today, Elsie showed it off with pride.

She walked around the kitchen island and took in the O'Connor townhouse for the first time. It warned Colin about the darkness within Elsie—her interests an inkling like his own.

Colin's fingers tapped the countertop methodically as he looked up at Elsie with heavy eyes. Elsie was rough. Kathleen had been rough, but she was missing the grittiness that exuberated around Elsie's presence. The only thing about Elsie that bothered Colin was It's pause as if he didn't instinctively trust her.

But It rarely trusts anyone. He didn't even trust Julie.

The accusation swirled in his mind. Colin wanted to trust Elsie. He was optimistic about her, and she worked tirelessly to gain his trust over the last few weeks. And a part of Colin wanted to let go of the deviousness that kept The Legislature running. He had other plans for him and It.

And for Julie, if she ever returned.

"How do you do it?" Elsie asked in a faint voice. "How do you know when you're pushing someone too far?"

Colin smiled and rounded the corner of the island, standing inches away from Elsie. She would shortly meet with the man at FACERE on behalf of the governor.

"You must think about the bigger picture. When the lines are blurred, that's when you make mistakes. And mistakes are unacceptable. I've built a legacy here—you cannot ruin the reputation of the governor's office."

Elsie shook her head, unsatisfied with the non-answer Colin provided her.

"That's where I struggle. I don't have a lot of self-control."

"It takes practice." Colin smirked.

He watched Elsie walk toward the living room with her eyes dancing around his home. Her fingertips lingered above Julie's sweatshirt, which was laid out on the arm of the couch. Elsie looked back at Colin before swiftly averting her eyes.

"What's bothering you?" Colin asked, feeling guilty for not offering better advice to his willing legislative aide.

"I promised Commissioner Jones, but my loyalties lie with you. What I'm about to share with you isn't easy," Elsie responded, her eyelashes long and elegant compared to the rest of her persona.

Colin raised his brow. Trust worked both ways, and Elsie was about to betray Jones and bestow her faith in Colin. He needed to offer her something in return.

Elsie walked over to him with Julie's sweatshirt in her hands. The soft and worn material provided comfort once in Colin's.

"I know where Julie is."

Her words sharpened Colin's senses, and his heart thumped loudly in his chest.

"Have you spoken to her?" His eyes turned toward the carriage house, and he wasn't sure why.

"Yes, I communicate with her every day," Elsie responded. "Would you like the number?"

She held her device out to Colin, but he couldn't find the strength to take it. A million possibilities raced through his mind. He hadn't spoken with Julie since the night he drugged and stabbed her.

Colin shook his head no. "Julie and I have a very complicated relationship right now. Something happened between us." His eyes glossed over, this was the truth he needed to entrust with Elsie. "You must know she time travels. I'm not sure what happened, but back in January, I attempted to kill her. I brought her to the woods and stabbed her. I didn't want to, but The Supreme transformed Julie into a hybrid. I thought she would betray me. But now I know that assumption was wrong."

A small tear escaped the corner of Elsie's eye, and she placed her device back in her pocket. Colin appreciated that Elsie didn't respond to him.

"Is she safe?" Colin asked.

"Sort of." Elsie shifted her weight back and forth. "You won't like it, but she's safe enough while I work on getting her out of her situation. I wasn't sure if I should share this with you now or when I had a better plan. Jones told me not to. He said it would unhinge you, but I'm wasn't sure what he meant by that. I didn't know the full story."

"Where is Julie, Elsie?" Colin pushed the question harder this time. His fists clenched together tightly in a ball.

"Again," Elsie cautioned, stepping away from him to widen the space between them. The move of a smart fighter. "You won't like it, but Julie is hiding out at Joel Kennsington's house."

"No."

Regret flashed across her skin in a shade of pink.

"I'm not sure how she wound up there from when you . . . from when you stabbed her. But you have to do something. We have to do something. Joel Kennsington is a monster."

"We can't let our emotions get too involved." He was angered that Julie was trapped with that scoundrel of a man, but he was held at Joel's mercy too.

Elsie laughed. "Because you've clearly never made a decision that wasn't driven by emotion?"

Colin dropped Julie's sweatshirt on the couch and walked over to Elsie. He stood uncomfortably close to her, his towering presence clearly concerning her as she backed up against the kitchen island.

"Jones was right; this does unhinge me. But I don't think you truly understand how that could be a good thing."

Colin grabbed his device and headed toward the door to the garage. A twinkle in Elsie's eyes grew as she followed him down the stairs and over to the vehicle.

"Are you coming with me?"

Colin tossed the vehicle's key fob to her before answering. "I want to see what you're capable of, but I won't infringe on your opportunity to truly prove yourself. I could go for a ride, though."

Once they reached FACERE, Colin stopped in the small parking lot. He didn't want to risk running into Maggie. She lingered in the hallways; he was certain of it. And Elsie's scheduled meeting with Paul didn't include Colin—his massive presence would ruin whatever Elsie's plan was to get the man to confess his knowledge about the riots and murders.

Colin looked down at his notes on Paul McGuire. In the photo, he sat in his office with a stone-cold facial expression. Colin's eyes wandered down Elsie's arms, then back at the photo of the horrid man who worked with Kennsington. He had broad shoulders and a rough square jawline. The massive size of the man, even while sitting, indicated a sheer strength.

Colin's eyes lingered and she cleared her throat. Colin opened the glove box and grabbed Elsie's hand. A coolness from a tiny syringe passed between him and her.

"A sedative. Trust me, while I admire that you're a boxer, you're no good to me dead or severely injured if things go . . . awry," he whispered into Elsie's ear.

She nodded curtly and placed the syringe in her bag.

"I think I truly understand now. Meet me at my place in The Monument in an hour and a half," Elsie said with her hand on the car door handle.

Her witchy smile mirrored back at Colin, and he couldn't help but chuckle.

"Before you go," Colin said, looking around cautiously, "do you know where in The Monument the Walsh family lives?"

Elsie's body tensed, and she nodded. The Monument was one of those neighborhoods in The City where everyone knew everyone—families stayed with families, and neighbors helped one another. They were a close-knit community.

"I do. I'm not sure what your intentions are, but you're giving me a bad feeling."

Colin averted his eyes from Elsie, unable to handle the truth in her questioning glare. He closed his eyes briefly and let out a large sigh. A warm feeling spread from his icy hand, and when he opened his eyes, he noticed Elsie's hand squeezing his own.

"Southside of Monument Square," she said, letting go and pushing open the vehicle's door. Colin waited and watched her walk into FACERE before turning the car back on and punching Monument Square into the navigation.

***

Julie's childhood home was a corner unit that shone dimly in the dark and dusky shadows of the evening sky. This was the home Julie spent her formative years in, a home her father provided when he made the difficult decision to move his family from The Outskirts to The City for her mother to receive the care she needed.

The Walshes weren't poor by any stretch of the imagination, but looking at their humble double-decker, Colin recognized the vastly different upbringing Julie and he had from one another.

A young woman, remarkably similar in resemblance to Julie except for her brown hair, fumbled outside the front door. She checked over her shoulder toward the abandoned street. Colin presumed this was Becky, Julie's younger sister.

What are you doing out past curfew? he wondered as she promptly disappeared behind the front door.

Julie had shared with him the falling out she had with her sister. The two didn't really speak anymore, and Julie only came over to the house on Thursdays to have dinner with her father.

Colin looked down at his watch; he was due at Elsie's condo in an hour. Elsie lived in The Monument, only two blocks away from her mother, former Representative Sullivan. Colin wasn't sure why he was sitting here in the dark, alone in his car.

He contemplated knocking on the Walshes' door and seeing if Patrick, Julie's father, was home. There were many things he wanted to say to the man.

Colin longed to apologize. He imagined the turmoil Julie's father faced thinking his daughter was dead. There was also another side of Colin that wanted Patrick's approval—a person who wasn't his sister with whom he could honestly share his love for Julie with.

He pulled the emergency brake on the vehicle and got out onto the hilly, inclined street. Colin strode past the brick home but stopped to take in the red-painted door. His eyes paused at the open window, the shadow of a man in his late fifties behind it walking from the kitchen to the living room.

Patrick Walsh wore a polo and khakis. His red hair paled in a soft gray, and freckles danced across his skin, spreading from his nose and across his cheeks just like Julie's.

Self-control prevailed, and he turned away from the temptation. He meandered the somewhat empty streets of The Monument, only distracted by a few humans who huddled in alleyways behind their homes. Eventually, Elsie's condo stood before him.

Colin pressed the keypad and punched in her security code. Elsie's home was fairly empty. She kept a couch in the living space and a side table and chair in a dining nook. The kitchen was painted a bright yellow, which made Colin laugh. Elsie wasn't the kind of woman who adored color palates and fancy decorations, so she must have purchased the home painted this way.

He settled into the couch and closed his eyes. The temptation of sleep teased him. The sound of the front door opening pulsed in Colin's ears, and he sat up alert. Looking down at his watch, an uncertainty seeped through his body.

"You're a bit early, Elsie," Colin said, turning his body to face the front door.

"You're not who I was expecting to see on my daughter's couch, Governor," Former Representative Sullivan said in an accusatory tone. Roslyn Sullivan stood in Elsie's doorway with a casserole dish in her hands.

Colin was used to seeing Roslyn dressed for a legislative Session, but it'd been years now since she served a term. Elsie's facial features were the same as her mother's, but the woman stood much shorter than her daughter.

Colin rose to his feet and approached her.

"I'm sorry," she said, moving toward the kitchen. "You startled me, is all. Sitting there like that, you looked just like your father."

"Sadly, I'm aware." Colin grabbed the casserole dish out of Roslyn's hands and placed it on the kitchen counter.

She still looked distraught. Colin sensed the words lingering on her lips—words that she didn't want to say out loud for fear of speaking poorly of the dead.

"I hated him, too, Ms. Sullivan. You don't have to sugarcoat anything about my father to me. There's not enough innocence in the world that could ever transform him from something other than a villain in my eyes."

Roslyn grabbed Colin's hands in hers, and a smile slowly crept across her lips. She shook her head in disagreement.

"He was only a monster after your mother's disappearance. And even then, the line was blurry. He was like a water paining, the good and mean in him blended. He was a different man, but maybe you were too young to remember. Once, he was vibrant, youthful, and enthusiastic. He wanted to help society. We were all intoxicated by his optimism. You remind me of him."

Colin had never accepted anyone speaking of his father with such kindness.

"I'm nothing like my father."

Roslyn let go of Colin's hands and walked to the other side of the kitchen. She pulled out Tupperware from a cabinet and carefully scooped the contents from the dinner she cooked into the containers. Colin stood beside her in silence and watched her strangely. He'd never known what it was like to have a mother take care of him for most of his childhood, let alone as an adult. And while that was his own fault to some extent, he couldn't help but harbor a bit of resentment mixed with longing.

"What Maggie Rivera and FACERE have done to you is unfair," Roslyn said with a close of the refrigerator door. "Ethan is a fine android. I think he will make a great supreme someday, when he's ready. I just hope that whoever replaces you in the years to come can fill your shoes. Or at least, attempt to. I heard about Celine's baby boy. Have you thought about children, Governor?"

Colin had only recently thought about children. Throughout his life, he was reminded that old bloodline families were expected to pass down their legacies through their children. Colin never felt the desire to raise a child with Isabella. Lingering moments of longing for a family only occurred when he was with Julie. But having Henry Jr. and his sister living with him now had opened his eyes—Colin felt awkward and bothered by the experience, but It handled the stresses better, the baby boy smiling whenever Colin released the other side of himself.

"I have."

Roslyn shifted her gaze and looked across Elsie's minimalist home with laughter.

"I never thought I'd raise such a rambunctious young lady. But I suppose parents end up raising a similar version of themselves to some extent."

"Rebel is a better word for her."

"I agree," Roslyn said with a hint of proudness. "Is she a good aide to you? She's only spoken highly of working for you, but I know it hasn't been all that long."

Colin grinned. Roslyn asking him this question rose an odd sense of belonging in his veins. On the surface, Elsie wouldn't have been Colin's first choice as Kathleen's replacement. Now, he couldn't imagine anyone better suited for the role.

"Elsie is fantastic. My schedule has never been more meticulous and well planned. And everyone leaves me alone. She's tough to persuade when it comes to time on my calendar." Colin smiled as he spoke the words.

Roslyn moved over toward the door. "Well, it's awfully late, and if it's Elsie you're looking for and she isn't home now, she probably isn't coming home tonight. You'll have better luck getting in touch with her tomorrow."

"Let me walk you home, Ms. Sullivan. I don't want you out on the streets alone." Colin guided Roslyn out the front door and down the steps.

***

In true Elsie fashion, she arrived back at her condo exactly one hour and thirty minutes from when Colin left her at FACERE. In between now and then, Jones also stopped by. They sat together on the couch and Jones's foot continuously bounced up and down.

"This is a lot worse than we thought." Elise's robust voice broke Jones's and Colin's silence.

Elsie raced for the kitchen, roughly opened the refrigerator door and yanked out a bottle of white wine. She aggressively removed the cork and drank straight from the bottle, not offering either of her guests a glass.

Her hair was still pulled back in a ponytail, but the edges were loosened and stray chunks framed her face. Gloves hung from her back pocket, and her white blouse was stained with bright red blood splatter. A small bruise started forming on her left cheek.

"Did you . . . did you kill Paul McGuire?" Jones asked, addressing the elephant in the room.

Of course she did. Colin groaned.

He could have answered Jones's question even if Elsie had changed her shirt before getting home. The disheveled appearance was a giveaway, but Colin focused more on the look in her eyes. The same look he had after his kills.

"I had to," Elsie responded and took another swig from the bottle.

No, you wanted to.

"Elsie!" Jones cried out, placing his head in his hands.

"Why is this much worse than we thought?" Colin asked, defusing Jones's unsatisfactory response to Elsie's admission. Elsie placed her bottle of wine down with purpose and looked at them.

"There's a whole backdoor deal happening among Joel Kennsington, Maggie Rivera, and many higher-ups at FACERE—all of which were appointed by her. Some Humanizers in The Legislature are also involved. There's a conspiracy theory regarding The Supreme and her predecessor's microchips and a tie-in to her posse hominem creation. They believe androids created posse hominems with a switch so that they could control them. So, if they terminate The Supreme, all hybrids will die."

Colin looked over at Jones, hoping for some kind of emotional response from the android. His scales did flicker briefly, but he seemed otherwise in control of his emotions.

"Well, what kind of evidence do we have? Is there anything recorded? Anything we can use or plant for your detectives to uncover while investigating Paul's death?" Colin asked Jones.

Colin needed to formulate a plan, and he preferred using Paul's death to their advantage.

"That's a possibility and something we could orchestrate," Jones said, crossing his leg and leaning back into the couch. His body shook. "But can I propose something a bit more radical?"

Elsie glanced at Colin with wide eyes filled with shock. While Elsie and Jones worked closely together, she and Colin often found pause in Jones's strong moral compass—one driven by both the emotions programmed into him and his android tendencies.

Colin walked over to the kitchen and opened Elsie's fridge. He needed something strong, and he needed it now. The inside was sparse with only the casserole her mother made, a few bottles of white wine, and a six-pack of beer. Colin contemplated the beer with a raised brow.

It drank beer; Colin didn't. Colin consumed wine or harder alcohol, while It kept to mild IPAs.

Colin's hand gravitated to a bottle of wine but ultimately grabbed a beer and popped the top off. The slight fizz of the beer touched his lips in a familiar yet distant sense.

Since he stopped taking the antidote, Colin made the conscious decision to live his life with It as one rather than fight him. He needed control over his other self and a way to fully understand and live in sync. Sharing all parts of his life with It was one thing: It also needed to share all parts of his life with Colin too. Colin drinking a beer felt like the first step in his control.

"We need to do this carefully," Jones said, his eyes observing Colin's behavior. "I think we can all agree that FACERE is beyond corrupt at this point, and that's dangerous for humans, androids, and posse hominems. We need to break into FACERE and kidnap The Supreme. You know your way around the building and so do I. But we need to cause a scene. This can't be a light, violent-free manner." The room grew quiet, a silence so loud they didn't even flinch at the sound of sirens wailing outside the windows.

"We need to do this when Joel brings Julie to FACERE. We can rescue her then too. If we create chaos and madness within the building and she slips out with us, Joel won't know where she went," Elsie noted, seeming enthralled with Jones's suggestion.

"Joel will know. We'll have to think on that one," Jones interjected.

"What do you mean when Joel brings Julie to FACERE?" Colin asked. His grip tightened around the glass beer bottle.

"Paul mentioned it when he was—indisposed. Joel plans on bringing Julie to FACERE for Maggie. It's part of the bargain he made. FACERE wants a hybrid in their possession so that they can deconstruct her and determine how The Supreme created the species."

Colin's eyes slowly shifted to Jones. The commissioner hadn't told Elsie that Julie's microchip was removed. He wasn't sure why, but now both he and Elsie had their own secrets with Jones.

"This needs to be executed perfectly. I can't get caught being wrapped up in this," Colin said, pointing his finger in Elsie's direction. "And neither can you."

"FACERE plans on experimenting on The Supreme for the next month, running tests and evaluations on her processor. They will update her to the newest model configurations, but they won't make a final incision and analysis on her microchip until The Legislature approves," Jones responded and approached Colin.

He took the beer bottle out of his hand and eyed Colin carefully before walking to the sink and dumping the contents down the drain.

What do you really know, Commissioner Jones? Colin wondered in agony.

"I need you and Elsie to push off The Legislature's decision until we know when Joel plans to bring Julie to FACERE." Jones looked down at his feet, tormented by this terrible scheming.

"I think Elsie and I can handle that," Colin said, and Elsie nodded in agreement.

Chapter 28
Julie

May 1st, 47 A.R.

The carriage house felt homier tonight as Julie removed the bottle of wine from the cabinet and poured herself a glass. The note she found underneath it a few weeks back provided her with a sense of curiosity.

The weeks blended together as the images of a life she so desperately wished was hers appeared before her eyes in the window across the courtyard. Her isolation made her drearier by the day.

She pulled out the note and brought it to her chest. An odd smile crept across her face as she reread the familiar handwriting. The blood sample that had been secured with the note shifted inside the small tube as Julie held it up to the light. There wasn't anything obviously different about this blood, but she cherished the gift and promised to only use his blood for the correct time travel purpose.

Julie suspected the note was written by It. While at first Julie wished the words were Colin's, her heart knew only one person would dare tempt her with flirtatious sarcasm.

Her fingers brushed against the edges of the time travel glasses, and she continued thinking about him. With theoretically all the time in the world, Julie never opted to go back to that night of her death. Part of her didn't want to witness the horrid act—that the person she loved more than anything could do something like that to her.

By not continuing treatment with the antidote, Colin chose to keep It as part of his life, and Julie still hadn't sorted her feelings out on this matter. She needed to accept or not accept Colin's change in heart. It was justified in asking Julie if she trusted him, because without trusting him, she ultimately could never trust Colin.

Julie looked out across the courtyard at Colin's study. It sat in the chair, brushing his hand methodically across the mahogany desk. His head turned up, and he looked out the window directly toward the carriage house.

He'd left her a note weeks ago, and she'd yet to communicate back. Colin might not know yet that Julie was back to save him and The City, but It certainly did.

She downed her glass of wine, and the confidence from the alcohol buzzed through her. With light footsteps, Julie puttered down the iron stairs and strode across the courtyard. She climbed the tiny fire escape with ease and reached the study's window.

It stood on the other side, already opening the window for her.

"Julie."

He stood out of the way to let her climb inside. The warmth of the townhouse kissed her skin as the cool night air cascaded off her body. A nervous hum ran through her.

"Can we talk?" Julie asked, allowing her hands to briefly brush against his.

"I suppose," It responded before sitting back down in the desk chair.

Julie walked toward the other side of the desk and leaned on the sturdy, hand-carved wood. She felt It's icy eyes focus on the scar cascading down her neck.

"I won't stay long. I received your note, and I'm ready to talk," Julie said without looking him directly in the eye. He didn't respond, so she continued, "You're right. We need to trust each other to put an end to the madness happening. We need to work together."

It remained silent. Her heart grew heavy in anticipation. She needed him to accept her just as much as he needed her to accept him. If not, they couldn't save society.

Julie walked over toward It and squeezed into the space between him and the edge of the desk. She lifted herself up and sat on the edge, matching It's seated height. Her challenging stare propelled It to inch closer as her legs dangled off the edge.

"I know I hurt you," Julie admitted, the tips of her fingers brushing against the hem of her shirt. "But I only wanted to help Colin because I love him. More than anything."

It's eyes never left her.

"Even after attempting to kill you?"

The words spoken out loud caused a physical pain in her heart. Hearing them in Colin's voice made them even more difficult. Everything about the man before her was daunting, his eyes, his mouth. He was familiar, yet the way he spoke was vastly unaccustomed to her.

"Yes. I accept him. I forgive him," Julie answered in a whisper before grabbing It's hands. "And I accept you. I forgive you too."

It didn't respond. But his steel-blue eyes softened, and his lips parted.

"I should have known you wouldn't turn against me," It admitted. "I hurt you, and I'm sorry. I've never really said those words before, but you deserve them more than anyone else. At The Oceanside, you created a time loop to try to save The City from The Supreme. To save me. An ultimate sacrifice. Watching you push yourself off the cliffs provided an insight into you I never expected. The raw truth about you. About me. About us. That was exactly what I needed to see."

"You don't hate me for what I did?"

"No," he answered and let go of her hands. His fingers brushed affectionately against the edges of her jaw. "I see you for what you really are. I trust you, and I think I have a plan. But I need you. We can save The City, but only if you can trust me."

Julie looked down at It and slowly removed his hands from her face and placed them in her lap. Julie pulled at the edges of her blouse and lifted the silk above her head to expose her pale, freckled skin.

The scars along her abdomen and ribcage shined against the small lamp on the desk in a unique hue. They stretched up her whole body, dancing all the way up underneath her camisole and disappearing beneath the soft fabric.

It regarded Julie with large eyes in a silent ask for permission. She nodded, and his eyes wandered away from hers and took in each mark, each imperfection. It's hands felt warm against her skin, and goosebumps rapidly spread across her body as he traced the outlines of all twenty-three scars. It didn't hesitate until his thumb lingered at the base of her neck.

Flashbacks flooded Julie's mind—not from the night Colin stabbed her. She had no recollection of that evening. Her mind brought her back to the night It strangled her in her sleep. The night he'd killed Kathleen.

The memory remained vivid and horrible in Julie's mind, haunting her more than any other night in her life. With It's touch close to this sensitive spot, Julie realized she forgave Colin for taking her to woods outside The City and stabbing her. He did this believing she was a hybrid controlled by The Supreme. The night It strangled her was what she'd been unable to let go of.

Colin willingly handed over full control to his other side that night, and his inability to separate himself from It truly terrified her.

I can forgive him. After everything that's happened, I need to trust him.

Julie nodded her head slowly, and It cupped her neck with his large hands. Colin's hands. Hands that were light and inviting, with thumbs tracing small circles on her skin.

Julie was pleasantly surprised by It's touch with only a slight pressure radiating from beneath his fingers. It didn't intend on anything violent, and she appreciated him waiting for permission before moving forward in each step of the way.

Loosening his grip, It slipped his hands away from Julie. His absence startled her, but he didn't stray for long. This time, It approached her differently. He purposefully traced her scars again as sorrow but acceptance danced across his face. Julie embraced the moment and leaned into his body. She allowed her lips to brush gently against his.

Their hold was anything but tame. The smell of him, the feeling of his tongue against her neck and body was a sensation Julie craved—one she needed. Her gut told her to run away before she traveled too far down this unfamiliar and dangerous path, a place she couldn't return from once she took the next step. But when It dove deeper into Julie at her allowance, she didn't ask him to stop.

For any redemption between them, any chance of moving forward, Julie needed to embrace everything about Colin: including It.

For the first time, what was Colin's also became It's.

***

Julie lay beside Colin's body in the comfort of his bed. A smile spread across her face as she listened to his peaceful deep breathing. She waited many months for this moment—possibly longer if she included all the time travel in between the physical dates.

She missed him.

Colin's arm draped possessively over Julie, and she relaxed into the concave of his body. Her device lit up on the nightstand, bringing her back to reality. She had stayed too long.

Julie carefully crawled out from Colin's grasp and reached for her clothes as soundlessly as possible. Being here when Colin woke up ignited a deep dread within her belly. She didn't know how he would take knowing what they did.

The events of the few hours before flashed through Julie's mind: how It traced her imperfections with his lips, how they ironed out with ease and willingness some more details to save The City and place the right individuals into the spotlight, and how they promised to visit one another in the past to solidify the rest of their plans.

There was something different with this experience, and the words It whispered in her ears left chills on her skin. *You've always been mine, not his.*

"Julie?"

She froze at the sound of her own name. Colin reached out toward her body and allowed his hands to track the shape of her through the light darkness of the early evening dusk.

"You're really here."

Julie turned to him and his expression changed at the full sight of her. Colin's eyes paused on her naked body, the flushness of her skin, the small marks and slight bruises across her collarbone and thighs. His body shot up from the bed, and he clenched the soft sheets.

"Did you . . . did we . . ."

"Yes," Julie interrupted softly.

Her hands cupped the sides of Colin's face with a softness as reality set in. Colin pulled her into his body and gripped her tightly in his arms.

They remained silent for a while, embracing the sounds of each other's beating hearts.

Julie kissed him gently, hoping her gesture calmed the millions of thoughts she imagined ran across his mind.

Acceptance from Colin freed them.

Julie let his fingers run through her hair, and his heartbeat eventually soothed against her ear. She let out a sigh of comfort into his chest, and his hands felt warm against her skin. Colin continued holding her, nuzzling his face into her neck.

"I can't stay. I'll come back, I promise. There are a few things I need to do before I let The City know I'm still here."

Colin nodded slowly. "What do you need to do?"

Julie gulped as a lightheadedness blurred her vision. Broaching the subject of the antidote with Colin worried her, but she refused to conceal the truth from him.

"I'm fixing the antidote," she answered with caution. The antidote meant the world to her—she needed to perfect the drug. "That doesn't mean you have to take the antidote once it's fixed. I'll always leave that decision up to you."

Colin rose from the bed and placed his head in his hands.

Julie kept no secrets from Colin, but Colin wasn't always as open with Julie. He had spent his whole life keeping his true self hidden—but the sinking realization that this approach wasn't sustainable forever was a reality they both understood. Colin walked to where Julie's clothes lay haphazardly on the floor and picked them up with care.

"I know about Joel," Colin said as Julie stood to meet him, letting the uneasiness about the antidote linger between them.

Colin swallowed Julie with his large steely eyes and pulled her close once again. Julie propped her head against the lower part of his chest, and he leaned down to kiss the top of her head.

"Elsie told me she's been in touch with you, but she still seems to think you're a posse hominem. Why is that, Julie?"

Julie grabbed her clothes from his hands and dressed herself.

"I doubt Elsie told you everything, then." Julie gripped Colin's shoulders in seriousness. "Elsie is a posse hominem. At some point, The Supreme transformed her."

His jaw tightened, and his teeth grinded against one another at this revelation.

"I didn't know."

"There's a specific reason Elsie hasn't told you. She's ashamed. I trust her," Julie said, sensing disappointment rising within Colin. "I think she will tell you when the time is right. Give her the chance?"

Colin nodded before speaking. "If you trust Elsie, I'll continue to trust her too."

"Thank you," Julie said, softly kissing his lips. "I don't want to leave you."

Colin smiled brightly, his hands sliding down her back. He embraced her possessively, not wanting to ever let her go.

"I don't want you to leave either, but soon we won't be without one another and then we'll have all the time in the world together," he said reassuringly.

Julie kissed Colin once more, tasting the sticky-sweet lie hanging on the edges of his lips. She smiled faintly.

"The plan will work. We'll make sure. I'll see you at FACERE."

Chapter 29
The Governor

May 17th, 47 A.R.

A single light shone in the study as Colin approached the townhouse. The rest of the street was completely dark, and he was able to make out the silhouette of his sister through the window. He parked the vehicle in the garage and walked up the several flights of steps until he stood in the doorway of his study.

"You said we need to be on the same page," Celine said without turning to address him.

"We do," Colin said as an unsettled sense of adrenaline rushed through his veins.

The day was already daunting. The Legislature ran wild while FACERE faced media coverage over the death of Paul McGuire. Having them delay any decision on The Supreme's microchip was a daunting task that took all his energy and time. Jones planted the right puzzle pieces into the scene, but Colin's inner demon spiraled without full control. Allowing Celine to do the same would only exacerbate It.

Colin walked over to his desk and sat down, waiting for his sister to join him. Eventually, his silence agitated Celine enough that she turned around, walked over to the chair he kept opposite the mahogany masterpiece, and plopped down.

"What are you doing about Emilia and FACERE?"

Colin kicked his feet up on the desk and leaned back. He filled his sister in on what he, Elsie, and Jones discovered about FACERE. Outlining the plan, Colin assured her that they would take The Supreme out from the facility and ultimately bring her back to the townhouse.

"What are you doing about FACERE? What if they decide to alter her microchip without The Legislature's approval?" Celine asked, her eyes darting to her hands, which rested in her lap.

Colin looked down, unable to answer his sister. The three of them grew up together, held a strange symbiotic friendship that wasn't normal or easily describable. Colin made peace with Emilia as best he could but couldn't fully forgive her for driving the ultimate wedge between him and the only person he had ever been capable of fully loving.

"I'm not sure we can do anything about that."

"Who modified Jones's microchip?" Celine asked with a slightly higher-pitched tone to her voice. The desperation in her eyes hurt Colin's heart—he didn't like seeing his sister in distress.

"Julie."

"Then she'll modify Emilia's microchip if need be? Right? I know Julie was here. I've heard her; I've sensed her. I know you've found each other."

Colin sighed, leaning back in his chair before kicking his feet off the desk. He hoped his sister hadn't noticed Julie's return or had an inkling of what Julie and It—what Julie and Colin—discussed. Colin trusted Julie, and she trusted him. She allowed all of him to encompass her and hadn't bolted. Pure acceptance. Much like Julie would allow Colin to make his own decisions about the antidote, he didn't want to ask her to do something he knew she wouldn't want to do: help The Supreme.

"I can't make any promises, Celine."

Celine's lower lip pouted as her eyes glanced away from Colin's. She stood and walked over to the cabinet at the far end of the room, punching in the security code that was originally their father's. One of the many aspects of the home Colin never changed.

"Do you remember when Father taught us all how to shoot?" Celine asked, opening the double doors with a strange sense of elegance.

Colin remained in his seat as his mind wandered to the memory he believed Celine referred to. They were out at the estate at The Oceanside, the air crisp and salty at the end of summer. Colin had been fifteen at the time, his sister and Emilia seventeen. The three had run to the backyard after hearing the sounds of a gun popping. They watched as Henry fired his shots at the target at the far end of the estate.

Henry hesitated at first when Celine asked if he would teach them, but Henry was feeling generous that day and he could never say no to Celine. He lined the children up and taught them about the safety, aim, and power of the weapon. They all practiced that day, the next, and for the rest of their time down at The Oceanside.

"I do remember. I've not fired a gun for a few years, though. I recall that you always had better aim than I did," Colin said with a slight smile.

Celine's eyes longingly looked at the various guns displayed inside the case.

"I practiced every single day that summer, but I haven't held one for some time either. But I love the weight of it in my hands," she said, her fingers lightly tracing the large long-barreled firearm inside the case. "I wanted to impress some guy. How dumb is that? I don't generally even like men."

Colin laughed as Celine removed her hands from the rifle. She wandered over toward the revolvers at the bottom of the shelf. Celine grabbed one, checked the safety, and removed it from its position. She followed suit with another revolver.

Colin watched as his sister placed both on the top of his desk.

"These two should work."

"I only need one," Colin said, reaching for the gun. "I'm not skilled enough to shoot with two separate hands."

"Take them both, Colin," Celine commanded before placing them back in the curio cabinet.

The sound of the heavy wooden doors closing rang in Colin's ears alongside the otherwise silence that encompassed his study.

Celine sighed deeply, and her shoulders relaxed. When she turned around, Colin saw the tears streaming down her face. Sadness crept into her voice.

"I know you want to do it, but it needs to be me."

Colin closed his eyes before lifting his head out from his hands. His heart raced energetically in his chest.

"You're right. You should be the one to have the honors."

***

The next morning was a blur. Tiredness consumed Colin's mind, and his concentration waned. He read through proposed increases to the android police budget and opposition from Humanizers about reintegrating humans back into the force.

A slight knock on the door of Colin's office in The Capitol Building drew him out of his concentration. Elsie's head peeked in, her eyes feverish.

"Colin," she said, her voice was uncharacteristically timid, "Dr. Peter Schneider and Dr. Anna Garcia have made an unexpected visit and request your presence."

Colin straightened his posture in his seat.

"Let them in."

"You don't mind?" Elsie asked, a hint of confusion emulating from both her voice and the look in her eyes. "I can send them away."

"No, it's all right."

Elsie closed the door, and the next time it opened, two of Colin's least favorite people graced his office with a sense of entitlement and inexperienced charm.

Peter was an arrogant prick, one who thought he was morally superior to a man like Colin—but Peter traveled time and fussed with components of the past that he shouldn't have, and that made Peter equally responsible for fallouts that occurred now.

Then there was Anna Garcia. The two never got along, most likely due to the feud between their families and the more recent separation between Colin and her sister, Isabella. Although Anna was very tough on the exterior, her eyes cast only an icy glare in his direction.

"Dr. Garcia and Mr. Schneider, how can I help you today?" Colin asked without looking up from his device.

"It's Dr. Schneider." Peter's voice sounded agitated as he corrected Colin's incorrect address.

"We're here to ask a few questions regarding COLI*GO and the ongoing investigation into the lower lab and posse hominems." Anna's voice sounded softer than Colin expected.

The two took seats across from Colin, but Peter's smug grin revealed more than the man could ever imagine. Colin smiled slyly, his fingertips brushing against the desk.

"Whatever I can do to help," he answered with as little sarcasm as possible, "but I'm surprised this is your top concern with a recent murder investigation."

"I'm highly capable of handling both roles, but thank you for your concern, Governor," Anna replied with retort. "Right now, I'm here to discuss COLI*GO and what you know about the lower lab."

How does she not know her sister is the one who has all her answers? Colin wondered, deciding he would respect this secret.

Isabella did wrongly help The Supreme, but he would be a hypocrite if he turned her in. He still held affection for Isabella, the person he had spent so much of his life with, even if the affection was now only platonic.

"We believe the person helping The Supreme was tied to old bloodline families," Anna said as if she wasn't of old bloodline lineage herself. "The Supreme denies Julie's involvement, but we still can't locate her, which is suspicious. Do you think it's plausible that Julie is somehow involved in all of this?"

Colin's lips tightened, and anger escalated in his body.

"Do you know where Julie Walsh is?" Peter asked, his eyes glancing down at his watch with annoyance.

"You mean, Dr. Walsh?" Colin raised his left brow.

Anna's eyes grew wide and a small chuckle formed on her lips, but she suppressed her laughter. Peter glared up at the governor, fury clear as a cloudless day in his eyes.

"She wasn't involved. I know that for a fact. Julie believed in full transparency; that's the reason my sister and The Supreme disagreed with some of her choices as CEO. But it's also why the public loves her. Sadly, I don't know where Julie is, and I grow more worried by the day. But I believe you know where Julie is, Mr. Schneider, considering you had the engagement ring I gave her in your possession."

Anna's body visibly shook from the shock of Colin's open admission. When she opened her eyes, she no longer looked annoyed or angry with Colin. Anna's rage was now aimed at her partner.

Good, Colin thought smugly, *someone needs to put Peter in his place.*

"You openly admit to your affair?" Peter asked, deflecting the menacing glare from Anna.

"An engagement is hardly an affair. It's only a small signing of a dotted line away from a marriage."

"I think we're done here," Peter said, rising from his seat and heading toward the door.

Anna didn't move—her body stiffening in her seat and her eyes directly locking in with Colin's. Her fingers tapped carefully against the arm of her chair. Peter paused, realizing Anna wasn't directly behind him.

"Go ahead, Peter," Anna said without looking back. "I'll catch up with you later. I would like to speak to Governor O'Connor alone."

An audible sigh came from Peter as he slammed the door shut. Anna didn't look away from Colin and her breathing increased in speed before she spoke.

"You know something. You know who helped The Supreme. I can feel it."

Her words pierced Colin's heart. His relationship with Isabella was always complicated from the day their partnership began until now. They were much younger back then—he looked for stability in his image to help win him the election, and Isabella looked for a way to increase her publicity. Their relationship blossomed from that initial need of one another—that initial intention—into something more. Regardless of both of their wrongs, they still cared about one another. If she hadn't cared about Colin, Isabella wouldn't have helped him in one of his darker times. And she wouldn't have helped Julie. He would never place Isabella in danger and would viciously defeat anyone who threatened her—even her own sister.

"I do," Colin admitted, tilting his head to the side in intrigue.

"But you won't tell me."

"Why would I do that? My knowledge is irrelevant," Colin answered, searching for recognition in Anna's face.

A small twitch crossed her lips, but Dr. Garcia held her cards close to her chest.

"You don't really know where Julie is? And you're saying Peter does?" Anna asked quietly.

"Yes."

"I know she isn't involved. I was there on the scene when they found Lexi Pvadinish's dead body. I don't believe anyone would voluntarily opt for that kind of transformation, let alone support it moving forward." Anna bit her bottom lip and looked up at Colin.

"I agree with you, Dr. Garcia." Colin stood from his chair. "Unless you have any more questions for me, I have some meetings to attend to. I really would like to find light in all this darkness."

Anna stood, her short frame hauntingly familiar next to Colin's.

"How is Isabella?" he asked, looking down at her as they walked toward the door. "I haven't heard from her since she returned to The Island. I promised to help her find a new home in The Hill when she returned."

"Yes," Anna said with kindness. "She's still on The Island. I'm not sure when she plans on coming back."

Colin opened the door, and Anna slowly stepped through.

"Thank you for your time today, Governor. Your insight is as convoluted as always."

Colin chuckled, glad that Anna returned the favor with a kind laughter as they said their goodbyes.

Chapter 30
Peter

May 20th, 47 A.R.

Celine, Martin, and Marta were in each of their offices on the 101st floor, alone in their own frosted glass bubbles. All Peter and Anna could see were feet—two sets of high heels and a pair of loafers touching down on the cool-toned tiled floors.

"Who do you want to interview first?" Peter asked, grabbing Anna's shoulder. He squeezed her, and her eyes looked up at him, thanking him.

"I'm not sure, but my gut tells me Celine O'Connor. Did you confiscate their devices?"

"Yes," Peter answered, pointing toward the table at reception. Three devices lay face down against the sleek, chrome desk.

Anna nodded and followed Peter as he led her to Celine's office. He knocked on the door before opening it, hoping he wouldn't startle his boss. Anna took in Celine O'Connor with her big, brown eyes. Celine was a beautiful woman in an elegant manner, not a vivacious one. She sat with her back completely straight against the chair and held her hands together on top of her desk. She didn't flinch as Peter and Anna walked into the room, but a small chuckle escaped her lips once she realized the identity of Peter's consultant.

"Dr. Anna Garcia," Celine said without motioning to stand or shake the other woman's hand.

"Ms. O'Connor."

"I don't want to take too much of your time," Peter interjected, "but let me introduce you to our consultant, Dr. Garcia. She's providing great insights and leads into the lower lab investigation, and we're now at the point where she needs to speak with each Board member individually."

"I understand," Celine responded curtly, glancing to the side.

"Let's get started," Anna said, sitting down across from Celine. Peter remained standing. "Your official statement to The Legislature claims you had no idea that The Supreme was experimenting on humans in the lower lab of COLI*GO, is that correct?"

"That's correct."

Peter watched Anna fight against rolling her eyes.

"But aren't you and The Supreme close?" Anna leaned closer over the desk.

Celine remained calm, and Peter stepped back, intoxicated with the tense exchange between those two powerful old bloodline women.

"We are. Which is why I know she had help. She couldn't have done this alone. She doesn't have all the capabilities."

Peter moved backward, surprised by Celine's response. After reading the files of Celine's testimony to The Legislature, she insisted on no knowledge of these experiments and remained confident that The Supreme had no co-conspirers. This change in narrative made Peter's stomach turn.

"Do you have any idea who that could be?" Peter asked before settling into a chair.

He smiled warmly at Celine when her eyes gravitated toward him. Peter couldn't deny he felt an affiliation with Celine. She believed in him; she recommended him for this promotion. Celine was nothing but a supportive mentor.

"I do."

The room grew still, the silence penetrating against Peter's skin, and his thumbs rubbed together in anticipation and suspense.

It can't be this easy, Peter thought while glancing over to Anna.

He couldn't read Anna's reaction accurately, unsure if she was pretending to be surprised by Celine or if she truly anticipated this response all along.

"Your brother said something similar," Anna spat.

"And which associates do my brother and I have in common?" Celine challenged, a smirk growing on her angular face.

"Too many for me to weed through."

"Okay," Celine said, crossing her arms. "Which associates do I, my brother, and you have in common?"

Anna's face paled, and Peter felt her leg shaking next to him.

"Think back to your own training, Dr. Garcia." Celine smiled wickedly. "Would you say you're equipped to perform surgery on humans? That you possess the abilities someone like The Supreme needed? I don't think you need to even bother with my other colleagues today."

Peter's heart beat rapidly in his chest.

"Isabella?" The name was a whisper from Anna's throat.

"I think our conversation is over," Celine said, standing. She looked over at Peter and addressed him directly, "Please escort Dr. Garcia out of my building. Immediately."

***

Peter held Anna's hair back while she vomited in the bathroom on the 101st floor. At first, she threw her fists in the air and punched at nothing for minutes on end. The tears and hysterical screaming exploded from her small body.

"Why?" Anna cried out in between bouts of sickness. "Why would Isabella do this?"

Peter didn't have any siblings and didn't understand the ins and outs of those complex relationships. The pain on Anna's face appeared more prominently than he expected as if she already had an inkling of the answer and Celine's confirmation was the final nail in the coffin.

The final, ugly confirmation.

"We have to still confirm this. We can't just go off a jaded accusation from Celine-fucking-O'Connor." The words were vile as Anna spoke them.

"What did Colin O'Connor say to you?"

Anna lifted herself from the edge of the toilet seat and wiped her mouth with the back of her hand.

"What is it to you?"

Peter sighed. His hatred for Colin O'Connor grew with each trip he took on Mick's time travel device. He was exhausted from the time he and Julie were spending in the lab, agitated that his work with her seemed fruitless if she was going to forgive a serial killer.

Her admission to Colin's betrayal helped Peter place those puzzle pieces together—Jeb Taylor wasn't The City's infamous serial killer; the beloved governor was.

"There's something weird going on here, and I don't like it. To be honest, I thought working with Jones had its ups and downs, but having you as my partner on this case is way more agitating," Anna said, exiting the stall.

Peter heard the door to the restroom close. Standing alone and walking toward the mirror, Peter groaned, closing his eyes. A small hand fell on his shoulder, jolting him back to reality. Celine's reflection shone back at him in the mirror, her eyes round and curious.

"Why?"

"I've always hated the Garcias. For good reason." Celine backed away, leaning up against the sink. Her eyes looked Peter up and down before picking at the corner of her perfectly manicured nails.

"They tried destroying my family. Colin was an idiot for entertaining Isabella for a decade. They claimed I was the one who was society's 'evil genius,' yet Dr. Filipe Garcia was the one who experimented on my brother. Anna was the one who cut into dead humans, was unable to identify their murderer. And Isabella has decided to play God and make her own creations."

"Why do I have a sinking feeling you're not mad about The Supreme's involvement in this?" Peter shot back, stepping closer to Celine. The space between them was dangerously close.

"Emilia was always fascinated with human emotion. She believed androids were treated as second-class citizens. And they are." Celine's eyes narrowed.

"Emilia?" Peter asked, never hearing The Supreme referred to by her given name. Celine placed her hands on Peter's chest and pushed him away.

"The Supreme cared for COLI*GO the way I did; she helped me build this legacy. She would have never deliberately tried to hurt this place or me." Celine grabbed Peter's hand in a fleeting moment of reconciliation and in search of forgiveness. "We must protect COLI*GO at all costs. FACERE is doomed. Corrupt. We were hoping if this was successful, COLI*GO could take over all android-being responsibilities. We need to take down FACERE."

Peter's heartbeat increased rapidly. The room spun around in his line of vision as Celine's words sunk in.

Power, he realized. *Everything is about power. And Celine wants all of it.*

Chapter 31
Commissioner Jones

June 2nd, 47 A.R.

Jones looked up at his ceiling and stretched his body out on his bed. Maggie's oddly loud footsteps sounded on the other end of the apartment, opening up kitchen cabinets before allowing them to shut. She never remembered where anything was in Jones's kitchen.

Maggie's footsteps quieted, and Jones closed his eyes. He didn't enjoy their affair and wanted to find a way to end things without causing more issues. But after dropping off The Supreme at FACERE, he couldn't stand the thought of things going too awry with Maggie in the event he had any sense of influence over the confusing woman.

There were too many hurdles in Jones's life right now; he didn't have the bandwidth to deal with a scorned ex-lover too. He hoped they could end things still on a professional note, considering she didn't seem to be overly enjoying herself in this affair either.

Each time her biometrics appeared in Jones's new eyes, he had to close them.

The silence shifted uncomfortably within Jones, and a growing anxiety elevated in his gut. Maggie was never this quiet for this long.

"What is this?" Maggie's voice called as she walked across the apartment toward the bed.

In her hand, she held the journal. Jones shot up from the bed and met Maggie's eyes.

"I can explain," Jones said as she closed the gap between them.

Maggie's face was uncomfortably close to Jones's, and he smelled the scent of espresso on her lips.

"That's good, because I have a lot of questions as to why you have a notebook that belongs to a missing woman."

Maggie placed the journal on the night side table with a loud thud and Jones's jaw dropped.

"Wait, what?" Jones asked, his hand reaching for what he assumed was Mick's journal.

Maggie was quicker—her hand firmly held the journal as she opened it for Jones. Jones spotted Julie's handwriting. The words were those of a madwoman. Her scribbles appeared quick and furious across the pages. Most of her notes weren't about time travel but instead the clinical words and diagrams of cells and receptors.

The pages were covered in her own depiction of a newly modified drug.

"Look, Julie and I are friends," Jones said, his scales uncontrollably flickering a deep shade of emerald green as he continued reaching for the journal. "But I thought this was Mick's journal since he left it here."

"Who is Mick?" Maggie asked, finally relinquishing her hold on the leather-bound pages.

"Mick is . . . well, Mick was, my partner. Things ended this winter between us."

Maggie stepped backward and sat at the edge of the bed. Jones opened the journal again and peered inside. The dates didn't make sense to him—the year was marked in 37 and 38 A.R.—and they would have been in their first years at The University. But on the pages, Julie was in the lab at COLI*GO, working on the antidote. Her study was in the errors that Mick often discussed with Jones right before they broke up.

"She's missing, but I know she's still alive. I just don't know what else to say," Jones tried explaining to Maggie. Her furrowed brow deepened.

"I don't think others would find this excusable, Commissioner Jones. There are so many people trying to find Dr. Walsh. Peter Schneider is looking for her, Celine O'Connor is looking for her, apparently so is the governor, and you're looking for her. I wonder if I should be too."

"You?"

"Yes," Maggie responded with a sigh.

"Why are you looking for Julie?" Jones asked again, unamused with Maggie's brushing off his question.

"The Supreme made her a hybrid. There are many components to The Supreme's doing that were immoral and wrong but also fascinating. In the future, FACERE might want to invest or propose some type of advancement on what The Supreme started. When I heard that Dr. Julie Walsh was one of The Supreme's victims, I started reading up on her. I've studied Julie's career closely, observed how she rose from the bottom ranks at COLI*GO to the interim CEO. It didn't add up to me. Until now." She held up the journal.

Maggie lifted herself off the bed and walked to the couch, picking up her neatly folded blouse and pants.

"Julie discovered something even greater than the antidote. Or at least, that's what I understood from the nonsensical writings in the journal. Along with her other admissions. There's clearly a connection among her, The Supreme, and Governor O'Connor. He's involved in this. Did you know all of this, Jones?" Maggie's eyes gazed out the window and across the street at Julie's apartment. "Does she ever go back there? Is that why you moved here? To watch for her?"

Jones looked down at the leather journal and back up at Maggie.

"Yes" was all he could say in response. It was the only answer that provided the truth behind all Maggie's questions, and Jones was tired. He was stressed and unhappy, juggling problems he didn't think he had answers to.

"Well, I have to get going," Maggie said, walking back to Jones.

She kissed his cheek, her soft eyelashes fluttering against his scales.

***

His apartment was dark and lonely. There would be no Maggie, at least not for a long time. Jones couldn't stomach the thought of her in his home. He walked over to the journal and held it between his arms, hugging it close to his chest.

He inhaled the scent of the journal, its old mildew pages, and the musky leather binding the admissions inside together. A tear trickled down his face, a sensation Jones hadn't allowed himself to feel or experience in a very long time.

"Please don't cry, Jones," a familiar voice said in the darkness.

Jones stopped crying and opened his eyes. His shadow hung back by the window, leaning against the frame with hesitancy. Jones wasn't sure if he wanted to scream or cry more.

"What are you doing here, Mick?"

Mick's heavy breathing slowed, and he shook his head slowly.

"I don't know. I made a mistake. I was wrong. I know that now. I want to fix things."

"I don't believe you," Jones said, placing the journal down in his lap. Mick didn't try to approach him, giving Jones the space he needed.

"We need to find Julie," Mick said, finally inching his way closer to Jones and approaching the foot of the bed. "We need to save The City. I know you might not be ready to forgive me. I don't expect you to take me back. I don't expect you to love me anymore. But I need you."

Jones closed his eyes, unable to look at Mick for a moment longer.

"Something bad is about to happen, Jones," Mick pleaded, stretching his hands out closer to Jones. Jones ignored the motion and shifted his glance away from the confusing man he still loved.

"Have you seen The City? Have you seen the streets? How bad things are now? How could it get any worse?"

Mick gulped and stood, pacing Jones's tiny studio apartment.

"You think the streets are chaotic now?"

Fury and anger fluttered through Jones's processor, but disappointment raged beside these emotions. Colin was finally back in control at The Capitol Building, working with The Legislature to ensure safety in not only The City but also the rest of The Constituency. Jones was close to making more arrests and lifting the curfew.

"Then change it, Mick!" Jones screamed, frustrated with how Mick had meddled so much with the past—and probably the future—but wouldn't, whatever catastrophe plagued him now.

"I can't, Jones. I really, really can't." Tears escaped Mick's eyes, hitting the corner of his glasses as they cascaded down his cheeks.

"Then what do we do?" Jones asked, walking over to Mick.

A small glimmer of hope passed through Mick's eyes at the use of the word "we," but reality sunk back in and his smile faded as quickly as it arrived.

"You're not going to be overly fond of it, but we need to free The Supreme," Mick answered, placing his hand on Jones's shoulders.

Jones already didn't like what was happening to The Supreme. She deserved to be treated better even if she was a criminal. He couldn't imagine the uproar if the roles were reversed and Colin was put through extensive testing. He had already planned on freeing her.

"Surprisingly, I don't hate your idea. I've been thinking about that myself," Jones admitted.

He grabbed Mick's hand in his own and squeezed it. Jones wasn't ready to forgive him or let Mick back into his life completely in the ways he knew Mick hoped for. But the idea of having a part of Mick back here with him, away from time travel, soothed Jones.

"I know you're . . . close with Maggie," Mick said, averting his eyes before closing them. "But I don't think she'll hand The Supreme over."

"She won't. We'll have to actually break her out of FACERE," Jones said, not ready to apologize to Mick about his relationship with Maggie.

"I'm not sure how we can do that," Mick replied with a sigh, fidgeting with his glasses. "And we'll need Julie. To restore The Supreme's microchip. I can do it, but I'm not as talented as Julie."

"What if I told you I had Colin's support?" Jones asked, noticing the stiffness in Mick's shoulders at the mention of the governor.

Mick nodded silently before quietly leaving Jones's home.

Jones looked down at the journal once more, the smell of ink and paper filling his nose as he opened to the first unfamiliar journal entry written by his friend Julie.

PART SEVEN

Mick's Journal

"Everybody has an agenda. Except me."
—Michael Crichton

Entry Ten:

January 29th, 47 A.R.

Dear Colin,

I hope this makes its way to you at some point—I'm not sure where or how many versions of Mick's journal have ended up in the various dimensions of time, but here we are.

Here is a confession: I don't know how long I'm going to live in this world. Each time I have died, I ended up back in the woods. Mick's theory, according to this journal and what he's shared with me, claims invincibility to a certain extent for a time traveler. He claims that if you die, you always end up back to the time and location of your "true death" unless another time traveler kills you.

But why did I end up back in the woods? The place where you left me? You technically didn't kill me, Colin. Mick saved me before I died. There must be something incorrect about his theory.

Unless . . .

No. Never mind. I won't go there. Not tonight. Not in this journal entry. I must concentrate on the road ahead. On how to save you and The City.

You won't like what I'm about to do, but I have my reasons and I think you know me better now. I think you still trust me, or at least, I hope you will once you realize I am no longer a pawn on The Supreme's side of the chessboard.

But I hope you realize I am not a pawn on your side either.

*Joel Kennsington is evil, but there are some components about the lies and deception at COLI*GO that I wasn't able to fully uncover before you took me to the woods. It helps to understand what went wrong fully, so I've written down all the evidence, the inconsistencies, and the proof needed to put The Supreme away.*

I plan on going back in time and giving them to you, along with a letter I've written. The concept is so hard to wrap my brain around sometimes. I realize you already have the documentation sitting in the bottom of your desk drawer in your office at the townhouse. You only have that evidence because I plan on traveling back in a few days and giving it to you. But I also need to give the documentation to Joel, or at least some of the documentation. He'll get it tomorrow, and I know what you'll do. You will go to Joel and the rest of The Legislature and confess your crimes. This way, when Joel presents his request to arrest The Supreme for all of hers, she has nothing to use against you.

You've already laid out your hand.

See, Colin, I can play this deceptive game. And I might actually be very good at it because I have no skin in the game—I do not wish for power or prestige. I just want to do the right thing. I'm better than a pawn piece. I'm a player too.

Entry Eleven:

March 22nd, 47 A.R.

Dear Colin,

I won't travel to the future, but I find myself continuously going backwards. I want to preserve the present, so I don't intend on changing anything while I'm there. Instead, I look at my adventures as a way to learn and understand.

This also helps me escape from Joel and his awful house. I'm a prisoner here, and I'm counting the days until my time here is over. I never travel to the future. I will only travel to the past. I fear all the side effects Mick described by going to the future.

I will only allow myself to use your blood once. Mick gave me some of it, but only a small amount. Enough for a couple of trips, at best. I want to see you when you're younger. I want to understand what happened to you on June 23rd, 12 A.R.

Do you hate me yet? Do you realize what I've been up to all this time?

If you don't hate me now, you might hate me in the future. I feel that's inevitable, although I don't want you to feel this way toward me.

I must be careful when I travel. Mick is also traveling, and it's an observation I will add to the beginning of the journal: I can feel when another time traveler is with me. It courses through my veins, aches my bones, and causes an indescribable sense of uneasiness and pain.

Entry Twelve:

Actual date: May 5th, 47 A.R.
Date I returned to: October 28th, 37 A.R.

Dear Colin,

I'm working on the antidote again. I'm sure you have mixed feelings about that, and I wouldn't blame you. You trusted me, and I broke that trust. I provided you with a drug that, while seemingly appeared helpful, never really cured you.

And while you asked me to treat you with the antidote, I think now you wouldn't want to take it again. I support whatever decision you make.
I know about Paul. I know about your work with Elsie. You may not physically have Paul's blood on your hands, but metaphorically, you do. Which side of you propels this kind of behavior? Is this strictly just It? Or is there some gray to this equation? You never stop It. You never had.

And I think you could.

Here on out, I will place all my findings on the antidote. There is an answer; the error has a solution. I know there must be one. There is always an answer to every question. One cannot be without the other, similarly to how good cannot exist without evil.

Additionally, I think it would be smart for me to catalog all our interactions. Or more accurately, the interactions I have with It. I need to document this for both you and myself. I'm not sure I trust myself anymore with you. I can distinguish when It controls your mind and when you control your mind (at least, I can most of the time).

What I underestimated was how intoxicating It can be. Persuasive, charming, thoughtful, careful, and calculated. I'm afraid one day, I won't be able to make a distinction, which sounds preposterous.

I know you're It. I know It is you.

There's only a matter of time before one of you grows stronger than the other. Until you truly cannot coexist together.

I don't know which one of you that will be.

The antidote is tricky. Trauma is even trickier. I have to look for the tiny fraction of genes with so much variation. If I can reengineer how the drug identifies the injured neurotransmitters, I might be able to fix this. But just like how you are so good—so damn good, by the way—at convincing everyone else around you that you're Colin when really you're It, injured neurotransmitters are fantastic at convincing the antidote that they are the healthy cells. The ones they should use to fix the rest of the dendrites, the part of the brain used to collect information from other neurons, are misguided. I need to reconstitute the drug—I need to construct it in a way where there is a single injection.

I don't know how I didn't notice this before.

As for It, we're formulating a dark plan. You didn't seem bothered by the bond I'm forming with It. Truthfully, I was surprised but also grateful that you trusted me with all of you. And that all of you finally trusts me. Working with It is strongly mind-altering. It doesn't hold anything back.

I don't trust The Supreme. It doesn't trust The Supreme. But you, Colin, you want to save her. Jones wants to save her. Why?

I am willing to help you when it comes to her, to an extent.

Entry Thirteen:

Actual date: May 19th, 47 A.R.
Date I returned to: November 2nd, 37 A.R.

Dear Colin,

I never thought of myself as a jealous person. I suppose I am. I should have known better, especially with how I felt after witnessing you and Isabella in the townhouse. I know there was nothing romantic there, but that feeling, Colin . . . Is that the feeling the darker part of you feels sometimes?

I spent time with Amanda today. There is something very charming about her.

I know It loved her, not you. I'm still trying to remember to simultaneously think of you as the same but different. For some reason, that bothers me more. I've seen you love Isabella. I've seen you love (even though it's a different kind of love) your sister, your nephew, your mother.

I've never seen It love anyone except me. But which one of you loves me? It? Or you? I can't tell anymore. And that terrifies me.

I felt a fury so blinding that I gave Amanda the information about COL2120. I didn't mind, knowing that her knowledge of the drug's true powers would be the reason you and It ultimately destroyed her. Actually, it wasn't her knowledge of the drug that killed her; it was what she decided to do with that knowledge.

Maybe that's how I'm justifying this in my head because it's too late. I've been time traveling too long and I feel incredibly guilty about my travels, but I like to think we still make our decisions. We still craft and have some control (even if it's only a little) over what happens despite the interference of time travel. We still have a choice with what we decide to do with the information we possess, the information we learn. The secrets we know.

I interfered in a way I shouldn't have with the past. I made a promise to myself when I first started time traveling I would try to keep things in the past as pure as possible, that I would fix Mick's mistakes. But it's impossible to not interfere. The littlest things have the biggest impacts. I've made a breakthrough in the antidote, an unconventional breakthrough. I discovered its toxin, the opposite composition. I wasn't looking for this answer, but I messed around with compounds and ended up here. The toxin is testing successfully in simulations and meeting its desired end points. The toxin is allowing for the complete takeover of the damaged neurotransmitters, letting the disease consume the mind.

The most amazing thing about the toxin is that it's a single dose.

I've attached a copy of the simulation results in case they get lost along the way somewhere. I cannot afford to lose them. Society cannot afford to lose them. Now that I have identified the opposite, I can work on deconstructing and reconstructing the opposite of the toxin. This will take time, trial and error, testing.

I'm so close. I'm closer than I've ever been before.

Entry Fourteen:

Actual date: May 25th, 47 A.R.
Date I returned to: December 7th, 37 A.R.

Dear Colin,

The toxin is continuing to test fantastically in the simulations. Peter is excited by this advancement and may finally have something to bring to Martin back in the present. This should keep things at bay for a bit.

*Peter mentioned all this pushback from The Board and the executives to get the antidote back on track for bipolar disorder and depression indications. I'm glad that we won't be changing the antidote for those with Alzheimer's and that the antidote works there, but that's never good enough for COLI*GO, is it? No matter, together, Peter and I are beginning to make strides with the antidote, too.*

I forgot how wonderful it is being in the lab. I like the hustle and anticipation in the work. I wonder what would happen if I never left, if I hadn't agreed to lead the program, and never was considered as the CEO while Celine took her maternity leave.

*I'm enjoying spending the days at COLI*GO and then heading to The Oceanside to be with you—to be with It. Everyone has their part in the takedown of FACERE. I miss seeing you in the present, but I'm also finding myself getting sentimental knowing my time with you—with It, alone at the estate—is coming to an end.*

*Setting up Maggie Rivera and FACERE makes the most sense. The loose ends are already somewhat attached—Paul is linked to the riots, and there needs to be a fallout for The Supreme's experiments that don't link back to COLI*GO. None of this is ethical, but the end result is bringing peace back to The City and even The Constituency.*

I still haven't found any answers to my existence and why I seem to have a different experience than Mick's observations in death and time travel. At least there aren't too many time travelers. Me, you, Mick, and Peter.

Entry Fifteen:

Actual date: May 28th, 47 A.R.
Date I returned to: January 8th, 38 A.R.

Dear Colin,

It's missing. The plans for the toxin are missing. I'm glad I saved them here because I'm not sure who stole them. I'm not sure where they would go.

I should have known better. Only two people have access to the toxin: me and Peter. We were supposed to bring it back to the present today, and now I don't know what to do. I've had a feeling someone has been watching me, and I'm wondering if Mick has returned.

If Mick found me.

What would Mick do with the toxin? This could be detrimental. Especially if he gave it to The Supreme. I wouldn't put it past her to control humans with the toxin. If someone takes a single dose of this, what they have been working so hard to cure in their mind will take over.

I should have destroyed the toxin. I should have completely obliterated it once I had the chance. We can't live in worlds of absolutes, of pondering about "could haves" "would haves" and "should haves," because of time travel.

Should I go back? Should I stop myself from discovering the toxin?

Entry Sixteen:

Actual date: June 23rd, 47 A.R.
Date I returned to: March 4th, 47 A.R.

Dear Jones,

How is it you're the one who always ends up with the journal? Is it because we all trust you? We all know you'll do the right thing? I'm not sure, but I'm very distraught right now and I need your help.

I spoke with Mick a while back. I believe you've spoken to him a few times, but it's so challenging to understand with time travel which Mick you talked to and would he know already.

We've been trying to make amends. I find it hard to trust Mick even with his apology. I really want to, Jones, but do you? Do you trust Mick? Mick's time travel observations are inconsistent. I don't believe he's purposefully misled us, but I think he didn't do the required amount of experimentation and observation.

Jones—I am about to give you three pieces of bad news.

First, I need to know what happens to a time traveler's body when they die but go back to another dimension, when they try to kill themselves as I did on the cliffs that night at The Oceanside versus when someone else kills them. Can we figure this out? Can you and Anna look into this for me?

Second bit of bad news: My toxin is still missing. I can recreate it, but I need to know who now has the recipe for creation. The toxin would give whoever holds it a terrible power—a power to completely ruin and control the minds of all humankind. Last, we need to find Peter. I can't find Peter.

Entry Seventeen:

Actual date: October 25th, 47 A.R.
Date I returned to: January 28th, 47 A.R.

Dear Colin and Dear Mick,

I suppose it's a good thing I haven't really changed too much of the past in my previous time travel. If I am going to ask for forgiveness, it would be for what I'm about to do now. I plan on returning to January 28th, 47 A.R.

I will make the right decision that night. Mick, you told me this was the only way, and despite everything, I have to believe you. There is no one else to believe but you.

This isn't an easy decision by any stretch of the imagination. I know I'll wonder if I made the right choice for years to come afterward. But I have a solution; I have two solutions. I just need to choose the correct one. Subconsciously, I know I've already made the choice. A choice that you, Colin, may never forgive me for, but I cannot allow you to continue the way you have.

I've left everything here in this time dimension in good hands. Capable, trustworthy hands, with people and androids who will work tirelessly to make society whole again—to help everyone, regardless of what they are. Jones. Elsie. Even Isabella and Anna.

But in terms of you, Colin, in terms of us, there needs to be some responsibility at some point. This goes beyond you. This goes beyond me.

We deserve a real chance, not only for ourselves but also for what's coming in the future.

PART EIGHT

The Past

"It'll all end in tears, I told them. But they wouldn't listen, and they went ahead, and the rest is theology."
—KJ Parker

Chapter 32

Peter

January 8th, 38 A.R.

The lower lab was quiet with Julie absent from the building. She never seemed to grace the place with her presence on weekends, a secret Peter didn't like. He wasn't sure where she went, if she chose to stay in the present or if she found another destination in her time travel.

Julie's more recent discoveries provided Peter with a sense of purpose in the past—a reason to risk everything about his own sanity and end up here. Even with all the known side effects of time travel, but for some reason, Peter felt a monstrous exhaustion that couldn't otherwise be described. He didn't age, agreeing to only travel on his own blood. He hated how time travel made him feel, as if he were weak, but in reality, he claimed a superiority. There was a protection of sorts, an invincibility that made him fume with an indescribable anger knowing who else participated in these unsavory acts.

The City never changed much whenever he time traveled. Especially to ten years in the past. COLI*GO was newer in society, the building a bit shinier in its inhabitant across in The River. The fancy and ostentatious design set the standard for the rest of the development in The City, the next generation peering with excitement over the anticipation of what new building design represented for prosperity and wealth for inhabitants to come.

He never expected himself to reach out to Dr. Filipe Garcia, but after his friendship with Anna blossomed, he wondered what the deceased man would have to say about the innovations happening at COLI*GO.

Peter was vaguely aware of Celine's hatred for the Garcia family, but that only heightened his curiosity. He almost felt a cemented respect for the former psychologist. Amanda hesitantly invited Dr. Filipe Garcia to COLI*GO headquarters, a strange invitation considering Dr. Garcia made himself publicly known for disliking the core values of COLI*GO.

Filipe Garcia was a shorter man, but his stature was still confident and strong, even in his old age. His daughters were young and so was his wife in comparison. Filipe had spent most of his youth perfecting his career and subsequently traveling the world to tout his new, unreviewed treatment ideas. His eyes grew wide at the high-tech machines, the equipment that Peter didn't find overly exciting since it was something he had been used to in his youth.

"I never pictured Celine capable of such greatness," Filipe said, his hands touching the walls beside him as he entered deeper into the COLI*GO building.

The walls were cool and harsh to the touch, but the old man didn't seem to mind.

"I always assumed she would fall victim to her father's guilt or the guilt of her brother."

Amanda's eyes narrowed in Peter's direction, uncomfortable with Filipe's perception and depiction of the O'Connor siblings. Celine doted on Amanda; the pure affection, care, and kindness showed him there was something more than just an employee and boss. He wondered to what depths, the concern none of his own.

Celine was happily married to Martin Borges, and in the present, where he came from, the two built a family together. Her son was the reason she didn't want to time travel at first, only succumbing to the idea after Peter showed her the lack of consequence when she used her own blood to go back in time and exist in the past.

"What do you mean by Governor O'Connor's guilt?" Peter ventured, hoping to coax a secret out of Filipe Garcia. Felipe laughed as if they shared an inside joke.

"I don't think it is best to speak of that now."

Filipe placed his hands on a test tube of Julie's toxin, his eyes growing wider as he read through the device's screen, the results of the toxin's simulations filling wildly across the screen.

"Who created this?" Filipe asked, his eyes watering in the corners. "This could hurt so many people."

Amanda's body stiffened, an unfriendly sentiment compared to how she behaved moments ago with the two men. She strode across the room, her eyes trying to read the results of Julie's drug. Amanda wasn't technical enough or trained to understand the meaning behind the simulations. The impact Julie's antidote could have on people in society was lost on her. Not because Amanda wasn't smart; she wasn't trained on this particular faction of pharmaceutical drug making. The molecule was just as good as a foreign language to her.

"Would you like for me to explain this to you?" Peter whispered to Amanda.

She didn't respond, anger flaring in her eyes at the assumption she didn't understand what was displayed on the screens in front of her.

Filipe looked over at Peter with a sharp set of eyes. The harsh overhead lighting in the lower lab highlighted the gray hairs on Filipe's head.

"I understand what I'm looking at, Dr. Schneider," Amanda said with a hint of arrogance that only a woman as beautiful as herself could get away with. "COL2120 might change patient lives, but it's still far from perfect. There are various defects here."

Her words were harsh, with a bitter bite behind her teeth.

This isn't COL2120, Amanda! Peter wanted to yell. Peter strode to the device and turned off the machine.

"I think we're done here," he said without hesitation.

Amanda and Filipe looked at him in disbelief as if he were a large disappointment to them both.

"I'm not stopping until The Legislature knows the true creation COLI*GO is producing. It's got to be maintained at some point. Celine won't listen to me, but I'm sure her brother, the governor, would lend an ear." Amanda's words pierced in a tone beyond defiance, one of hurt and heartbreak.

Chapter 33
Mick

June 23rd, 12 A.R.

"Julie! Stop!" Mick called out after her as Julie ran away.

She raced across the green lawn of the O'Connor estate, well aware none of them could see her, none of them know of her presence. Except Melanie O'Connor.

Mick, on the other hand, was all they could see. Mick was conscious of this fact, allowing the distance between him and Julie to extend as he gathered himself up off the ground.

A vibration shook Julie, causing her to trip over into the grass. The color stained her jeans as her knees collided with the ground. Julie's eyes darted around her, looking for the other time traveler. The feeling was all too familiar, one experienced each time glasses were placed over the eyes. The options were limited, and the answer appeared.

Colin's familiar frame loomed near the edge of the cliff, facing the ocean. His gaze shifted, focusing in the opposite direction from where Julie and Mick stood. Her eyes followed his as she rose. Henry and Melanie hastily running along the edges of the cliffs filled their vision. Julie's concentration on the scene abruptly changed focus as Mick's hand reached out from behind her and held her tightly.

"Please, I'm not trying to hurt you." Julie didn't resist Mick's restraint. "Let's get out of here. Things are about to get—"

"I know," Julie interrupted.

"You can't stop It." Mick's truth hung hauntingly in the air between them. "I've tried."

Mick grabbed Julie's hand, and together, they wandered away from the horrid and jagged coastline. They moved slowly toward another property. The limestone structure reminded Mick of a chateau that belonged in another world, not their own.

Everyone believed It was impossible to stop, the sheer evil of him an ever-lingering presence that couldn't be shaken. Colin didn't believe in himself to outdo the other person who occupied his brain. He wanted to, but in the very end, the want didn't matter. Julie was close—her antidote could forever shatter the idea of It, bring him to a well-worthy demise. But the idea of ending It made his friend pause in a way that terrified her own morals. There was an unexplainable pull, a fascination.

"Julie, I need your help," Mick said, pushing his glasses up the bridge of his nose.

His eyes zeroed in on Julie's feet, the shame creeping up his neck. The sun shone brightly in the sky, and in the natural lighting, a small nick on Mick's neck exposed itself.

"We're not all that different, you and I."

"Is that why you save me? Is that why?" Julie eyed Mick suspiciously.

"Sort of," Mick hastily interrupted her. "That's part of the reason. The larger reason is that you're my best friend."

Julie didn't respond, lying down in the grass and allowing the sun to prick her skin with its warmth.

"I miss you. And I miss Jones. More than anything," Mick said, lying down beside her and gazing up at the sky.

The fluffy white clouds rolled along the vast blue expansion.

"I have my reasons for why I help The Supreme. Just as you have your own reasons for why you help It."

"I help Colin."

"That's the same thing," Mick challenged, cocking an eyebrow up in her direction. Julie looked away, not wanting to admit defeat. "I, someday, will transform into a posse hominem. I worry about Nolan. His work without Isabella and The Supreme was a bit shitty, at best. The headaches and the dry skin are from not placing the microchip in the exact spot it needs to be. But if I do this, I need to know that you can adjust my microchip. That you can reprogram me."

"You want me to remove your future microchip?" Julie asked, turning her head against the soft blades of grass so that Mick was in her full view. Mick shifted away, a large sigh leaving his body.

"I'm not sure I want you to remove it permanently," Mick responded truthfully before gaining the courage to make eye contact with her again.

"I don't know if I can help you. I'm not a surgeon. I'm not even sure where the microchip is supposed to go inside humans."

They watched clouds for a long time in silence. The peacefulness of a warm summer day engulfed them even though they both knew back on the coast that the man Julie couldn't shake from her heart was committing the most unforgivable act.

"I want your forgiveness, but I don't know how to ask for it," Mick finally said, a small sob escaping him.

Tears spilled out of Julie's eyes. Mick, Julie, and Jones were the perfect trio. Their friendships were intertwined with all the gaps that each missed in their lives, the comforts of support, stability, and understanding.

Mick followed her through her time travel. Much of Julie's perspective changed in the last few months, but the core of who she really was fought its way out, clawing against the rough, deceitful exterior she'd built to protect herself.

"I'm not sure how you should ask for my forgiveness either," Julie said to Mick, reaching over and wiping away the tears hanging on to the bagginess of his eyes. "But we can try to figure it out together."

***

Against his better judgment, Mick spent the remainder of the summer in 12 A.R. Then, summer rolled into fall, and soon he was halfway through December. The carriage house had another inhabitant more often than not—Colin—and each time, Mick had to force himself to not interfere. This chipped away at his soul. The wails and cries pierced through Mick's body as he stood in the alley-way below, waiting for Dr. Garcia and Henry to leave.

Each time Mick went back into the carriage house, Colin seemed in worse shape than before. His wrists were always red and raw from thrashing in the constraints, but his gangly body remained passed out, exhausted from whatever torment occurred not only in his mind from It but also from the realization that his own father didn't love him and would rather make him a prisoner than get the boy the real help he needed.

Mick never woke Colin. Colin despised Mick in the future, thinking he was the reason behind the chaos and uncertainty with Julie. But Mick always untied Colin's restraints and sometimes stayed to watch over him for a few hours. He never feared getting caught, knowing that if he somehow did, Colin or It wouldn't remember him. Mick didn't look much like himself anymore anyways.

Pacing up and down the street, Mick waited an ungodly amount of time for the light to turn off in the carriage house, but it never did. He peeked into the townhouse across the courtyard, and there at the dining room table sat Henry and Filipe, sharing a bottle of expensive red wine, laughing like they didn't just strap Colin to a bed, place him under sedatives, and shock his body with electric currents.

Mick peered up at the carriage house and swiftly climbed the circular iron stairs. He wasn't sure what to expect this time, but he was shocked to find a young Celine sitting at the end of the bed, slowly rubbing her younger brother's ankle, with tears streaming down her face. Mick lingered in the shadows outside the carriage house, watching as Celine untied an unconscious Colin, placed a glass of water on the nightstand beside him, and grabbed a blanket from the chest at the end of the bed. Tucking him into the makeshift covers, Celine smiled sadly before climbing out the window and scaling down the side of the structure.

***

Supreme Edward and Governor Henry O'Connor sat next to one another in the O'Connor box at Symphony Hall as Mick sat behind them. The loud shrill of violins and cellos filled the room, making Mick's pulse beat rapidly along with the racing crescendo.

Only six months had passed since Melanie O'Connor went missing, and Henry grew more sinister each day: in his own self-destructive behaviors and in his treatment of his son.

Henry suffocated his townhome with cigar smoke and force himself to sleep by drowning himself in expensive whiskeys.

He whored around, first with his legislative aide and then with various women Mick didn't recognize as he peered across the courtyard from the carriage house. Mick's eyes always averted away. The women all had one thing in common: they were blonde and fair, tall and lanky, just like his late wife.

When Henry couldn't indulge in his habits, his actions became more fluid and common. He was a functioning alcoholic, passing legislature with ease and keeping an active social calendar.

Colin and Celine watched their father knock back another drink at family dinners. At his father's dismissal, Colin hid in the corners of the home with a book. The pure mistreatment made Mick sick to his stomach. Henry was never this way with his daughter or even with Emilia. He doted on them.

Why? Mick wondered. *Does he see himself in his son? Colin is too young.*

Edward turned around and grinned in Mick's direction, his hand gently gripping Henry's bicep.

"This is my associate, Mr. Jeb Taylor." Mick still hated being referred to by his uncle's name, but the false identity provided him with shelter from the real truth.

His uncle was roaming around somewhere in The City now, but being his doppelgänger wasn't overly difficult. Jeb ran in different circles, at least during this point in his life.

Mick stretched out his arm and shook the governor's hand.

"A human working for an android?" Henry asked with a raised brow.

Mick chuckled and replied, "I find Edward's logic grounding. As if I know what to expect from him."

Edward's scales flickered before dimming back down, joining in as the two human men laughed.

Mick and Edward discussed at length ways to infiltrate Henry O'Connor's life, to better understand his weaknesses and use time travel to help bring down the wretched man.

Creating cracks in the foundation is essential to long-term success, Mick had said to Edward, hoping the android didn't apply as much pressure on him as his successor would.

"How is your son faring? Is Dr. Filipe Garcia any help at all?" Edward's question was asked with the pointedness of a double-edged sword.

Henry laughed sarcastically, slamming his empty glass down on the small table between the two. Looking between Edward and Mick and narrowing his eyes, Henry finally let out a sigh.

"He rarely speaks. Keeps his head down in books."

Maybe he doesn't speak because he saw something horrific and because you hit him and trap him inside the carriage house overnight. No child that young should be subjected to that kind of torture.

Mick closed his eyes and toyed with the idea of speaking up. The ramifications could hinder him and the identity he worked so hard to build here in the past.

"Have you considered any kind of creative outlet for him to express his emotions?" Mick ventured. "I'm not a psychologist, but I am an artist. I find my work comes straight from those dark corners in my mind. It releases them."

"You're an artist? How come I've never heard of you before?" Henry posed, signaling for a refill of his drink as the waitress entered the box.

"I've just opened a studio in The Port."

"How do you like the neighborhood? We've been putting lots of legislative funds into building up that area and modernizing it," Edward interjected, steering the conversation back to politics as he normally did.

"The neighborhood is fun. A step up from the artist community in The Harbor where I started when I moved to The City," Mick answered almost robotically, trying to stay as close to the truth as his uncle's actual story.

"Do you have any images of your work?" Henry asked, unwilling to continue discussing The City neighborhoods and development.

"Yes," Mick replied, pulling out his device and bringing up his uncle's website.

Serene paintings appeared at the top, and Henry scroll further down, his eyes widening while taking in Jeb's more artistic expressions. Henry's fingers slowed in movement, pausing over a few obscure pieces.

"You created these?" Henry's words slurred, too distracted from what was right in front of his eyes.

Mick nodded, his eyes glancing over toward Edward who had scales shimmering so beautifully, so wildly and majestically, Mick was surprised Henry hadn't noticed.

He stretched out his arm again and shook Mick's firmly.

"Welcome to the inner circle."

***

Speaking to the real Jeb was never a challenge for Mick. Jeb was so high out of his mind most of the time he never questioned the similar-looking old man who sat on the edge of his bed. Mick imagined his uncle found these as "introspective" conversations with himself, waking up the next morning swearing to change his ways. This circle started optimistically but rounded a corner a few days later when he saw his friends or needed inspiration for his artwork.

But Mick needed to secure his future. His uncle wouldn't make money on his own. Jeb had the talent, but he lacked the networking skills, lacked any sort of marketing or word-of-mouth campaigns his creativity needed.

Mick knew better.

"You've just secured a contract with Governor O'Connor," Mick said, placing his hand on top of the blanket sheltering Jeb's legs.

"I did?" Jeb asked, his hands grasping his cheeks and touching his face to see if he was really awake or if he was dreaming.

The color drained a bit from his face at the realization he wasn't asleep.

"He will introduce you to all the old bloodline families. They are very interested in your artwork. And so is Supreme Edward."

"My work?" Jeb asked, his eyes bugging out of his head and his hands itching at the scruff on this jawline.

His fingers twitched slightly, the effect of some black-market drug coursing through his veins.

"You need to make good connections here, Jeb. These will help you in the long run. You'll become rich if you can just concentrate on this opportunity."

"Why does this matter? I only need enough to survive, to have some fun." Jeb grasped the corners of the blanket on his bed, his eyes darting from Mick to the rest of the room.

"Listen to me," Mick said, leaning in so that he was only inches away from his uncle's face. "You have responsibilities. You've stolen from your family. You're a piece of shit. But I intend to make you a better person. Or at least, a better one for the person who needs you the most: your nephew."

Jeb's eyes blinked, the strain on his face evident. He wouldn't move away, terrified by the experience in his incredibly intoxicated and high mind, fueled by a mixture of youth, drugs, and alcohol.

He reached out and placed his hand on Mick's face, feeling his skin with his coarse, pruned fingertips.

"You are my rook, Jeb." Mick's words hissed off his tongue. "You will behave like one. You will not mess up all my hard work on the chess board. Do you understand?"

Chapter 34
Julie

December 10th, 37 A.R.

The waves crashed outside the O'Connors' Oceanside estate, violently pushing against the coastline, demanding more consumption, inch by inch. The grass in the yard appeared yellowed and browned from the harsh fall air while storm clouds rolled in off the nasty cliffs. The darkness added an illusion of secrecy to the candles and small fire dimly lighting the inside of the house.

After solidifying their intentions, It and Julie used their willingness of time travel to meet here. No one came to the estate in The Oceanside during this time of year, the property abandoned except for the occasional housekeeper or gardener. Julie traveled back to 37 A.R. frequently in her mission to fix the antidote, something she'd been upfront and honest with It about the entire time since their reunion. The destructive, potent drug should have driven a wedge between It and Julie, but he seemed to accept her quest to better the whole of society and her purpose and drive.

Julie thought back to the night of their reunion, how somewhere in the future she watched him for weeks and weeks on end before finding the courage to face him. But once she did, the opportunities were endless. They could save The City, or at least together, they were strong enough to unify it.

"We should stop doing this," Julie said breathlessly as It's fingers lingered across the scars on her stomach.

She felt her heart beating erratically against his chest, the heat from his bare skin keeping her warm under the covers.

"Why?" he asked, leaning into the crook of her neck and gently kissing the base of her scar.

"I'm afraid you'll fully corrupt me."

It let out an honest, deep-rooted laugh before pulling her body closer to his, engaging her in an adoring embrace.

"Are you telling me," he said, pulling away from her lips, "that I'm growing on you? That you're starting to like me more?"

Julie kissed him back, silencing any other words he dare tempted. The rain puttered outside, hitting the large glass French doors in a steady, soothing pattern. His fingers combed through her hair, the silky strands helping avoid thoughts about how this arrangement was soon coming to an end. They lay there together in comfortable silence, the only sound coming from the crackling fire.

"Well," It finally said, his body moving on top of hers, pinning her down before a small chuckle broke free from his lips. "Why don't you relax? You've been very busy, and anyways, I think it's too late for your innocence."

Julie leaned into the moment, enjoying the feeling of him, the feeling of her, the feeling of them. She didn't want to admit It was correct: There was something about him that wasn't the evil villain everyone else made him out to be. In these past few weeks, he'd shown her nothing but support and encouragement, willing to put her plans before his own. He saw the good and immoral in her, and he understood what sacrifices were needed for peace in The City. An undeniable trust forged between It and Julie, stronger than the one she had with Colin. She loved Colin without a doubt, but there were always a few secrets, a full picture never painted, never shared with her.

It was willing to expose himself to her, both the good and the bad.

***

"How is the antidote coming along, by the way?" It asked, pouring the coffee pot over a pale blue mug.

The morning sunrise wasn't visible from the storm last night, but a small haze rolled across the cliffs, the mist hiding all the imperfections along the harsh landscape outside.

"I've made a significant breakthrough," Julie said, looking over at him from her spot on the living room couch.

She was curled up in a blanket, her thick cable-knit sweater hanging loosely off her right shoulder.

"I discovered the culprit that originally compromised the drug."

It raised a brow, pouring a second cup of coffee for himself. His bare feet puttered across the cool tile floor until he reached the refrigerator. He grabbed a few apples from the drawer and brought them over to the cutting board. Slicing the fruit, the juices bled onto the tips of his fingers as Julie continued sharing her thoughts on the drug that once held him captive.

"Now I can fix the antidote. For good," she said, looking toward the mysterious and intriguing landscape outside. "Unless someone tries to stop me. I can't explain why I feel this way, but sometimes, I feel like someone is watching me. Someone who wants me to fail."

Her words rang across the room, and his face contorted with hurt and agony, along with a slight hint of fear. He grabbed the mug he poured for her and walked from the kitchen to the living room.

"I keep the knife in the bottom left drawer in the study," It said, his lips brushing against her cheek as he placed the coffee mug on the end table beside her.

Goosebumps spread across Julie's skin, and his breath intoxicatingly lingered down her neck.

"You think I'll need it?" Julie asked in nearly a whisper.

He grinned, the metal spoon clinking against the edges of his own coffee mug in slow circles as the milk mixed in. "Yes."

It handed her the plate with apple slices, and Julie grabbed them willingly and without question.

"Have you thought about what you'll do?" It asked, settling in next to her on the couch, wrapping his arm around her shoulders. Julie relaxed into the comfort of his chest.

"Peter and Celine want me to provide the biologics and a reconstitution of the improved antidote once testing is complete on the single-dose injection."

"Is that attainable?" It asked, his knowledge of this part of Julie's world minimal. "A single-dose injection?"

"Yes, or at least that's what I'm working toward. I was able to develop a single-dose injection of the antidote's opposite, the toxin."

Well," It said, a seriousness in his tone, "I don't trust Peter."

"Jealousy isn't a good look on you," Julie countered, squinting her eyes with a playful grin.

"I'm not jealous of that man." It's eyes furrowed. "I'm not sure I trust how close he is to Celine. And how close Celine is to The Supreme."

Julie considered his words of advice for a moment, sipping her warm coffee. Peter's constant nagging for information didn't sit well with her, but she hadn't noted a particular strain between Colin and Celine. Her observations from the carriage house confirmed that the siblings finally patched up their grievances.

She had to remind herself that It and Colin weren't necessarily on the same page. And while Colin and It blended their consciousness lately more than she had previously ever witnessed, that didn't necessarily mean they had the same intentions.

***

The lab was quiet, the machines humming wildly in the lower lab. Julie grew concerned by the lack of Peter's presence. She needed another scientist to validate her, to tell her she was on the right path. But the differences between Julie and Peter when it came to her personal life seemed to impede her professional status.

Typical, she thought, thinking back to her time as the interim CEO of COLI*GO, *men are more than willing to chat with you but only if you're a man.*

Julie's eyes narrowed as she looked at the screens of the various lab equipment. Finding the answers that bothered her about the antidote wasn't easy to come by. If a scientist without expertise in neurological conditions was looking at her work, she might not see the strange inconsistencies Julie observed. Instead, Julie dealt with cryptic messages from Peter about how The Board wasn't satisfied with her advancements.

As if they even know these are my advancements, Julie wanted to argue.

She was supposed to be missing in the present, so Peter considered her breakthroughs a part of the generalized teams. This infuriated Julie, but with her journal entries, she could eventually prove her own success here if need be.

The trust between Julie and Peter faltered. She wanted to trust Peter but found his distaste for Colin—and his strong affiliation with pleasing The Board—a weak quality of his. If Julie was in charge, she wouldn't let The Board boss her around this way.

Julie didn't want any part of the power struggle between COLI*GO and The Legislature. Nor did she want any involvement in the fight for power between Governor O'Connor and The Supreme. Those were their battles to fight, their own games to play. All Julie wanted was peace for humans, for androids, and for hybrids. No matter what that meant.

Finding the solution for the antidote was Julie's first logical step. If she could create a perfect antidote for the oddities clouding human brains, she could essentially eliminate evil from people. The lack of sinister thoughts in one's brain could lead to better outcomes. A better future. Androids, if their microchips were programmed correctly and without complete abomination, could aid humans. Together, Julie felt like there was a great opportunity.

"What do you see?" A small voice came from the shadows of the lower lab.

Julie felt her hands still against the machines that she was testing the toxin on.

"The toxin is performing almost perfectly."

"Good."

Celine's figure emerged before Julie, taunting her with shadows.

"I didn't realize you time traveled," Julie paused, looking over at Celine from her spot near the lab equipment.

Celine smiled briefly, her eyes looking upward from where she stood. Celine was beautiful, the true definition of charming, old-world class, and prestige with a stylish long bob and high cheekbones.

"Recently. That's how this lab was set up for you." Celine smiled, her eyes twinkling in the soft lights of the lower lab. "What are you working on?"

Julie grabbed a chair and pulled it closer to herself and the large monitors on the desk beside her. Celine sat eagerly, her taller frame towering over Julie even in a seated position.

"I've discovered the inverse of the antidote. That means, with a bit of trial and error, I will have the antidote fully constructed." Julie couldn't help but grin at her discovery, the simulations of the toxin dancing around the device.

"What does the toxin mean, though?" Celine asked, her delicate and long bony fingers pointing to the screen before them.

"The toxin takes the defected cells and activates them, making them gain control. The purpose of the antidote is to make the healthy cells take control. Especially, this drug is the inverse of what we would ever want to happen."

"And what happens if a healthy person ever took the toxin?" Celine's words sounded curious in a bothersome way, leaving Julie feeling awkward and insecure.

"I'm not sure. I'd imagine if someone even was predisposed to a disease like Alzheimer's or dementia or even a psychological condition like manic depression, they might be affected negatively. That's why this can never escape the lab. It would be dangerous otherwise, and I plan on destroying the composition once I have the antidote corrected."

"That's a good idea," Celine said with a grim smile.

Julie desperately wanted to fall in step with Celine. She wanted the two of them to come out on top as two strong women in science. But Celine didn't seem too concerned about the actual science and use of the antidote. Only its success.

"Peter hadn't mentioned the potential here," Celine said, standing from the lab stool and striding over to the other end of the glass bubble that made up the lower lab. "Why is that?"

Julie paused. She allowed Peter access to all her working documents. Essentially, he knew everything as soon as she had discovered it. Peter's reasoning for holding the information back from Celine made Julie suspicious.

"Well, with every positive there should be a negative. We need an understanding. That doesn't mean the negative needs to be shared with the public. I know Peter well enough now, and I don't think he would do anything to ever jeopardize the health and safety of another person."

Celine nodded, her body moving from one end of the lower lab to the other. Julie followed her, watching as Celine's eyes grew larger taking in the countless notes and observations Julie conducted with only the simulation device.

There were much more complex approaches to the antidote and what needed to come next. He wouldn't test her drug on humans for a long time—there were validations and steps in the process that needed to occur first—but by the look on Celine's face, Julie was cautious in thinking the proper protocols would be followed with COL23. Especially when COLI*GO had so much at stake with the asset.

"How did you discover this?" Celine asked, a grin widespread on her face.

She approached Julie with an ease and stealth that Julie was used to when it came to the O'Connor siblings. Celine's hand rested on Julie's shoulder encouragingly, a feather-like appearance spreading through Julie's mind.

"I was testing the antidote, understanding the failure rate. I magnified the failure, allowing a full 100 percent range. And the simulations provided this type of result," Julie answered hesitantly, her hands trembling as she pointed to the parts of the antidote that made up her new toxin. "I don't want the toxin to ever see the light of day, but at least the toxin will provide a good roadmap for myself and Peter as we reconstruct the antidote. And with a new antidote, we can promise a full, single-dose solution to manic depression and potentially other psychological conditions."

Celine looked at Julie in awe, her jaw slightly ajar and her eyes wide with anticipation and excitement.

"Julie, you're a genius." Celine flashed her pearly whites, which contrasted against the dim lights. "I imagine you're so close with the antidote. And then not only can you cure society but also can you cure Colin."

"Is that what he wants?" Julie asked, her eyes hesitating before landing on Celine's.

"Does it matter what Colin wants? If that's what The City needs, then we make that happen. Society needs Colin, but he can't be his best until he's cured. Don't you agree?"

The question hung in the air with a sharpness akin to the knife in the bottom of the desk in Colin's study. The heaviness and the gravity of Colin's actions as a vigilante weren't forgivable; they weren't something Julie could condone on her own, no matter how much she wanted to.

"I want what's best for him," Julie finally answered, looking away from Celine's deep stare.

A quietness followed the women as Julie continued tinkering with her simulation process and Celine paced back and forth on the tile flooring. Her high heels sounded pointy and sharp in Julie's ears.

"Good. Then keep working. You're almost there."

Chapter 35

It

November 4th, 46 A.R.

It looked over at Julie's sleeping body in the bed beside him, her breathing a smooth, soothing sound. Deep and calm. Reaching out, his fingers grazed her smooth skin.

He walked out of the room before his irresistible urges took control. This was his darkness, a feeling he wanted to shove deep down inside his chest but instead bubbled up like an overflowing river.

It's feet carried him down the stairs to the first floor and into the kitchen. An ominous glow illuminated around him as he opened the refrigerator door. He found a beer, popped off the top, and took a slow swig. His eyes glanced to the drawer in the kitchen island where empty bottles of the antidote collected dust. He felt an irresistible urge to reach inside and laugh, a deep-rooted chuckle showcasing how he really still stood here, how Julie's experimental drug failed. How someday, she would be grateful for this failure.

I assume, It thought, closing the refrigerator behind him.

It traveled back up the stairs but stopped on the second level and headed for Colin's study. The room was completely dark, and he turned on the small lamp placed on the desk. It's fingertips itched for the bottom drawer, the place he kept the nifty time travel device.

He made a promise to himself he wouldn't use the device for his own personal convictions. He would only use time travel as a mechanism to help Colin's cause, to save The City from The Supreme. It had visited her earlier in the day, hurt and conflicted by the knowledge she passed on to him about Julie, the antidote, and how Julie wasn't entirely human anymore.

I have to kill Julie. I don't want to kill Julie. But I have to convince Colin we must kill her.

The time travel device fit perfectly in It's hands. The intricate markings on the device showed It how much Mick took care of his craft—Mick was proud of what he produced, the small moments etched and engraved inside the frames, telling a story. A story It couldn't quite piece together.

Anger and hurt erupted inside It's body again. The ache teased him, his constant back and forth made him want to do unexplainable, horrific things. He needed the outlet. Having been locked up for so long inside Colin's mind made this newfound freedom a wonderful, vibrant feeling. But It felt too much now. He closed his eyes, hoping the impulses would wane.

Julie was the last one I strangled. Kathleen was the last woman I killed. I can't have Julie be the last feeling in my hands. I can't have Kathleen's blood be the last stickiness on my blade.

It grasped the knife in his dominant left hand, Colin's reflection shimmering against the shiny steel. Pricking his right index finger, his blood emerged as a tiny dot at first before gurgling down his long finger. It filled the small space on the overly used slide with his blood and placed it between the time travel glass frames with a sense of ease and familiarity.

The chrome box offered him options for his time travel destination, the date options making him stiffen in his seat. A small, bottomless pang in the pit of his stomach grew, and It took a deep breath.

It opted for the past, selecting March 14th, 38 A.R.

It was used to the vibrations, the oddness, and idiosyncrasies of time travel spreading through his body as he made his way further back in time. The townhouse felt vaguely familiar to him, his eyes drifting to the documents on Celine's device, which she casually left in the dining room.

How she doesn't even know, It thought.

Celine's company, COLI*GO, would present its first pharmaceutical asset to The Legislature in the coming days. COL2120 would eventually become the company's legacy asset, but right now, COLI*GO had nothing to show for any approved drugs of their own. COLI*GO purchased up the rights to manufacture drugs that had already been created, drugs that couldn't be trusted by some of these bloated, biotech companies anymore. But without the approval of COL2120, COLI*GO would fail.

*And Amanda plans to burn Celine and COLI*GO to the ground.*

Her threats were simple in the message. A final, desperate warning. During this time, both Celine and It lusted after this wicked, intelligent woman, a woman not good for either of them. A woman who was determined, selfish, and ready to ruin them all.

How did she ever uncover the real truths behind COL2120? It wondered, unsure how Amanda connected the dots.

While she was a brilliant woman, Amanda wasn't a scientist; she wasn't a researcher. She was a creative thinker, one who belonged on the business side of things. Not the technical side.

It forwarded the message to Colin's device and promptly deleted the note from Celine's. Walking briskly from the dining room and rounding the hallway toward the living room, he found Colin on the couch, his eyes buried deep within legislative documents.

"Amanda," It spoke the forbidden name, and Colin looked up at him.

Playing with Colin's mind wasn't something It should have done to his friend. To himself. Colin was somewhat aware of how It was only a figment of his imagination, but Colin often recalled thinking about It as another ominous figure he saw standing in front of him rather than just in his mind.

Time travel explains those instances, Julie. Colin isn't completely out of touch, It desperately wanted to share with her.

But he couldn't.

Colin sighed, throwing his device to the other end of the couch.

"Why? I don't want you with her, but I can't do that to Celine."

It couldn't share his true longing. The irreversible itch running through his body, how if he returned to 46 A.R., to the bed beside Julie, he would do something more horrific, something completely unforgivable.

It couldn't kill Julie. That was why he left, why he returned to the past. He still had this violent, devious need. He had to take care of these desires, to satisfy them or face far greater repercussions that neither he nor Colin could recover from. At least by channeling his anger and using his power for the betterment of society, It could justify his raw, animalistic needs. He hated and loved how Julie brought this urge out of him. A dirty, terrible little secret he wanted to wrap around her like a sheet and lose himself in a tryst together with her. Not that she would ever knowingly allow him.

"Amanda's going to take down COLI*GO. She's already hurt your sister. I do enjoy her; she treats me differently than the women you choose. She's fascinating and stimulating compared to Isabella, compared to Maggie. But we have to end her, or she will end the O'Connor legacy we've worked so hard to secure." It's words weren't lies, and his venom cemented the bite. "We can't prove Henry right. We aren't cowards."

"When?" Colin asked, his hands grasping one another, fingers interlacing and releasing in a nervous tick that both thrilled and terrified It.

"Now," It answered. "She will go to The Legislature tomorrow. This is for the best."

Colin stood, making his way to the garage door in only a few strides. The decision was made.

Together, It and Colin meandered over to Amanda's apartment in The Bay. Her place was a bit closer to The Symphony and removed from Commonwealth Avenue. The separation of Amanda and Julie was important to It, especially in this moment when all he could think about was Julie.

A sense of relief filled It's body as the car continued weaving through the narrow city streets with Colin in the driver's seat.

When they arrived, It closed his eyes before making his way up Amanda's front steps. He needed to keep his persona up, needed Colin to still hate how whorish he could be, the uncontrollable longing resembling a drug withdrawal rippling under the thin layer of skin on the human body.

It reemerged in the vehicle, half of his shirt buttons undone, his overall presence in disarray. It smiled at Colin falsely and nodded his head, making sure Colin was ready.

Amanda lay completely unconscious on her bed. It dressed her with ease, the woman he once obsessed over, in Colin's mind, at least. Amanda's dress slipped on with ease, professional and unassuming, with its wooly black fabric and minuscule zipper that cinched against her shapely, voluptuous figure. While she was a conniving, back-stabbing genius, Amanda deserved dignity in her death.

Slipping high-heeled shoes on Amanda's feet, It felt her smooth, delicate, and pale skin limp under his firm grasp. She wasn't dead yet—the sedative he and Colin used, the one he injected into her skin, made its rounds in her body. Lifting Amanda up in his arms, It paused.

Does she deserve this? he wondered for a moment too long before agreeing she did, before agreeing that if he didn't fulfil his need, he would strangle Julie again.

It would hold her down roughly, lashing out his anger meant for The Supreme on Julie. While he was intoxicated with and intrigued by Amanda, It didn't love her.

He loved Julie.

And that's why this is even more painful, It wanted to scream.

It carefully placed Amanda into the back of the vehicle. Colin nodded at It, his hands gripping the steering wheel with confidence. Henry taught Colin how to drive a car manually back in his youth. This wasn't something many drivers with self-driving vehicles knew how to do, but by turning off the self-driving function, the vehicle's device wouldn't track their movements.

They made their way to the back of The Capitol Building, stashing the car in the garage at the townhouse. Easing their way through the back alleyways was familiar and made the adrenaline coursing through their veins briefly slow down. It and Colin's footsteps were drowned out by the lively night air around them. Remaining hidden in the shadows was even more important tonight.

"I don't want to do this," Colin admitted, looking gingerly over at It. "Celine will be devastated."

"But she will ultimately be thankful even if she never knows why. Amanda was planning on exposing the issues with COLI*GO's new drug asset, COL2120. The drug won't get approved if Amanda brings the documentation she had before The Legislature."

Colin nodded, looking up toward the starless sky. The knife trembled in his hands, and the familiar blade shone brightly in the darkness. The sharpness of its pointy end illuminating against the old gas lamplights lining The Hill neighborhood.

"Give me the knife."

Amanda's skin felt cold in It's hands, his thumbs gripping the sides of her neck, strangling her. The sedative did its job, keeping her asleep and unaware as she slipped into darkness. It found solace in noticing how she didn't flinch, how she didn't even care as he violated her in the most violent way.

The knife pierced through Amanda's skin and sliced with an echo. The markings were deep and aggressive compared to the way It planned for their next victim. He would put on a lovely little show but would refuse to destroy Julie even if she threatened to destroy him.

One. Two. Three. Four. Five . . . The number continued climbing on Amanda's abdomen until he reached twenty-three. Sprayed with the aftermath of Amanda's death, It looked up at Colin.

Colin's eyes were closed, his feet inching back farther and farther from where It and Amanda lay. The moonlight lingered across Colin's face, and for a moment, he thought he witnessed Julie's shadow behind his friend. In It's imagination, Julie smiled slightly, the corners of her mouth upturned hesitantly at the scene in front of them.

In an act of defiance, It grabbed Amanda's silver key necklace. The piece always hung delicately from her neck, but instead of unclasping the chain, It gripped the key tightly and yanked the jewelry from her body. Colin's eyes opened widely at the noise.

They discarded Amanda's bloody, exposed body near a dumpster behind The Capitol Building and made their way back to the townhouse. The venture wasn't far, only a few blocks, but the silence between It and Colin reminded him of after they killed Kathleen.

It watched Colin strip his clothes, his fingers shaking while placing Amanda's necklace into the little drawer in the laundry room.

Their private stash of trinkets.

A smile spread across It's face as Colin continued their ritual. The sound of the wine bottle opening echoed in It's ears, and the beers left on the counter enticed him. Clanking the bottles, he grabbed one, consuming the contents with almost too much ease. Shame filled It, but he pushed the unwelcome visitor down into the deeper depths of his mind. A place that Colin could unlock later.

Naked, Colin continued up the stairs.

Isabella was in the bed, fast asleep and unaware of the disturbance of a missing body. She was so obtuse with this side of Colin, with It. It wanted to shake Isabella and yell at her for her inability to understand him—to understand Colin.

It reached into his pocket, holding up a pill from the stash Colin kept from the future. A hallucinogenic that promised sleep even if rocky. He placed the pill in Colin's palm, the chalkiness of the drug rubbing against his rough skin.

"Take this," It whispered in Colin's ear. "This will help."

Colin dry-swallowed the pill without any hesitation and looked into the darkness of his bedroom. It backed away, but oddly enough, Colin reached out and grabbed his shoulder. Shock spread through his eyes, recognizing that he was physically feeling someone else in his grip.

Chapter 36
Mick

December 19th, 37 A.R.

"Is this the only way?" Mick asked nervously, shifting his weight side to side on the cot inside the lighthouse. He was trapped, sweat pooling on his brow.

Julie held the knife against Mick's throat, her hand shaking from a mixture of nervousness and adrenaline. Mick's breathing slowed, but he tried to remain calm despite the closing, palpable tension around them.

"Julie," he said slowly, feeling her grip tighten against the knife's handle. Julie's arm secured itself in a stronger hold of his neck, bringing him closer to her chest.

A soft grunt came from a dark shadow on the other side of the lighthouse floor. The massive, looming figure sat in the wooden, rickety chair: Colin O'Connor.

Or rather, It.

"Why couldn't you just leave me alone, Mick?" Julie's voice trembled with a bit of a cry in between her words. Mick closed his eyes.

"You can kill me, Julie. But I know you don't want to." He granted her the permission more easily than either of them expected. Julie's breaths grew angry and harsh in response, but she remained silent.

Mick wanted to shake Julie; he wanted her to realize this was madness. If she could let him go, they could calmly work out their differences, come to a solution.

"Each time I go back, I'm smarter. I know more about the future. I can change it. We can change it together, Julie. You don't need him," Mick cooed.

"You wouldn't dare," Julie said through clenched teeth.

The cool metal blade sliced into Mick's sticky, warm skin. He felt the blood gushing from his throat, spitting out profusely like a dam releasing a river behind it.

Mick's eyes darted open into darkness, and he violently shook from the horrid dream. He was in the carriage house, not at The Oceanside. His neck stiff from falling asleep on the couch, Mick fumbled for his device.

Just a dream, he reassured himself. *That's not how this ends for me.*

Mick had died hundreds of times during his time travel journeys. He always ended up back to where he was supposed to die—a true sentiment that horrified him still, but it wasn't this moment that he pictured in his dream.

This wasn't a recollection of how he truly died. Or at least, not how his experiments told him how he would die.

Escaping death was something only individuals with the ability to time travel had the special abilities to foresee. They would "die" and then end up back to where they were supposed to die—fully alive and well. Nothing about their original, god-intended death inflicting them from moving forward. The only time they could actually die was at the hands of another time traveler.

Mick still hadn't figured out how this worked between Julie and Colin. Colin essentially almost killed her but at least hadn't completed the act. As an unknowing time traveler, Colin could have permanently killed Julie if he tried hard enough.

And he didn't. It regrets his decisions. And I saved her.

Mick was so familiar with his own death now that facing it when the time came didn't bother him. He knew he would travel; he would be able to still influence the timeline of society and life in his own way, no matter how much his actual death hurt him.

***

"What's wrong?" Julie asked as Mick's body twisted and turned.

She was up on the other side of the room, brewing them coffee, her delicate hands clasping the pot with a grip so tight that Mick wondered what kind of trauma preceded this version of Julie.

"Nothing," Mick replied, not wanting to relay the dream he experienced.

This dream tormented Mick's soul, creeping up during times of insecurity and reminding him desperately of a future that could happen if he wasn't careful, if he didn't convince Julie to leave the caress of Colin and It soon enough.

"Okay," Julie replied, not believing Mick's response to her question. Her hands held the warm cup of coffee aggrievedly before relinquishing the mug to him.

"I have a secret, a request," Mick responded after Julie poured herself a cup.

Julie sat beside him on the cot, her eyes kind and soft in the morning light.

"Isabella fixed you," Mick said, his free hand creeping up the side of his neck. "Do you think she would fix me?"

The smile dropped from the corners of Julie's mouth as Mick spoke, his words striking an odd chord with her. Julie's small hand lifted to Mick's face, cupping his cheek in the cold palm of her hand. He shivered at her touch, always a cold one compared to what he was used to.

"I'm not the person to ask that question to," Julie answered before releasing her hand from his face. Her eyebrows danced in a furrow, the honesty in her response true.

The waves crashed alongside the lighthouse outside, the afternoon tide coming in with a swift and powerful vengeance. Julie would leave him again, insisting on heading back to the O'Connor estate on the other end of the beach. He didn't want to blame her for spending her time traveling through dimensions with It. He would gift Julie with a part of herself that she would cherish forever.

Julie knows so little about the future.

This could explain to her why he would fight so hard to make amends, for a slim chance of redemption with the people and android he loved the most.

"I also don't know why Mick said, breaking their silence.

"What?" Julie asked, her fingers tracing the scar on her neck.

There was so much complexity to Julie since her return to the world from when she nearly died in the woods.

Nearly died, Mick reminded himself.

"You didn't die in the woods that day. I saved you. You

shouldn't have ended up back there after pushing yourself off the cliff." Mick pushed his glasses up on his nose, standing to finally meet Julie's questioning gaze.

"I must have died. Maybe there's something strange in the dimension that neither you nor I understand, Mick," Julie replied, her eyes glazing over in confusion and sadness.

Mick didn't enjoy seeing his friend this way. There was something heartbreaking about her, a piece that had always connected them even after her mother's death.

Julie and Mick hadn't been part of one another's lives yet, but Mick recalled the moment with certainty. He traveled time, hoping to better understand not only Julie but also Jones. Julie had recently reprogrammed Jones's microchip to understand more human emotions and feelings. And by the stroke of irony that the world often offered, Julie's mother committed suicide.

Jones was there for Julie in every way that mattered, holding her while she cried, actually feeling the pain that seeped through her body to some level of understanding. Mick watched from afar. He was always jealous of their bond, their closeness.

They would never have that if it weren't for that decision, Mick realized.

He wasn't sure how he felt about this, his mind toggling back and forth between wishing Julie never bonded with Jones because she changed his microchip versus how she provided Jones with the gift he required to be the partner Mick needed.

"You wake up where you are supposed to die," Mick said with confidence. "I know this. I've experimented on this several times at this point."

"It doesn't matter anymore anyways." Julie sighed, watching the ocean from the small window in the lighthouse's circular walls. The portal was oval shaped, placed directly in between several layers of bricks.

"Do you trust me?" Mick asked, his heart beating fast under his chest.

"Truthfully?"

Her eyes held confusion, fear, and a hint of uncertainty. Mick hadn't seen this expression across his friend's face in a very long time. Mick nodded, unable to vocally answer her in his nervousness.

"I'm not sure."

"Is it only because Colin hates me?" Mick asked, his hands grasping the edges of his T-shirt.

"No, Mick," Julie answered, approaching him cautiously and slowly, each step taken with careful consideration as she closed the gap between them. "You lied to me. After you rescued me from the woods, you sent me back in time, hoping I wouldn't escape a loop I created. Somehow, I did. Somehow, I ended up back at that spot in the woods, rather than the place you intended for me. And you still won't tell me where that is."

Because I don't even know where that is, Mick wanted to confide in her. *You have defied every single rule and observation set by time travel. Every single one of them, Julie.*

"Then what are we going to do?"

Julie looked at Mick, and a small grin crept across her beautiful, freckled face.

"Next time we time travel together, we're going to The Island."

Chapter 37
The Governor

November 10th, 46 A.R.

Colin had never time traveled before, leaving the contents of those adventures to It. This was an exception, and the sheer idea that he and It were becoming so blended together lately uncomfortably tickled his chest. He knew where It kept the device, and blood was still on the slide.

The sensation of time travel was puzzling to Colin, a familiar but distant recollection in his physical body. The momentary silence providing peace in his otherwise noisy mind.

Former Representative Roslyn Sullivan looked over at Colin from the other end of the hallway within The Symphony. Colin felt tired from the day, wondering if being back in time was what drained his body of his typical vigor and energy. He nodded at her and smiled.

She had been kind to him in his youth and had once looked up to her. He never understood Roslyn's willingness to work with his father when he was the governor, but he appreciated her kindness toward all constituents, even androids.

She approached Colin slowly, a small smile spreading across her freckled face and the paleness of her aging strawberry blonde hair shining against the harsh lighting.

"Governor O'Connor." Roslyn hugged him, an informality he was used to and one he treasured even more after spending more time with her daughter, Elsie. Roslyn raised a fierce, strong woman, and he admired her for it.

"How are you, Roslyn?" Colin asked, leading her to a quieter end of the hall.

"I'm all right. I'm still shaken up by what happened with Jeb Taylor and poor Kathleen Murphy's family."

The mention of Kathleen sucker punched Colin in his gut. He missed Kathleen terribly, the images of holding her while she asked him to kill her painting vividly in his mind.

"No one could ever replace Kathleen," Colin said reflexively, his hands trembling. "She was like family to me."

"Jeb Taylor makes sense in my mind, but I remember him being a timid man, not a violent one. It's all so odd to me." Roslyn looked away. "When I was younger, I remember your father being the one who helped launch his career."

"I'd prefer not to talk about my father, if you don't mind," Colin replied with an icy tone.

Roslyn sighed heavily, grabbing Colin's hand in hers.

"I loved him once, you know. But you're right; he threw away all the good things in his life because of his inability to express his pain, his suffering. Had he not been so afraid to do so, I think things would be different. For you. For your sister," Roslyn said before lowering her voice to barely a whisper, "for me and maybe for Elsie too."

Colin's heart stopped beating in his chest, and he felt the color drain from his face. Elsie appeared in his mind: her uncanny height for a woman—much like Celine's—her larger hands, her wicked smile, her fierce attitude.

Colin backed away toward a more crowded part of the hall, adrenaline flooding through his body.

Elsie is my father's bastard child. That's why Roslyn was so candid and unassuming with me in the present the night Elsie killed Paul McGuire.

"I need to get going, Ms. Sullivan." The words barely escaped his lips before he dashed to the other end of the hall.

Colin fumbled in awkward conversations with others wishing to speak to him, the social element of The Symphony a constant reminder why coming here while time traveling wasn't his best idea. When he finally reached the townhouse, the number of lights on confused him, the heat cranked up higher than when he left it.

The real Colin, the Colin from this time, wasn't here; he was with Julie, trying to cherish every waking moment with her while struggling with telling her how the antidote didn't work, how It made himself free.

"Colin," Martin Borges's deep voice echoed soundly from the kitchen. He stood in front of the open refrigerator, and upon closing the doors, he held two beers in his hand. Martin cracked open the tops of the glass bottles and gingerly handed one to Colin.

Colin studied the beverage in his hand for a moment too long, the silence growing more awkward between the two men who never hated one another but never seemed to get along. There was no secret that Colin found Martin fickle and weak, a jellyfish of a man.

And in return, Martin always considered Colin to be harsh and unforgiving, monstrous even.

"What are you doing in my house, Martin?" Colin's bite a bit harsher than he intended.

"I need to talk to you," Martin said before taking a swig of his beer. His deep eyes furrowed with conflict and confusion. "It's about Celine."

Colin nodded and placed his untouched beer on the countertop.

"Is everything okay with Henry?" Colin asked.

Martin didn't respond and concern grew across Colin's chiseled, stone-cold face.

"I'm very worried. I found some troubling information. You might want to sit down for this one."

***

The documents saved inside Colin's device felt heavy in his hands. He illicitly extracted Julie's signature from another document and placed the structured letters on his new one. Julie would never incriminate him for his wrongdoing.

The crisp fall air swept across the streets of The City, making Colin quicken his pace. He tried enjoying the scenic walk, especially given the circumstances back in the present where he came from. Sometime during this part of the previous fall, It emerged from the confines of Colin's brain after Julie trapped It in there. Exactly when It escaped remained fuzzy in Colin's memory.

The Courthouse came into view, a large structure with white pillars and crimson brick walls. The steep steps were an intriguing pain on his sore and tired legs. While exhilarating, time travel was exhausting. Between It and Julie, Colin was aware of some guidelines. Following the rules promised to help limit the changes in physical appearance, but Colin still felt like his blood sloshed inside his body, angry with him for abusing its capabilities.

A familiar face from his present greeted him at the front desk of the Record Department: Elsie Sullivan.

Her tattoo was raw and fresh, the skin blotchy and slightly bruised around the edges. Colin didn't know the timeline of when Elsie realized she had a microchip in her brain versus the actual occurrence of the surgery.

Did Isabella do this to you too? Colin wondered. *Did Jeb Taylor kidnap you? Or was he already dead?*

"Governor O'Connor!" she shrieked as if a child caught reading under the covers with a flashlight when they should have been fast asleep. "I don't have an appointment scheduled for you."

"You're right," Colin cooed, lowering his voice and placing his hand on her desk. "Is that a problem?"

"Of course not," Elsie replied hurriedly, pushing the mess on her desk to the side. "What can I help you with today, Governor?"

The mural of the high judge—the android who occupied the position while The Supreme was still in power—hung on the wall behind Elsie, the dim light illuminating the softer colors of his scales.

Colin pulled out his device, motioning to the sharing drive. Placing his device on top, he watched it scan the document. Elsie's large monitor flickered to life, the screen filled with the simple one-page certificate.

"Could you please notarize this document and file it?" Colin asked, looking away from her.

He liked Elsie; regardless of her status, she eventually fought for his trust. But they had no bond on this day in the past. The importance of this step in his plan was essential.

Elsie's eyes furrowed in confusion as she read through the file before printing it. Knowing Elsie's typical abrasive and flippant personality, Colin respected her for not making any kind of comment to him. Instead, she grabbed the notary stamp with ease and pressed down with her large hands.

The stamp punctured the bottom of the crème paper before Elsie scanned the document again, uploaded it into the cloud, and placed the cardstock into a sealed envelope. A copy of the scan transferred over to Colin's device, and he smiled slightly as the green check mark appeared on his screen. Safe and sound, the document was officially his.

"Thank you, Miss Sullivan, for your help and your discretion," Colin said, placing the device back in the pocket of his suit jacket.

"Of course, Governor O'Connor," Elsie replied, sitting back in her seat. The tips of her fingers grazed the edges of the snake on her tattoo before she looked back up at him. "And congratulations."

PART NINE

The Present

"Man cannot change or escape his time. The eye sees the present and the future."
—Salvador Dali

Chapter 38
Julie

June 5th, 47 A.R.

Mick grabbed Julie's hand as they exited the aircraft and walked on-to the dock. The landing was jittery on the water, an exhilarating rush causing an uneasiness she hadn't experienced in months. There was a slight chill from the lingering spring air, although The Island typically remained moderate throughout the year.

Julie had never been to The Island before—a place her family couldn't afford to visit during her youth or while her father was paying off her mother's medical bills.

But she understood why those who could vacation here would, similarly to how those who afforded The Oceanside spent their weekends and summers there too.

The waves on The Island were peaceful compared to The Oceanside. The sandy beach beyond on the coastline looked pristine and welcoming, the color nearly white from the paleness of the rocks and the brightness of the sun shining down on them.

People were bustling around the streets, weaving in and out of shops and restaurants while chatting and laughing comfortably with one another.

The overall peacefulness soothed Julie compared to the dangers occurring in The City. Being removed and isolated from the mainland helped shield the people and few androids who lived here from the horrors their neighbors shared.

Mick and Julie strolled from the small downtown area toward windy streets following the coastline. The homes were beautiful, all well-kept and manicured.

The Garcia family enjoyed living here, and yet, Anna insisted on staying away. If Julie had the choice, she would escape here.

Julie slowed her legs, noticing how Mick struggled to keep up with her. He was frail from the effects of time traveling on other people's blood. His normally deep-colored hair was freckled with silver specks, and the lines on his face were profound, stretching across his forehead.

When they finally reached the Garcia home, Julie stopped. While they were an old bloodline family built on prestige and wealth, the purely gorgeous home in front of her made her pause. From the outside, the house rivaled the O'Connor estate in The Oceanside.

Peeking into the large glass windows showed that, instead of history and charm, the home was modernized and updated. The idea of so much glass and open space reminded Julie of contemporary museums back in The City, and she instantly wished she didn't need to venture inside.

The seashells in the driveway crunched beneath Julie's and Mick's feet, and they finally reached the door.

"We're doing the right thing," Mick said, the words low but not directed at Julie.

The front door opened, and Isabella stood on the other side as if she were expecting them. She looked relaxed compared to the last time Julie saw her.

"I knew I hadn't seen the last of you," Isabella said to Julie with a hesitant smile.

The two women would always share an awkwardness: they were supposed to hate one another, being pitted against each other because of a man. But for some reason, there was little animosity. Julie previously felt jealous watching Isabella take care of Colin, but she didn't hate her for doing so. Isabella previously disliked Julie for taking the affections of the man who was supposed to fit her perfect old bloodline family heritage, but she found she couldn't hate Julie.

"You look good," Isabella noted, her fingers reaching out toward Julie's neck. "I'm sorry I couldn't prevent the scar."

Julie chuckled before replying, "Actually, it gives me a bit of character. I've grown fond of it."

Isabella welcomed Julie and Mick into her home, the deep chocolate hardwood floors shining with a brand-new coat of wax against the gray-toned walls and white woodwork.

"I wish I could properly show you around The Island, but I'm afraid your visit isn't purely pleasure," Isabella said, walking into her kitchen, turning on the stovetop, and settling a kettle down.

"You're correct, but I do wish we had more time. I've never been to The Island before," Julie noted, "and it's beautiful here."

Mick awkwardly paced between them, his hands in his pockets.

"I need some air," Mick declared, walking himself out the back door to the patio.

He continued pacing around the in-ground swimming pool. He stopped to touch the beautiful plants surrounding the lawn chairs and then continued on his exploration of the grounds. When the kettle whistled with boiling water, Isabella finally settled down in the seat next to Julie.

"What brings you here?" Isabella asked, her eyes never leaving Mick.

"Mick needs your help in the future. He's hoping you can help transform him into a posse hominem. He has concerns about Nolan. And selfishly, I'd like to observe the process."

Isabella sat back in her seat, her hands gripping her warm mug closely. "Mick shouldn't become a posse hominem."

"Are you sure?" Julie asked, a red skepticism showing on her flushed cheeks. "That's not what he's led me to believe. He said he must in order to continue on."

"I don't think Mick will ever truly understand what he is or what he needs. Time travel has changed his physical and mental being too much, as far as I'm concerned." Isabella frowned.

"He told me he has a microchip inside of him in the future, that he becomes a posse hominem. Why would he lie about that?"

"I'm not sure, but I never made him into one."

"That you know of. Maybe you do in the future."

Isabella and Julie looked at one another.

"I have a time travel device, Julie. How else do you think I saved you?" Isabella's hand gravitated toward her face, tracing the small delicate crow's feet in the corners of her eyes.

Isabella was vain when it came to her beauty—an element of her personality that Julie assumed Isabella was constantly aware of.

So, Isabella has the remaining time travel device Peter mentioned.

"Then maybe Nolan does help him in the future," Julie posed, her eyes finally finding Mick again.

She barely recognized her friend, so much about him constantly changing. Julie could hardly keep track of how many times Mick experimented with time travel on his own, forcing his body into catastrophe in the name of research and science.

"That's a possibility, but I assumed FACERE deprogrammed him."

"You're probably correct on that front. That's what they plan to do with The Supreme."

"I wonder if I should be there," Isabella said, her hazel eyes wet from holding back tears. "I believed there was good. I knew that what The Supreme wanted to do at COLI*GO wasn't just a creation of her own. I had an opportunity to finally impress a person who spent her whole life hating me: Celine. I finally had the ability to show my craft, my skill. To empower myself. To highlight I was more than just a pretty, philanthropic face in The City. I grew stronger as a surgeon with each operation. I perfected the procedures, and I wouldn't change that experience. The only regret I have is with The Supreme herself. If she never grew selfish, if she never wanted to use these creations to destroy humans, I would have continued. I would have gladly helped create a better version of society."

Julie grabbed Isabella's free hand in hers and gave her a gentle squeeze. Isabella was a tiny woman, but her words took up the space of the entire room. An odd sense of understanding passed between Julie and Isabella.

"This had nothing to do with Colin. When will everyone learn that not everything has to do with a man in power? Sometimes, women want to leave their own mark on society. We want our own command. I never had the opportunity before. I lived in the shadows of my father, and then I lived in the shadows of Colin. I wanted my own legacy."

"I agree," Julie responded, smiling slightly at Isabella. "That's all I've ever wanted for the antidote. And then everyone else got involved. I wanted the antidote to save people, and instead, the antidote killed me."

"The antidote didn't kill you, Julie," Isabella said with an upturned brow.

"That's why Colin killed me. Because of the antidote."

"You didn't die; he didn't succeed. I'd argue he didn't want to kill you at all based on how shallow your wounds were."

"Then what happened to me?" Julie asked. "I don't follow Mick's rules of time travel. Each time I have died in a past dimension, I end up back in the woods on that night."

The mug slipped from Isabella's grasp. The crash of ceramic hitting the hardwood floor rang loudly in their ears, and even Mick looked back toward the house from his position outside. Steam from the hot liquid rose from the dark wood, and the smell of the tea was instantly stronger in the air.

"You didn't die that way, Julie," Isabella insisted as both she and Julie picked up the broken shards off the ground. "At least, not in that body."

Chapter 39
Peter

June 20th, 47 A.R.

"Elsie Sullivan?" Peter asked, his eyes barely moving upward while he sat behind his desk.

The woman in the doorway was roughly his age, her height a bit intimidating, but he was a tall enough man where that didn't bother him. Her black fitted suit jacket hung proportionately with a black skirt, tailored closely to her body and extenuating her lovely features. She wasn't from a popular old bloodline family, but he was aware her family name worked with the elite in The City.

"Hello, Dr. Schneider," she answered with a small chuckle while her delicate hands closed Peter's office door behind her.

Peter liked to believe he never objectified women, especially having worked for intelligent, strong leaders like Celine and Julie. But Elsie Sullivan differed. The air around her was bitter, and a mysterious shadow lingered behind her. Peter was simultaneously attracted to Elsie and afraid of her.

"I'm here on behalf of Governor O'Connor. He mentioned the two of you have a bit of a strained relationship and that I might not receive a warm welcome."

Her words were like honey against Peter's ears. He hated Colin O'Connor with a passion, but he wasn't willing to make the same assumption about this woman.

"That's an understatement."

Elsie laughed in response, her small chuckle kind and endearing in Peter's ears. A small smirk crossed her face, and there was an edginess to Elsie that Peter wanted to like.

Peter motioned for her to step into his office, and Elsie approached. When she came face to face with Peter, her body relaxed into the seat opposite his desk, her smile never ceasing.

Elsie's tall frame reminded him of Celine's. While she was lanky, Elsie also held herself with ease and comfort, much like his boss. Peter continued observing Elsie's body more closely this time, having been too distracted the last time he saw her. His eyes narrowed in on Elsie's tattoo—the black ink stark against her otherwise pale skin.

"But why are you here in my office?" Peter asked, leaning into his hand as he stretched across his desk.

Elsie looked up at Peter with large eyes, and Peter could hear his heart beating in his chest in anticipation of what she might reveal. After a few moments of silence, Elsie stood, the hem of her skirt riding up her legs as she walked to the other side of the desk.

Peter's eyes didn't leave her as she sat in his lap, her right hand securely gripping his shoulder. The move felt natural until Elsie strengthened her grip. The air escaped Peter's lungs, but he wasn't afraid. Elsie inched her face closer to Peter's, and the edges of her lips brushed against his earlobe.

"I won't ask this more than once, Dr. Schneider," Elsie said with an intoxicatingly husky voice, "but I need to know the truth of what's happening with Dr. Walsh."

Peter paused, his pulse stilling from Elsie's request. She released her grip on him before escaping from his lap. She has large hands, especially for a woman. Her actions confused him. He wanted to slap her and simultaneously kiss her.

"There's nothing happening between me and Dr. Walsh," Peter reassured Elsie, his body stiffening at the sound of Julie's name.

"I didn't mean like that," Elsie said, her gaze stretching out to the floor-to-ceiling windows just behind Peter. "I know she loves him, not you. I want to know what kind of threat you are to her. I know you travel time together."

Peter held his breath, unaware of the lingering knowledge Elsie possessed. She looked over at him and smiled wide again before saying, "I just need to know if you're the one who ruins everything, for everyone."

Peter stiffened in his seat, confused by Elsie's cryptic accusation.

"I don't know what you're referring to," Peter finally answered.

Her eyes wandered across Peter's office with uncertainty. Peter wasn't sure what to make of this woman—she was powerful in the sense that she reported to Governor O'Connor, but otherwise, she didn't seem to matter in the grand scheme of things.

At least, not yet, he thought, uncertainty clouding his mind.

"What do you know about the toxin?" The words finally left Elsie's mouth: an inkling that she was, in fact, a larger piece on the chess table than Peter initially anticipated.

"Julie's toxin would negatively change The City if it was ever exposed," Peter answered truthfully. "But the antidote is what we're after. We need her antidote to save people from Alzheimer's. To save people from manic depression and other psychological conditions. To save the human brain from self-destruction. To save The City. And to save Colin."

Elsie leaned against the window. The look in her eyes was empty, distant. She gazed at the lighted buildings across The River. Concern ruffled Elsie's brows, but Peter felt troubled too. He and Julie were running out of time between the toxin and the antidote, the inability to test on a larger array of simulated patients in fear that someone besides Amanda MacDonald might know of their unwelcomed presence at COLI*GO ten years in the past.

Peter couldn't afford to see the slowdown in any asset, regardless of if he worked on them personally or not. He learned in his short tenure as COLI*GO's CEO that when it came to having influence and power, there was a specific, calculated reason why. Martin prioritized assets logically and strategically, willing to put everything else on the line for the antidote, COL23. There was something so intoxicating about that drug that even Peter was immune to his own logic. The simple fact that Julie proved the concept of a single-dose injection of antidote demonstrated how powerful and impactful this innovation would be.

*COLI*GO needs to launch the new and improved COL23, and soon.*

"What would the antidote do for Colin?"

Peter laughed, his chuckle deeper than he anticipated.

"I don't know much about your boss other than that he hates me. Sounds like a personal matter you should ask him about."

Elsie turned her smile upward, a devious grin spreading across her cheeks.

Peter continued, "But I imagine the antidote would cure Colin of whatever infliction it is that Celine won't admit to. One you're probably too familiar with but realize if you ever exposed, you'd be responsible. Something far more sinister than even Julie would confide in me with."

Elsie returned to Peter's lap, her hand grasping his throat in a delicate but serious manner. There was vulnerability and exposure in Elsie's action as Peter gripped her waist, careful not to touch her inappropriately. In response, she tightened the strangle she had on him. Elsie's thumbs pushed against his skin, the seriousness in her small threat escalating in a matter of seconds, a tendency of outward bursts of anger Peter recalled from both Colin and Celine.

"You have a very familiar grasp to another O'Connor," Peter threatened as Elsie strengthened her grip around him.

Her eyebrows furrowed in response to Peter's accusations, words she didn't want to believe.

"What are you insinuating, Dr. Schneider?" Elsie asked in a threatening tone, her voice soft while retaining a strong manner.

"I'm not sure, Ms. Sullivan," he responded in a strained voice. "Wasn't someone in upper management at FACERE recently strangled and stabbed in a similar fashion to The City's infamous serial killer's murders?"

Peter smiled, regardless of the helpless position Elsie held him in. He was invincible to her touch, even with her thumbs squeezing closer together and the blotchy red marks on his skin becoming more visible as each second passed. While Elsie didn't intend to cause him too much harm, she had an undeniable and uncanny charm to her.

Elsie's taut and muscular body leaned in against his, her fingers refusing to let go of his neck. Something made Peter remember there was more to this world than his role here at COLI*GO, his duty to Celine, his hatred for Mick, or his desire to help Julie. There was simplicity in being the prey and not the hunter.

The thought of what Peter needed to do in the coming days exhausted him and made his hands shake with uneasiness. He had made a promise and couldn't back out now; Elsie was right to accuse him of unsavory intentions.

"I think upper management at many of these companies that line their pockets with representatives from The Legislature should watch their backs," Elsie hissed. "Especially you."

Peter couldn't contain himself anymore—he leaned in and kissed her.

***

Anna sat in silence on her couch. The loft apartment was spacious, deceiving the inhabitant of more space than what was really there. Peter and Anna hadn't spoken since her time at COLI*GO with Celine's interview and untimely and unflattering consequences that made Anna sick in the bathroom.

The woman sitting on the white leather sofa grasped a stemless glass of red wine with authority, her eyes hollow but fast-moving. Peter didn't doubt that Anna was crafting a devious plan or, at least, thinking about what she wanted to occur next.

After discovering a potential connection between his consultant and a potential suspect aiding The Supreme's crimes at COLI*GO, Peter swiftly handed the case back over to Commissioner Jones. Technically, Anna still worked for Jones, but Peter felt the only politically correct answer that wouldn't land him in some kind of predicament later was to give the case back.

After his encounter with Elsie Sullivan, Peter was convinced everyone at COLI*GO and in The Capitol Building was connected when it came to the creation of posse hominems. He wasn't sure where to go next, except for wishing he had an explanation or a larger picture drawn for him by Isabella Garcia herself.

"I haven't talked to her," Anna admitted, finally acknowledging Peter's presence in her home.

Peter didn't respond; he was afraid any noise might tip Anna off, and he didn't put it past her to insist on him leaving, to insist he knew nothing about Isabella and her involvement in the creation of a new species that spread throughout The City. Peter didn't know the full implications behind posse hominems, wasn't sure of their capabilities or motives now that The Supreme was back at FACERE.

"I'm not sure why she would choose to help the O'Connors. But I suppose I understand why she would transform Dr. Walsh into one of those creatures." Anna's words were suggestive and harsh, something Peter was used to after working with her for a few months.

"Doesn't explain the some-thousand number of hybrids out on the street," Peter commented, finally finding his footing with this complicated woman.

"Are they really that different from the rest of us?" Anna asked, taking a large gulp from her wine glass.

I suppose not, Peter thought.

Elsie didn't feel any different to him than the other woman he had been with. Women who weren't hybrids. There was nothing stiff or different about her. Nothing he could tell except for the tattoo on the side of her neck hiding her incision scar.

"I feel like The Legislature and the COLI*GO Board of Directors are sending me on a red herring of an investigation," Peter responded, taking a seat beside Anna on the couch and grabbing her glass of red wine from her smooth but dark hands.

Peter took a deep gulp, remembering the taste of this very red when he and Julie were closer. She exclusively drank red, her lips barely wanting to touch the varietals of white wines. Her only exception was with champagnes.

"I wouldn't be surprised. I imagine they were in on this. They probably knew everything from the beginning." Anna stood from the couch and walked to her front door.

Commissioner Jones entered Anna's loft with a sense of familiarity that was deeper than that of a colleague relationship. Jones and Julie had always been close, but Peter barely remembered spending time with Jones or Mick when dating Julie. She kept her world of friendships away from him as if she knew that he and she were never going to make it as a couple.

Jones's scales were a brilliant emerald, barely peeking out from his long-sleeved collared shirt. The calming but classic android facial features betrayed Jones for what he really was: an android. One that would never fully understand the implications of all human emotions.

"I'm not surprised," Jones said, still ignoring Peter's presence on Anna's couch.

"I am," Anna responded, smacking her palm flat against her marble countertops.

The slap echoed across the room, making all three of them stiffen into a silence, waiting on a cue from Anna before ending the razor-thin silence surrounding them.

"Isabella always wanted to help people. When I spoke with the few victims of this crime, they all expressed the terror, distaste, and confusion that followed their experiences. Why would my sister contribute to that? Why would she ever help the O'Connor family? Especially when all Colin did was do her wrong?"

"But what do we do now?" Peter asked, standing from the couch. He approached Anna swiftly, his face growing more concerned with each step.

"I don't know," Anna answered honestly. "I think she needs to come clean."

Chapter 40
Commissioner Jones

June 20th, 47 A.R.

After reading Julie's entries in Mick's journal, Jones placed the leather notebook in the bottom drawer of his office desk at police headquarters. He contemplated for days if he should give the journal to Colin—the recipient Julie initially intended for her confessions—but something about the last two entries made Jones pause.

When Mick asked for his help in the journal, Jones obliged, and instead of saving The City, he contributed to its downfall.

I'm not going to do anything, no matter how sincere I think Julie was with her request.

He looked out the window and sighed. The sun shone brightly in The City today and the temperatures promised a warm summer. He wanted nothing more than to lift the curfew on human and android residents.

And posse hominems. I can't forget about them, either, Jones thought as his scales flickered a deep hunter green.

His scales betrayed him more frequently. Julie reminded Jones of his ability to continuously learn, improve, and optimize his understanding of human emotions over time. When she initially reprogrammed him, the bar was set at just over 60 percent. But now, Jones wasn't sure how much he comprehended.

The knowledge of The Supreme's ability to recognize all human emotions, even if not fully experience them, still struck Jones as odd. Jones doubted humans understood all their emotions, but he knew they still experienced them.

He picked up his device and scrolled through Peter Schneider and Anna Garcia's latest report. They discovered who aided The Supreme in her creation of posse hominems: Isabella. Both Peter and Anna asked for guidance from the commissioner, but Jones cautioned to do much with the information himself. The investigation was nowhere completed, and Isabella would need to come to The City from The Island for questioning as a first step.

Peter and Anna uncovering the truth about Isabella wasn't part of the plan they crafted the night Elsie killed Paul.

They needed Isabella's involvement to remain under wraps and hidden from the public.

I should have known better. Anna is amazing at uncovering the truth.

A small knock on Jones's open door startled him. He shouldn't have been surprised to see Maggie Rivera, polished and attractively put together in a violet fitted dress with black pumps. They had this meeting scheduled for a long time, ever since The Legislature agreed to send The Supreme back to FACERE for evaluation and reprogramming.

Tension and awkwardness filled Jones's office as he realized they hadn't spoken to one another since the morning she left him with Mick's journal.

"Commissioner Jones," Maggie addressed him before entering the room. "I wanted to discuss our initial findings from scans and testing of The Supreme's processor and the evaluation we did based on her predecessor, Edward."

Maggie sat down and handed Jones her device. On the screen, Jones examined various lines of coding and programming that made almost no sense to him, but as he continued scanning each line, his eyes widened.

This is similar to the coding Julie used to program me. Jones's placed the device down steadily.

"Some of our engineers suspect once I remove The Supreme's microchip, we will see similar results to Edward's. What puzzles me, though, is that Edward went on this long undetected, but I suppose I should be encouraged he never behaved in a manner like Emilia."

"How did his coding manifest in this way?" Jones asked, trying to seem inconspicuous and unassuming.

"I'm hoping his processor didn't just evolve on its own. Then we would have a large problem on our hands." Maggie looked up at the ceiling before dropping her eyes back down to Jones.

"Do you know I have always been intrigued by how some androids are more in tune and empathetic than others but I haven't been able to figure out why? There are always issues with hackers on the dark web offering androids a piece of freedom with new programmed microchips, but FACERE has been cracking down on that more lately. We've successfully identified and taken down those terrorists with ease."

The way Maggie spoke so freely about androids as if they weren't conscious beings and as if Jones wasn't one himself spurred a flare of rage across Jones's processor. He tugged down his sleeves and removed his hands from the top of the desk when he felt his scales pulsate and swell.

"I think reprogrammed microchips are probably the correct assumption for the culprit," Jones answered as flatly as he could.

"But who reprogrammed Edward? Who reprogrammed Emilia?" Maggie's eyes were accusing and focused, a sharpness shimmering from her irises.

"I'm not sure, but I'm assuming you want my department's help in investigating the manner?" Jones inquired while shifting uncomfortably in his desk chair.

"I read the whole journal, Jones. Not just Julie's entries."

A stillness sliced through the room like the sharp blade Colin and It used on their victims. Jones's own entries were problematic and overly vulnerable, and Mick revealed secrets, especially with the entry where Mick retold how Julie reprogrammed Jones's processor. Jones almost felt the burning sensation of the journal in the desk drawer beside him as if it were igniting an explosive fire no one could ever put out.

A small cat-like smile purred across Maggie's face. Crossing her legs and leaning forward, Maggie made direct eye contact with the commissioner.

"I'm convinced more than ever that Dr. Walsh has a bit more explaining to do."

Jones gulped, sitting up taller in his seat. Maggie might know his secrets, she might know too much about Mick and Julie, but he was still in possession of the physical journal. Plus, he had a strategically thought-out plan. Jones believed in Colin, and he believed in Julie, regardless of how unhinged some of her journal entries were.

"I've arranged for Julie's transportation to FACERE. She will have to answer to me about posse hominems and explain time travel, a construct I know Joel has hidden from me for far too long. FACERE will be the one to put a controlled end to the madness The Supreme created, and all of The Constituency will thank me for it."

Maggie stood and made her way around Jones's desk. Perching herself on the edge, she leaned in closer and engulfed Jones with the smell of her floral perfume. Jones looked away from Maggie, disgust with the woman she turned out to be ricocheting through his processor.

When Jones didn't respond, Maggie continued. "I've always been intrigued by your kind. I might know how every single circuit board version works, the importance of each modification and improvement to processors, microchips, and scales, but I still relish the drive, the commitment coded into your brain to please humans. I find a small thrill in the way you unknowingly seek my approval and place my interests over your own. That's why I enjoyed our little trysts. Not because I actually care for you, Jones. I understand now why this felt different compared to the others. You fascinate me even though I created your kind, but you're nothing more than a glorified pet even if you do understand more emotions than most androids. With a simple extraction of your microchip, I can change you and shape you into whatever I want you to be. Which is why I never desire to be one of your kind or anything close to it. I've never wished for a microchip to be placed in my brain. No respectable human ever should."

"Governor O'Connor was correct in his accusation," Jones finally butted in, not caring that his scales flickered. The bright greens reflected off Maggie's smooth, dark skin, casting shadows in the dim office. "You're a shameless, self-serving, despicable bitch."

Maggie laughed, but her eyes remained defensive and narrow. "I promised you I would be the one who lit the fire to the demise of the O'Connor family. Don't worry, Jones, I've doused them with lighter fluid. Once I'm finished with The Supreme and Dr. Walsh, I'm coming for you."

Her threat hung in the air, lingering like an unwanted visitor in the room even as the sound of her heels told Jones she left.

Chapter 41
The Governor

June 20th, 47 A.R.

Elsie sat quietly beside Colin in his office at The Capitol Building. He couldn't stop looking at her and wondering how he hadn't noticed all the similarities before.

Her sheer height should have been a dead giveaway, but even now, Colin zeroed in on the small things. Elsie's uncharacteristically strong facial features, the shape of her nose, and even the largeness of her hands. And those were just the physical traits; Colin didn't want to venture down the rabbit hole as to why he and Elsie shared similar drives and needs—why their instinct was violence when it came to protecting those they loved and the things they cherished.

"What is it?" Elsie asked, tucking a piece of her chestnut hair behind an ear.

"Why were you so willing and insistent on killing Paul?" Colin asked, but the words sounded more like a statement as they left his lips. Elsie looked down at her hands in her lap and sighed.

Her large fawn eyes, a trait she obtained from her mother, were wide but serious.

"Paul isn't the first person I've killed. And he won't be the last."

Colin stilled in his seat. While he and Elsie had only known one another more personally over the last few months, he felt a kinship and responsibility to her. He wanted to be the person his father couldn't—he desperately wished to help her even if this meant fueling her inner It too.

"When did these urges start?" Colin ventured, hoping Elsie would open up to him more easily if he remained unbothered by her confessions.

Elsie's hands let go of one another, and her left hand automatically brushed the tattoo on her neck. She closed her eyes and said, "I have a confession. I'm a posse hominem."

Colin raised his eyebrows softly, leaning in with a sympathetic smile. Before he could decide if he should tell Elsie he knew this already, and admit to Julie telling him of her secret, Elsie rose from her seat and walked over to the window facing the courtyard. Her gaze longingly lingered toward The Supreme's empty, dust-collecting office. Elsie looked back over at Colin with a deep sigh, ready to make a confession.

"I've always been rough around the edges, a rebel with a small tick toward anger. You have to understand, I've never known my father, and my mother, while she loves me, wasn't always around. She still pined after whoever he was even though he left her. Even though he never gave a shit about me. But I never wanted to kill. I never thought it would feel satisfying to grip someone by the neck and watch the life slip away from their eyes. Not until after that damn microchip was placed in my brain."

Colin froze in his seat and his heartbeat raced in his chest. While he was honored Elsie trusted him enough with this secret part of herself, this devious monster inside her brain, he never expected this.

Did The Supreme program Elsie's microchip to have the tendencies I have? Is she even capable of doing that?

The Supreme knew about It. She knew the truth behind the mystery in Colin's mind, the one that haunted his soul and triggered dark desires while also mending the pieces of his broken heart back together.

If Emilia knew Elsie was my father's daughter, I wouldn't put this past her.

But Colin couldn't tell Elsie this. He couldn't explain all of It, The Supreme, and the messiness of their figurative chess game to Elsie. He didn't have enough time.

"I remember when I found out I had a microchip placed inside me. I awoke with the worst headaches after an event hosted by your sister and her husband, Martin. I barely recall the actual evening itself other than how excited I was that the high judge invited me. I'd been trying to get myself into The Capitol Building for a while, but I didn't want to use my mother's influence as the reason why a representative might hire me. I didn't care about the big wigs from

COLI*GO because there were plenty of old bloodline families with power and influence. People were just enjoying themselves and the booze. But everything else went fuzzy after I met The Supreme and that famous artist."

Colin sucked in a sharp breath, automatically knowing where Elsie's tale was headed.

"After waking up with a pounding headache, my skin grew drier and drier, but with much persistence and constant moisturizing, it's manageable now. Then I noticed the scar. I hated it so much even though it was only a tiny imperfection. I knew something was terribly wrong, but I was too afraid. I got the tattoo to hide it after the most peculiar thing happened. I came home one night, and on my couch sat that artist I recognized from the party and from the papers. But he was supposed to be dead. It all felt so surreal and as if it were a fever dream. Who knows, maybe it was. But he told me about what The Supreme did to me and handed me two letters from her. One to open right away and one to open at a later date. I still have both the letters but haven't opened the second one yet."

Elsie wove the missing pieces of the story together so perfectly that Colin felt like he was witnessing her experience first-hand.

"When are you supposed to open the second letter?"

Elsie's eyes grew wide with terror.

"In a few days. June 23rd, 47 A.R."

Colin looked away and nervously stroked his chin.

"I need to confess something to you too," Colin said, approaching Elsie by the window. They looked out together and stood in silence for a few moments. "I know who your father is."

Elsie looked up at Colin with an upturned grin. He could see the suppressed excitement Elsie tried hiding from him. He didn't blame her; she had gone thirty years of her life not knowing the man who made the other half of herself. The man who caused the tension and rift between her and her mother.

"Henry O'Connor. My father."

The color drained from Elsie's face, and she took a few steps back, her hands reaching for the corner of Colin's desk to steady herself.

"What?" Elsie asked with a tremble. "How? Are you sure?"

"I'm positive. You can ask your mother at some point if you want the confirmation. She knows I know." Colin spoke softly and placed a steady hand on Elsie's shoulder.

"Who else knows?"

"No one I'm aware of, but I have a sinking suspicion The Supreme does. I think that's why she programmed your microchip to emulate my personality, my own troubles. There's always an ulterior motive behind her actions. I haven't told Julie or Celine. It's not my business to share. And knowing Celine, it might not be best if she knows before others."

"Why are you telling me this?" Elsie asked, her eyes darting around the room.

"Because you deserve to know and because your mother has zero intentions of telling you. I'd rather you hear this from me and know that I would welcome you into the O'Connor family with open arms if that's what you wanted."

Elsie closed her eyes and tilted her head down.

"I need some time to decide if that's what I want," she finally said. "Does this change things between us?"

"No," Colin said with a reassuring smile. "I would still like to keep you by my side as my aide and hope that someday, you might be on the Session floor yourself. You're smart, Elsie. You have a knack for politics."

"What about the way we handle our aggressions?" Elsie asked with a mischievous grin, and Colin chuckled lightly at her question.

"I don't think that has to change either. If it did, how would we help The City?"

***

Darkness set upon The City later and later as summer approached. Normally during this week, Colin would find himself lingering in the freshly cut grass and glossily manicured estate at The Oceanside. Each year since he could remember, Colin ventured back on the anniversary of his mother's death and birthday and allowed himself to mourn her.

The last two years, Julie joined him. She was the first person

Colin had ever opened up to about his mother's death and the reasoning behind his infliction of It. The relationship he maintained with It now differed from ever before, and the idea of how close he let It inhabit his mind both scared and excited him.

Colin opened the refrigerator and looked at the mostly empty shelves inside. He had grown accustomed to Isabella's constant presence in his home this late winter and early spring and the terribly cooked meals she prepared for him.

Before Isabella came back to help, Colin used to cook for himself and Julie so frequently that the fridge was always stocked.

He smiled, thinking about how Julie would come to the townhouse well past seven, her hair a rumpled mess and small markings around her eyes from the protective eye goggles she wore in COLI*GO's lab.

When he opened his eyes, the bareness of the townhouse consumed him. An untouched six-pack of beer sat on the bottom shelf next to a container of takeout and a fruit drawer with a handful of apples. Colin took a beer and studied the bottle of IPA for a moment before popping off the top and taking a large swig. The hoppy taste foamed in his mouth and buzzed its way down his throat.

Colin didn't need to turn around to know who sat on the countertop behind him. He grabbed a second beer, opened the bottle, and handed the contents off to It.

"Are you ready?" His voice echoed behind Colin.

Colin never understood why sometimes It was one with him and other times It stood before his eyes the same way anyone else would. The insanity in his own mind bogged him down, pushing deeper and deeper into both madness and darkness.

"Yes. The plan is solid," Colin responded with hesitancy.

The plan was solid, but only if everything happened in a timely fashion and if everyone played their parts correctly. Colin believed in Jones and Elsie. More importantly, he believed in Julie. What he didn't trust were the other pieces on the board: The Supreme, Celine, Isabella, Peter Schneider, and most importantly, Mick Taylor.

"Good. We only have one shot at this."

Colin pushed himself up on the countertop and sat beside It. He studied It with precision: the exact mirrored image of himself. Speaking with It was always an odd experience, one that wasn't necessarily bad but came with a promise of unsettling discussion.

"You love her, don't you?" Colin asked, referring to Julie.

The room stilled, and silence followed Colin's question. It took a long sip from his beer and sighed. While It was a part of him, Colin never liked the idea of sharing all of himself with It. They needed separation, or Colin was afraid he would lose himself in It completely.

Sharing Julie skirts that line too closely.

"Do you trust Julie?" It finally responded.

"Of course," Colin replied immediately.

"Do you trust me?" It asked, his question hanging in the air between them with a sense of strange ambiguity.

Colin looked out the window toward the carriage house. None of the lights were on, and the emptiness disappointed him. Colin reserved his strong hatred for Mick Taylor and was glad the time traveler didn't linger in the shadows there, but he was saddened to not see the familiar figure of Julie bouncing around the open room.

Learning this was where she had spent much of her time at night over the spring made Colin feel a sense of abandonment, knowing she hadn't returned in over a month. Julie watched over him and It, learning more about him without even being inside the confines of the townhouse. She trusted all of him, and in return, he trusted her judgment.

"Yes," Colin finally answered.

"Then you have nothing to worry about."

PART TEN

The Past

"The distinction between past, present and future is only a stubbornly persistent illusion."
—Albert Einstein

Chapter 42
Mick

January 28th, 47 A.R.

The bitter air wrapped around Mick's skinny body with an astonishing amount of pain. The sound of the snow crunched against his boots and he picked up his pace. Climbing the side of the hill remained a difficult task for him with his out-of-shape body. The slight elevation didn't help his cause and his lungs ached and burned inside his chest.

*Why here, Colin? Why not The Oceanside? Why not The River? Why not COLI*GO?*

What didn't matter was how many times Mick came back to this moment to find his friend. He needed this version of Julie alive or the future where he came from would cease to exist. The dimension would close. But Mick also needed to find the future Julie—the Julie who traveled time and wreaked havoc on all his thoughtfully laid-out plans.

Lights from The City twinkled in the distance as Mick finally made it to the top of the hill. He now knew his way through the paths and trails, which were popular with humans and androids in the summer months and which now in winter were more forgotten and abandoned because of the dangers of slick rocks and sharp corners. The first time Mick came and saved Julie, he barely knew these woods. He didn't know where she was other than that she was here and he needed to save her.

A sharp vibration hurled through his already fragile body. Another time where too many time travelers came together for one reason or another. Julie's supposed death was a delicate topic amongst the key players, himself included.

"Which version of you am I speaking to?" Julie's soft voice

sounded from behind Mick.

Mick turned his head in her direction and pushed his glasses up the bridge of his nose. He smiled lightly at her, knowing that this was the Julie from the future based on the scar on her neck.

But I wonder, How many times does Julie visit this date? How many times has she been back here?

"Are you the same Julie who went to The Island with me?" Mick asked, taking in the sight of his unrequited friend.

Julie was dressed more appropriately for the weather. She wore a large puffy coat, which protruded awkwardly around her normally tall and narrow frame. Julie held the time travel glasses in her left hand, but in her right, were two syringes.

"What is it you need to do, Mick?" Julie asked, her eyes wide and her breath misty around her face.

The wind picked up, howling loudly while he remained silent. Mick wasn't entirely sure why he kept coming back here, similarly to why he wasn't entirely sure why June 23rd, 12 A.R., also remained an important date for him.

"I'm looking for a different version of you," Mick answered, walking over toward Julie's familiar figure. "There's another you I expect to come back here. But I don't know where she comes from. You do. You were once her."

"Ah," Julie responded and slipped the syringes into her jacket pocket. Rubbing her hands together to combat the cold, this Julie smiled softly at Mick. "Yes. I do come back here. Twice. First, after I tried killing myself in the past. I attempted to create an infinite time loop. I failed."

"You're right. You did, but I can't figure out why," Mick said, reaching out for her hands. His large ones engulfed her hands with warmth. "But that's the version of you I'm looking for. Do I find you?"

"You do not find that version of me, but you do find the next one. I come back once more before now."

Mick looked up at Julie with confusion and curiosity. Julie hated time travel, how she thought it wasn't ethical. Mick didn't disagree with her assessment, but he wasn't overly excited by the idea that Julie now played with the past, that she now changed the outcomes and decisions of the future too. He was used to that role being his and his alone, with few but necessary exceptions from It.

"What are you planning to do?"

Julie tightened her grip on Mick's hands. There was so much back and forth between Julie and Mick over the years, but in his heart, he felt his friend still cared for him. They had gone from being on opposite sides of the board, passing one another in swift, elegant moves. Mick and Julie were equally responsible for one another's many deaths, the hollow versions of themselves that traveled time, changing dimensions for the better and worse. They brought each other back too. They saved one another, and while there would always be differences and opposite loyalties, Mick and Julie could never truly hate one another.

"You'll know when the time is right. You're the one who tells me to come back. You're the one who tells me this is the only way to fix It." Her words were a trembling, cryptic whisper. "Just stay here. I promise."

Julie let go of Mick and backed away, leaving small footprints in the snow. Mick held his breath and waited in the darkness to face one of his largest fears.

Chapter 43
The Governor

January 28th, 47 A.R.

Julie was unconscious in the back of Colin's car. He didn't bother to tie her hands together; he didn't think that even if she woke up that he was in danger. It shook his head from the passenger seat, annoyed by Colin's innocence and naïve nature when coming to the woman he loved.

You were also this way, It. Especially about Amanda.

Colin was unsettled by Amanda's death, a stain on his long line of victims. If Colin was honest with himself, he never would have killed the woman who meant so much to his sister. Who meant so much to It. But It insisted on her death, resulting in his massive struggle with those consequences indefinitely.

The vehicle pulled into the small parking lot off the side of the main road. The trailhead started here, and the hike up the hill was short and slightly strenuous. Colin rarely came to the woods, and It's insistence on this place bothered him. There was nothing significant about the reservation except for its serenity and isolation even with being so close to The City.

Colin turned off the car and let out a large sigh. He didn't want to kill Julie and had spent the last month wondering why It told him this was necessary. A month of not knowing when It would return and insist upon this horror.

It remained silent beside him, and Colin felt the uncomfortable urge to reach out toward him and grab his hand. Colin shook off the feeling and opened the driver's side door. The parking lot was empty, and relief flooded Colin's body.

Maybe there is a valid reason It picked this place. And I'm sure someone will discover her in the morning. This place is popular for marathon runners to train even in the winter.

Cradling Julie in his arms, Colin began the ascent with It.

Colin veered off the main trail and sank deeper and deeper into the woods. When he came across a small clearing next to the path, he gently placed Julie down in the snow. Goosebumps were raised all over her skin, cold from the lack of proper clothing. Colin wanted to touch her with his bare hands, not ones covered with leather gloves. He wanted to kiss her, wake her up, and curl up in a blanket beside the fire with her. He wanted things to go back to normal, back to how they were a few hours ago. He almost felt her warmth despite the bitterness of the cold winter air around them. But It wouldn't allow her as a permanent part of his life, and he should have seen that earlier. He was being selfish and greedy, risking her by wanting her. By wanting them.

"I can't do this," Colin said.

It sighed before parting his usual wisdom on Colin. "Of course we don't want to do this. But we have to."

Back to the ritual.

Colin grabbed the knife from his coat pocket and studied the pointy steel blade. He sharpened it a few days before, unsure when he would need to use the weapon but knowing the day was coming soon.

Closing his eyes, Colin thought back to earlier in the evening to him and Julie sitting across from one another in the dining room with It's looming figure stalking behind her chair. It had leaned over, his face inches away from Julie in her seated position. She did not see It. She did not feel It's presence. But It's presence overwhelmed him.

When Julie kissed him, he wondered if she knew what was about to happen. Their kiss had been filled with passion and desire, a feeling he wanted to indulge wholeheartedly in, especially at that moment. This feeling would haunt him for the rest of his life.

After opening his eyes, Colin focused. This wasn't what he wanted, but he could blame The Supreme; he could blame Emilia for all her hatred and bullshit, her quest for power.

Fueling himself with hatred and anger, Colin made his first slice on Julie's skin. The marks were shallow compared to his normal rough and heavy strokes. Defiling Julie in this way didn't sit right with him; she differed from all the others, even Amanda. And even Kathleen. Julie's body remained still and silent as he continued marking her otherwise perfect milky skin with slashes. After twenty-three stabs, Colin leaned back and looked at the woman he loved.

Shaking, Colin felt the vomit rise in his chest. He swallowed it down, unable to get rid of that evidence if he allowed himself the release.

"I hate you!" Colin yelled out into the empty darkness. Tears sprung to his eyes, and his skin grew blotchy. "I hate everything about you! I never want to see you ever again!"

In a quick, deviated moment, Colin dipped his gloved finger across Julie's soiled shirt, lifting it to get a look at the fresh wounds. With his pointer finger covered in her blood, he traced her beautiful lips. A small sigh sounded from beside him, and Colin looked at It with narrow, square eyes. He was beyond angry with It. Colin refused to let this experience be easy for It too. It needed to suffer just as badly as him.

Colin reached out toward It, but nothing was there.

He was alone.

Chapter 44
Julie

January 28th, 47 A.R.

A chill from both adrenaline and the harsh winter weather ran through Julie's body as she took off the time travel glasses. Celine's condo was much different from the O'Connor townhouse. The decorations were modern, and the glass structure was harsh with cold colors that allowed all the light from The City into the living space.

The sound of baby Henry wailing muffled in the background as Julie continued toward the large windows. She had spent little time here, only a guest on a few rare occasions with Colin.

But I'm not here to see Celine.

Martin sat cross-legged on a yoga mat on the floor, his floppy brown hair and olive skin radiating in the dim lamplight. He was a strange man, very logical and scientific, but rumors in the office circulated about how much of a hippie the head of Research and Development truly was.

Julie learned little of Martin's personal life over the years, other than he was married to Celine and the father of the next in the O'Connor bloodline. Colin didn't particularly care for him but didn't hate him. And at work, Julie always noted how introverted and quiet he was in the lab, how he barely participated in any of the lively debates in the Board room.

"Dr. Julie Walsh," Martin said without opening his eyes. He turned his palms upward and took a deep, breathy inhale. "I've been expecting you."

As if he truly was expecting her, there was a second yoga mat beside him with candles burning on the corners. Julie approached him and sat down, crossing her legs. Julie refused to close her eyes, and the awkwardness between her and Martin settled around them.

Martin opened his eyes and smiled warmly at Julie. He reached behind himself and held his hands out toward her.

Her gaze followed his, and she slowly saw what Martin possessed in his hands.

"You've come seeking answers," Martin said, his eyes wide with a still fear. "I didn't ever imagine being a part of this mess, but I suppose the moment I agreed to help Celine, I didn't really have much of a choice. I tried to warn Colin, but he won't do anything about his knowledge. He will always protect his sister."

The leather-bound journal made Julie's heart stop beating, and she flipped through the pages. Mick's scraggly handwriting consumed most of the journal, followed by the perfectly legible entries from Jones. Her own writing. She stopped after reading her last two entries, rereading the all too familiar words.

But Julie's pulse quickened when she reached the next set of pages, one dated nearly four months prior to the date she traveled.

Entry Twenty-Three

June 23rd, 47 A.R.

Dear Julie,

I don't know if you'll ever forgive me—but I have to do this. I've played this game long enough to know that anyone who wants the victory so badly is a liar, a cheater, a murderer, and someone willing to create chaos. And they don't deserve it.

The rest of the lines that followed were structured as an ambiguous confession, both harsh and heart-wrenching. Julie continued reading on, unsure why forgiveness was requested and if she hadn't granted it. She was aware of the events, and seeing them after relentlessly trying to uncover the truth behind them for so long made her shake. Tears flooded her face, outbursts of cries erupting from her tiny mouth.

When Julie finished reading the journal's last entry, she closed her eyes. There were no answers here, only a ridiculous number of vague premonitions of what could go wrong in the future. She didn't hesitate a moment longer and quickly tore out the last entry.

Martin looked up from the ground and nodded his head. The sounds of Henry crying in the background escalated, and Martin motioned to find and comfort his son.

Gripping the journal tightly in her arms, Julie ran out the door and pulled her device out to request a ride. She was already running behind.

The warmth of the vehicle welcomed Julie, but she still shivered in the backseat. The driver took them through the heart of The City, neglecting the underground tunnel system and remaining on the open surface roads. While it was a chilly night, Julie smiled softly at the people and androids wandering into restaurants and bars and leaving some small shops closing up for the night. They reached the highway and quickly exited into The Outskirts. The presence of triple-decker-style homes eased into houses with small yards and a bit of space between.

With a sharp transition, the vehicle approached the woods, and trees climbed high into the sky, thickly nestled together. The driver pulled over to a parking lot.

One recognizable vehicle was parked at the farthermost edge, and Julie rushed out of the car, slamming the door with emphasis and confidence.

She had only been here once before, arriving after killing herself at The Oceanside. Julie's lips trembled as she made her way through the woods. She was unfamiliar with the terrain, having been too afraid the last time to really absorb all her surroundings.

The path was well marked, and old footprints guided her in what she hoped was the right direction. Everything was so dark, and the lights from The City weren't visible in the deepness of the woods. Looking up above, Julie wasn't surprised to find a blank sky, the stars hiding from The City's proximity. Julie's breath surrounded her, the cool air freezing her face and making her exposed hands dry and itchy.

A clearing ahead made Julie pause, but she continued on, optimistic when the view of The City started meeting the skyline.

This was a night full of regret, misery, and mistakes. Necessary actions were taken, but regardless, Julie didn't like the strange feeling hanging in the air up on top of the hill. Somewhere on the side, deep within the trails, her body was bleeding. Colin was stabbing her. But that wasn't why she came here.

The outline of a figure ahead made the blood course louder in Julie's ears, her heart picking up its pace. She expected to find Mick and wondered why she was so nervous. Goosebumps prickled her skin, and the two friends approached one another.

"Julie," Mick said, extending out his arms for a hug.

Julie embraced him, the tears already trickling out of the corners of her eyes.

"Mick, the journal. You need to give it to Jones." She handed him the leather-bound book, but Mick's eyes never left hers.

"Julie . . ." He trembled, with eyes wide and full of fear. Mick backed away slowly, his mouth open in awe and terror.

Julie turned around and gasped.

Chapter 45
It

January 28th, 47 A.R.

Julie's unconscious body lay in the week-old snow in almost an angelic way. Her strawberry blonde hair was fanned out around her face, brushing against her shoulders. She wasn't wearing a coat, just a sheer, silky blouse and a pair of black fitted jeans. Her blood seeped and stained her shirt, dribbling into the harsh white snow around her.

It knelt next to her and lifted her blouse, counting all twenty-three stab wounds. Fumbling for his device, he checked the time.

The sedative Colin gave her will wear off soon. I don't have much time.

Reaching into his jacket pocket, a small pocketknife emerged in It's hand. He stalled, looking at her bright red lips. They spent over a decade killing either powerful women or the women who belonged to powerful men.

But Colin was gone, already on his way back to the townhouse.

Julie's small breaths were slowing, but this was a side effect of the drug Colin placed in her drink earlier that night. From there, he brought Julie to the woods and did this to her. But in Colin's haste and heartbreak, he forgot the most important part: the microchip in Julie's brain.

The moonlight reflected off the knife against Julie's pale skin, now purpling from the freezing temperatures and cold, hard snow beneath her. The blade pierced Julie's neck lightly, in the spot where a small, almost unnoticeable scar resided. Blood bubbled to the surface swiftly, but It didn't flinch. He had seen and experienced much more gruesome events, especially when it came to Julie.

It didn't intrude on his new incision, the mark that would stain her lovely, elongated neck. He simply left the mark as he made it.

Julie needs to know for herself, but she needs to discover what truly happened to her on her own.

It's hands trembled from the cold. The pocketknife was stained with her blood, dripping small droplets into the white snow by his feet. A harsh vibration pulsated through his body, the warning sign that another time traveler arrived.

Grabbing the glasses and chrome box in his free hand, It tilted the knife toward the slide and watched as a droplet of Julie's blood soaked through the glass. It placed the slide in between the glasses frames and secured them on his face. He looked at the chrome box and the dates provided.

It needed to get back to the present, he needed to not stick around too long in the past, but there was one more place he needed to visit before he could go home. And he needed Julie's blood to take him there.

PART ELEVEN

The Present

"I'm afraid in order to escape this place, you will need to suffer more."
—Dr. Robert Ford, Westworld

Chapter 46
Julie

June 22nd, 47 A.R.

Julie woke to a message on her device. The sun was already shining brightly, but her clock exposed the earliness of the morning. The sounds of Joel puttering around the kitchen shook across the hardwood floors as Julie hastily read the message.

To: 617–333–2985
From: 617–345–8709
Date Sent: June 21st, 47 A.R.
Subject: John Hancock

{Message Encryption}
Julie,

The governor has requested your signature on the attached documents. Please sign and return ASAP—they are urgent and need filing before you are brought to FACERE. I'm glad he knows you're back. We must be unanimous; there must be no pulling different ways; we must hang together.

I'll see you soon.

Regards,
Elsie Sullivan
Legislative Aide & Secretary to Governor Colin O'Connor
24 Beacon Street

Julie followed the instructions carefully.

Why does Colin want me to sign a document granting me permission to The Oceanside estate as a new legal residence? She still owned her apartment in The Bay and didn't intend on letting that go.

Slipping her device deep into the waistband of her pants, Julie prepared herself. Joel planned on dragging her to meet with Maggie Rivera. As if sensing she was up to no good, Joel barged into her room without knocking. He stopped and looked horrified at the sight of her. Julie spent nearly every day sneaking back to 37 A.R. when Joel left for The Capitol Building and he hadn't noticed the deep-set purple circles underneath her eyes. He was too preoccupied with The Legislature, which grew anxious after the body of Paul McGuire was found in an alleyway behind FACERE.

The media raged with speculation of someone inspired by The City's former infamous serial killer. One they believed was Jeb Taylor but the credit belonged to Colin and It. Paul was killed in the same fashion: twenty-three stab wounds and strangulation marks. The chief medical examiner—Dr. Anna Garcia—noted a smaller set of hands had gripped Paul, possibly a woman's. A different, new threat to The City emerged, one piling on top of another.

"Glad to finally leave my house?" Joel asked, glancing out the window as his vehicle navigated its way across The City.

Julie sat quietly in the passenger seat as they crossed the bridge leading to The River. The COLI*GO building was dark except for the 101st floor as everyone continued hunkering down at home, avoiding the threats of mobs and protests.

"Yes. I can't wait to get out of your ashtray," Julie said with a bite. Joel laughed, pulling a cigarette from his pocket and lighting it up in the car.

"You're the only one complaining, darling."

They continued in silence until the vehicle reached FACERE. The building was larger than Julie anticipated. She'd never made it this deep in The River neighborhood, always staying close to the actual waterway.

Joel rolled down the window, greeted by a full security detail. Dozens of tall, burly men and women escorted them across the lobby. Perspiration pooled under Julie's arms and at the base of her neck. The thought of Jones, Elsie, and Colin entering this highly secured area soon caused her hands to shake uncontrollably.

"I have an appointment with Maggie Rivera," Joel said, flashing his device. The man looked over at Julie but, after reading Joel's credentials, didn't question her presence.

"Pull forward," the man instructed, and Joel rolled up the window and parked his car in the underground garage.

FACERE didn't resemble a building like COLI*GO, and instead, she was greeted with palm trees in large old-fashioned styled pots, bright florescent lights, and carpeted floors. No androids loitered in the lobby, and only humans mulled around the mostly empty space.

A receptionist eyed Joel with enthusiasm as if he knew Joel from multiple visits before. The man's eyes lingered on Julie, recognizing her from the multiple "MISSING PERSONS" fliers littering the streets and occupying the end of the nightly news segments.

Julie didn't sign her name in the register and followed behind Kennsington with ease. Her eyes paused on the security camera, noting the red recording light was turned off.

Every camera inside the building is, she noted as they continued walking through the lobby.

The elevator ride to the top floor took longer than the ride in COLI*GO's elevator, escalating her nerves even greater. Once they reached the top, Joel walked briskly to the left and a small sign displayed Maggie's name in all caps.

"Joel!" Julie heard the voice from behind the door shout as he entered.

Julie went in after him, her eyes large at the difference in design from the hallway.

Maggie Rivera's office was cold and composed of mostly metal furnishings. There were two chairs sitting opposite her desk, one for Joel and one for Julie. Julie looked around hesitantly, noting the small bar cart with various liquors, a leafy plant off in the corner that looked like it hadn't been watered in nearly a month, and a stack of devices piled neatly on the corner of the desk.

"And you're the infamous Dr. Julie Walsh." Maggie's voice filled Julie's ears.

"In the flesh," Julie responded, outreaching her arm to shake Maggie's hand.

Maggie stared at her hand curiously and clasped hers together behind her back. The gesture was rude and intentional.

"You smell good," Maggie noted, an eyebrow raised. Julie flinched at the odd remark and took a seat beside Joel.

I'm a prisoner in Joel and Maggie's eyes.

"I was surprised when Joel told me you traveled time. I was even more surprised to discover during The Supreme's trial that you are a posse hominem," Maggie said, leaning forward in her chair and resting her elbows on the edge of her desk.

Julie paused, the scar on her neck viciously burning on her skin. A microchip didn't occupy her brain anymore; when Isabella removed the technology, she informed Julie it wasn't activated. The memory made her think of Mick.

Mick crossed Julie's mind often these days. She was angry with him, upset her best friend betrayed not only her but also many humans. She tried empathizing with Mick's desire for more liberties and freedoms between androids and humans but wished he hadn't taken the bait so easily in aiding The Supreme's ulterior motives.

But he didn't tell anyone about Isabella fixing me, Julie thought, acknowledging that Mick truly brought her back from the dead.

Without him, she would have bled out in the snowbanks. If he didn't care about her, why would he have done all of this for her?

Then why did he lie to me about so many aspects of time travel? Why is he chasing me through time?

"I'd like to run some tests on your brain and have our researchers look at your microchip, but," Maggie started, her body slightly shaking at the sight of Julie's scar, "I also don't want to be responsible for being the person who kills the infamous and beloved Dr. Julie Walsh. Everyone is still convinced on finding you, even six months later."

"Seems like you're in a bit of a pickle then, Ms. Rivera," Julie responded sourly.

Keeping the world believing she was a posse hominem was imperative to her and It's plan.

"We can't kill her," Joel said, alarm sounding in his raspy voice. "She's no use to us dead."

"What use am I?" Julie asked, her eyes scrunched together in confusion.

"Let's bring her down to the experimental lab. I need The Supreme to walk me through the process of creating her specimens before I dissect one," Maggie said to Joel, ignoring Julie's question.

The three headed downstairs, fear tingling through Julie's gut.

Joel dragged her aggressively by the arm as if she could even run away.

The experimental lab was enormous, with various androids in liquefied circular holding tubes. Several had talons, feathers, wings, and tails. The smell of antiseptic filled the air, and Julie felt vomit rising from her stomach, her deep breaths doing nothing to relax her. The experiments around her were truly from stories and nightmares.

Her eyes quickly glanced over at the clock before she threw up at Maggie and Joel's feet.

Chapter 47
Peter

June 22nd, 47 A.R.

Peter was still shaken by Elsie's unannounced visit, but spending time down in COLI*GO's lab provided him a serene sense of security and calmness. He missed the scientific work he used to perform, recalling the long hours in the lab as a researcher with happiness. At the time, he wished for nothing other than to be a program director and didn't expect to lead the whole biotech organization.

The toxin and the new under-development antidote simulations danced around Peter's computer screen. Various machines with organic matter and some robotic arms moved quickly back and forth across the lab. He wasn't supposed to take the toxin out of the past, but the technology, even only a decade later, was much more advanced and reliable than the testing environments he and Julie were using in 37 A.R.

A small knock sounded on the glass door, breaking Peter away from his deep concentration on the new assets. Mick stood on the other side, asking for Peter's permission to enter. Peter waved, and the sound of the massive glass door announced Mick's formal presence.

Mick approached Peter and sat beside him on an empty stool. He wore his white but stained lab coat, his name embroidered in thick blue letters above the pocket on the left chest. Peter didn't trust Mick, or at least, Peter didn't trust the version of Mick he met up with while traveling the dimensions of time. But there was something about the present Mick that eased Peter, reminding him of a simpler time when they had a strange sort of banter. Back before Mick identified some of the errors in Julie's promised drug.

"What are you working on?" Mick asked with a raised brow.

Peter could see Mick's eyes moving rapidly behind his glasses, taking in all the simulation lines on the screen.

"A single injection of the antidote," Peter responded with a smile. He moved the device closer to Mick so he could see what took place on the screen.

Mick pushed his glasses up further on his nose and studied the compounds on the screen. The silence between them wasn't awkward as Peter initially expected. The clatter of machines running and the bubbling of liquids and testing labs filled the empty rooms, providing them with a sense of companionship while alone in the laboratory.

"And this, what is this?" Mick asked, his jaw slightly ajar. "This looks magnificent."

Peter hesitated. He didn't want to divulge all the secrets behind Julie's plan for the antidote and her discovery of the toxin. Peter and Julie spoke often about how if the toxin was delivered to the wrong hands, The City would be in danger. Whoever had possession of the toxin could essentially empower the darker parts of the human brain to flourish.

"That's just another variation of the antidote. There are a few, especially since there is a lot of trial and error with the single-dose injection," Peter explained, hoping Mick wouldn't press harder on the topic.

"I think the single-dose injection is the correct way to go. Nip the damaged receptors in the brain as early as possible without giving them a chance to regenerate and regrow again. And it's more patient friendly," Mick said, handing the device back to Peter. "But this, this version here, I'd get rid of it."

Peter paused as Mick pointed to the second line on the screen. He expected Mick to refer to the toxin, not the antidote.

"What do you mean?"

"Well," Mick said, opening the notes application on his device and reaching for his stylus. "The compound is still a bit weak looking, and if it's weak, the mechanism of action might not regulate correctly. The half-life of the drug might be compromised."

Peter narrowed his eyes and focused on the screen as Mick highlighted and jotted notes on the side.

There could be no room for error a second time with the antidote. The antidote needed to work, or Martin and Celine could insist on canceling the program.

"This one is strong. This version is nearly perfect. Look at how it binds," Mick said with a large smile on his face.

The toxin simulated with ease, doing the job Peter and Julie wished for the antidote.

***

A sharp ring shrilled from Peter's call box. He stood from his couch and walked over to the buzzer and paused. He didn't remember ordering anything or placing a delivery request at any of the local grocers or shops.

"Hello?" Peter asked into the intercom.

A monotone voice emerged from the other end, "I have a package for Dr. Peter Schneider."

"From whom?"

When silence followed, Peter unlocked the building door and waited on the other end of his closed apartment door. The noise of heavy footsteps approaching filled the hallway, and a soft thud sounded on the other side. Peter debated on opening the door while the presence of another lingered just beyond. Against his better judgment, Peter unlocked and opened it.

On the other side stood an android with vibrant yellow scales. He was tall and boxy, his strange figure awkwardly standing behind a large metal box.

"The Supreme sends her regards."

He disappeared as quickly as he came, and Peter grabbed the heavy package with both hands. Peter was in great shape and wondered what kind of contents must have been inside to make it so heavy. An envelope was taped to the top of the box, and his name was typed in the center.

How did The Supreme send me something?

The last he was aware of, The Supreme was back at FACERE under supervision. She was still a prisoner, still found guilty of all her crimes.

Peter stared down at the note and ripped open the envelope. The words were handwritten inside, a familiar script he knew all too well.

Dear Peter,

On June 23rd, please bring this box and its contents to 15 Beacon Street. Do not open the box. Do not tell anyone about the box.

You will know what to do. I trust you'll make the correct decision.

The box burned on the other end of the apartment as Peter walked toward his bedroom. His curiosity was what made him an intelligent and successful researcher. He didn't want to ignore his hunch, his gut feeling that he should look inside. There were too many twists in turns in this city, one where he never thought time travel was real, one where an antidote was supposed to save its inhabitants, not have its toxin developed, and another where The Legislature and Governor O'Connor were supposed to save people, not corral them into confinements while terrorists roamed the streets. Peter didn't want to be surprised anymore by those who controlled The City. He wanted to be among those with the control.

Peter walked over to the metal box and kicked it gently with the edge of his foot. The sound of clinking glass made his brow raise, and he leaned down, his thumbs rubbing the metal latches. The top popped after Peter unhinged the locks and lifted the lid.

He took a deep breath at the danger that lay inside.

If Peter was correct in his assumption, he held on to something that would destroy any shred of stability left in The City.

Chapter 48
The Supreme

June 22nd, 47 A.R.

The room was quiet except for the small beeping sound coming from the machines hooked up to The Supreme's body. She'd been through hundreds of tests at FACERE since the commissioner handed her over to Maggie Rivera and her team.

The Supreme was all too familiar with the experimental lab. FACERE did everything in its power to shield The Legislature from what really occurred here. A man came in and scanned her scales several times, extracting the silver liquid from underneath her scales and dispersing it into various test tubes. Her eyes flickered with his biometrics—an update she neither liked nor thought she'd ever get used to.

The sound of Maggie's shrill voice filled her ears and The Supreme's body perked up at the sight of Julie Walsh. She hadn't seen the scientist since before her disappearance in the winter. The ugly, hellish scar on her neck reminded her of their confrontation in Julie's office at COLI*GO that past winter.

So she is a time traveler. The Supreme confirmed her suspicion when Julie leaned over.

The smell of vomit lingering with the strong scent of the experimental lab made The Supreme's nose scrunch in discomfort. The Supreme watched as Joel Kennsington shuffled Julie to a chair and placed the back of his hand against her forehead.

The Supreme closed her eyes, the flashing biometrics revealing all of Julie's secrets buzzing across her line of vision similarly to Joel and Maggie's. Julie did travel time, and she no longer had a microchip inside her brain. Julie was no longer a posse hominem.

"Hello, Representative Kennsington," The Supreme said before opening her eyes and looking directly at Julie. "And Dr. Walsh."

The technician beside The Supreme glanced at her with disgust. He puttered around with the tray of surgical instruments behind him. The shiny silver tools glimmered in the bright overhead lights.

"I'd like for you to walk us through the process of developing your prized creation, Madam Supreme," Maggie said as Joel and the tech began strapping Julie into the chair.

The Supreme noted Julie didn't put up a fight, and suspicion flashed through her processor.

"I didn't perform the surgery on Dr. Walsh. I'm not a surgeon," The Supreme answered flatly. "And I won't tell you where the microchip is. You'll have to run a scan to find it yourselves."

"Are you really going to be this difficult?" Maggie asked angrily, walking over in her loud, clunky heels. "We want to help posse hominems who don't want microchips in their brains anymore. That will help bring peace to The City. Why don't you just tell us who helped you, walk us through the basics, and then we can discuss the next steps for you. Maybe we can even come to a deal."

"You're going to wipe my microchip clean even though the commissioner has asked you not to," The Supreme answered in a huff. "And you only want access to Julie's microchip so that you can control her, not because you're interested in helping posse hominems."

Maggie rolled her eyes and walked back to the technician. Her hand rested gently on his shoulder, and the man gazed up at Maggie with a smile.

"Please remove the microchip," Maggie said before glancing back at Emilia, "from The Supreme."

Julie's eyes grew wide alongside Joel's. Neither expected the escalation to happen so quickly. The man walked over to The Supreme with instruments in hand. Julie squirmed in her seat, finally showing resistance.

"Don't worry, Dr. Walsh. You can still save The City from him. I believe in you," The Supreme said with a small smile.

Joel and Julie watched in horror as the man sliced the back spot of The Supreme's neck and placed the skinny tweezer-like tool inside. He removed the microchip in a swift motion.

The Supreme's eyes fluttered for a few more minutes and she

watched as Maggie pulled latex gloves on her hands and delicately grabbed her microchip. Maggie pulled a swab off the tray and cleaned the technology of The Supreme's silver fluid.

"Holy shit," Joel said, a maleficent grin spreading across his face. "I never thought I'd see the day where The Supreme was silent."

Julie looked down at trembling hands and back up on the wall. Maggie placed The Supreme's microchip in a small device and the screen illuminated her face. The microchip stored an incredible amount of data—years and years of memories, experiences, and code linking The Supreme's understanding of human emotion, now proudly live on the screen.

"He wasn't lying," Maggie said, her jaw dropping as she digested the code on the device.

"Who wasn't lying?" Joel asked, his body a bit too close to her.

"Colin."

"What does this say?" Joel grunted, ignoring Maggie's answer.

"She understands 100 percent of human emotions but doesn't experience them all herself."

"How is that even possible? That's well over the limit FACERE programmed in her!" Joel exclaimed, circling in a panic. "Are you telling me this is why she was just so . . ."

"Aware? Manipulative without understanding the consequences?" Maggie finished his sentence.

Joel nodded.

"I don't know how this happened, but someone reprogrammed her. I'll have to weed through her memories. I'm sure it's logged in there somewhere. But that's going to take time."

The device roared with The Supreme's conscious. The machine slowly detecting coding used to help The Supreme understand human emotions—a coding that was familiar to Julie.

Chapter 49
Commissioner Jones

June 22nd, 47 A.R.

The doors to the lab exploded open, the metal colliding with the walls. Colin and Jones stood in the entryway, swiftly approaching Maggie, Joel, and Julie with a timid and cowering FACERE employee in tow. Maggie stiffened at the sight of them, and Joel crossed his arms in an attempt to intimidate them.

"I'm fairly certain I didn't invite you to FACERE today, Governor O'Connor," Maggie said, her eyes wandering from Colin to Jones. "And what are you doing here?"

Jones shifted, his police-issued holster showing openly on his waistband. "We've come to reclaim The Supreme," Jones said stiffly, "with orders from The Legislature."

"I don't think so." Joel reached into his suit jacket and a small revolver emerged.

The room stilled as he slowly walked back over to Julie and placed the muzzle against her temple.

"You might want to rethink that one, Commissioner," Joel said as Jones's jaw dropped at the sight of his best friend.

Her heart rate wasn't elevated as Jones anticipated. She was a time traveler now, and Jones suspected Julie knew about her certain level of invincibility from a man like Joel Kennsington. But his friend wasn't the same as the last time he saw her. So much about Julie had changed, and nothing about her and her condition was what he expected.

"Drop the gun, Joel," Colin said strongly, the fierce anger visible in Jones's line of vision.

"Not the loving reunion you hoped for, Colin?" Joel asked, removing the barrel away from Julie and pointing it at the governor

"Drop your weapon," Jones declared, finally drawing his and pointing it at Joel.

"If you were really here to detain The Supreme, wouldn't some members of your police force be here with you?" Maggie asked, crossing her arms.

The screen beside her illuminated, declaring it successfully removed 50 percent of The Supreme's microchip coding.

"Don't make this more difficult than it needs to be, Maggie," Colin said, inching ever so slowly closer.

"I think you're forgetting your place," Joel said, his eyes glancing over at Julie, hitting her in the side of the head with the butt of his revolver.

Colin's swift confidence surprised everyone as he grabbed Joel's jaw in his large hand, the gun falling to the ground in a large crash.

"I would gladly rot in a prison cell for the rest of my life for killing you, knowing it'd mean you never get the chance to try to hurt Julie again." The words echoed loudly in the room as Colin's hand squeezed tighter around Joel's neck.

Joel kicked and attempted a scuffle, but Colin overpowered him, his left hand joining his right around Joel's neck.

"Colin!" Jones shouted in almost a plea, glancing at Julie to see if she'd intervene.

This wasn't part of his and Colin's plan, but Julie's silence confirmed to Jones all he needed to know.

Colin dropped Joel to the ground with a thud as the man gasped for air. He walked toward Maggie, and she backed away slowly from him. The intimidating man largely filled the room with his presence. His height emphasized his rage, the sheer strength of his frame more prevalent with a struggling Joel still heaving for air.

"Hand over Emilia," Colin's voice boomed. Even Julie shuttered in fear.

"No," Maggie said sternly, her hand reaching for a button on the side of the wall.

A loud alarm rang through their ears, and both Jones and the technician raced toward Julie. Scalpel in hand, he sliced in Julie's direction, but Jones was quicker. The pop from his gun caused everyone in the room to freeze and look in his direction. The technician's body fell to the ground.

The single shot spiraled into a fury of events.

Joel crawled on the floor, reaching for his gun, but Colin's foot collided with his hand. The crunching sound of breaking bones followed by Joel's howl ignited a cry from Julie. A single shot silenced Joel's screams, and the pool of red blood quickly haloed around his body.

"That felt really fucking good," Colin said, walking over to them.

Jones released Julie from her restraints, and immediately, she rose into Colin's arms.

"Stay over there and hide behind one of the desks," Jones instructed.

"No," Julie spat. "I'm helping any way I can."

Panic and dread filled Jones's processor, his scales erratically shifting through different shades of green. The bright emeralds cast a glowing hue against Julie's skin.

"You can't. Please, Julie. I didn't realize," Jones said as a loud buzzing noise exploded around them.

The hundreds of tubes in the experimental lab drained themselves and the doors swung open. The many eyes of androids holed up in those containers flickered wide. Maggie let out a cry as the androids released themselves and assessed the situation, instinctively looking at Jones.

"They're attacking me!" Maggie screamed, but none of the androids even glanced her way as security guards rushed down the hallway toward the lab.

"They'll hurt you," Jones said to the hundreds of eyes on him, and they nodded in return.

Androids stormed the door, holding it closed with their strength and odd figures, and three others with snakelike tails cornered Maggie against the wall near The Supreme. Jones looked back over at Colin.

"We don't have much time."

Colin nodded.

"Julie," he said, his voice softer as he spoke to her. "I need you to recode Emilia's microchip and insert it back into her."

"What?" she yelped.

"We don't have much time," Jones nervously reminded them, his eyes finding the door again. "Just do it, and we'll explain later."

Jones kept himself busy as Julie and Colin hovered over The Supreme. The other androids in the room were connected to him, and he couldn't explain why. They trusted him—he was the only one here of similar species—and they looked to him for guidance.

"Jones, I was never trying to hurt Julie. That was all Joel!" Maggie pleaded.

"You're no better than her. You were going to hurt thousands of people. You let Joel in on your schemes," Jones said, backing away from Maggie and the androids.

"What are you going to do? You can't let FACERE burn to the ground." Maggie's eyes darted toward a fleeing governor and supreme.

Jones's hand shook for the first time as a group of security guards stormed the room.

Chapter 50
The Governor

June 22nd, 47 A.R.

Colin guided Julie over to the large device beside The Supreme. Her hands shook as she furiously typed.

"The coding, it's similar to my coding," Julie said to Colin. "Similar to the one I placed in Jones's processor fifteen years ago. Except this code is missing a single triangulation connecting the understanding of feelings to the actual ability to experience them."

Colin watched Julie hurriedly alter the code to add an extra line. The microchip circled inside the device as the sounds of security attempting to breach the room wafted around them. Julie carefully removed the microchip and walked over to Emilia's lifeless body.

With unsteady hands, Julie placed the microchip between the tweezers, and as carefully as she could, she inserted the technology back into The Supreme's processor. Julie stitched the razor-thin incision closed with the silk thread from the surgical table.

Time froze around them as Colin waited to see if Julie saved Emilia. Her eyes darted underneath her eyelids before vividly opening. Emilia took a large breath and smiled at Julie as Colin untied her restraints.

The sounds at the front of the room grew louder, and Jones panicked as a security guard snuck through. Jones begrudgingly fired his weapon, picking off the guard with ease. The Supreme brought her hands to the base of her jaw, her fingers fluttering down her neck as she looked up at Julie.

"Thank you, Dr. Walsh."

Julie pursed her lips together tightly. "Don't thank me. I didn't want to do this."

Julie then shifted her gaze to Colin, and he reached his hand out to her.

"Trust me?" Colin asked, offering his charming smile as an explanation.

"I wouldn't have done this if I didn't," Julie said, squeezing his hand.

"You saved me," The Supreme said, standing on solid ground for the first time that day. She wobbled a moment before gaining her footing. "Now let me save you."

Julie scrunched her face in confusion as Emilia swiftly lifted Julie into her arms in a large embrace before directing her toward the emergency exit elevator at the back of the room.

"What are you doing?" Colin pleaded, as Emilia shoved Julie inside the elevator and pressed the lobby button.

"When you get to the lobby, exit through the back, not the front. Head to the townhouse," The Supreme said and closed the door.

And as quickly as Colin had reunited with the woman he loved, she was gone. The sound of the small elevator descending sounded briefly before he turned back around to the other side of the laboratory. The androids in the front had lost their battle in keeping the door secure.

"Run!" Jones yelled.

Colin and The Supreme raced for a door in the back. The dimly lit back entrance led to an empty office, ducking down to hide from the window in the door. Footsteps raced down the hall on the other side of the door. Colin glanced at Emilia and handed her the second revolver he carried with him. The one Celine insisted he bring with the other.

The sounds behind the door quieted, and Emilia poked her head up through the window in the door.

"All clear."

"The elevator is down the hallway to the right," Colin said as The Supreme's hand gripped the doorknob.

They tiptoed to the elevator and shifted in with ease as sounds of people approaching began filling their ears. The doors closed, and the car descended.

"It's good to have you back, old friend," The Supreme said, her fingers quickly inspecting the gun in her hands.

She grinned up at Colin, releasing the safety. The ride from the top floors of FACERE to the main lobby took an excruciating amount of time, and the two hadn't been alone since that fitful day in February.

"Fuck FACERE, fuck Maggie Rivera," he said crisply, a smile forming in the corners of his lips. "And fuck The Legislature."

"That's the spirit," The Supreme responded, lifting the gun up as the elevator doors opened to a flurry of chaos and madness.

The android police force surrounded FACERE employees, some fighting back aggressively and others surrendering. Detained employees were seated on the floor, their hands cuffed behind their backs. Colin grabbed Emilia's arm and dragged her toward the front exit, colliding with a few security guards who fired at him. They both shot back, avoiding as many casualties as they could and dodging stray bullets.

The journey to the front exit was longer than the journey to the back exit from this area, but Elsie was waiting in the passenger seat for them in Colin's vehicle outside. He'd previously disabled the automatic driving function so that no one could track the vehicle's location.

None of the police officers interfered with Colin and his path, a few small nods of approval in his direction as he and The Supreme finally made it through the large glass doors.

The vehicle was a roomy sedan, and Elsie smiled as her superiors settled into their seats. She opened her mouth to ask the question both Colin and The Supreme anticipated, but Colin—being the only one who knew how to manually drive—slammed the car into gear and turned the wheel before she could ask why Julie wasn't with them.

Chapter 51
The Supreme

June 22nd, 47 A.R.

The townhouse was the same as the last time Emilia had been inside it with the addition of Celine and her son's belongings. Celine's stiff body rose from the couch as her disheveled brother and her friend both approached her, the baby fast asleep in her arms.

Julie lay on the couch, small bruises forming against her wrists and chin. She held an ice pack against her temple, and Colin immediately raced to her.

The Supreme paused and took in the humans in the room. Her eyes scanned Elsie, able to identify her microchip with ease. Celine's temperature and biometrics popped up, but Emilia closed her eyes and opened them again until the information disappeared.

"What happened to you?" Elsie asked Julie, breaking the awkward silence in the room.

"Joel Kennsington."

"That fucker," Elsie said, her stare shifting to Colin. "Did you at least kill him?"

"Yes," Colin answered, a warning glance passing between him and his legislative aide.

"We need to talk," The Supreme said to Colin, and he nodded. "Privately."

"I'll make us some tea," Celine said, her warm smile spreading to Elsie and Julie.

"I'm going to need something stronger than tea." Elsie laughed, her hands already scouting for a bottle of red wine in the beverage fridge.

The governor and The Supreme ascended the stairs until they reached the third floor and study. Colin closed the door and ran his hand through his hair. He was a mess, blood splattered against his suit. He uncuffed his shirt and rolled up his sleeves, slouching into his chair.

The Supreme rummaged through the drawer and smiled.

Henry O'Connor always kept his secret stash in the bottom, underneath a box of fountain pens, and she suspected Colin did the same.

Like father, like son, she thought, dropping two cigars on the desk in front of Colin.

Her grin grew from ear to ear, and the golden hue of her scales illuminated brightly.

"I haven't smoked one of these in years," he said with a raised brow, slowly picking up one with his long fingers.

"Well," Emilia responded with a smirk, "we're celebrating."

Colin chuckled, leaning back in his chair as he cut the ends of both with a knife he pulled out of the bottom drawer. He inspected his perfect slice before lighting a match and puffing. The smoke smelled delicious and forbidden, delicately swirling around Colin's square jawline and into his nose.

"I'm not sure I'd use the word celebrating to reflect on this morning's events."

The Supreme held the cigar Colin cut for her between her fingers, the golden scales on her hands shimmering with excitement. The feeling of tension combined with glee not only registered in her processor in understanding. She fully experienced the feeling. A new indulgence to add to her list.

"We're not celebrating the events of this morning."

"No?" Colin asked, his eyes zoning in on The Supreme with the intensity she missed from her former friend. "Then what is the occasion of interest?"

"We're celebrating the future."

Confusion crept across Colin's face, and he didn't respond.

He doesn't know, Emilia realized as she inhaled the spicy smoke. *But how could he?*

The innocence of Colin's unawareness made Emilia smile brightly. There was a piece of information her friend was blissfully oblivious to—and knowledge was power in the game to control The City. Emilia wasn't sure exactly how she would use this information yet, but having a secret move on the board always served her well.

"To unity," she said with a slight nod.

Colin bowed his head and took another puff.

"So you have a plan, I imagine?" The Supreme asked with a small breathy chuckle.

"I do." Colin leaned back, a grin spreading across his square jawline.

"Well?" The Supreme asked, excited by the opportunity to scheme with her favorite opponent. "Are you going to tell me?"

Colin laughed a low chuckle with a sarcastic undertone.

"Now where would the fun in that be?"

***

The Supreme turned the corner of the wooden steps, stopping at the sight of Julie perched on the kitchen island. She turned her head toward The Supreme, but her lips remained a straight, firm line.

In the short amount of time between leaving FACERE and now, The Supreme felt like a new android. Her eyes buzzed with human biometrics at nearly every turn and while her ability to understand a vast majority of human emotions wasn't new, feeling every emotion startled her.

"I want to make one thing clear," Julie started, her eyes caught on The Supreme's beautiful scales. "I wouldn't have restored your microchip if Colin didn't ask."

"But you didn't restore my microchip," The Supreme responded, approaching Julie with caution while she stole the untouched glass of red wine from Julie's grasp. The intoxicating liquid left a purposeful and bursting flavor on The Supreme's lips. "You could have reversed the damage, but instead, you wrote your own code."

Julie chuckled softly, toying with the ends of her hair. The purple bruises shone brightly in the daytime light, cascading down the side of her face. Between her slightly swollen eye, the bruises, and her scar, Julie looked monstrous and nothing like the missing photos that lingered on the daily news.

"The code in your microchip was mine, only it was missing a few lines. I added those back in." Julie pushed herself off the island, her body mere inches away from The Supreme.

Julie wasn't a short woman like the Garcias, but Emilia's android height toppled over the scientist. The Supreme gulped the rest of the wine and walked over to the other end of the kitchen, the empty glass echoing as she placed it in the kitchen sink.

"Why?" The words escaped Emilia's lips liberally, loosened from the alcohol.

"Because you need to understand the consequences of your wickedness." The response was cold and harsh, slicing through the air with authority and clarity. "Now when you hurt someone, you'll experience why it was wrong."

The Supreme chuckled, but the tenderness in her belly swelled: an experience of nervousness and uncertainty that she was unfamiliar with.

"You'll be up to no good soon enough, but I'm not a pawn anymore, Madam Supreme. I'm a valuable piece in the game," Julie said, her iciness physically cooling Emilia's scales and she shivered.

"Oh, Dr. Walsh," The Supreme responded, walking back toward Julie. "This game is far from over, but I look forward to your next move."

"I don't intend on letting you win," Julie asserted.

The Supreme extended her hand, waiting for Julie to grab it. The scientist did, her handshake firm and confident. The two didn't break their stare for a long while.

Julie shifted past The Supreme as she headed up the stairs to find Colin, and Emilia's ears perked up at the sound of Celine and Elsie in the back dining room. Their voices drifted, a friendly reminder that not each moment required full attention to detail.

Emilia poked her head through the door and was greeted by Celine's small but familiar smile. She recognized the pearl necklace around Celine's neck, a gift from her husband. Elsie shoved her device into a small bag and let out a large sigh.

"I'll take this to The Capitol Building," she said to Celine, not even acknowledging The Supreme's presence at the other end of the dining room table.

The air grew heavy in Elsie's absence, her footsteps loud and powerful as she exited the O'Connors' townhouse. The last time she and Celine were alone, she'd hastily given her the time travel device Mick created.

I wonder if he'll still come for me.

The Supreme couldn't help but think of Mick as her own impossible human—one who followed her without hesitation in hopes of full acceptance of Commissioner Jones.

"I still can't believe you're really here," Celine said, her very small smile brightening her face.

"I can," Emilia answered, her rough, scaly fingers brushing the edges of the mahogany dining room set chairs. There was so much about this house that stayed the same from her childhood, and a sickening feeling that Colin would always keep it this way seeped through her. "I just wish I didn't have to spend months in that tiny prison cell."

"Did you miss me?" Celine inquired, placing her hand on top of The Supreme's. Celine's long delicate fingers wrapped around Emilia's, tightening their grip before letting go completely.

The Supreme looked away, the rawness of her new ability to experience these emotions flashing through her. She always understood the closeness she felt toward Celine—a woman she grew up with, a partner in crime, and her best friend. They'd been through so much together, their memories unable to fit in a single recollection or moment.

"I honestly didn't fully experience the feeling of your absence until Dr. Walsh reprogrammed my microchip. I felt this the whole time; I just didn't know what it meant."

"So you still understand human emotions?" Celine asked, the pitch of her voice higher than normal. Emilia nodded silently. "Remind me to thank my brother's fiancée."

The Supreme's laughter filled the dining room before her embrace engulfed Celine. Her body eased into the hug, Celine's narrow frame breakable against The Supreme's build.

A silky smoothness collided with the scales on Emilia's cheek, a tender and innocent kiss from Celine's lips. Celine leaned away, and her steely eyes locked with Emilia's. Celine's manicured hand traced The Supreme's cheekbone with a touch as light as a feather's.

Fireworks exploded in Emilia's chest, and her hands trembled slightly. She backed away from Celine with wide eyes, unable to trust her own instincts with the hauntingly posed woman who stood before her. The Supreme always loved Celine, and with months of solitude and reflection, she realized her attraction and desire were woven into that emotion of love.

"If this is what intoxication of another feels like," The Supreme said with a toothy grin, "then yes, as much as it pains me to say this, please thank Dr. Walsh for me."

Without second-guessing her move, Emilia leaned in, and their lips collided. The abrasiveness of her scales rubbed against Celine's porcelain skin, but that didn't stop her. Celine's hands were fast and meaningful, exploring the body The Supreme barely knew herself as her scales swelled, a slight pleasurable pain protruding from the amber colors.

Emilia's knees weakened, the room spinning around them as her lips pushed harder against Celine's skin.

In response, Celine's body edged closer, her fingertips loitering against the hem of Emilia's shirt. In a sharp movement, The Supreme pulled back from Celine and shook her head. Nervousness consumed her.

"I've never been with an android or a human before," she admitted to the only woman who knew all her other secrets. "Much less a woman."

Celine smiled at her gently, brushing stray strands of hair away from Emilia's face. She nodded and grabbed The Supreme's hands within her own. Celine's eyes were wide and honest, never leaving Emilia's.

"I remember my first time. With a man. With a woman."

Trust, The Supreme thought, reeling over the all too familiar word. A concept she logically comprehended but never knew the magnitude of until looking into Celine's eyes.

She was the only person Emilia had ever trusted, the only one she wondered if she ever could.

"That's the beauty of intimacy. It's yours, and you don't need to explain it to anyone. I promise you'll like it. Let me show you." Celine's words were meaningful and enchanting, eliciting a certain promise Emilia had previously believed wasn't attainable.

***

Emilia awoke in Celine's bed alone, the remnants of their endless night of lovemaking apparent through wrinkled sheets. Celine had kept her promise, and The Supreme sensed an understanding of why humans risked everything for the ones they loved. She empathized with Jones and his love for Mick and smirked at the idea of her opponent Colin and his thirst for the scientist. This unfamiliar lightness intrigued The Supreme as she climbed out of bed and wrapped herself up in Celine's bathrobe.

The townhouse remained eerily empty, but muffled voices from the first floor taunted her. When she reached the bottom of the steps, Emilia's eyes widened at the television monitor on the wall. A headshot of Julie appeared on the screen beside the news anchor, and his voice boomed from the speakers.

"Breaking news: Sources tell us Dr. Julie Walsh, the missing interim CEO of COLI*GO, was found alive behind the walls of FACERE during the commissioner's raid of the facility yesterday. Little is known regarding the raid of FACERE's facility, with insider sources claiming a connection to the terrorist group behind The City's mass riots and recent violence. The governor's office, in conjunction with the commissioner, will hold a press conference today at noon at The Capitol Building on the matter."

The news anchor looked down briefly at his device, the morning clouds breaking into wispy white streaks while the golden dome of The Capitol Building shone brightly behind him.

"Dr. Walsh's health and status are unknown at this time. During The Supreme's trial, we learned she was transformed into a posse hominem. Our investigative team brings additional insight into this strange case. Leaked documents from The Courthouse's Records Department tell us two months before Dr. Walsh went missing, a marriage certificate was filed between her and Governor O'Connor. If true, Dr. Walsh holds extreme power in The Constituency; as an influential executive at the largest biotech conglomerate, Dr. Walsh would carry even more privileges if she were in union with Governor O'Connor. Our analysts urge The Legislature to evaluate the validity of these documents, especially if she is in fact still a hybrid species. In other breaking news, the whereabouts of The Supreme remain unknown, and The Legislature is offering a five-billion-dollar bounty reward. We'll bring you more information after these messages from our sponsors."

The Supreme smiled at the screen before settling into the comforts of the couch. She doubted she'd ever step into The Capitol Building again, wondering how long the O'Connors would shelter her in the confines of the townhouse. The game was why she wanted to live, the back and forth, the deals, and the surprise maneuvers. This turn of events wasn't what Emilia expected, especially not from the information Mick told her regarding the future.

Where is my time traveler? The Supreme wondered, turning the volume up on the television when the news anchor's face appeared back on the screen.

Chapter 52

The Governor

June 23rd, 47 A.R.

Julie fidgeted in the chair across from Colin's desk in The Capitol Building. She hadn't appeared in public for six months. Colin reached for her hands, firmly engulfing them in one of his. Julie looked up at him, and warmth spread across her eyes.

"Are you ready?" Colin asked without breaking eye contact.

Julie nodded, glancing one last time at the arrangement of photos on Colin's desk. Not much had changed in five years. The antique chess board remained in the corner, a photograph of Colin and Celine from their graduation at The University was situated beside it, along with the lovely photograph of him from his childhood with his mother at The Oceanside.

Colin twirled the ring on Julie's finger slowly before letting go of her grip. When he'd first proposed to her, she insisted on wearing the emerald stone on her right hand, but since the winter, Julie exclusively wore the ring on her left. Where it belonged.

He glanced over at the hologram photo on the corner of his desk. In it, his mother wrapped her arm around a much younger version of Colin, and his smile was so wide and happy. Colin loved this memory of her and just as much adored the memory of the first time Julie was in his office. She had mentioned the photo with a warm, genuine smile. That was the moment Colin knew there was something special about Julie. This was clearly a premonition of what they would become and what Julie would ultimately mean to him.

Together, they were in the home stretch of Colin's elaborate plan. The pieces of the puzzle fell so perfectly together when he, Jones, and Elsie mapped it out.

Originally, they planned on rescuing The Supreme from

FACERE and wove the other loose threads together. Joel needed to be silenced, Maggie needed to be stopped, and the chaos in The City needed to end. Her involvement with Joel was her undoing; pinning all the crimes on her was unfair, but after her cruel demeanor to The Supreme, no one argued the morality of their choices.

When Julie came back into Colin's life, he pledged to free her from hiding. The Supreme was correct: Julie was the missing piece that could unite The City together—unite androids and humans. Conspiring the lie that Julie had always been at FACERE fell easily on Colin's board after careful scheming and protected Isabella from an unsettling fate, one that would send her to prison and prevent her from being able to help save Julie in the future.

The only vulnerability in the plan was Colin's knowledge of Julie and It's involvement. It lingered hesitantly after Colin discovered he shared all of himself with Julie. The details were fuzzy in his mind, trying to blend the two personalities that lived there into one. They time traveled to meet during the month after she left Colin's bed. But Colin wasn't sure why. The plan they developed, the one he championed and crafted, didn't require additional conniving.

Julie needed the time to work on the antidote, to fix the drug that he needed to end the evilness in his mind. She promised he didn't have to take COL23 if he didn't want to once she'd solved the scientific riddles the drug tormented her with.

But I want to. The words crept into Colin's mind. *Time to say goodbye to It, to evil, for good.*

Elsie knocked quietly on the door before letting herself in. She uncharacteristically wore her hair in a sleek ponytail, and the threads from her tailored skirt and blazer shimmered against the harsh light.

"They're waiting for you."

Colin and Julie nodded, heading out of his office and down the empty halls. Everyone waited for them outside The Capitol Building. Jones stood at the podium at the top of the worn and weathered marble steps, his voice echoing across the silence of a large crowd. News reporters, citizens, and The Legislature stood below in a galley, thousands of eyes glued on the commissioner.

"I bring great news," Jones said, his scales flickering before calming down. "With the intelligence and due diligence of detectives on the force, we were able to identify the leaders of the terrorist group murdering The City's citizens and rioting across neighborhoods. The head of FACERE, Margaret Rivera, and her Finance Operations lead, Paul McGuire, conspired with Representative Joel Kennsington to follow out on numerous crimes across our great City. We have Margaret Rivera in custody, but unfortunately, Representative Kennsington did not survive the raid. We're working with the coroner's office and looking into the connections between Mr. McGuire's death and other potential ring leaders in Ms. Rivera's operations. In the raid, we rescued Dr. Julie Walsh, but The Supreme escaped."

Jones paused, looking down at the podium before lifting his head to the whispering crowd.

"We're looking for her and offering a reward to anyone who brings her in. Her microchip was reprogrammed before we arrived, meaning we cannot track her from it. Even with this slight setback, I'm pleased to announce the end of the curfew in The City and welcome all of our citizens—humans, androids, and posse hominems—to enjoy their lives freely and without pause again." The commissioner smiled, and the crowd cheered. "I'd like to hand over the podium to Governor O'Connor now for a statement. Afterward, we will answer your questions together."

Jones backed away and looked at Colin and Julie, the pair in public for the first time an intriguing sight. Colin traced his left hand to the small of Julie's back, leading her to the edge of the steps with him. Looking down at her, he smiled as the kindness and awe he remembered from six months ago returned to her presence. The softer Julie, the Julie not weathered from terrible, traumatic experiences.

Experiences I put her through.

Colin cleared his throat and leaned down toward the scattered microphones on the podium.

"Good afternoon," he said as the crowd quieted. "I am pleased and excited by the commissioner's grant to end The City's curfew and for life to resume to a new sense of normalcy after these daunting months."

The sticky summer air hugged him, constricting his throat as he tried to speak. The faces before him showed nervousness and an invincible excitement, and the forbidden acts that could now be everyday occurrences shadowed across their grins.

"The commissioner's mission at FACERE was completed, the incident exposing former Representative Joel Kennsington and the head of FACERE as the leaders of the movement that conspired against innocent citizens across The City and kidnapped and experimented on my wife, Dr. Julie Walsh."

The crowd exploded with murmurs, the reporters elbowing one another as they inclined closer to the steps.

"Are you still a hybrid?" a voice yelled from the mass of people and androids in front of them.

Julie looked up at Colin, and he nodded, moving off to the side.

"I involuntarily was turned from a human to a posse hominem by The Supreme," Julie replied, her voice sturdy. "I didn't discover this until I was taken to FACERE. Like many of you, I lived my life unaware that the transformation happened to me. I still considered myself a person. A human. The experience changed me, as I'm sure many other posse hominems could attest to. While at FACERE, my microchip was removed. I'm not sure what that makes me in the eyes of others anymore, but I ask you all to consider, Does it matter? Did it ever truly matter?"

Everyone quieted from Julie's answer and Colin noticed that the stillness mixed with the humidity paled Julie's face as her hand lightly clutched her stomach. Cheers and clapping sounded loudly. Julie turned to look at Colin. He smiled widely at her, grabbing her hand in his as his constituents' overwhelming support and awe of Dr. Walsh flourished like a vibrant garden around them. People and androids cheered and chanted, optimism for a better, stronger future breeding around them.

They believe again. There's hope.

A loud pop crackled in the air, and darkness lingered in Colin's eyes before he comprehended what was happening. Another blast sounded loudly in his already ringing ears.

Before everything transpired to blankness, Colin noted Julie's mouth was slightly ajar, her arms reaching out to him, catching him as he came tumbling down.

Shouting and crying erupted from the crowd, and fireworks exploded in Colin's mind, flickering and tormenting his line of vision until it turned to complete blackness. Colin never experienced this sensation before.

Nothingness completely consumed him.

Chapter 53
Julie

June 23rd, 47 A.R.

"Julie, I need you to tell me what happened," Jones said calmly, but his hands grasped Julie's tightly, trembling while holding her. "Or at least what you remember."

The moment burst vividly in Julie's mind at Jones's request. Julie closed her eyes, recalling the scene as if she were still on the steps of The Capitol Building. Her whole body trembled, and nausea filled the pit of her stomach with a swift and harsh urgency. But reality didn't shake from her mind.

Colin smiling at her and the crowd, hopeful and happy. Then, the bang vibrating across her whole body, from her ears down to her feet firmly planted on the marble stone.

The spray of warm, sticky splattering residue and droplets across her face, the rapid blinking of her eyes, instinctively unsure if she should keep them closed or witness what transpired around her.

Another bang. More splatter, now consuming her clothes and her hair. Everything froze around her, time standing still for once in Julie's life.

The look in his eyes.

Julie couldn't stop seeing the way Colin looked at her no matter how many times she shook at the thought. How wide his eyes grew, painfully acknowledging what occurred, before disappearing in an instant.

Colin's hands reaching for her jaw, fingertips brushing against her skin before the violent, harsh weight of him collapsed on top of her. Scaly hands grabbing for her, arms wrapping around her, trying to pull her away.

Jones.

A screaming crowd dispersing around them. Complete madness.

Julie's guttural scream, an ungodly sound exploding from her throat. She wouldn't let go of Colin, cradling him in her arms.

I'm not leaving him here. Julie wasn't sure if she thought or said the words out loud.

Tears streaming down her face, mixing with the blood on her cheeks, the cold and hot sensations on her skin and lips causing her to shake uncontrollably. Her fingers digging deeper into Colin's hair while she screamed louder, hoping the volume of her voice would keep him awake, but instead, the feeling of his labored breaths ceased in her arms and the stillness of him solidified this reality.

He was dead, both bullet wounds having sliced through his head.

No. No. No. No. No. No.

She cried out once more, so loudly she was sure her wrath vibrated across The City.

The next thing Julie remembered was this hospital room, her feet dangling off the side of the bed as her hands fisted and pulled the red-stained sheets. Her clothes sodden, Colin's blood still painted on her face, bits and pieces of him embedded deep in her hair and under her fingernails.

So much blood. Too much blood.

A nurse tried convincing her to change, but Julie refused. She would only listen to Jones. And now that he was here, she didn't know if she had the courage to say anything at all.

"Who did this?" were the only words she could force out loud, the only words her mouth would speak.

Jones closed his eyes and shook his head. "We don't know."

"Mick," Julie cried out. "Where the fuck is Mick?"

PART TWELVE

The Past

"You have been the last dream of my soul."
—Charles Dickens

Epilogue
It

June 23rd, 46 A.R.

It walked down the wooden steps hugging the sides of the cliffs. The crying present version of Julie kneeling on the edges didn't notice him, her eyes covered by her hands, her wails so loud and terrified they consumed her. The steps creaked beneath the weight of him, the waves crashing loudly around him.

But there she was. Julie's body, mangled, tangled, and bleeding on the rocky shore.

It stepped carefully over the slippery rocks, the water creeping in along the shoreline. But he didn't want to miss her; he needed to see her. He needed to know if this was real, if Julie really died the same way Colin's mother died.

Her body twitched, but her eyes were still open. It knelt beside her, brushing the loose hair from her face and running his thumb against her cheek. Blood seeped from her body, broken limbs, and gashes deep from her fall down the cliffs.

An overwhelming feeling flooded It, and he pulled her into his chest, shivering from his exposed chest and arms. She was already gone; there was nothing he could do to save her at this point. His eyes lingered on her neck, taking in the scar he was unfamiliar with. It traced the scar lightly with his index finger.

Love was a rare feeling for It. He didn't believe in love—he didn't believe that there was a person out there who could ever love him.

Yet here she was. And she was dead; he had killed her again. He would kill her multiple times, and in return, she would destroy any chance she had. Capturing him and holding him hostage was her specialty.

The Oceanside was still dark, the sun hiding behind the world in bashfulness. Her skin was bloody and blotchy, pale and purple, but he couldn't stop looking at her. Her hair was now damp from the spray of the ocean water around them.

It let out a cry that surprised even him. Holding her tighter in his arms felt right even though her blood poured all over him. She stained the bare skin of his chest, the gym shorts he wore as pajama bottoms. Everything about Julie's dying body coexisted with him.

Without warning, the skin on her body evaporated in the air, peeling off her bones and dissipating around him. Her blood and ligaments exploded around him, disappearing for a moment before igniting.

It looked down at Julie's body disintegrating around him like pixels on a computer. He wasn't sure what was happening to her, but her blood left its trace on him. When she was completely gone, he closed his eyes.

Upon opening them, It found himself in the prison he didn't know Julie put him in. The prison that was Colin's brain. The pulsating walls around him vibrated a squishy substance, but he felt Julie on his skin.

It raised his hand, yelling and screaming, hoping someone would hear him.

Silence followed.

I will not be quiet any longer. I will fight my way out. I will persist. She needs to know.

Julie's blood seeped through the lines on his palms, staining him with the remembrance of her death, even though her death wasn't physically his fault.

He slammed his fists into the wall, covering the veiny surface with her, smearing it around like paint on a canvas. It was determined to make Julie part of Colin and Colin part of Julie.

The walls absorbed her blood, feasting on the substance like it hadn't eaten in decades.

Coming Soon

REVIRESCO

Book Three of the UNITAS Series

November 2022

For more information, please visit:
LeeSHannonBooks.com

The toxin is missing. In the wrong hands, the drug could spark biological warfare across The City. Dangerous time traveler Mick Taylor knows who holds the toxin and believes his rescue mission will reunite him with his estranged friend, Dr. Julie Walsh. But Mick faces a larger issue: He is slowly disintegrating through dimensions of time.

At The Capitol Building, Commissioner Jones and The Legislature investigate a recent act of terrorism. In order to understand the gravity of the situation, Jones must uncover the truth behind the supposed invincibility of time travelers—and why The City's infamous serial killer has reemerged.

In a bloodthirsty grab for power, the O'Connor siblings face off in the gubernatorial election—both vying for Dr. Julie Walsh's public endorsement. Unsure where her allegiance lies, Julie must decide if she honors old bloodline families or will forge her own path.

Across The River at FACERE, newly appointed leader, Dr. Isabella Garcia, forms an uncharacteristic partnership with her sister Anna. With guidance from The Supreme, Isabella is convinced her new, secret creations are the answer for peace and prosperity in The City.

Acknowledgements

I cannot thank everyone enough for their love and support as I began writing UNITAS, Book Two of the UNITAS Series. This was a much different experience from COLIGO, Book One of the UNITAS Series. I handed off my manuscript to my editor, Jenny, as I released COLIGO and I'm so glad for that timing or I would have tinkered with UNITAS to the point of exhaustion.

First, thank you to my readers. I can't believe I created a world and characters that people not only believe in, but enjoy. I hope you stick around for the full UNITAS Trilogy. I'm glad to fast-release this world and these characters for you.

Thank you to my mom, Linda Smith. There is no one else I would ever want to dedicate this book to. Not only did you re-read COLIGO, you read UNITAS with such enthusiasm several times. Sequels are hard, and I am so excited that you love UNITAS more than COLIGO. This book is truly for you.

When it comes to theories, I have to thank my father, Geoff Smith because you've created rabbit holes upon rabbit holes and are always willing to talk through the insanity that is time travel with me. My parents are my number one supporters and I love you. Thank you for everything.

A sincere and heartfelt thank you to my cover artist and one of my closest friends, Tori Mulhern. I almost gave up on this series and I'm forever grateful that you talked me out of giving up on this story and my dream of creative writing. Our friendship makes holding physical copies of these beautiful books so much more special knowing you're an integral part of them.

Special shout-outs to my "OG" COLIGO beta readers. Many of you beta read or advanced read UNITAS and your insights, opinions and excitement helped shape this whole trilogy.

Yes, I understand you hated the ending but keep going—you'll see why saying goodbye to Colin (for now) is important to this story. A special shout out to: Barbara, Cathy, and Kirstie.

This story wouldn't be where it is today without my amazing editor, Jenny. Thank you so much for all your hard work, catching the mistakes and making them beautiful—I'm so glad to have you through this process because you're one of the rare gems who champions writers and I couldn't be luckier.

Thank you to my fantastic graphic designer, Keir DuBois. Without him we wouldn't have the map that everyone loves! It is truly stunning and I'm forever grateful that you helped visually build the world of the UNITAS Series.

I took various creative liberties while writing about specific topics but would like to acknowledge the research, studies and papers that enlightened and educated me in areas where I'm not a subject matter expert.

Thank you to my grandmother, Idella White. I miss her so much. She is truly the inspiration for my publishing company and its namesake. Thank you to my grandfather, James White for the unconditional love and support.

Thank you to my friends, family, co-workers, and BookTok friends/community who have listened to me talk about my writing journey (probably too much) and have been huge cheerleaders regardless. In no particular order, rhyme or reason: Rachel, Jonathan, Emily, Kimberly, Jessie, Joshua, Holly, Anu, Ranga, Josh, Andrea, Rachel and the whole US RBD team, just to name a few.

Lastly, thank you to everyone who relates to someone in this story. I see you, I believe in you, and I accept you.

I hope to see you on the other side of REVIRESCO, Book Three of the UNITAS Series. I can't wait.

Sincerely,
Lee S. Hannon

About Lee S. Hannon

While not a time traveler yet, Lee S. Hannon works in the biotech & pharmaceutical industry, helping launch and sustain novel therapies within rare diseases.

She writes fantasy, speculative & science fiction.

Lee S. Hannon resides in Boston, the city inspiring the world of the UNITAS Series. Her passion for crafting thought-provoking stories with her background in biotech inspired her ideas on time travel through blood and a cutting-edge world desperately wishing it was better than our own.

When not working or writing, Lee S. Hannon can be found at a spin class, trying a new recipe in her kitchen, or adventuring to a new coffee shop.

Lee S. Hannon loves hearing from readers. Please reach out at sleehannon@gmail.com or follow her on social media platforms: Instagram, TikTok, Twitter, and Facebook (@LeeSHannonBooks).

www.ingramcontent.com/pod-product-compliance
Lightning Source LLC
Chambersburg PA
CBHW020304030826
48979CB00027B/2092/J

* 9 7 9 8 9 8 5 1 1 7 5 4 7 *